SUNRAY

SUNRAY

Vincent Taylor

Macdonald Publishers · Edinburgh

Published by
Macdonald Publishers
Loanhead, Midlothian EH20 9SY

ISBN 0 904265 49 8

Any resemblance to any person, living or dead, is entirely accidental.

Printed in Scotland by
Macdonald Printers (Edinburgh) Limited
Edgefield Road, Loanhead, Midlothian EH20 9SY

SUNRAY

PROLOGUE

THE SIX MEN were dressed identically. Throughout the five minutes it took them to complete their tasks they didn't exchange a single word or command. The silence added menace to their preparations and they looked almost unreal and disembodied as a low ground mist enveloped them from the waist down. In the distance the lights of Edinburgh were dimming against the sky as the darkness gave way to dawn. There wasn't a cloud in sight. Scotland's capital city was going to have another beautiful September morning—the sort of bright morning that often changes to rain by about ten o'clock.

Old army blankets spread on the ground deadened the sounds of the car wheels as the Rolls Royce and the BMW were rolled slowly into position. There was a faint hiss almost like a tight zip being undone as razor sharp scalpels sliced through the leather seats in the two cars and the tightly packed man-made fibre spilled out like blood from a wound. Paraffin bubbled with a bluish tinge in the growing light as it was poured over the slashed seats and was soaked up in the padding.

The blankets were rolled up. Simple explosive devices—armed—waiting for their radio-activated instructions were thrust into the petrol tank of each car. The paraffin-soaked padding lit easily without exploding as lighted rags on six foot canes carefully touched the front seats of each car through open windows. The six men melted away into the trees and waited for the signal to complete their demonstration. They would detonate the bombs by remote control thirty seconds after they heard Sunray's telephone call being answered.

*

Mark Armstrong was wakened abruptly by the telephone at his bedside. As he reached for the receiver, he took in the time from the green, glowing digits of his electronic alarm clock. In spite of the lingering effects of sleep his heart began to race with apprehension. Why would somebody be calling him at five o'clock?

'Mr Armstrong?'

'Yes.' Mark tried to place the voice as he struggled to pull himself together.

'I hope you and Clan Oil are able to raise all that money you need from the Scottish National Bank, because we want fifty million pounds of it. Otherwise all that oil of yours is going to stay where it is – at the bottom of the North Sea. Your schedule will be put back at least another two years.'

Mark was now wide awake. 'What is all this? I don't think this sort of thing is funny. Who are you? What do you want?'

'This is no joke, Mr Armstrong. Take a look out of your window and you'll see how serious we are.'

Mark dropped the receiver on the bed and crossed to the window. There in the circular drive in front of the house his Rolls Royce and BMW Coupé were burning fiercely. He knew they had both been in the garage at the back of the house when he'd gone to bed. As he watched, the Rolls Royce – followed a second later by his BMW – exploded with a deafening roar. He ducked as debris rattled on the window-pane. He was appalled by such a direct attack and by the planning he recognised had gone into co-ordinating the destruction of the cars with the telephone call.

Shaken he went back to the telephone.

'You see what we mean?' The voice was flat and noncommittal.

Even though he was naked and felt threatened, Mark repeated his question. 'Look, what is it you want?'

'We want fifty million pounds. We will confirm our demands – and our conditions – later.' The voice was deliberate, emotionless. 'We'll be in touch. Our code-word will be Sunray.'

Then the line was dead and Mark was left holding the purring receiver. He gripped it tighter and tighter, making the veins on his arm stand out. Tension gripped his whole body. The muscles on his flat hard stomach clenched and unclenched and the sinews on his neck were like wires. Then he crashed the instrument back down onto its cradle.

He ran his right hand through his thick black hair a couple of times as he collected his thoughts. Christ, as though I don't have problems enough. Now this! What will the Bank's reaction be? I'm asking them for an extra thousand million pounds and now some maniac's obviously going to attack us in some way. He was worried by the threat, and by the attack on his property. From the diary on his bedside table, he found the number of the head of security at Clan Oil, and dialled it. As the phone rang in his ear he noticed that his hand was shaking with anger and resentment.

John Graham, his security chief, a blurred, sleep-laden voice at the other end of the line, listened in silence as Mark told him what had happened.

After a pause, to Mark interminable, he said thoughtfully, 'Stay where you are, Mark. I can be with you in fifteen minutes. Before I leave I'll get in touch with the police.' The increasing assurance in the security man's voice calmed Mark down. Throwing on a dressing gown, he went down to look at the two burning wrecks. As far as he could make out from a cursory survey, nothing else seemed to have been touched and there was no sign of any attempt to break into the house. He realised that he'd better not touch anything and went back upstairs to shave and freshen up, deciding that his usual morning bath could wait.

A few minutes later, as he was pouring himself a glass of grapefruit juice, he heard two cars draw up. He went out of the house to greet Graham, and found him staring at the wrecks, with a second man, broad-shouldered, burly, by his side. Without taking his eyes off the smouldering wreckage, Graham introduced the stranger to Mark.

'This is David Mackay, Chief Superintendent David Mackay. He's a rather unusual policeman. I've been in close touch with him over the last few months and I rang him right away just in case this is more serious even than it seems.'

When Mackay turned, Mark saw a striking man – six foot four, tough and muscular, his angular face pale and lined, his hair thick and black, traces of grey at the temples. He looked more like a successful businessman than a senior policeman. He stepped forward, holding out his hand. 'Good morning, Mr Armstrong. Unusual is not the word I'd have chosen, but I have had some special training.' Mackay's Hebridean childhood showed in his soft West Highland accent.

'This certainly looks as if it is David's department,' Graham said as they walked round the two wrecks, the acrid smell of burning rubber, scorched paint, and the fumes from the melted upholstery padding making them all draw breath. 'David's the local expert on our friends.'

'Our friends?' Mark was puzzled.

'Terrorists, subversives, urban guerrillas,' the policeman said quietly. 'I've studied the lot and their methods, all over the world. For some time now we've recognised that the techniques of modern terrorism would sooner or later spread to Scotland.' The Chief Superintendent peered cautiously into the gutted interior of the Rolls, his face screwed up against the heat. He shook his head sadly. 'What a waste.'

'But surely it can't be terrorists?' Mark was incredulous. 'Not here in Edinburgh?'

'Well, the whole thing has been very carefully planned,' said Mackay as the three of them turned away from the still-smouldering wreckage. 'The cars moved round to the front of the house and without making a noise on the gravel. I would guess they laid blankets or something like that to mask the sound.' Mackay scuffed at the stone chips as he spoke. 'The fact that you were not telephoned until they were burning. The demand for fifty million pounds. No, this is no bunch of amateurs we're dealing with. Also, their choice of code-word is suggestive. Unless there is some other special-interest meaning that escapes me for the moment, Sunray is military wireless procedure for Commanding Officer. It's the code-word meaning the CO is on the air.'

Graham butted in. 'That's right. I remember Sunray from my National Service days.' He was obviously feeling guilty and his whole manner showed it as he moved restlessly beside Mark and the policeman. He knew that the resources of his small security force couldn't cope with what had just happened and he nodded as Mackay went on.

'To my admittedly over-suspicious mind, that seems to indicate well-prepared planning and direction.' Mackay shrugged, with a rueful downturn of his mouth. 'But, to begin with, we will be trying to read every detail, to build a picture which will allow us to out-think whoever Sunray are. Every little thing we can add to our bank of knowledge will help. My forensic people will be here shortly so don't touch or move anything, not that I expect they'll find much to work on. In the meantime, can you fill me in on your side?'

Mark described what had happened in detail – missing nothing out.

'What did they mean about your schedule, and putting it back?' Mackay asked.

'I can only guess. It's fairly common knowledge that my company, Clan Oil, is running behind schedule on the development of our finds in the Scotia Field. We've been badly affected by unusually harsh weather, by late delivery of platforms and by strikes, and we're two years behind in bringing on-stream what is accepted as the biggest field so far discovered in the North Sea. It's also pretty well known that we are trying to raise an extra thousand million pounds to finance our operations.' Mark paused as Mackay reacted to the amount of money needed. 'But I can't see what any outside group could do to delay us further. We've almost got our first platform in production, and the other three will be coming on-stream within a year, provided we can actually get the extra financing.'

'What about sabotage?' asked Mackay.

'Well, we accept that there is always a possibility of that, but we take all the precautions we can. We have our own security people under the direction of John here – both out in the North Sea and at our landfall base. But I can't believe that anyone could really threaten our platforms. We have regular inspections . . .'

Mackay interrupted. 'Believe me, Mr Armstrong, your whole operation is now under threat. As John knows, we've just completed a joint exercise with the Royal Navy and the SAS – the Special Air Service – to test how secure installations in the North Sea really are.' He turned to Graham. 'I think you'll agree, John, that Exercise North Sea Tapestry confirmed our worst misgivings?'

The security man agreed gloomily. 'Yes. Yes, it did. You remember, Mark? I sent you a report on it. The results were rather inconclusive. Short of having the armed forces on each rig and platform permanently, there seemed to be nothing we could add to our normal precautions.' He looked to the policeman for agreement.

Returning his attention to Mark, Mackay went on, 'And of course the government wouldn't agree to that – mainly because of cost – so unfortunately we've had to recognise that apart from their isolation and sheer size, most of the installations in the North Sea are pretty vulnerable. Our only real hope would be to respond instantly to any threat or attack as it happens. John told me he's warned your platform people already.'

Even as he finished speaking, Mackay was already planning what he would have to do. He could be back in Edinburgh in quarter of an hour; his first call from the office would be to his Chief Constable. After that, he would contact in turn all the other sources and facilities he might have to call on if there was a political angle to all this. There would be a telephone call to the duty officer at Army HQ outside Edinburgh – just a precaution at this stage – and a request for standby services from the Post Office and the Navy. Those were the preliminaries. The most important of all the calls would be to an army barracks outside Hereford, where twenty four hours a day there were small groups of men on constant alert – the Tactical Response Groups of the SAS. With any luck, he might get through to one of the officers he had worked with on North Sea Tapestry, someone who agreed with his own view of how to tackle things.

He looked at his watch. 'Can I suggest, Mr Armstrong, that we meet in an hour's time at your office to discuss the whole thing? I'm going to have to know all there is to know about your business and I'm going to have to know it today. Out of the blue somebody is about to attack your company. And I for one believe that they are highly organised.' Mackay strode towards his car and made ready to leave. His hand was on the door handle when he paused pointedly and turned. 'A few weeks ago a large amount of small arms, ammunition and high explosives was stolen in a number of separate attacks, obviously co-ordinated, on the same night here in Scotland. We've hushed the whole thing up, but I've known since then that something was about to break. I didn't know when or where. Well, the when is today; and you, Mr Armstrong, you and your company are the where.

'Somehow you're going to have to carry on your business while I try to set up an operation to protect you.' He smiled gently, as though to take some of the sting out of what he had just said. 'And I'm not going to be popular with my fellow officers. I'm going to need a lot of men for this operation and the force is already stretched to the limit dealing with the tens of thousands of extra visitors in Edinburgh for the Festival. But that's my problem,' he said, as he got into his car, 'and it's nothing compared with yours.'

SUNRAY

LIEUTENANT COLONEL BILL GORMAN looked every inch of what he wasn't – the successful landowner. Dressed in sober tweed, knickerbockers and matching jacket with green stockings and gleaming brogues, he was wearing as he always did his old school tie with its distinctive pale blue stripe. As he stepped out of his front door, a dark green Range Rover drew up with a crunch on the sparsely gravelled oval at the bottom of the steps. As he leant against the iron railings on the edge of the steps, Gorman's weather-beaten face, a mass of broken veins, broke into a smile. The driver of the Range Rover leapt out of his vehicle and threw him a smart salute. He was smiling triumphantly. Taking the steps two at a time, he strode up to the Colonel and reported, 'It went like clockwork. Not a hitch in sight. Someone should be doing a bit of thinking right now.'

Gorman chuckled. 'Well done, Douglas.' He clapped the man on the shoulder. 'Now, come and have some breakfast.' He turned and went back into the house, leaving the driver to follow him.

Douglas McQuillan glanced at the men getting out of the Range Rover. 'Breakfast,' he said sharply. McQuillan's tense abruptness and aggression contrasted with Gorman's easy, almost nonchalant, self-assurance as he emphasised his order by waving the men on in an agitated way. The men followed him into the house in disciplined silence. Trooping into the once-elegant dining room with its wide sideboards and heavily framed sporting prints, they seemed curiously out of place. As they came in, they exchanged glances with the fourteen other men already there, some of them seated at the long shabby table, others still standing behind their chairs.

Gorman smiled round at them all. He alone seemed to be indifferent to the almost tangible excitement. 'Right,' he said cheerfully. 'Tuck in. We must keep our strength up—we've only just begun. Having saved this benighted country's neck time and again I think they owe us our fifty million and a new start somewhere—somewhere where the old values still hold good.' He sat down at the head of the table and began his meal. McQuillan sat at his right, reaching greedily for two slices of toast from a broken silver toast rack and pulling his plate of bacon and eggs towards him as the cook for the day laid it down.

For almost all of his adult life, Gorman had served his country with distinction and bravery—as a soldier in the Black Watch, that famous Scottish regiment, into which he had followed his father and grandfather; then in the SAS and a number of other very specialised groups that the British Army never talk about and which aren't even mentioned in the Army List published each year to show where every officer is currently serving.

In more than thirty years of active service Gorman had been in the front line as Britain's once-mighty Empire declined. From time to time he had been seconded in a way that would have greatly surprised our allies and horrified our liberal-thinking Establishment had either ever known. In what was then Palestine, in Korea, Malaya, Kenya, Aden and Borneo, he had won, as an officer in the regular army, grudging although suspicious respect as a ruthless but brilliant commander, a man the generals and the politicians knew could accomplish the seemingly impossible with small, highly mobile units of hand-picked veterans—carrying out tasks which were often beyond the ability, or perhaps more importantly beyond the conscience, of bigger, more structured forces where reports and details of operations are carefully and properly recorded for future scrutiny.

Seconded to the SAS, and other still more clandestine *ad hoc* units, his covert service had included Vietnam, Cuba, Israel, Chad, Biafra, Nigeria, Algeria, South Africa and Ireland, north and south.

But even for a man with his record there was a limit. Over the years only highly placed friends had saved him from the consequences of impulsive, even erratic, indiscipline. Brother officers, his contemporaries, who now out-ranked him, who envied him, but who realised that they always needed to have peple like Gorman to do their dirty work, started to have misgivings. He was too tough, too ruthless, too prepared to get the job done at any cost, too willing to bend the rules; above all, altogether too willing to kill. He never took prisoners – all Gorman's enemies were dead. Even when the cause or the result was right or good, Gorman spoiled it by overkill.

In the end they had to get rid of him. They didn't dare promote him above field rank – they were too worried at the influence that that might give him. They seized the opportunity to force him to leave after an incident with a visiting coloured General, who had once served under Gorman. At a dinner at Sandhurst, Gorman, somewhat the worse for drink, had slapped the man when they were both in the lavatory after he had taken offence at what the General had meant to be good-humoured banter about Britain's shrinking influence and the lack of opportunities for Gorman in the future. 'No more glory,' he had suggested, 'no more black men to call you sir.' Three times Gorman had slapped him with the back and front of his hand, reducing the man – even to Gorman's consternation – to tears. Quietly invited to resign, Gorman had gone with bad grace, feeling, rightly, that he had been manoeuvred and that a few years earlier, in a different political climate, he would have been protected, the whole matter hushed up and made light of. The Army to which he had given his whole life, his whole being, had turned its back on him.

On retirement he found himself in an alien world, completely at variance with his values and standards, with no discipline, no sense of common good, everyone obsessed with his own interests. He couldn't understand people who seemed to run Britain down, people who didn't want to play any part in the national life, who seemed only to find fault and to want to be spoon fed. He detested the resignation with which he saw central government allowing authority to be eroded and standards lowered.

He found he was cut off from the rest of society. In the beginning there had been people who had rallied round him. He was, after all, a tall, good-looking man, still only fifty-five and the owner of a large estate. But he was his own worst enemy, his roughness, ruthlessness and incongruous – and outspoken – idealism out of tune with civilian society. He offended people and himself took offence on the slightest pretext. Much of what he did, and more of what he said was unacceptable to the kind of people he saw as equals. As a guest on a grouse shoot in the Highlands he had appalled everyone by shooting a young Labrador pup which had run-in before the end of the main drive. The dog had been excited and had slipped its lead. Its owner, the teenage daughter of Gorman's host, had stared in horror as Gorman had blasted its head off at a range of only a few feet. He had put his own pleasure and a momentary slip by an untrained dog above everything else. He had been asked to leave the moor, and for one terrible moment, as the disgrace sank in and his temper took control of him, it looked as though he might turn his gun on the man standing shouting in front of him.

On another occasion a huge salmon had won a tussle with him when he was a guest fishing on the Tweed. He had gone back to the pool that same night with a grenade. The explosion had brought the ghillie running from his cottage and he had heard Gorman shouting as he lifted the dead salmon from the river, 'I told you I'd get you, you bastard.' The incident had become a scandal. People just could not understand how a gentleman could use such a method on the world's greatest salmon river.

The final straw, the incident that more than any other confirmed him as a social outcast, occurred at a dinner party where he had lost control and assaulted the butler for nothing more heinous than spilling soup in his lap. Gorman had leapt wildly to his feet, knocking the rest of the soup over the lady on his right. Using all his strength he had punched the poor man in the stomach, so severely that he had to be taken to hospital with internal bleeding. After that the diminishing flow of invitations stopped abruptly and nobody ever seemed to be able to accept any of his.

Gorman found that he had nothing to say to people, had nothing in common with them. Bit by bit he became completely self-centred, wanting to create a haven for himself in a world he didn't like and didn't want to come to terms with, a haven where he could do and behave as he wanted. He frittered away his time, arguing with himself that he couldn't take on a job because he was needed on the estate – which he wasn't – it was slowly running down from the years of lack of investment.

Even his home, his very background, wasn't safe in this new world. Four years before he had left the army, he had inherited Glenn House and the Glenn Estate – six thousand acres at the foot of the Pentland Hills, twenty miles south west of Edinburgh – on the death of his father. His father had made no provision for capital transfer tax and Gorman had had to find two million pounds to meet the tax, for which he was now being pressed by the Inland Revenue, or to sell the estate. He couldn't bring himself to sell, and he had found it impossible to raise the money. As a last resort, he had spent an awkward three hours with a man in Edinburgh who described himself as a 'landed property specialist.' It had been a useless and humiliating exercise. The 'specialist' had offered to arrange for the property to be mortgaged to the hilt to an industrialist who would also acquire immediate rights to the occupancy of the house. Gorman would be allowed to stay on the estate, but would have to occupy the old manager's house. As he studied the terms offered to him, Gorman suddenly realised what he was – a man going into a pawnshop. Thirty years as a success in the army was now all too clearly irrelevant. It certainly had not provided the means of securing the only thing he really wanted.

For weeks on end he had walked the solitude of his moors and woods as he tried to think of a means of raising the money. A lonely man who had never married, he had no-one he could turn to for help, no-one whose advice he would value.

I've given my life to the country, he thought, and now the country is going to take my home from me.

His bitterness grew, nurtured on his self-pity, until even his sense of values was called into question. Then, on a visit to Edinburgh, ten months before the attack on Mark Armstrong, he had come across an old friend from the army, Douglas McQuillan, who was visiting the city. The two had met by chance outside a pub just before opening time and had spent the next four hours reminiscing about the old days. They had served together many times both in regimental service and in the SAS and other undercover units. They shared a common belief in the elitism of the SAS and similar groups and their pursuit of excellence—but from different standpoints. Gorman believed that the best was the only standard that would do. McQuillan was an opportunist and liked to surround himself with hard toughened men, men with whom he shared violence as a way of life, whereas Gorman saw violence and massive retaliation as a means to gain the end he wanted.

In Aden McQuillan had saved Gorman's life. Gorman and five of his men had been captured in an ambush in the Radfan mountains and taken back to the tribesmen's base where they would be tortured before being killed. The favourite method was to cut off the genitals of the victim which were then stuffed in his mouth after he had been buried to the neck in the desert sand and left in the burning blaze of the sun. On the first day this was done to three of the soldiers with Gorman and the two others watching, knowing it would be their turn next. But during the night McQuillan had led a rescue party of ten into the base. It had taken him and his men two hours of silent slaughter to free them. On McQuillan's instruction, not a shot was fired. Every tribesman—twenty two in all—whether sleeping or on guard, was garroted or knifed to death. Neither Gorman nor McQuillan had ever mentioned the incident again but Gorman felt McQuillan was the one man in the world to whom he owed anything.

When they were finally pushed out of the pub they had gone back together to Glenn House. McQuillan had suggested a walk to clear their heads, and as they walked Gorman had told the younger man of his problems. McQuillan listened to Gorman's story of frustration. A few years before he would have thought such feelings pathetic and would have been tempted to tell Gorman, as tactfully as he could, to pull himself together and stop complaining. Now he understood. As he brought Gorman up to date with what had been happening to him, the experiences of the two men seemed remarkably similar.

'As you know,' he began, 'I had to leave the army after I refused to go to Belfast. Sometimes I regret it, but I was born in the South, you know. And now I haven't been able to fit in to civilian life. Nobody seems to need a forty-five year-old ex-major whose only skills are a great many different ways of killing people, although at one time they were queueing up for my services.

'I got a job selling insurance, but it was hellish – touting something I didn't believe in to every friend and every casual acquaintance I could drag up. I'm not doing anything now – just sponging off old friends. What I'd like to do is get some money together and try to start something new, like farming in New Zealand. It's too late of think of Rhodesia – I can't get used to calling it Zimbabwe – or even South Africa.'

They had talked on into the evening. Gorman could no longer afford any help in the house and they had fixed themselves a supper of baked beans on toast with fried eggs on top and a couple of bottles of cheap red wine which they would have dismissed as sergeants' mess claret a few years before. Slowly it dawned on them both that they were saying the same things for different reasons. They both wanted money – lots of money – and both of them had only one talent – fighting, killing and leading men.

'Douglas,' Gorman said, half way through the second bottle of wine, 'I'm fifty-five. You're forty-five. If we don't do something now, we never will.'

'But what? What can we do?'

'Let's put the talents we have to work. Let's fight for what we want.'

But it wasn't that easy. Even the days of the mercenary seemed to be over. There were no more Congos or Biafras, no more chance to choose the cause with the most money and with the bonus of unlimited opportunities for looting on the side.

They tried placing an advertisement in *The Times*. All it produced was an enquiry from an effeminate Arab middleman who didn't inspire them with confidence, either in himself or in his employer whose reluctance to be named was only equalled by his eagerness to replace his ageing uncle as absolute ruler of their tiny country; and a number of equally uninteresting responses from companies in the oil industry, the electronics industry and the growing business of electronic surveillance, who were really only looking for some security men tougher than the usual run of ex-policemen. They were being offered jobs, admittedly highly-paid jobs, but nothing that would create the sort of wealth they were looking for.

Eventually they took stock.

'We've just got to face it, Douglas. If we're going to fight again we're going to have to do it for ourselves. We're going to have to take what we want – nothing else will pay enough. I started off wanting to protect this house, now I just want a new start somewhere, with enough money to have to rely on no-one, to be able to do what I want, where I want, on my terms.'

McQuillan agreed. They started to examine how they could freelance, as they put it. They looked at everything. Ordinary crime was too much for them to swallow. But in their self-absorption they began to justify to each other the idea that since most other people seemed to be taking what they wanted in life, why shouldn't they? Why not for a short period put to use all the skills they had, to ensure a new future? Why not take what they needed from someone or something so big that it would never be noticed?

Idea after idea was rejected. In the end they found themselves looking with envy and calculation at the immense wealth and potential of the North Sea. For Gorman it meant an opportunity to strike a blow for Scotland, or at least, his idealised view of his country; for McQuillan, it spelled cash, in huge quantities. From different motives, the two men became united in a single resolve.

'Thousands of millions of pounds there, Douglas. All we want is a few millions of it for ourselves.'

They had spent a miserable day at Glenn House. It had been cold and wet and they were huddled in front of a fire which threw out no real warmth. Gorman read out loud an article he had marked earlier in the Sunday paper.

'"The development during the next few years of the rich natural resources beneath the North Sea is going to alter forever the economy of Britain. Almost ten thousand feet below the sea-bed are proven reserves of more than sixteen thousand million barrels of oil."

'It says later on,' said Gorman, interrupting himself, 'that a barrel is the accepted measurement for oil – equal to thirty-five imperial gallons, or forty-two US gallons. This oil will have a total value of more than six hundred billion dollars at today's price.'

McQuillan cut in. 'And didn't that Arab middleman we met say that today's price is more than three times what it was only a few years ago. Twelve dollars a barrel then, and now almost forty dollars a barrel.'

'Yes, which means that what they've got now is a gigantic windfall in value just because the bloody Arabs are pointing a gun at our heads,' agreed Gorman and carried on reading.

'"As well as the oil, there are in the North Sea proven reserves of over fourteen hundred billion cubic metres of natural gas.

'"Britain uses just under two million barrels of oil a day and thirty-seven billion cubic metres of gas a year. This means that the oil is going to last for at least twenty years and the gas for thirty-eight years.

'"These huge natural reserves are going to revitalise our economy during the eighties, strengthen sterling and provide the base on which future generations will build a great new prosperity far beyond anything we envisage now. We will once again become a great trading nation, operating at a surplus and extending our influence throughout the world."'

'So maybe then,' Gorman said as an aside, 'we'll sit at the centre of the top table again, instead of being there on sufferance.'

'Too late for you and me, though,' said McQuillan, his mind set, not on national prestige, but on personal prosperity.

'"And that is not the end. So far we have explored only a small part of the total British sector in the North Sea – we may well find even greater reserves as we explore the rest over the next few years.

'"To date, only the British and Norwegian sectors of the North Sea have proved to be oil- and gas-bearing – nothing of commercial quantity has been found in any other sector. This means that Britain alone in the Common Market can be self-sufficient in energy. In fact, Britain can be in a position to be a net exporter of oil, and, if we seize our opportunities can become again the strong-man of Europe.

'"It is against this background that the giant oil companies and dozens of small exploration companies are working in the North Sea – twenty-four hours a day, seven days a week, fifty-two weeks a year – non-stop effort to wrench from under the sea the greatest commercial prize of the second half of the twentieth century.

'"In the harsh and hostile environment of the North Sea, technology and capability are being pushed to new heights, breaking new frontiers as the oil companies grapple with, and overcome, all the problems related to the depth of the sea, the force of the wind and the freezing temperatures, the like of which have never been experienced by their industry anywhere else in the world. Here men and machines are being stretched to their absolute limits.

'"The North Sea will provide much of the drama and rewards for Britain in the eighties and the nineties. More than twenty thousand million pounds will have to be invested before all the known fields can come on-stream – more money than has even before been spent in any similar commercial enterprise – and all since the first major discovery in 1970."'

Having decided on their target area they set out to find their quarry. For weeks they studied the oil industry. There was no lack of material and they became regular readers of *Petroleum Times* and *Petroleum Weekly*. They spent long evenings in the pubs of Peterhead and Aberdeen, buying easy friends and information from the men off the exploration rigs and production platforms. Bit by bit, all the publicity surrounding Clan Oil and the Scotia Field, and all the dozens of conversations began to point in one direction.

They laid their plans with infinite care. Gorman raised two hundred thousand pounds as working capital by selling a small outlying farm on the estate to one of his tenants. He realised that what they were planning would not save the estate as he had first hoped, but on the contrary would mean losing it forever. Even with this knowledge, however, he had been insulted and enraged by the smugness with which the tenant had driven a hard bargain, feeling he was in control and that Gorman had to sell.

Together, McQuillan and he bought six second-hand Range Rovers and modern two-way radio equipment. They stocked Glenn House with food and other provisions to cater for a group of twenty, and then they set out to recruit the rest of the men they would need. Drawing on a lifetime of experience in the trouble-spots of the world, they gathered into their group like-minded men with a bond of violence.

Slowly and carefully they went about the task of identifying and recruiting each man, often rejecting men they felt were unsuitable rather than let them know the details of what they were planning, pretending initially that they were trying to put together a special mercenary commando force.

They had disagreed at first on how to recruit the men they needed. McQuillan had wanted men they each knew personally—men they had already served with. But Gorman insisted that that was too risky and might make it easy for the police to identify them. 'We must avoid all the mistakes everyone else makes in this sort of operation—and when it's finished.' He had laid down the recruiting guidelines. 'Each of us, Douglas, will approach the one man we are absolutely sure about. Then, working as teams, you and I and our first recruit will identify another perfect candidate. Then you and I with the newest man will target another, and so on. It should mean that we cast a very wide trawl with few common denominators apart from ourselves.'

The method worked well and threw up hard, bitter, lonely men who shared a common background of isolation and who were introduced to their new comrades only by their first names. There was Ishmail who had been too much of a killer even for the PLO; Roger who had been a captain in the Marine Commandos and was cashiered out after an indecent incident with his batman in the shower—and later asked to leave the French Foreign Legion for the same offence; two Irishmen, John and Paul, one from each side, who had proved their callousness in Belfast, Paul having the added bonus of being an ex-Fleet Air Arm helicopter pilot; Gorman's one-time batman, Mac, who had risen to colour sergeant but was reduced to the ranks for striking a private soldier in a public house; and, a piece of good fortune, a former French paratrooper, Henri, who had been fired as a watch-stander from a French exploration rig off Aberdeen for taking marijuana on board in spite of the strict 'no drink, no drugs' rule.

Thc others were all in the same mould: experts in cars, explosives, radios—and killing; men whose specialised training had been designed to protect their different societies but who in changing times found themselves dinosaurs, rejected by the societies they were conditioned to protect, and thrown back on their own devices.

All of them had certain things in common: all were between forty and fifty years old; none had any family ties; all were ruthless and self-centred; all of them were willing to do virtually anything to make a lot of money.

Under Gorman and McQuillan they were forged into a single-minded unit. They trained for months over the length and breadth of the Glenn Estate, fired by the idea of a million and a half pounds each, with ten million each for the two leaders.

Gorman and McQuillan reverted to their erstwhile Army roles of Colonel and Major, driving their men forward in a training programme that started at six in the morning and lasted until dusk, and beyond as they practised working together in the pitch dark. Over the weeks, they all became hard and fit again, grew to rely on each other, and became completely self-reliant as they learned to do everything they needed for themselves—they even took turns at being cook, sometimes living off the land for days at a time. The experts in unarmed combat revised or taught new skills to their colleagues. They practised using weapons again, to begin with using Gorman's shotguns and hunting rifles. Local misgivings about the greatly increased amount of shooting on the estate were explained by Gorman's story of a private shooting club, which he had indeed taken the precaution to set up. As an extra safeguard he had dismissed his few remaining estate workers.

Radio techniques, use of explosives, car maintenance and much else were dinned into them all, Gorman and McQuillan included, by each specialist. Nothing was left to chance, no detail was too small to consider. Nothing, when it came to the time, was going to fail for lack of know-how or rehearsal. Each expert in the end had two equally qualified back-up men. They all did four hours back-breaking physical training every day carrying sixty pound rucksacks and, slowly but surely, even the drunkards and drug-takers, who were compulsorily on the wagon until after the attack, became fit and hard and tough again. They helped each other, and through the sweat and dirt and effort friendships and alliances grew. But they also criticised each other with some prodding initially from Gorman, and the criticisms became a spur to even greater effort. Operating together as a group they forged a presence of violence, tension and menace. They became what Gorman wanted—a finely-tuned team, working together, able to solve any problem that arose. There was nothing they felt they couldn't tackle. As they prepared and rehearsed for the action that Gorman wanted to limit to only forty eight hours to deny the police the opportunity to counter their safeguards, speed in action would be their best defence.

'The smallest group I've ever worked with, but perhaps the best,' Gorman said to McQuillan, the old decisiveness back in his voice. 'A crack unit if ever I saw one.'

In teams, they spent weeks reading old newspapers and news magazines, absorbing every detail of every hijacking and kidnapping over a period of three years; seeing where the strengths and weaknesses were in every action; drawing up plans and working models; forcing themselves to think as the police would think. They hired from the Central Film Libraries in Glasgow and London every available film about the North Sea oil business and production platforms, running them sometimes as many as twenty times each, until each man, even those who had never been near a platform, came to know every detail of layout to the point where they could, if necessary, find their way around blind-folded. Every day Henri would test their knowledge with a series of different questions: pass mark was one hundred percent; error was punished with extra physical and weapons drill.

'We've got to make sure our plan is foolproof, Douglas,' Gorman insisted, again and again. 'We've got to cover every angle, make sure we can't be forced into a corner. At all times as our operation gets under way we must hold the initiative—we must be in charge. And if anything does go wrong we must have a fall-back plan that will protect us, because that's where everybody else fails.' Gorman drew on his vast experience of the working methods of most of the police and military forces of the West as they planned to ensure that the initiative would always be theirs; trying to second-guess the counter measures that would be taken against them; preparing even for a disastrous end by clearing a three hundred yard area around Glenn House of all obstructions—bushes, buildings and trees—to create a huge flat killing ground, just in case they had to defend themselves at the finish, although Gorman was sure his precautions would ensure that it was a genuine safe house which would never be connected to them.

Three months before Mark Armstrong's early morning phone

call, they were ready for Phase One: the action necessary to arm themselves for what they planned.

In two simultaneous raids they got what they needed. McQuillan led an attack on a large quarry on the outskirts of Glasgow from which he and his party stole ten wooden cases, each holding forty sticks of dynamite. The sixty-seven year old night-watchman at the quarry was in hospital for twelve weeks afterwards, and his pet collie's neck had been broken by McQuillan himself with one savage jerk and pull. They were back at Glenn House before the incident was even reported to the police.

The other raid was led by Gorman. He and his men overpowered the night-guards at Fort George near Inverness. The Fort was being used by a volunteer reserve battalion for two weeks of annual training. No-one was seriously hurt. The guards had been completely surprised and were picked off one by one, with a single blow from behind, as they stood watch with empty rifles. They were easy prey for the experts. The off-duty guards had been dealt with just as easily as they slept in the guardroom. From the armoury Gorman and his men had taken twenty 9mm SMGs, twenty cases of ammunition and twenty hand grenades for each member of the group, and two ·38 calibre revolvers and ammunition.

Now they had the firepower they needed. But Gorman was not quite satisfied. 'I know these SMGs are good. But I prefer their predecessor, the Sterling machine-gun. I've stopped a lot of people dead with it in the past. They'll do though. Nobody is going to expect the sort of offensive we'll mount. Nobody at Clan Oil will even be armed. Stupid buggers. They deserve to have the whole thing taken away from them – they and others like them are risking the whole country's future just to save the cost of a decent defence system.'

Now they had their weapons and the next ten weeks were spent honing their expertise with them. In the outbuildings behind Glenn House Gorman and McQuillan recreated the killing house of their own training procedures with the SAS. Using first of all dummies, and then as their confidence and ability grew, each other, they perfected their close quarter battle techniques. Their final ability in this was awesome in its witness to training and commitment. In the darkened killing house each man could with his SMG on single shot move continuously from room to room and six times out of six hit the head of a dummy positioned right beside their colleagues with two rounds separated by less than two inches.

CLAN OIL'S CLIMB from obscurity to its present potential as one of the richest oil companies in Europe had been the result of a mixture of opportunism, genuine ability, chance and an amazing combination of fortuitous circumstances that could only be described as the luck of the devil—the sort of luck that real success in business always needs.

Mark had seen, sooner than most, the scale of the opportunities that the discovery of oil in the North Sea would open up. Although he had trained in his native Edinburgh, after taking a business degree at Harvard, as an accountant, and indeed was a very successful one, he had sold out his interest in his flourishing practice to his partners and had thrown himself into setting up an oil service company—operating out of two small depots in Peterhead and Aberdeen, on sites which originally he had rented but now owned and which now had a value of several times what he paid for them.

He promised his customers that the Clan Oil Service Company, as he called his firm, would offer a 'twenty-four hour, seven days a week, twelve months a year' service, to supply anything and everything that the exploration companies out in the North Sea needed, and always needed fast. He was a success. Sometimes at the beginning it meant working himself for forty-eight hours at a stretch, but no matter what the problem, he was always able to deliver the goods. He realised that for the exploration companies the requirement was speed, not economy. When it was costing a hundred thousand pounds a day to run an exploration rig the companies would pay anything for the vital services, spares and repairs needed to keep the rigs running. Because he never let anyone down, Mark was able to charge almost anything he wanted for his service—and did.

Mark's character and make-up suited the oil business well. He responded to the idea of complete commitment to business, to the belief that family and outside interests have to come a bad second. Even the exercise he took—squash, tennis and golf—was always with customers or potential customers and provided excellent opportunities for pushing his case and his company. Lunch every day from Monday to Friday and at least four or five dinners a week were given over to business. He was tough and resourceful and oilmen admired his straight talking and the way he conducted his affairs.

He expanded. With the help of his friend, Bob Robertson, the dynamic development director of the Scottish National Bank, Mark's empire and influence grew. He leased, and then bought, his own supply ships, four of them, and helicopters, six Sikorskys at nine hundred thousand pounds each. And although he never courted it, he was the darling of the press. Every imaginable newspaper, from the smallest locals to the Sunday qualities, wrote articles about him and his company. He seemed to have a Midas touch—everthing he did, or was associated with, turned to gold.

But like so many men to whom success has come early, he became curiously dissatisfied, felt he needed new fields to conquer. And like most men who are in any way associated with the search for oil, he became obsessed with the search itself. Bolstered by his success in the service area, he felt he could turn this into even greater success in the exploration field. He shortened the name of the company to Clan Oil. He brought in a general manager to run the service side and set about finding a way to develop his new interest, which he saw as a means to achieve his now all-absorbing ambition—to create a great company from nothing, an extension of his own self, a company that would achieve financial success on a scale never before seen in Britain.

Looking for oil in the North Sea is no game for beginners or amateurs and in a way, certainly at first, Mark was both—but he struck lucky.

Mark's luck came in two entirely separate, but as it turned out, related ways. First of all, Cromarty Promotions, an exploration company which really only existed on paper—it had been set up by three diverse and unconnected organisations as their way of 'getting into oil'—was running out of time. It had the licence to explore in the Scotia Field, only five miles offshore from the Fife coast and the area so far licensed closest to the British mainland. Cromarty had been granted those rights in one of the recent rounds of licensing but a stipulation of that round had been that the licensees had to begin actual exploration drilling before a tough deadline; otherwise half the block would revert to the British government. Also, most people in the business realised that any company which didn't meet this date would incur official displeasure, and would be unlikely to be granted any further licences in the North Sea. All the member organisations of Cromarty Promotions relied on government contracts in other areas for their normal businesses, and therefore didn't want to upset their existing relationships.

So, acutely aware of their vulnerability, they offered their rights to Mark Armstrong and Clan Oil for virtually nothing—if he could get them off the hook by drilling before the deadline. The deal was simple—nothing for the rights themselves, but if oil was found in commercial quantities, Cromarty were to have a first option of buying a ten per cent share in the company set up to develop the oil field. In this way they preserved their interest in the North Sea, but at the same time they were able to get round their obligation to set up and finance their own exploration operation.

At the same time, Johnson and Baird, the famous shipping line based in Edinburgh, found that they were going to take early delivery of a new drill ship—*Marine Knight*. *Marine Knight* was a dynamically controlled drill ship: that is, with the help of ten computer-controlled propellors and thrusters, it could remain virtually stationary at depths of up to three thousand feet, in waves of up to sixteen feet. In an emergency, it could break off drilling in four seconds and automatically seal its wellhead. Johnson and Baird had been under contract to lease *Marine Knight* in ten months' time to a company in the Middle East—and those customers had refused to take delivery early. This meant that Johnson and Baird were open to an offer from Mark Armstrong to lease the drill ship for six months' exploration in the Scotia Field which, being so close to the shore, was in relatively sheltered water.

Built at a cost of £18 million, to lease *Marine Knight* at the going rate of more than one thousand pounds per day per million pounds of cost had meant a bill of over £20 million in total, including the operating costs, for the five months it had been drilling for Clan Oil. Mark had taken his credit limit at the Bank to the top and over to fund this operation. Based on his success in the service area, they were happy to allow this, knowing he had collateral and security in his ships and helicopters, and in the value of the business he had built up already.

And like a fairy tale come true, *Marine Knight* hit the big time in its fifth month of search—against all expectations, she found oil. *Marine Knight* had never been intended for use in the North Sea—only the close inshore position of the Scotia Field had allowed her to work there—since she could not have coped with the weather conditions a hundred and forty miles offshore, where most finds in the British sector are. And it was against all the odds that she struck oil. More than a thousand exploratory wells have been drilled in the North Sea and less than a hundred of them have been found to be oil-bearing.

Tests later showed that the find was probably the biggest single field in the North Sea. Extraction could take place at the rate of 1.1 million barrels a day with an expectancy of at least twenty-five years of production. With crude oil commanding a price of almost forty dollars a barrel, the field had a potential annual turnover of over £16 billion at a profit of almost thirty percent—at present prices. But to bring the field on-stream meant raising a staggering amount of working capital.

Mark Armstrong now found himself in control of potentially one of the richest companies in Britain—if he could raise the extra capital required.

On the strength of the proven reserves in the Scotia Field, Mark had originally persuaded Bob Robertson and the Scottish National Bank to help him raise the initial five hundred million pounds needed to develop the Scotia Field in the late seventies.

The prospects had been dazzling. There seemed to be no risk for the Bank—they had set up a syndicate of major Scottish financial institutions and the money had been raised in less than a week, the whole loan and interest to be repaid in Clan Oil's first few years of oil production. But things had not gone according to plan. For two years running there had been exceptionally bad weather in the North Sea—much worse than anyone had ever expected. The four production platforms thought necessary to develop the field had not been delivered in time because of strikes and late delivery of the special steel needed. Each platform cost over £100 million just to build and each on its own was a massive job to control during construction. The first was now just coming on-stream; the other three lay like exaggerated metal sculptures in construction yards in Scotland, Norway and Germany. None of this was the fault of Clan Oil. But business is business, and Clan Oil's lack of experience was blamed for the delays. They just hadn't been big enough to cope with the extraordinary demands of such an enormous oilfield development nor had they been tough enough or experienced enough to make the penalty clauses in the platform orders stick. There had just been too much to do.

Now Mark Armstrong and Clan Oil needed more money and more time to develop the Scotia Field—another thousand million pounds and another two years. The obvious source to turn to for the money was the Scottish National Bank. But there was a complication. Mark's wife, Sara, had left him and was having an affair with Bob Robertson who, as development director at the bank, was the one man whose help Mark now needed more than anyone else.

*

John Graham took Mark to Clan Oil's headquarters on the western outskirts of Edinburgh. The hundred-acre site was just in the country, fifteen minutes from the city centre and had originally been the home of a famous Scottish judge who had played host for a night to Boswell and Johnson on their renowned journey around Scotland in 1773. The original house had been burned to the ground in 1969 whilst standing empty. Mark recognised that this site was ideal for Clan Oil—they could build their own new building and have ample parking and a private heliport for the continual journeying to and from their platforms and landfall base.

Scotia House was a tall slim tower in brushed steel, its lightly bronzed glass reflecting the traditional skyline of Edinburgh with its classical spires and the Castle on one side, and on the other the two bridges over the Firth of Forth—the single span road bridge with its new clean lines and the railway bridge, completed in 1890, with its familiar giant pink-painted fretwork. Over in the distance, to the south, stood the Pentland Hills.

The building was handsome and elegant in its own way—symbolic of the new age of corporate financial muscle. The main tower rose from a circular cluster of offices, a reception area and conference rooms, to a height of twenty floors. On the top floor was the boardroom and the directors' dining room. Mark had his office one floor below with separate offices for his assistant and his secretary and two smaller conference rooms for important visitors and less formal meetings. There were car parking spaces all round the building and the company's heliport and radio control office were across the old parkland, tucked away behind a screen of oak trees, some of which were more than three hundred years old.

The entrance foyer was busy and bustling as usual. The uniformed security men even checked, to John Graham's relief, Mark's identity card and passed it through the personnel monitor without any prompting from him. Mark greeted half-a-dozen men by name, and several others gave him a brief comment on their own areas of responsibility within Clan Oil. He and Graham stopped for a moment at the large visual display unit beside the lifts which gave a constantly updated status report on every aspect of the company's activities, key personnel, platforms, pipeline progress and landfall base. Even as they watched, their own names flashed up showing 'known location' as headquarters building. Having told the receptionist to send the policeman straight up as soon as he arrived, Mark and John Graham took the lift to Mark's office.

The Chief Superintendent was a couple of minutes behind them—and with him he had a dozen policemen all wearing civilian clothes. He apologised for bringing such a large team and explained that there would be even more arriving soon. 'If it's OK with you, Mr Armstrong,' Mackay said, 'I'm going to set up my headquarters here in your office. I've told your people in the foyer to send my men up as soon as they get here. The next contact is almost bound to come to you here and we'll have a lot of equipment to set up before then. Can we isolate your phone from the main switchboard?'

'Yes, that should be easy, and I have a private number too,' Mark replied. 'And for God's sake, call me Mark. Everyone else does.' He gestured for them all to sit down and asked Mackay, 'What do we do now?'

'We wait. We've got nothing to work on. We have to wait until they contact you. But they'll be short on the phone—they won't run the risk of being traced. We just have to wait and see what they do next. We need something to build on before we can make any move at all.' Mackay looked around Mark's office as he sat down. The modern stylish furniture, which he correctly guessed to be imported from Scandinavia, was set off by the large picture windows all along three walls. On the fourth wall was a huge back-lit map of the North Sea showing exactly where existing and planned operations were—not just for Clan Oil but for all oil companies. On a table to one side was a beautifully scaled model, four feet high and perfect down to the last detail, of Clan Oil's first production platform, Delta One.

Mackay leaned forward in his seat and asked Mark, 'Can you tell me about Clan Oil and your operations? Where do you think you're vulnerable?'

Mark thought for a moment and then shrugged. 'John and I have been talking about nothing else since we last saw you. And I think the real answer, if you're right about how professional this Sunray thing is, is everywhere—this office, our landfall base, our pipeline, the three platforms under construction, and Delta One too.' Mark pointed to the model platform across the room. 'We're just a normal commercial organisation. We can't possibly protect ourselves against armed attack—you must know that better than anyone—no business can.'

Mackay agreed. 'Don't I know it? After North Sea Tapestry, I and a number of senior colleagues made the most urgent representations to the government that, with thousands of millions of pounds to be invested in the North Sea before 1990, we should give considerable thought to positioning a genuine defence system on every major installation—platform or exploration rig. There's even talk now of floating airports being positioned a hundred and fifty miles out to take short take-off and landing, fixed-wing aircraft.' He shook his head. 'But so far the answer is no. The cost of such a defence system is apparently unacceptable. It's going to take a major disaster to change their minds. I presume you agree, though, with their point of view that the sheer scale of most platforms and rigs makes them immune to anything other than a massive attack?'

Mark got up and went over to the model of the platform.

'Yes, because the demands of the North Sea are the most extreme that the oil industry has ever had to cope with—the winds stronger and the waves higher than anything that has been tackled before, allied to freezing temperatures. The offshore industry grew up in the Gulf of Mexico in depths of only twenty feet or so, with warm and kind weather. A hangover from those early days is the description of this production platform as a platform jacket. In those days the jackets were little more than templates to keep the piles of the rigs in position. In the North Sea these jackets are thirty five thousand ton monsters costing a hundred million pounds and more each. Some of the main steel in the legs, for example, is eight inches thick and welded to standards that would satisfy the Atomic Energy Commission. They operate in water up to five hundred feet deep.' Mark ran his finger down one of the main legs of the model. 'Eight inches thick, almost six hundred feet long and wide enough to drive a double-decker bus down inside them when they're lying flat in the construction yard.

'In most months of the year the weather out there is so severe that many major operations such as pipelaying and placing platforms in situ have to wait for what is called the Weather Window—the few weeks in the year during the summer when these operations can be done, when the weather conditions could be described as being reasonable, not that you and I would think them reasonable. So yes, I agree with you, it would damn near take an atomic bomb to damage the structures themselves.

'And,' Mark went on, 'it's not just the equipment which has to be tough. If a man falls overboard from a rig or a supply boat his instructions are to swim away from both the boat and the rig. In his protective clothing he can last for forty five minutes in the freezing hell of the sea but he could be mangled by the propellors of the boat or smashed to pulp by the force of the waves against the steel legs of the platform. Without protective clothing he'd die in five minutes. That's why there is what we call a shepherd boat patrolling each rig or platform twenty four hours a day.'

John Graham cut in. 'But the safety standards are very high.' he said. 'Almost as many men died in the seven years it took to build that bridge out there,' he pointed to the Forth railway bridge in the distance, 'as were killed in the first ten years of exploring and developing the North Sea fields. Also, our security clearance for personnel is second to none—it's my main function. Every employee, no matter how junior, is checked and double checked by an independent security company. Everyone no matter who they are or how senior they are is subjected to a full body search before they're helicoptered out to the platform. There are no drugs, no drinks, no guns and no explosives on Delta One—I can guarantee that.'

'The problem is,' Mark continued, 'the whole set-up is just so complicated. For a start, much of the technology in the North Sea is new. For example, no-one had ever had to build thirty five thousand ton platform jackets and then float them out over their position. No-one really knew until the first time that BP actually did it with Graythorpe One if the crash dive theory would work—the whole thirty five thousand tons might have sunk to the bottom of the sea. All the practice in the test beds might have been wrong. What worked with the model might have failed with the real thing.

'Most production platforms, ours included, have three levels of deck area—each deck almost two hundred feet square. Normal manning level is usually about a hundred men who have to be catered for twenty four hours a day with food, clothes, entertainment and sleeping accommodation. Most platforms, would you believe it, have even more up-to-date film shows than the cinemas in the West End of London.'

'The platforms have to be able to stand up to the worst weather that can be expected and they can. BP based their designs on the assumption that the worst wind and wave combination that could be calculated during the next hundred years would be a simultaneous wind gust of a hundred and thirty one miles per hour with a wave height of ninety four feet and they designed their platforms to be able to withstand that combination and more. We made pretty well the same assumptions.

'So when we're fully on-stream, although it will take two years to get all four platforms up to maximum flow, we'll have nearly four hundred men out there, spread over ten square miles, working twenty four hours a day in cramped and exposed positions—an almost impossible complex to protect. And, as you know, we're already planning to have more platforms.

'But, and this is what has always led us and, incidentally all the other oil companies, to be optimistic about sabotage—if they can stand up to what the North Sea subjects them to, no small group of men is going to be able to do any significant damage.'

'But there must be certain operations that are crucial,' Mackay interjected, 'some areas that are more vulnerable than others?'

'Yes, there are. But it would take an expert to identify them and to know how to damage them. Do you really think these men know enough about a platform and oil extraction to attack the few vital sections that could slow us down or stop us completely? Remember Delta One is like a miniature town—even finding your way around all the different levels is difficult until you've done it twenty times.'

'Well,' said Mackay, 'we can't rule out the possibilty that Sunray has such experts. What else is there?'

'Our landfall base is a much more likely target. The pipeline comes ashore at Ochiltyre and we have storage and pumping facilities there to pump the oil almost a hundred miles down to our refinery. All we have to protect that is a twelve-foot high fence, with security men and dogs patrolling the compound twenty four hours a day.

'And, of course, there is this office with the helicopter terminal on the far side of the car park. We use the helicopters to ferry people up and down to the landfall base and to supply the platforms. We're a little bit unusual in that. We have our own helicopters and we're lucky in that the field can be directly serviced from here in Edinburgh because we're so close to the mainland. Almost everybody else uses Aberdeen which explains why it is now the busiest heliport in the world.'

Mackay prowled around the room turning over what Mark and Graham had told him. Then he sat down and said, 'Right. I'm going to have to go over the detail of every one of your operations with John Graham. I'm going to have to bring in even more people and equipment than I thought originally. Is that OK? Can we use the other rooms on this floor?'

Mark nodded. 'Sure. Do anything you want. Anything you feel will protect us—just in case you are right and this whole thing is serious.'

'I am right,' Mackay insisted. 'One other thing. What about communications?'

'We're in constant touch with both the platform and the landfall base—by telephone and radio. And we have a thirty minute check procedure. John can explain all of that to you.' Mark sat forward in his chair. 'One thing interests me. How do you think you can protect all this? We don't know when or where we might be attacked. The whole thing might drag on for weeks. Has John told you by the way that the weather out in the North Sea has closed in—thick fog—and the platform is now cut off until it clears? We got that on the VDU as we came in. How can you protect us there now? Who will you use?'

Mackay was emphatic. 'We'll use our own men. The public always thinks in a situation like this that we will call in the Army, but that is always a last resort and only if the nation's security is threatened or there is a political element to the terrorists' demands which are following the classic pattern of coming in stages. In this country there is a tradition of using the Army only when one absolutely has to. We have to think of the possible implications of doing so. Let's hope it won't come to that, although I have taken the precaution of alerting a number of other services. In the next few hours there are going to be men with very special talents turning up here.' Mackay paused, hesitating. 'I, em, have been wondering if we should give you some sort of personal protection.' He held his hand up placatingly as Mark jumped to his feet in protest. 'You might not like it, having a couple of my people with you all the time, but it could become essential. For the moment, however, I don't think Sunray will do anything against you personally. They'll need you to raise the money. If they'd meant to kidnap you they could have done it easily this morning, instead of burning the cars. But what about your family—your wife and children?'

Mark's face set into much harder lines as he answered. 'I don't have any. And my wife and I are living apart, and have been for a while.'

Mackay apologised. 'Oh, I'm sorry. I didn't know.'

'There was no reason why you should.'

Mackay turned to John Graham. 'Well, we can do something about this building and the landfall base, and I'll get other police forces to mount guard on the other three platforms that are still under construction. I'll get men onto it right away. Can you explain to your own senior people what is happening and get them to co-operate? Tell them only what they absolutely need to know. For all our sakes, we want to keep a tight lid on the whole business.'

Mark agreed. 'It's your show. Run it as you like. Right now I've got to see my bankers.' He hesitated, wondering whether he could confide in Mackay. He decided that he could – there was something about the policeman which inspired complete confidence. He went ahead. 'Believe it or not, your terrorists are only a minor problem. This company is facing a much bigger threat. We're running out of time and money. And only the Bank can help – if they've got the guts.

'Just before I left home the head of the Bank rang and said he wanted to see me at ten. It didn't sound like a request – as least not one I could refuse.'

DELTA ONE

BRUCE BARR, THE production director of Delta One, was shaken awake by a roustabout who gave him an insulated mug full of scalding hot black coffee with no sugar and said, 'You're wanted in the radio room.'

Barr glanced at his watch and saw it was just after five twenty. He'd only been asleep for a couple of hours. What now, he wondered, as he dressed quickly and set off for the radio room two floors above his tiny cabin, taking the coffee with him.

In the radio room were Sparkie Brown, the radio operator, and Peter Klein, the toolpusher. Klein was a grizzly haired American from Texas who had spent forty years in the oil business from the age of fourteen.

Klein was reading a telex which he and Sparkie Brown had just decoded using Clan Oil's own cypher. He handed it to Barr. As Barr read the message Klein wondered where he got his reserves of energy. He knew that Barr had only gone off to have some sleep just before three o'clock and yet, as usual, he looked fresh and capable—although a small man at just five foot six, he radiated authority and command. The telex read—

SOME FORM OF THREAT TO COMPANY STOP EXTRA VIGILANCE ESSENTIAL STOP ACTIVATE THIRTY MINUTE REPORT PROCEDURE ON RECEIPT OF THIS MESSAGE STOP NO UNAUTHORISED PERSONNEL TO BOARD PLATFORM STOP POLICE INVOLVED NOW STOP DON'T KNOW IF DELTA ONE THREATENED BUT BETTER SAFE THAN SORRY SIGNED JOHN GRAHAM.

Barr stuffed the telex into his pocket and said to Klein, 'Get the four drilling supervisors who report to you and the two watch standers responsible for security and carry out a complete physical check of the platform now—no exceptions, everyone to be accounted for and every facility checked during the next hour. Any questions?'

Klein shook his head and said, 'Within the hour, boss.' As Klein left the room, Barr turned to the radio operator, 'Get the rest of your people up here, and from now until I give you the word to stand-down, I want the television scanners operating on all legs constantly.' He opened the door to leave and said, 'I'll be along in my office until we get this sorted out.'

Barr's office was an addition at the corner section of the top level of the three main decks of Delta One. The strengthened glass windows looked out on miles of empty North Sea in one direction and down over the complicated mass of the entire platform in the other. In the centre of the office was a working surface twelve feet square, with underneath it sixty-four built-in drawers with the working diagrams and blueprints for every part and every function of the platform. Every drawer held at least three hundred sequentially numbered plans—more than twenty thousand in all.

Barr sat down at the table and drummed his fingers on the surface as he worried that his massive responsibility might be threatened. He was too much of a pragmatist to go charging round the platform himself checking only what he could reach. He knew that the training and trial runs that he and Peter Klein had developed were the quickest way of getting the most complete check.

A petroleum engineering graduate of Heriot Watt University in Edinburgh, Barr had created Delta One from first design concepts to the point where it was now almost ready to go into full production. To him Delta One was not a giant inanimate structure

—it was a small town with the almost unbelievable ability to suck hundreds of thousands of barrels of oil a day from far beneath the sea-bed.

At thirty-three Barr was young to have such responsibility, but his pedigree with Exxon in America, Canada, South America and the Far East had made him an easy choice for Mark two years earlier when Clan Oil had first struck oil with *Marine Knight*. He had always wanted to come back to his native Scotland and knew that he would get his chance after the first major North Sea oil field was discovered by BP in October 1970 in Block 21/10 which is now called the Forties Field. For some time then, Barr had, like other experts, a growing conviction that there was oil off the Scottish shores. But not everyone believed in the potential of the North Sea. There were many sceptics, and Barr had been tremendously excited when the details of the find in Block 21/10 were released—a natural reservoir, oval in shape and measuring ten miles long by five miles wide, more than seven thousand feet below the sea bed and holding an estimated 4.6 billion barrels of oil. At the time he was working in Venezuela and had said to a colleague, 'In a few years there will be a major Scottish company working there that I can go back to.' And like others he had laughed at the legend that the BP Board of Directors at a late night meeting had decided, because of ever-rising costs, to withdraw from exploration in 21/10 the day before they struck oil. Fortunately the decision to cease operations was not relayed to the exploration rig *Sea Quest*.

He had been excited by the prospect of producing oil from his own backyard. He had studied every facet of the new technology of offshore production right back to the first discovery of gas in Groningen near the Dutch coast in 1959 which, when allied to a small find in Yorkshire, proved the prospects for the whole North Sea. He studied the results of the thousand wells that have been drilled there since the International Convention on the Continental Shelf in Geneva laid down which sectors belonged to which countries—and in particular the only commercial ones which were all in the British and Norwegian sectors.

He had been on leave in Scotland when the first oil came ashore from the Forties Field on the third of November 1975. And less than three years later he had got the job of overseeing the designing of the Clan Oil platforms, their pipeline system and their landfall base.

Delta One, the first platform, had been the biggest challenge. He had seen it through construction with frustrating delays because of labour problems followed by bad weather when they were ready to float it out. He'd experienced the tension when the complete thirty five thousand tons was manoeuvred into position by half a dozen heavy duty sea-going tugs and then had to be turned through ninety degrees to get it upright. He had personally directed the complex operation of taking the ballast out of the two enormous pontoons on which the whole thing floated. The computer in the base of one of the giant legs had controlled the activating of the valves and the de-ballasting of the platform itself and the grouting which directed the piles which, with the full weight coming onto them, had penetrated the sea-bed under their own momentum to a depth of eighty feet. The crash dive had been a complete success. The £2.5 million computer in the leg had been used only once for ninety seconds. If it had malfunctioned Barr had designed in a manual back-up system. He had finished the operation by activating the electric charge to fire the explosive bolts that released the flotation pontoons away from the main platform legs.

He had designed the extraction pattern for Delta One to overcome as far as he could the problem that there is always more oil in a field than can be recovered because of difficulties of the shape of the reservoir, its varying depth, the structure of the surrounding rock and the danger of part of the well collapsing as extraction takes place. Millions of years ago layers of dead organisms, mainly plankton, simple plants and bacteria, were deposited on the sea bed; later movement caused these sediments to be buried and later still compacted, until under pressure they became oil and gas which moved through faults and porous rock to form the reservoirs where it was trapped beneath a cap of impermeable rocks with a structural form that allowed the hydrocarbons to accumulate. This very process, which created oil in the first place, means that the recovery system for every platform has to be individually created. For Delta One Barr had dictated a circular pattern of thirty wells all at different angles from the vertical and with this had hoped to recover more than sixty percent of the available oil—a slightly higher percentage than is normally recovered. All of the oil collected from Delta One would then flow through a thirty-two-inch diameter pipe made of three-quarter-inch thick steel for more than ninety miles—first to the landfall base and then to the refinery near Edinburgh.

Barr was dwelling on all this planning and design and his instructions to get Delta One—the major platform and control for the entire Scotia Fjeld—fully operational as soon as possible when Klein came back to report to him.

'Nothing, boss. Nothing. There isn't a can of baked beans on this beauty that shouldn't be here. We've checked the whole place—every deck, every storeroom, the generators, the fuel tanks, the blow-out preventor, the sleeping quarters, the cinema, the computer controls, the radar facility. Everything's working. And there's no-one or nothing anywhere on this platform that shouldn't be here.'

'OK. Send a telex to that effect at the next check-in time. And make sure that all your senior staff report anything out of the ordinary—anything at all—to you or me personally.'

'Boss, I've told them if anybody sneezes louder than usual I want to know why.' Klein grinned, and went on, 'But I don't think we're going to have any unexpected visitors for a long time. Look at that.' He pointed out the window. Barr felt a surge of relief as he saw what Klein meant. The bright sunshine outside stopped abruptly a mile away where dense grey white fog was advancing towards them in an impenetrable wall. 'You're probably right, but my instructions still stand until such time as we get an all clear.'

Barr walked out onto the deck to watch the approaching fog. Far below him the sea was a gentle heaving swell of even rounded waves glinting dully in the fading light. As the outer fingers of the fog reached him, Barr shivered in the colder air. Every light on Delta One was now blazing but he couldn't see a thing beyond the flashing perimeter indicators. Even the incessant noise of the busy platform with men working outside in bright fluorescent protective clothing seemed to be dulled by the fog. He turned to go back to his office knowing that until the fog lifted they were cut off from all physical contact beyond the platform. Shifts would change and men would be extra vigilant under the unforgiving direction of Peter Klein but, for the time being, he was content that the environment of the North Sea itself was protection enough.

SARA

SARA ARMSTRONG WAS tall, beautiful, with rich dark-red hair that tumbled to her shoulders in thick waves and wide-set grey-green eyes which sparkled when she was happy. Her lithe, slightly muscular body was tanned a rich dark-brown colour after her recent holiday in the Bahamas.

An American, she had come to live in Edinburgh four years before, in 1976, when she married Mark after a whirlwind courtship in which he had literally laid seige to her for three weeks in New York—calling her every day, sending her flowers, taking her out every night. They had been attracted to each other by superficial things like looks and clever conversation – they hadn't really had much in common outside a successful background – but that didn't seem to matter while they threw themselves into enjoying each other. Even though she had lived and worked there Sara had been amazed at how much there was to do in New York when Mark set out to lay it at her feet. Mark managed somehow to get tickets for the latest shows on Broadway – even though they'd been sold out weeks before. He took her to private previews at half a dozen art galleries, followed by equally private dinner parties; to premieres of two major films with celebrations afterwards at Sardi's; intimate dinners for two in restaurants ranging from a Japanese one just off Fifth Avenue to the River Café set beneath Brooklyn Bridge in an old barge moored opposite the glittering light-filled glass cliffs of Wall Street with the Statue of Liberty glowing green in its floodlighting off to the left; to late-night drinking sessions in fashionable bars like Maxwell's Plum; to baseball games at Shea Stadium, tennis Master finals at Madison Square Gardens; a cocktail party on the hundred and tenth floor of the World Trade Centre – a breathtaking fourteen hundred feet above the ground. All this and much more Mark had been able to pack into their first weeks together. Looking back later Sara realised that it had all been glamorous but brittle, and that she and Mark would probably never have adjusted to the slow pace of conventional courtship. It was almost as if Mark felt he had to sweep her up into a whirlwind of excitement in order to blind her to the reality of their relationship.

Sara worked at that time as personal assistant to a well-known architect who, although a good fifteen years younger, was a close friend of her father, one of the Republican Senators for New York. Mark was in the city tying up financial details of a complicated contract for his small oil service company operating in the North Sea which was just starting its first major phase of development. The deal later fell through, but Mark was able to re-arrange his important financing and a new contract through Bob Robertson of the Scottish National Bank. Bob was running the bank's New York office – downtown, just off Wall Street – a position from which he was promoted back to head office a couple of months later. They had met by accident – introduced by a mutual friend because of their Scottish background and Bob had been just as disappointed as Mark when the original deal collapsed.

The two men had hit it off together immediately and spent Mark's last working day in the city planning how they might work together in the future. Late that night Mark took Bob to Sara's apartment. The apartment was part of a rooftop penthouse, with a superb view over the Hudson River, which her father owned but used less and less as business kept him in Washington and the insistence of his wife and doctor kept him at home when he wasn't in the capital. Sara liked this second Scotsman in her life. The three sat and talked and drank whisky late into the night. She was fascinated to listen to these two men, so different in many ways, but sharing a common belief in the future of their country and the part they were going to play in it, confident of their own abilities, respecting each other but disagreeing a lot.

At that time Sara had never been so completely dominated by anyone the way she was by Mark – needing to see him, talk to him, touch him and share anything and everything with him, and knowing he felt the same. She would phone him constantly if they were not together, even during important meetings, and he was able to pretend to other people listening that she was part of his business razz-ma-tazz, at the same time returning her feelings and endearments in a language of their own.

But at four o'clock that morning when she and Mark went to bed together she was very conscious in a strange inexplicable way of Bob in the guest room next door. His presence intruded into the excitement of their lovemaking – particularly since Mark was one of those men who put all his energy into making love silently, showing his feelings and the depths of his need through his movements and his hands, and an impossible-to-define ability to talk to her without words.

After they were married she and Mark lived just outside Edinburgh – a city in which successful people, whether they are the new successful in merchant banking, oil, investment management or advertising, or part of the established successful in law, accountancy, insurance, banking or civil service, are obsessed with the need to live in the right sort of house in the right area.

Set in a total of sixty five acres of parkland, only twelve miles from the city centre, their Georgian house had an elegant entrance up a flight of seven steps. It had five bedrooms, and four bathrooms, the drawing room was over thirty feet long and was matched by the dining room in which Mark and Sara had at first given a series of very successful dinner parties mixing friends and business colleagues. The fabric of the house had been allowed to run down over the years and they had renovated it lavishly. Mark had insisted that everything should be restored to its original Georgian splendour, except for the fireplaces which he had had blocked up because of a phobia he had of open fires and his inexplicable fear of fires and flames in general. Outside there were stables, garaging for three cars, a one-acre walled garden and an en-tout-cas tennis court.

But the material things they had shared had not been enough. They had not had any children and Mark's almost total absorption with Clan Oil had come between them. They had no common interests. They had nothing to share, nothing to plan for, nothing to dream of together. Sara didn't know which of them was more to blame – she or Mark. Each of them started continually to find fault with the other and to take offence easily. They reached a point where for days on end they couldn't even talk to each other. The marriage had come apart at the seams.

Sara had left. One day during a blazing row she had shouted at Mark, 'I'm leaving. I'm going back to the States.'

'Go,' Mark had shouted back. 'Go. And good riddance, too. There's nothing to keep you here.' He had then turned and walked out and driven himself to the office as though nothing had happened. He had made no attempt to stop her. To Sara the end was an anti-climax. She felt nothing but relief – no remorse. Her marriage had failed because it had never really been a marriage in the first place – no sharing, no planning, no comfort – just a legal state of being together. That had been more than two years ago now. Sara had gone back to New York and had taken a job with one of the big investment banks on Wall Street. Bob Robertson had written to her after a few weeks, and, after he had broken the ice, did so regularly, sometimes telephoning her as well. On a visit to New York about a year after she had left Edinburgh, Bob took her out to dinner and listened whilst she explained with some self-recrimination why her marriage had been a mistake in the first place and how it had got worse and worse. Bob had said little but Sara had sensed his sympathy and understanding and his concern for her which she had always suspected.

A few weeks later Sara had gone off to see an old school-friend in the Bahamas. To her surprise Bob Robertson was a fellow guest. He, of course, had arranged the whole thing, and had got himself invited when he knew Sara would be there. His treatment of her was so different from Mark's, and this had its effect. Mark saw her as a possession, another jewel in his already glittering crown. To Bob it was all very different. Where Mark was obsessed with business and money, Bob seemed to have the time to have other interests and to want to share them with her. Even when the two men had been discussing oil in the North Sea, their particular business, financial, even patriotic interest, Mark had managed to exclude her from the discussion by his coolness and detachment whereas Bob always went out of his way to draw her into the conversation, trying to share the excitement of it all with her. She began to feel that she wanted to share the rest of her life with Bob, to do all the things with him she had somehow never planned to do with Mark, whose business and growing introspection had always seemed to get in the way. She knew what she wanted to do and had only hesitated in her resolve when she thought about the damage an affair might in turn do to Bob and to his prospects. Although he didn't let business dominate him to the extent Mark did, she knew his career was important to him, knew that he was aiming for the top job at the bank. And yet, thinking about it, she also knew how he felt about her and that he would be willing to take almost any risk to preserve what they now had together.

With Bob everything was exciting, everything had to be shared. Mark increasingly had had less and less sense of fun. Everything had narrowed down to his business, and life outside it had lost its sparkle. Even his work seemed to be something he did mechanically, brilliantly perhaps, but with no humour and no room for mistakes or for other people's feelings. Drive had become an end, rather than simply a means.

Bob had persuaded her to come back to Edinburgh a couple of months ago, after he had suggested that they would have another ten days alone together in the Bahamas. He had reassured her that he could handle the situation that would undoubtedly develop between himself and Mark, reminding her that Mark would put Clan Oil's dependence on Bob above his feelings about her. And he had convinced her that Edinburgh society would find it in their hearts to forgive them—particularly if he was the head of Scotland's biggest bank and therefore too powerful a figure to antagonise.

She soon found an old-fashioned flat in the centre of Edinburgh and, curiously, whilst Mark had had almost no contact with her when she was away except to reply, saying no, to her letters asking for a divorce, he tried to see her now. He pestered her on the telephone, wanting to meet her.

Bob had been forced to intervene and tell Mark that Sara wanted nothing to do with him. The two men had quarrelled badly, which was difficult since it was exactly the time that Mark was starting his negotiations with Bob and the Scottish National Bank for the huge extra funds needed for the continued development of the Scotia Field.

*

Sitting in the protected courtyard of the flat she was renting, Sara was having lunch with her great friend, Jenny Scott.

The two women had a special affinity. Just after she first arrived in Edinburgh Sara had helped look after Jenny and nurse her back to health and sanity after she had had to face, in the space of two years, both a messy divorce and the death from leukaemia of her young son.

Often such a close friendship between two women is based on one of them being particularly attractive and the other plain—with the less attractive one enjoying a vicarious life and excitement through association with her friend. But in this case Jenny was more than able to hold her own.

Although tiny, being barely five feet in height, she was lively, extremely pretty with dark good looks, thick, naturally curly black hair of which she was very proud, and at the age of twenty-eight had a figure that was the envy of most girls of sixteen. Wealthy in her own right, with a witty and clever turn of phrase, she and Sara shared many interests and all of each other's secrets. But they were very different from each other. Whilst Sara wanted a man to share her life with in the widest sense, Jenny was much more superficial in her attachments to men and had never made any bones about the fact that she was attracted to Mark and his successes. Perhaps this honesty and the differences between them was why they got on so well together.

Because Jenny had been visiting relatives in the south this was the first time they had seen each other since Sara's return from America. 'I could have died when I got to the Bahamas and discovered that Bob was there as well,' Sara said, remembering the curious mixture of embarrassment and excitement she had experienced. 'Apparently, he'd known the people for years, and when I was invited he moved heaven and earth to get himself invited too. What do you think of that?'

'Were there just the four of you?' asked Jenny.

'No, no. At first there was a whole houseful. It's a big house, swimming pool, tennis court, the whole thing.'

'So what happened? I always knew there was something between Bob and you. But I thought that nothing would ever come of it because of his friendship with Mark, and because they do so much business together.'

Sara smiled gently. 'You're right. I always thought that too. And I think Bob did as well. In fact, I've often heard him say that, no matter how much he fancied a friend's wife and no matter what the circumstances, he would never do anything about it—partly because of trust, and partly because he felt he wouldn't be able to look the other man in the eye again. He also always said it was a difficult rule to live by, since he usually finds himself fancying the wives of the men he likes and admires—presumably that's part of the reason why he admires them.'

Jenny laughed. 'Every man says that. It's the conscience act. It gives them a good out if they make a fool of themselves and then later regret it—the sobering guidelines of the morning after—although I admit it happens to us girls too.' She grinned. 'That's the only reason I've kept my hooks out of Mark as you know—our friendship.'

Sara laughed at her frankness and said, 'Feel free, although I think you'll only get hurt unless you don't get involved too deeply.

'Anyway Bob found it was too difficult a rule . . . something went wrong with his convictions. He said he'd got himself invited because he wanted to talk to me away from the pressures of New York and the ghost of Mark. And that's all we did at first—talk. For hours on end. He asked all about Mark and me, and what we were planning to do. And I told him how Mark had become more and more involved with his work and its worries, that we had drifted apart and had stopped being husband and wife except in name, that I had gone back to New York to sort myself out, and to rethink my whole relationship with Mark.'

'But he must have known all that,' protested Jenny. 'Everyone had noticed how you'd drifted apart. And after all, you had gone back to America.'

'Oh he did. But we talked for hours, and I was trying to explain how it had all happened bit by bit. Not that I made a very good job of explaining. It's so difficult to remember exactly how things happen. It's not as though with Mark and me it was a sudden thing, with rows and arguments and throwing things around. We just seemed to grow apart slowly and then one day it was too late and the rows and arguments were part of our life. We no longer shared anything.'

Sara paused, and for a moment or two, was lost in a world of her own thoughts—the happy moments of when she thought she shared bliss in the simple things like seeing early morning raindrops glistening on the rich green leaves of a clump of primroses, or long walks on a deserted beach; then the increasingly bitter flashes of realisation that somehow she didn't mean enough to Mark, that no woman could, that he wouldn't share his thoughts and plans with her, couldn't take the trouble to tell her what he had been doing all day, that Clan Oil had come to be the beginning and the end of his thoughts and dreams.

'Anyway, we talked and talked. He was very sympathetic and a good listener and I suppose he just let me talk myself out. Then one day I had nothing more to say. We were lying on a hot sunny beach, all the others had gone out fishing and left us there. We were lying side by side not touching in any way. He began telling me how, against his will and his better judgement he was in love with me.'

'And what did you say? What did you do? Did you encourage him? What happened next?' Jenny wanted to know.

'I can't really explain.'

But she remembered how they were suddenly in each other's arms; how he had held her head against his chest and in spite of what he was saying about not wanting to do anything, she knew he did—his racing heart gave him away. He told her how he had always loved her, always wanted her, but couldn't see what he could do about it, and how in the end his love for her was so great that he couldn't ignore it any longer—not for Mark's sake and certainly not just because a few stuffed shirts at the bank might disapprove.

He had whispered to her—the words hushed as though he was afraid that if he spoke them normally they would be robbed of feeling—told her how he felt, how he needed her, asked her what was to be done. What she was going to do about Mark. How did she feel? He told her that he wanted to share his life with her, to build a family with her at his home in the small town of Melrose, and to have her help him with his new job if he got it.

'And suddenly I was able to tell him that I wanted him, needed him, loved him—always had. And only convention and muddled thinking had stopped me seeing it sooner.'

'But Sara, what happened?'

'We made love.'

Sare could see that the three words did not do justice to what had happened. But there was no way she could bring herself to share it with Jenny: the warm sun; the sand hard against her back; the way he had run his fingers all over her—sometimes softly and gently, and sometimes harshly, making her call out as his fingernails traced deep patterns on her stomach, thighs and back. How with shaking hands he had undone the top of her bikini and run his fingers round and round her breasts until she thought her nipples were going to burst before he kissed them—gently at first, then catching them between his teeth and biting harder and harder until again she cried out. How she herself had pulled off the bottom of the bikini. How perfectly they seemed to match each other, he strong and masculine and she feminine in a way she had never felt before.

'We made love,' she said again. 'Many times and in all sorts of places, indoors and out. And for the rest of the holiday he looked after me. Because we were so far from home it didn't matter who saw us or what we did.'

'But perhaps it was only one of those holiday romances?'

'No. No. Would I have come back to Edinburgh for a holiday romance? We need each other. He loves me. I love him.

'I went back to the States again to give us all a chance to cool down. Mark tried to get me to come back. We had terrible rows at God knows what cost on the transatlantic telephone line. I think he accepts now that we're finished. But he won't agree to a divorce. He hates to give things up. But he will in time.

'Bob visited me in New York, of course, about half a dozen times in the last two years. Our love has grown. But for some reason—old-fashioned principles I suppose—he won't yet agree to our living together. He wants divorce, then marriage. But that hasn't stopped us enjoying each other. At the end of last winter we had a lovely romantic weekend in a skiing lodge belonging to friends in New England. It's cold there, you know, too damn cold really for good skiing. But it was wonderful. Bright sunny days and warm tender evenings with just the two of us lying in front of a huge log fire. A peaceful time away from everyone else.' Sara stopped to light a cigarette. 'Bob had to go home early and after he'd gone I wandered around the lodge for hours just touching the things he'd used and we'd used together. I remember standing with my face pressed against the cold of the window staring out at the snow and trees and reliving again the warmth and the closeness we'd just shared. I'll cherish those few days for ever. They were perfect in every way. Even if we never have anything like it again, we'll have had more than most people ever get.'

'What will you do if Mark won't change his mind?'

Sara's normally husky voice with its Bostonian traces took on a determined edge. 'What I should have done as soon as I came back. I'm just going to park myself on Bob and make him accept the situation for what it is. And I'm going to do it today. I don't care if they do still have to work together. Bob has told me he can manage it. And Mark needs his help. No-one else is going to give him all that money. So he is just going to have to see reason.' Sara paused and stood up as though to emphasise what she was saying. 'I'm sure he wouldn't have minded if I had stayed in the States. It's because Bob and I are here in his home town. That's really why he doesn't want to let me go. Well, for once in his life, Mr Mark Armstrong is going to lose.' She took Jenny's hand. 'Perhaps you can help. You can have him if you want him. I'll help. But don't love him – he won't love you. Use him just as he used me, as he uses everyone and as he'll use you if it suits him. You're much more beautiful than I am and perhaps it would salve his wounded pride.'

MARK

JAMES TENNENT, THE managing director of the Scottish National Bank, stood looking out of his office on the second floor of the Bank's headquarters in Charlotte Square. Like the rest of the Square, sometimes described as the most beautiful in Europe, the Bank's office had originally been designed as a gracious townhouse by the architect Robert Adam. Built in 1791, the Square, with its elegant symmetry, has been carefully preserved over the years and looks today exactly as it did when Adam finished it – even many of the original mounting blocks for carriages and horses are still there – except for the addition of electric lighting and parking meters, the darkening and weathering of the buildings and the change to asphalt from the original cobbles. Even from such a steep angle Tennent was able to recognise the man emerging from a car parked in front of the Bank as his most troublesome, although potentially his richest, customer.

Sighing, he reached behind him and buzzed his secretary.

'Ask Mr Robertson to come to my office,' he said as the girl came in from the connecting room. 'Tell him Mark Armstrong is just arriving.'

He knew that the coming meeting was going to be difficult and that there would have to be a lot of give and take on both sides. But he could see that the Bank would have to be careful. Armstrong wanted help and yet at the same time was in a powerful bargaining position.

He took a last look at his view of the Square and George Street beyond, turned and picked up the brief Bob Robertson had sent him first thing that morning. The factual and unemotional single page was an outline of the present state of Clan Oil's account with the Bank, together with what Armstrong was asking for and needed.

Tennent still found it difficult to come to terms with the demands of the oil industry in the North Sea – much of it was totally alien to his whole approach to life and business and very different from banking. On a recent visit in his capacity as head of the Bank to an exploration rig operating about a hundred miles off the Scottish shore, he had watched stores and equipment being unloaded from a supply boat. There had been a heavy swell running. Suddenly an enormous wave swept over the sides of the vessel and a large wooden crate that had not been lashed down slid over the open stern of the boat and disappeared beneath the waves. Standing next to him was a roustabout with a thick Liverpool accent who was directing the unloading operation on a two-way radio. The roustabout's only comment was 'I don't know what was in that. But it's no fucking good to us at the bottom of the sea. Get another one out here on your next run.'

Later Tennent learned from the American toolpusher who was in charge of the rig's drilling operations that the crate had contained over a hundred thousand pounds' worth of sophisticated measuring equipment. The incident had reinforced his misgivings as a banker about the whole oil industry where the cost of materials and the margin of waste is completely overshadowed by the need to keep the drilling rigs and production platforms running, and where the management attitudes are totally different from the ones he had encountered throughout his career. He had gone out to the rig to see at first hand what it was really like in the North Sea. A kindly man, he had been shattered to find men operating in sub-zero temperatures amid howling winds that never seemed to let up, always threatening to rip the unwary from the safety of the rig and into the boiling murderous seas below. The visit had given him some idea of the personal risks the oilmen took every day—risks that could only be justified by the scale of the prize they were ripping from almost ten thousand feet below the sea bed.

Below him Mark Armstrong had slipped the new Ferrari he had borrowed from one of his fellow directors into one of the parking spaces reserved for important visitors. He had killed the engine but continued to savour for a few minutes a Mozart horn concerto on the car's stereo—just as he had a few moments before enjoyed the recognition and salute from the commissionaire at the front gate and the unashamed curiosity the salute had brought from the casual passers-by. He enjoyed his success, even the little things like being allowed to use this reserved parking area and the comfort and luxury of the powerful car. And he had needed a little time to prepare himself mentally for what looked like being a daunting interview.

Getting out, he looked up at the imposing and in some ways intimidating facade of the Bank as he walked into the reception area where he was again saluted, this time by Tom Morrison, the ex-sergeant major from Glasgow who was the custodian of the Bank's foyer. Over the years Mark had struck up an easy-going friendship with Morrison, who had lost a leg fighting as a tank commander at Anzio and who still resented the fact that the British Army hadn't been able to hold on to his unit's original gains in that famous battle without reforming.

'Morning, Mr Armstrong,' Morrison said, clearly pleased to see Mark. 'See from the papers you're in the news again. Nothing serious, I hope. And remember I've got a little put aside if you need it. I always put a pound or two away every week, always have.'

'Thanks, Tom. I think this is going to take a bit more than your savings. But thanks again for the offer.' Mark smiled, sharing Morrison's good humour and appreciating the way the way the man's friendliness had unwittingly helped him to relax.

'I've got an appointment with Mr Tennent. He's expecting me. Can you let him know I'm here?'

'Certainly can, sir. Certainly can. And if you have any trouble with him, just let me know—I've got a lot of influence around here.' Morrison winked and grinned.

Laughing, Mark followed him as he limped across to the small lift that took visitors up to the executive floor of the Bank. Tom held open the door and said, 'You know the way? And remember, if I can help. I've got a lot of faith in you, Mr Armstrong. What this country needs is more people like you – people who get out and do things, get things moving. I'll let Mr Tennent's secretary know you're on your way up.'

In the small lift, finished in leather in the Bank's colours of deep red and gold, Mark marvelled as always at the fierce independence of a man who obviously saw his role as being every bit as important to the Bank as the managing director's, and had no doubt that he could put in a good word, an impression he probably gave in a similarly lighthearted way to the dozens of important customers who came to the Bank every week.

Tennent's office always seemed to Mark to be cut off from the harsh realities of life, cushioned from the outside world by the strength of the Bank. It was large, and the quiet, reserved carpeting and furnishings reflecting the owner's conservative taste must have cost more than most people would pay for their house. The Chippendale partner's desk from which he was rising was worth several thousand pounds on its own.

As always, Tennent was immaculately dressed, a small light-yellow rose in his buttonhole setting off his thin cultured face, complemented in turn by the mass of curly grey hair which he wore parted in the middle. Although he was a small slight man, everyone who had ever met him was always impressed by his strong character and his ability to handle the most complex financial affairs. He was a man who never in his business life had taken an unnecessary risk and always put the interests of the Bank before every other consideration.

Standing beside Tennent was Bob Robertson, his development director – tough, compact, heavy-set, like Mark, in his forties, lively and bristling with energy and enthusiasm, his square open face, deeply tanned, emphasised by his slightly receding hairline, his grey eyes gleaming. To the Bank Robertson was a rising star who, since joining the Bank from university, had packed a lot of experience into his career, including a stint in their prestigious London corporate banking office as well as his time in New York. Although he wore a conventional dark business suit like his superior's – his was better cut in a more modern style – at the same time he had the air of easy, informal self-confidence, of a man confident in his own abilities and sure of success in whatever he did.

Robertson had backed Armstrong in all his ventures since they had met in New York. But he knew that his affair with Sara was now so open that it could put an intolerable strain on their dealings with each other, and that, in spite of his reassurances to Sara, it was causing Tennent and the chairman of the Bank, Lord Drumsheugh, considerable concern.

'Mark, it was good of you to come round so quickly,' said Tennent, trying to soften the threat of his abrupt request for Mark to come to the Bank, only an hour before. 'And I was sure you wouldn't mind Bob joining us, since he is very much involved in the whole thing.'

Mark was careful to conceal any anger and resentment he felt. Only a slight flush deepened his naturally dark complexion. Tall and slim, at six foot two, he was much taller than both the other men and he acknowledged Bob with only a brief nod. He wore his wiry black hair slightly long, an informality emphasised by his habit of always wearing casual clothes. Today they were grey trousers and a dark blue jacket with hacking slits, which emphasised his slimness.

It was, of course, unusual for the chief executive of the Bank to be taking part in the sort of meeting that was about to follow, but the Bank's Executive—the senior executive directors who run the Bank on a day-to-day basis—had felt that this was essential in view of the scale of the operations concerned, the adverse publicity it could attract to the Bank if things went wrong, and the fact that he and Bob Robertson were the only people who, up until now at any rate, could handle Armstrong in an eyeball-to-eyeball confrontation.

'Just what do you propose to do about all this?' asked Tennent in his slightly prissy Edinburgh accent, indicating the newspapers scattered over his otherwise clear desk top.

'All this' was plastered over the front pages of the *Scotsman* and *Financial Times*. 'CLAN OIL UNDER PRESSURE' said the *Scotsman*. The *Financial Times*, with a little more elan and an eye for the true trouble had chosen to lead their report: 'CASHFLOW PROBLEMS FOR CLAN OIL'.

Mark answered Tennent directly, ignoring Bob. 'Both statements, as you know, are true in their different ways.' he said. 'The important thing is, which one do you want to help solve? Surely to God you are going to help. You've helped so far, all along the way. You're not going to withdraw your support now when I need it most?' His strong, classless voice seemed to add extra emphasis.

As Mark was speaking, Robertson's mind was considering the implications of their personal relationship. He felt that it was only a matter of time until Sara would want to live with him and wondered how the other man would take it. He won't like it, he thought, but he'll accept it in the end. He needs me, needs my help. Without it he'll lose control of his company. The Bank will never back him without my support; he's asking far too much. I think he'll put that first. But he never gives up easily. He knows that Sara is frightened of the effect our affair may have on my prospects here but he must see that that's a two-edged sword, and if I fall from grace he'll never get the money. The only time I've seen him scared of anything was the time he and I were on that other oil company's platform and he was worried by the flames from the flare stack. Strange, we were in no danger but when the crew lit it he seemed to shrink into himself. But he won't shrink from this.

Momentarily he reflected sadly on how well he and Mark had worked together a couple of years before. BP had just raised £380 million to help them finance the development of the Forties Field. That had been the largest loan ever arranged by a commercial company – with the entire loan including interest to be repaid by 1982. It had been relatively easy for them since they are one of the ten largest trading organisations in the world – the largest in Britain if Royal Dutch Shell is discounted because of its joint parentage. In comparison, Clan Oil was a tiny company. Its development costs would, because of inflation, be even greater than BP's for the Forties Field and the only way it could raise the money was with the fullest possible backing of its Bank. Its potential was tremendous, but to realise it would mean a level of funding never before attempted in Britain, or elsewhere for that matter, by a private company. To persuade the Bank to back them two years earlier had been the result of the closest negotiation and planning by Mark and himself working together as a team. Now Mark was back asking for twice as much, his schedule in tatters, no revenue coming in and yet the two of them would still have to work together in spite of what was happening between him and Sara.

Mark took off his jacket and loosened his tie. Tennent pretended not to notice that Mark had thrown his jacket on the floor – not because he disapproved, although he himself had never once in his forty years with the Bank taken his jacket off. No matter how hot it was – even in the scorching summer of 1976 – he had always been properly dressed according to his lights, a state which always included wearing a waistcoat. But he realised that with this gesture Mark had taken some of the initiative, shown his disrespect for the Bank's way of doing things.

Still unwilling to catch Bob's eye, he started to put his case to Tennent. 'As you're fully aware, we need another thousand million pounds to develop the Scotia Field – we're running badly behind our schedule. You know the reasons for that – exceptionally bad weather and late deliveries. As you know, both of these problems are all too common in the North Sea. Neither of them is our fault.' Mark clenched his teeth and swung his right fist in a chopping gesture to reinforce what he had said. 'But on top of that we now estimate that we will need an extra four production platforms, although the reason for that is good. We have now shown that the reserves are more than fifty percent greater than we first estimated.' They all sat down as Tennent fastidiously picked up Mark's jacket and hung it on his coat stand and indicated the chairs in front of his desk. For the first time Mark looked straight at Bob. 'But the big question is – are you going to raise the money for me? I know it will be difficult because we haven't lived up to our timetable and therefore the repaying of the initial loans will also be behind schedule. Your deputies and mine have been discussing this for weeks, but we've now got a crisis of confidence. Our big suppliers and sub-contractors are getting worried about whether we'll be able to meet our commitments. I'm glad James asked for this meeting, otherwise I would have. We've got to know where the Bank stands.' Mark's confident stance put his case well, though inwardly he knew Clan Oil owed a lot to the Bank and that he needed these two men on his side.

'But one thing you'd better realise,' Mark's tone became more aggressive as he pressed his case with an element of bluff, 'there are plenty of other banks I could turn to for help and a lot of them would jump at the chance. So don't bullshit me with how much I owe you, or how much you've done for me in the past. What you're going to do in the future is what counts now.' With an actor's skill he flattened his voice into a sneer. 'I know you've often told me that only three percent of the population change banks – well, I'm not impressed by that. Either you help, or I'll be seeing some of your competitors later today.'

Tennent could sense that Mark's personality and the obvious strength of his bargaining position were starting to dominate the discussion. He tried to regain the initiative. 'Naturally we want to do everything we can to help you, Mark,' he began, 'but I'm afraid that financing of the scale you now need is beyond the resources of this Bank – or any other single bank for that matter – so I'm unclear as to which of our competitors would welcome you so readily. And you must accept some of the blame for not sticking to your timetable. That sort of failure worries outside investors, and the downside is an understandable lack of confidence.

'If we are to help we will have to persuade, not only our own Board of Governors but also all the other financial institutions who put up the original loans, and the investing public as well. To raise a thousand million pounds in total, the company is going to have to go public.'

Mark interrupted impatiently. 'But how quickly can you do that? We are running out of time. I don't mind going public. I've always recognised that sooner or later we would have to. But you know yourselves that we're almost at the limits of our original loans. Our first platform, Delta One, is due to come completely on-stream in a few weeks. We're running final tests at the moment, but it will be two years now before we get the first four platforms up to maximum production. And our running costs are nearly a million pounds every ten days, let alone the interest payments to yourselves.'

Mark searched Tennent's expression for signs of a change of attitude. Seeing none, his exasperation broke through. 'Look, for fuck's sake, I've worked my arse off getting this company going. I saw the opportunities. All you've been asked to do all along is put up the money for something that carries no real risk – the oil's there. I know it and you know it. And in any case, you make your money out of lending money to other people, don't you? Well, here's a chance to make a lot more money – more extra business in one deal than the Bank would normally handle in a year. Are you going to pass it up?'

Tennent never liked to be reminded of the Bank's role as moneylender so he ignored the question. But he frowned and flicked at imaginary specks on his spotless desk to show his resentment of Mark's language. 'It will take time for Bob and me to prepare your case for consideration by our Board. Believe me, we'll work as quickly as we can – we've been doing a lot already. But it is beyond even our remit to sanction what you need. Don't you agree?' He turned to Bob who nodded in confirmation. 'And on top of all this are your very considerable personal borrowings from us – to buy your house and the land with it. And there is your guarantee to Gordon Advertising – it looks as though it may be called in. Not by us, we're not their bankers, but we understand the Caledonian Bank are very worried about their position. In all it means you are very stretched personally. We know how successful your company is potentially, I'm only putting the Bank's position. We may have to ask you to lodge some of your shares with us. I don't need to remind you that we can't separate your personal position from the wider discussion. It's not our own money we're lending and we must protect our deposit customers, whose money it is, and our own shareholders.'

Mark looked at them both in calculated disbelief. 'So what? My shares in Clan Oil are worth several hundred times more than my commitments – that's why I don't even bother about them. Just what the hell are you trying to do? Does Bob want my business as well as my wife? Do you want to have two fights going at once? Bob and I have a score to settle. Are the two things going to get mixed up?' He turned angrily towards Bob. 'And where do you stand in all this? What's the price of your help – my wife?' Quite deliberately he was striking at a weakness that might just give him an advantage provided he didn't go too far.

Tennent winced. But Robertson showed why he'd done so well, come so far so quickly. He met the challenge head on. He kept his voice even; he saw instantly that Mark was trying to rattle him to gain a temporary positioning advantage. 'Surely you don't want to have a personal row here? Do you want us to help or not? You and I have got to work together until we get this straightened out. Right? At the moment your company owes this Bank and others in the original syndicate more than four hundred million pounds. That is the extent of the indebtedness to us you have built up in the development period of the Scotia Field. Even if some of it is covered by your equipment, how saleable is it now? You know how little a forced sale ever brings. All right, I know we, myself in particular, encouraged you.' Mark grunted agreement and raised a contemptuous eyebrow. Bob leaned forward and tapped the top of Tennent's desk. 'This Bank wanted a major investment in the North Sea. Well, we've got it now, through you and Clan Oil. But we must be sensible and face facts. You are vulnerable and over-stretched financially. James has outlined your personal debt and liabilities. We know that given time you can cover most of your debts. But you may not be given time. What you obviously don't know is that you may lose control of Clan Oil. The government is considering nationalising the company in what it believes to be the country's best interest. Which means that we have to be careful. James has already been contacted this morning by Hamish Blair at the Scottish Office saying that they would appreciate our co-operation.'

Mark was amazed. He had often criticised the senior civil servants at the Scottish Office, saying that whilst theoretically they could wield enormous power, and were often criticised by Members of Parliament and the public for this, when the chips were down they usually shied away from it. Here for a change they were showing real teeth – but why the hell had they picked on him and his company? Why had he himself or any of his other people not picked up the whisper of such a threat which they had always recognised might be a possibility? And why had they contacted Tennent – were they hoping perhaps to squeeze him in a pincer thrust? Although he was shaken he didn't show it.

'That shouldn't make any difference. We'd have the government instead of thousands of investors as partners. They would have to pay the proper price if they bought control.'

Robertson shook his head. 'I'm afraid not. Naturally Blair was somewhat guarded in what he said to James, but we think the Treasury are arguing that they could make a case for buying you out, simply on your performance to date. They would put up the money for the rest of the development of the Scotia Field and launch the first really integrated government oil company covering everything from drilling, to marketing through their own filling stations. The justification, apparently, would be the precarious state of the country's economy and the fact that Clan Oil could radically alter for the good our whole government borrowing position. You personally might get virtually nothing – all the government would do is take over your debts and give you a nominal payment for the look of things. You might even lose your job.'

Mark was obviously taken aback. 'The devious bastard. And to think I took him to lunch only the other day and he didn't mention any of this.' His whole tone changed. 'What do you suggest we do, James?' Mark suggested by his deliberate use of the collective we that he expected the Bank to join with him in fighting off the threat from central government, always seen by banks and businessmen alike as the real enemy.

Tennent was relieved to see Mark's anger directed away from the Bank and his obvious reconciliation to the need for collective action.

'As I understand it, Blair didn't know anything about it until today. He got his instructions this morning.' He paused, then went on, 'I think we have to attack. We should fight fire with fire. You must get your side of things across, too – particularly to the general public. We must have public opinion on our side.'

Mark brought the conversation back to the purpose of his visit. 'And the money?' he asked.

Tennent was placatory. 'Look Mark, we're not going to abandon you, but our position must be watertight. It probably is possible for us to help you raise the extra money you need – you must leave it to Bob and me to put your case within the Bank. But to get the public on our side will be vital if we are to simultaneously fight off the government. I think we should hold a press conference – after all, it would be better to have the newspapers and television putting our case across for us. You should present yourself and your company as perfect examples of working capitalism attacked unnecessarily by central government. And above all as a Scottish business being interfered with from London.'

Mark and Bob could hardly believe what they had heard. Tennent was known to shun personal publicity – and the Bank had always kept a low profile with the Press, even when it was criticised by them. Now, although it went completely against his character and all his training, he recognised the special circumstances in this case.

Noticing the effect of his suggestion, Tennent smiled wryly. 'Not here, of course,' he said hastily, picturing with horror an unknown number of reporters rampaging throughout the quiet of his beloved offices. 'Perhaps you could arrange it under your banner, Mark? And Bob can be there to represent us as your financial advisers. It should be good experience for him, since I expect it will be increasingly important in future. Bob will keep in touch, and you let him know what arrangements you make as regards the press conference.' He got Mark's jacket and held it for him to put on.

'With a little bit of luck we'll both win,' he said. 'But don't underestimate the opposition. The prize is too great. The government may be willing to take great risks to win control of Clan Oil—risks they might otherwise be reluctant to accept. For our part, we want to help. But bear with us; we've never had to find funding on this scale before.'

'Well,' said Mark, returning to some of his earlier belligerence, 'you've got to find it now. I need a commitment in the next few days. I'm relying on you.' He hesitated, then decided to take them into his confidence. 'Oh, and by the way, we've had a threatening phone call. We don't know how serious it is. I can't tell you any more at the moment, the police are handling it and asked me not to say anything to anyone.' He was carefully off-hand. It would never do to indicate that the situation was potentially serious—he was certain the Bank would overreact just when he needed them to feel that Clan Oil's position was cast-iron.

Tennent stood up, rather formally shook hands to say goodbye, and added, 'Well, put us in the picture if and when you can. These things are best left to the experts. Presumably it's just a passing problem, no matter how tiresome and difficult it is for the moment. We for our part have always found the Scottish police to be most efficient whether in dealing with robberies, fraud, or the occasional bomb hoax.'

'I'll see Mark out,' said Bob.

Outside in the hall waiting for the small lift to come up, both men were awkward. The lift seemed painfully slow in coming. Mark broke the silence almost reluctantly. 'I need you, need your help. But I think you should keep away from Sara. After all, she's still my wife.'

Bob brushed the implied threat aside. 'I'm sorry, Mark. It's too late for advice like that. Things have gone too far. I'll do everything I can to help you and Clan Oil, but the business of you, me and Sara is entirely separate. I think I can help you keep control of your company—but that's where my co-operation stops.'

Bob turned back towards Tennent's office wondering how much of the argument had been overheard. With all the executive directors of the Bank sharing the same floor, there had been people coming and going behind them as they argued.

*

As he drove back to his office Mark thought about the peculiar relationship that was developing between him and Bob Robertson. In a way he understood. He knew that Sara and he had not made a success of their marriage. He neither knew nor cared whose fault it was, although he suspected it was his. Always he had put the business first. He had ignored the warning signs. He had accused Sara of not understanding, never being willing to make allowances. He wondered now if they had ever really been in love, or if, as he sometimes felt, he had seen her as the perfect wife: good family; classless; acceptable; a foil to his commercial success. But Christ, he thought, why did she have to choose Bob Robertson?

*

At eleven thirty a Range Rover turned into the gates of Glenn Estate. In it were four men who had driven up from London where for two weeks they had kept a constant surveillance on the night-time operations of the staff and security men at the headquarters of Independent Television News at their studios in Wells Street. They were well pleased with the success of their operation. They now knew the strengths and weaknesses of the security staff and the habits and timings of everyone who used the studios regularly. They were confident that their back-up action, if necessary, was feasible. The previous night they had carried out an unarmed rehearsal of their operation using an alternative form of deception and had, as they expected, encountered no last minute hitch.

Gorman saw them arrive from his desk in his study, but was prevented from going out to greet them by a telephone call which was short but which confirmed that the last piece in his complex defence system was now ready. 'Sunray? We are now on station at a berth in Stranraer harbour and will keep pre-arranged rendezvous.'

BOB

Bob Robertson was a rarity in a major Scottish Bank – he was an individualist, an extrovert, and wealthy in his own right. He was a man who always took instantaneous decisions, who knew where he was going and what he wanted.

Born in Melrose, he was the eldest son of one of the Border knitwear barons. Educated at Sedbergh in Yorkshire, which at the time was popular with wealthy Borderers, he was destined at first to follow his father into the family business, where after a few years of being bullied by the various section managers he would be appointed to the Board. But he didn't want any part of this apparently democratic nepotism; he had become fascinated by money, and announced that he was going to join the Scottish National Bank – Scotland's biggest bank, with a reputation for being more progressive than their rivals. He almost failed at the first hurdle – the staff department were understandably suspicious of his motives, particularly since they handled his father's personal and business accounts. However, he had won them over, and since then had blazed a meteoric rise up the Bank's hierarchy and was now held out by the staff department as a shining example of how to succeed in banking where everyone, including the most senior executives, has to start at the bottom.

His easy self-confidence fitted well into the world of modern banking where articulate young men conduct corporate finance and international funding with style and ability both on the customer side and for banks; where staggering loans and resources are negotiated with an easy-going charm that belies the hard professional edge that guarantees the self-assurance. Now he was being tipped as the obvious successor to James Tennent as the Bank's next chief executive – the top job in a Bank that had a staff of over 10,000. The one thing that might stop him getting this, the best job in Scottish banking, was his personal life. Still a bachelor at forty, and for that alone suspect in the eyes of a great part of Edinburgh's Establishment, his affair with Sara Armstrong was becoming common knowledge. It was an affair which he had found himself unable to resist – not because he ignored the dangers such an indiscretion might have on his career, but because he had analysed them and decided he was prepared to accept the risks because Sara was too important to him to deny what had happened between them. Only a few days before one of the Bank's customers – an old-fashioned whisky distiller – had vindictively brought up the subject with his boss, James Tennent, whilst the two were playing golf. Grasping Tennent's elbow in that annoying way Scotsmen do when they want to be conspiratorial, he said he was worried about young Robertson and Armstrong's American wife – thereby implying criticism of Bob because of his comparative youth, and of Sara for having been born anywhere other than Scotland. What he really meant, Tennent had thought bitterly, was that he hoped to be the bringer of bad news. Tennent had cut short the criticism in his usual brusque way, pointing out that with the social changes that were part and parcel of modern life a man was four times more likely to change his wife during his lifetime than he was to change his bank.

But Tennent was worried—a constant topic of conversation between him and Lord Drumsheugh, the Bank's chairman, concerned his possible successor. Robertson was the obvious choice—the natural front runner—but since Tennent and the chairman hoped to make a firm recommendation to the Bank's Board of Governors, as the Directors are rather pompously called, within a few days, any overt scandal associated with Robertson at this stage or later could be disastrous.

When Tennent brought up the matter with Bob, the younger man had been frighteningly honest.

'I am in love with Sara,' he said. 'She, I think, is in love with me. No matter what the consequences, I want her to divorce Mark and marry me.'

But Tennent fretted all the same. He saw Bob as his protégé, which he was—the son Tennent had never had—and he selfishly wanted to take credit for new glories through the younger man's successes. He had sought out his chairman, Lord Drumsheugh, in their shared club, the New Club, one evening after dinner and the two of them had sat long into the night discussing the matter.

Drumsheugh had won his spurs in banking when in the late sixties he had masterminded the absorption of two smaller banks into the much expanded Scottish National Bank. An accountant, he had spent his early years in London, carefully building his career and contacts, certain in his own mind that one day he would be the head of the biggest bank in Scotland—and therefore of the biggest business in Scotland. Curiously, he didn't in any way resent the size and scale of Clan Oil or of the business, actual and potential which it represented. Tennent shrewdly kept referring to the problems of the oil company as he gently pushed Robertson as his successor.

But Drumsheugh seemed to have reservations about Bob Robertson. He summed these up to Tennent as the two of them stood on the steps at the Club's entrance on Princes Street.

'As you know, James, my own wife was killed in a hunting accident only two months after we were married. I never felt the need or the inclination to remarry. For some reason I can't explain, this has always rankled with and intrigued the financial establishment in Edinburgh.

'Your successor must be the perfect choice. In the next ten years banking is going to be thrust more and more into the public eye. We're going to have to get used to having many of the decisions we used to take in private being the subject of public debate. The only query I have about Robertson is his private life. I am haunted by how cruel people in Edinburgh can be. It's a small city.' For a moment he was lost in a bitter memory. 'All the same, perhaps I'm wrong, perhaps people are changing. Dammit, I will not have the choice of the Bank's next managing director dictated by people outside – particularly people whose opinions I feel are suspect.

'Let's discuss all this as soon as possible. Can you set up a Board meeting, James, for late on Friday? Let's see if anyone can put up a better candidate. I doubt it. You've groomed him for this, haven't you? I can't believe that you have wasted all these years and all that effort. Let's see if everybody else has the same faith in him that you have. There's only the one doubt I have about him – and I'll give him every chance to prove I'm wrong. I want to mull it over for a couple of days before I decide whether or not I'll back you.' As Drumsheugh stepped on to the pavement his chauffeur pulled the Bank's Rolls-Royce silently up beside him. As he settled himself in the back he said goodnight to Tennent and left him with a sobering thought. 'But remember, no matter how much we may disapprove of the attitudes that seem to prevail in Edinburgh, we have to live with them and we won't change them.'

Tennent took a last chance to further Bob's position. 'You may be right. But that doesn't mean we shouldn't try, does it? You and I know who he's married to won't make one whit of difference to how well he'll do the job. Perhaps it would be cowardice on our part not to acknowledge that.'

'Perhaps,' said Drumsheugh, raising his hand to say goodnight and nodding to his chauffeur to drive off.

As he drove home, Tennent thought about Bob and his hopes for him. And his mind turned to Clan Oil and the North Sea. Earlier that day, he had been talking to the head of the Bank's oil division about rigs, about how they were built and how they were insured in view of the risks they represented. If a ship collided with a production platform, or if one of them broke loose, millions and millions of pounds would be lost, perhaps for years, until the operating company could reposition over the well – not to mention the spillage that would occur, and the damage which that would do.

'But,' said his oil expert, 'we are making advances all the time. Breaking new ground. Now to protect them from corrosion of the wind and weather most production platforms have their splash zone clad in a skin of stainless steel – the legs and all the braces. And much of the steelwork beneath the waves have special self-sacrificial anodes built into them. These anodes build up a reverse electrical field – electro-chemical reaction it's called. This means that the anodes corrode and destroy themselves instead of the steel to which they are attached. Perhaps in a few years it will be possible to do the same thing on motor cars.

'But in spite of all the research, people still make mistakes and a platform jacket just placed in position a while ago was ten feet higher than it needed to be. The operating company made a mistake in estimating the depth of the sea. And that extra ten feet cost them £5 million extra in production costs.

'Also, a couple of years ago a French company made a mistake in estimating the depth of water they were going to operate in. The water was thirty feet deeper than they thought it was. Under the extra pressure the legs of their £100 million platform collapsed and the whole thing was a write-off.'

As he turned into the driveway of his home in fashionable Gamekeepers Row, Tennent reflected on the dangers of the North Sea where daily fortunes were at risk. The conversation had done little to help him make up his mind. In fact, the opposite was the case as he saw the pressures building up to risk funds on a scale never before contemplated by any Scottish bank.

SUNRAY

GORMAN AND MCQUILLAN had spent months preparing every step of their intended attack on Clan Oil. Working in relays, they and the twenty men in the group had spent hour after hour, day after day, week after week, studying through high-powered binoculars the routines and operations of all the key personnel at the head office outside Edinburgh and at the landfall complex, as well as the Delta One platform. They had posed as birdwatchers and hikers as they checked and rechecked the entire length of the pipeline and the area round the landfall base. To get a closer look at Clan Oil's headquarters in Scotia House a dozen of them had gone there individually pretending to be looking for jobs, spinning out the time it took them to fill in application forms in fake names and when they got them taking full advantage of actual interviews. None of them, of course, accepted the couple of openings that were offered. Another four at monthly intervals posed as mature students from English universities and were shown over the entire building and given brochures and explanatory plans of the company's organisation by an anxious to please external affairs executive.

During a period of good weather in the early summer, Gorman

and McQuillan had taken it in turns to take three men at a time, all of them wearing dark clothing, out to spend the hours of darkness only a hundred yards from Delta One using an inflatable black rubber boat. On three occasions Roger used his Marine Commando experience and they hired a sailing boat and with five companions they had pretended, without causing any alarm, to be harmless deep sea anglers in the area around the platform, getting closer to it bit by bit and using a powerful Nikon camera with a telescopic lens to get detailed pictures of the platform.

Their notes had filled dozens of notebooks. They had identified the wave lengths used by the company for its radio links and had monitored them round the clock for weeks on end—eventually being able to imitate and recognise their check procedure. They knew Clan Oil, its strengths and its weaknesses, better even than anyone who worked for the company. Although only one of them had ever been on an oil platform, by the time they were finished all of them could have found their way around one backwards. The enforced study of books, brochures, magazines and the constant showing of the films they had hired had paid off as Gorman had known it would. Every test McQuillan and he set was completed successfully and with absolute confidence.

Sunray training had started in early March. By the beginning of August, Gorman had decided that his men were ready, and that if they spent any more time on preparation they would go stale. McQuillan, who by temperament was less patient, had wanted to begin three weeks earlier, but Gorman had insisted they continue with the routine of painstaking preparation. At last, on a warm Friday evening the men were gathered in the drawing-room of Glenn House for a final briefing. With his understanding of the art of leading men, which he had built up over a lifetime, Gorman had given everyone, apart from those involved briefly in the destruction of the cars that morning, two days off. The idea had worked. Now, relaxed and refreshed, his men were ready—their reflexes sharpening as the run-up to the action shortened. The exceptions were the men who had returned from London earlier and on instruction were sleeping and getting a good rest before they drove back there. Gorman had insisted they come up to give him a face to face debriefing, since their fall-back operation, if used, would be the key to freedom for all of them.

The scene was incongruous—the faded elegance of the once-grand room filled with fit healthy-looking men, all wearing corduroy trousers and tan shirts, their military appearance emphasised by the SMGs and other equipment stacked by the door.

'Right,' said Gorman, 'attention please. This will be our last opportunity to go over everything together. If you have any questions now is the time for them.' He paused to let anyone voice any last-minute misgivings. There were none and he turned to McQuillan. 'Douglas will go through everything in detail.'

As McQuillan started to speak, Gorman left his position by the fireplace and went to look out the window. Part of him was lost to the beauty of the rolling countryside outside but he still checked mentally every point McQuillan made. Gorman knew he was saying goodbye to the house and estate his family had lived in for over two hundred years. It was a strange thought, he reflected, since the estate had been the original reason for gathering together the menacing group of men behind. He felt no guilt, only a touch of sadness that his professionalism was now going to be turned against the country he had served so loyally for so long. But what the hell, he excused himself, I didn't know what I was protecting. The whole country's a disgrace now – everyone out for themselves. Well, for the first time, I'm out for myself. He was drawn back into listening to Douglas McQuillan speaking as the excitement at the thought of action, together with the huge ransom, added a harsh uncompromising tone to everything he said – the accusing way in which he queried that every member of the group had absolute understanding of their own role.

The plan was complicated. McQuillan took just over an hour to complete his check of the whole thing and deal with the few questions that inevitably came up – only a few, because every single move had now been rehearsed dozens of times.

'Well, that seems to be everything,' he finished.

As Gorman turned from the window Ishmail asked, 'What about casualties, Colonel? Not ours, I don't suppose we'll have any – we'll be armed and no-one else will. Do we shoot to kill?' It was obvious from the way he asked and was working and reworking the bolt on his gun that he was looking forward to the possibility.

The question hung over the room. Everyone looked to Gorman for guidance as McQuillan just grinned and made a throat cutting gesture with his right forefinger across his own neck.

Momentarily Gorman was perturbed and didn't answer. The implication of violence had been all too clear on the Arab's face. His pleasure in anticipating the power his weapons would give him worried Gorman – not so much what the man was thinking and planning but whether he could control him and all the others in the crises and changes of plan that were bound to come, make them bend to his will and his leadership at all times. He knew that the first test of that leadership was now posed, with Ishmail's questions.

His voice was confident. 'That is something Douglas and I have discussed for hours. Obviously we're going to destroy a lot of valuable property and terrify many people over the next three days. But it is vital we all know what is expected of each of us so we don't let each other down. To say, "No, don't shoot to kill," would be unrealistic. At first we will take people by surprise—people who have done us no harm. But within a day some of what we will do will be anticipated. The police will be armed within hours of our first strike. They may call in the army although they usually only do that for actions which have a political base.'

One of the men laughed. Gorman shot him a sharp look as he said, 'They'll need the whole army to stop us, Colonel.'

'We must face facts,' Gorman responded. 'None of us is a soldier any longer—we will have no sanction for what we're doing. We are about to become thieves and, I suppose, terrorists. Our plan must succeed—we must complete each part of the operation. But remember, if we are caught the authorities will exact a terrible revenge. In this country property is still held more dear by the legal system than life—and we will have betrayed the system.'

For a moment he allowed himself to become lost in his own thoughts. He knew he was turning his back on the ideals that had ruled his life, however dimly, throughout his army career. He knew just how destructive a small group like this could be. He remembered the effects of a ten-man cadre of communist insurgents who had swept through a sleepy trading post on a river in Malaya. When he had arrived later with a company of men there had been only one survivor out of nearly a hundred men, women and children. Even he had been chilled by the man's pathetic cry, 'They were only here for ten minutes. We did them no harm and they took nothing.' Would people one day think of him and his men with the disgust and despair he had felt for the insurgents? He knew in his heart that he had created a monster, and that when he slipped the leash the monster, and he as part of it, would undoubtedly grow and react with terrible savagery—especially if threatened itself. He forced the doubts away as he saw the men were restless, and anxious for his spoken approval for what all of them had always believed would be necessary.

He looked round slowly at all of them and said clearly, 'All I can do is tell you what I will do myself. I don't want to kill, but in the last resort, the end must justify the means. If possible, I will not permanently hurt anyone—but if the plan is at risk, no-one must be allowed to get in the way of it. You must each decide for yourself. Each of you is fighting for a new life, a new beginning: you will each have to decide what you are willing to do for the chance of that new life.'

When he stopped speaking the silence was complete as the men in the room mulled over what he'd said. There was no dissent. They had not been training for months for a picnic and they knew it. Each of them could and would take just as much reassurance from his actual words as they needed: a guideline to some, a licence to others.

There were nods of agreement all round as they took shelter behind his collective decision and their own thoughts. McQuillan felt reassured as he handed Gorman his gun – just as he always had in the past when they were going into action together. As he had in Aden two days before he had had to rescue him; in Borneo when with only twenty men they had held off a force of over three hundred natives for almost a week before being relieved; and in Vietnam when they were both only supposed to be observers with an American Ranger battalion but where Gorman had to take command, with the consent of the sole young American officer left, when all the senior officers were killed. Without being able to describe it he knew what real leadership was and how in its absence men can so quickly go off the rails and become unmanageable. As in Kenya, he thought, when they gave a bounty for each dead Kikuyu. The bounty was paid on the evidence of a human hand, and a group operating with the one he and Gorman had been in had had to be disciplined for chopping both hands of living natives and turning them loose in the bush. He had laughed at the story when they first heard it, but Gorman had rounded on him saying, 'If men get that unmanageable without check, then one day they will round on you and me. I want the perpetrators found and court-martialled.'

McQuillan wasn't the only one who appreciated Gorman's strengths in this area – others were bolstered and uplifted by it. John contrasted it with the amateurish and directionless way he had been ordered and bullied into doing what his supposed superiors had wanted and needed in Belfast, often with as many casualties to their own side as the enemy – to the point where the army ridiculed them by calling it an own-goal when they blew up their own comrades. Mac took strength from it as he remembered a titled major who had cracked in Malaya. He had leant back against a tree and alternately gibbered and laughed as the communist force attacking them hacked them to ribbons because no-one was co-ordinating their defence. They had only escaped because the RSM had shot the major through the head and taken command himself. Henri compared Gorman favourably to the Para colonel who had led him in Algeria – the only man he had ever been physically frightened of and who as a young officer had been one of the last to surrender in the terrible encirclement at Dien Bien Phu. All the others were having similar thoughts and memories, and all of them acknowledged Gorman as the best commander they had ever had.

McQuillan walked to the fireplace and turned to address them all. 'Everybody is to meet back here at the end. Colonel Gorman wants to be able to check that we have everybody with us. Leave the dead, but the wounded, no matter how bad they are, are to be brought out. That way we can all rely on each other. We won't be wearing masks as you know—the Colonel thinks they're too restricting—we should leave that to the death-and-glory boys of the SAS.' His voice became more aggressive. 'But that means that we'll run the risk of being recognised in the future. So as we've told you, everybody is to make his way abroad—we've made arrangements for the pay-out to be made, even if anything happens to the Colonel and me. As far as I know, we've left nothing to chance.' The men nodded agreement. 'And if anyone gets taken prisoner, they keep their mouths shut, no matter what happens to them. If anyone goes to jail, we'll have enough money to get them sprung if they haven't betrayed us. And,' his voice was deliberately matter-of-fact, 'enough to get them killed if they have.'

Gorman turned over what McQuillan had just said, realising again that, although he had set out originally to try to save Glenn House and the estate, this was now impossible. It had probably never been anything more than a sop to his conscience as he sought a justification for what he was doing. But he didn't underestimate the opposition. He knew how good they were and how they would react to one of their own changing sides and the consequent dangers there would be for them in that. He walked briskly towards the door and said, 'That's all, then. I suggest we all have a few hours' rest now. It's too late for changes. The plan will work. We make a great team. Tonight Sunray will be off and running.'

MARK

As Mark drove the borrowed Ferrari back to Scotia House he was reasonably pleased with the way the meeting at the Bank had gone. He was confident that Tennent and Bob Robertson, in spite of the situation with Sara, were both completely committed to helping raise the extra money and would do so if they could carry the rest of the Bank with them. The news about the government's plans to nationalise Clan Oil had been a bombshell and he could see that he would have to trust the two bankers to raise the financing whilst he tried to get the government to drop their grab at his company. He recognised that he would have to enlist the support of every opinion leader in Scotland, but decided to do nothing until he got up enough steam with the hoped-for results from his press conference. As he parked the car he decided everything was going as well as he could expect. When he got out of the lift to go to his office, he was immediately challenged by a pair of armed policemen in civilian clothes. His ID card got him past them and into his office which was swarming with police – he noticed that every other room on the floor seemed to be too.

Mackay was slightly apologetic as he greeted him. 'Sorry about the mess, Mark. But I've made this my headquarters.' He pointed to where several technicians were setting up what looked like an exaggerated and extended version of a tape recorder, except that this one had two tapes running in parallel in case of a malfunction. 'We're just linking this into your telephone,' he explained. 'Next door we're setting up a radio link with the army, the navy and the rest of my own force. They will be getting constant reports on anything suspicious at your landfall base, or the pipeline, from the three construction yards building your other platforms. And they'll be monitoring any attempted approach to Delta One which, incidentally, now has two frigates from Rosyth Dockyards patrolling about twenty miles out from it. Once the weather lifts they'll move right in beside it and put a detachment of Marines on board. In all, I've got about thirty of my own people here. Not that there's anything for them to do right now,' he said bitterly, 'but the way we do things is to have one centre co-ordinating everything. Although it's been done before in London, this is the first time it's been attempted for real up here. Oh, and by the way. Just in case it becomes a long drawn-out affair, we've set up a dormitory and we're using your kitchen across the hall.'

'Is there anything we can do to help?' Mark asked. 'Surely you could use our canteen for food – it's open all through the night.'

'No,' Mackay disagreed. 'We want to try and separate all our action and needs from the rest of the normal activity in this building as far as we can, although I'm going to have plain-clothes but armed policemen controlling your reception area just shortly with orders to be as inconspicuous as possible – no guns showing, just pretending to be extra security men. Their orders are to stay within this building at all times. Four other constables in an unmarked car are patrolling the grounds.'

'Yes, I was stopped by them,' said Mark. 'It must be easier for you in that all the staff here wear identity badges.'

'It is indeed,' said Mackay. 'And can I just explain why we haven't got the whole area around this building swarming wih my men? I want to contain this incident as much as I can. Only your security people under John here know there is something going on – they and the switchboard supervisor. We're going to programme the lifts so that don't even stop on this floor and anyone trying the stairs will be turned back by your own security staff on the excuse that there is a confidential meeting in progress. If we don't do this then rumour and gossip will be rife and within a couple of hours the press and media people will be here in dozens. I certainly don't want that – it would blow the whole thing wide open, and get in the way of any progress we might make.'

Mark went to talk to his secretary, who had been crowded into a corner of her own office by several burly policemen. He wanted to know if there were any messages for him. When he'd cleared up the few that she hadn't been able to deal with he came back to find Mackay sitting talking to John Graham who had an unfolded diagram on his knee and who turned to Mark as he approached.

'I've just been giving David some background to all the departments we have here,' he explained. 'He says he's got nothing to do until his people have finished setting up all their equipment.'

Mackay smiled ruefully. 'I am exaggerating. I've got to keep a whole army of people informed of what we're doing.' He became serious. 'I've just taken a message that our anti-terrorist unit – twenty of the toughest policemen I've ever met and all of them a marksman with both a rifle or pistol – have been called together at Police Headquarters. The navy has made a helicopter available for them so we'll be able to lift them into position the instant we know where the next attack comes from.'

'Well, let's hope it doesn't come to that,' said Graham. 'By the way,' he turned to Mark, 'how did the meeting go?' He had looked for some sign in Mark's expression that would give him a clue to the outcome of the crucial visit to the Bank, but Mark's face had given nothing away.

'OK, so far. I think we'll get it, even if we are going to have to give fifty million right away to Sunray. We'll be holding a Press conference here later today – upstairs in the boardroom.' Mark was deliberately cool. He now knew that any mention of the Press would not be welcome. 'I'm sorry, but I've no choice. I need to have public opinion on my side at the moment.'

'The Press in here?' Mackay was horrified. 'Look, we must keep this terrorist threat from them – we mustn't escalate this whole thing by publicity. I've told you we'll never contain it if we have to deal with the Press as well. I'm relying on being able to operate with a relatively small, tight team.'

'That shouldn't be any problem,' said Mark, 'we can just lock off this floor whilst it's on. Also, none of your people seems to be wearing uniform and the men in reception will just have to make themselves scarce whilst the conference is on – it's unexpected so Sunray can't use it to their advantage, can they? By the way, when do you think they're going to contact me again?'

'When they're ready. Obviously they are working to a plan.'

Mackay was perturbed but saw that he would have to agree to withdrawing his men on guard or the Press would see instantly what was happening – armed policemen do not walk the streets daily in Edinburgh.

'Have you anything other than the frigates to protect the actual platform?' Mark asked. 'Surely there must be more?'

'No,' Mackay explained, 'I've been in touch with my Chief Constable. And he and I in turn have spoken to all of the commanders who have had experience of this sort of thing in London. Their advice was to wait for Sunray's next move. It would take a massive military operation to protect the platform, and that would be bound to be noticed even if it could be done in the fog. We would have to explain what we were doing, and then every platform in the British sector would want similar protection. We just couldn't provide that. Our best protection for the moment is the fog.'

'I've been thinking about the demand for fifty million pounds,' said Mark. 'Isn't that a bit ridiculous? I mean, how would we get so much money together in a manageable form? And if it was in high denomination notes, they could be traced easily. I thought about that, first thing this morning, and it's been nagging me ever since.'

'I'm sure,' replied Mackay, 'that Sunray will have thought of that. That is usually where all ransom demands – if that is all it is to be – break down. The size of the sum involved, its bulk, picking it up safely, all cause difficulties. But I have a feeling that Sunray will have thought out answers to all that and will know what our counter measures will be and be able to top them. As I said before, to judge by what's happened to date they are not amateurs.'

For the first time Mackay seemed to have doubts about his own ability to cope. It was clear that he felt that he might have to use other than police resources, as he said, 'By the way, I was told by my Chief Constable that two people from the Tactical Response Group of the SAS will be joining us here before lunch. They will have authority to operate separately and on their own initiative to a certain extent. Just the sort of thing I don't like. Also, we can't rule out the possibility that you may be contacted away from this office. John tells me you have radio phones. I wouldn't put it past Sunray to contact you, since I understand all your cars have the same number. If so, you must get in touch with me here immediately.'

'Don't worry,' said Mark with feeling. 'I will. It's a company rule that we keep our car phones on at all times – we almost had a disaster last year when we couldn't contact one of our drilling experts. But this is not something I want to handle on my own.' He picked up his brief-case from the desk. 'Right now I've got to go and see some publicity people. I'll be back in the afternoon. My secretary will know how to reach me.'

As Mark left, John Graham, Mackay and his principal assistant, Inspector Jock Henderson, went back to their checklist of possible weaknesses throughout the entire Clan Oil operation even though they knew there was now nothing more they could do until they were again contacted by Sunray.

*

Earlier in the day, John Pallin, the recently appointed Under Secretary at the Scottish Office, had sat stiffly in the opulence of his huge office on the sixth floor of New St Andrew's House, conscious that the meeting he was meant to be chairing was in fact being dominated by his Permanent Secretary, Hamish Blair—an Eton and Balliol-educated Scot who although he had loathed the inefficiency of the previous Minister had discovered that he disliked even more the wishy-washy liberalism of his new master—and by Archie Donald, the Director of Information.

These two had bickered quite openly on how to handle the public stance of the Scottish Office, which only the day before had been asked amongst other things in a confidential memo from 11 Downing Street to examine the possibility of the government acquiring a majority holding in or complete ownership of the Scotia Field in view of the magnitude of the potential from this field and whether it was desirable for it to be developed for commercial gain. The memo had also said that Pallin, in the absence of the Secretary of State due to illness, was to report back to 11 Downing Street as soon as possible with recommendations.

New to his high office after promotion from the Department of Trade in London, Hamish Blair at fifty-four knew that he had reached, with his return to Edinburgh, the high point of his career. He was troubled by his Minister's instruction from Downing Street that morning. Later, in the privacy of his own office, he sat brooding to himself, turning over the alternatives open to him, wondering if the plan forming in his mind could be brought off.

It can be, he thought. With a little bit of help from just two directions, I'll stop this madness dead in its tracks. If James Tennent and his Bank are half as good as I think they are, I can do it. With them and a lot of understanding from my supposed colleagues at the Scottish Development Agency in Glasgow, I can do it.

BOB

AFTER MARK HAD left the Bank Robertson went back into Tennent's office. Each was concerned to protect the Bank's position—not financially since they didn't see any real risk there but on the public-relations front. A great deal depended on how the media and business community in Scotland would interpret their actions in relation to a customer in trouble. Because of the special relationship of absolute trust that exists between banks and their customers, a bank always finds it difficult to present its side of public debate on a customer. To do so would mean betraying earlier confidences which they would not do, in view of the implications this would have for the hundreds of thousands of other companies and individuals with whom they do business. Even when it seems to hurt them in public they are prepared to ride the storm—hoping that the rest of their customers will see that they would do the same for them if the circumstances were the same.

The younger man could tell that Tennent was agitated from the way in which he was constantly arranging and re-arranging everything on his desk with exaggerated exactness, and having thrown the newspapers in the bucket, lining everything up precisely.

'Well, Bob, what do you suggest we do now? In a way I can't help liking Mark Armstrong, and I think we should do everything we can to help. But of course we mustn't forget the Scottish Office's interest—we certainly don't want to fall foul of central government over this. Yet we must bear in mind that in theory Clan Oil will be the biggest company ever in Scotland and as such, naturally I want to keep it as a customer of this Bank—it would be a nice high-note for me to finish my career on. If you wouldn't mind me taking all the credit to myself?'

Tennent smiled wistfully at the thought that this would be the last, and the biggest, Boardroom drama he would take part in. Both men mentally rehearsed the cut and thrust of the next few hours. Bob spoke first.

'I think we should split our efforts. You contact as many of our directors as you can and sound out their feelings. Also, can you brief the rest of our own executive to keep them in the picture? Meanwhile, there are two things I'm going to do. One, I'm going to be at this Press conference Mark is going to call, and I'll see if I can help get the media on our side. Two, I'll have lunch with Hamish Blair if he's free and try and get some guidelines from him. I don't know him very well – we've only met twice, at receptions of one kind or another – but we've struck up a relationship of a kind and are on Christian-name terms. I think he might be sympathetic.'

The telephone rang. Tennent answered it, and said, 'Say that he is in a meeting and can't be disturbed, but he will ring back.'

He looked angrily at Bob, tightened his lips into a thin line, shook his head in a mixture of anger and disbelief and said accusingly, 'That was Sara Armstrong for you! Does she normally phone you quite so openly here? Everyone on the switchboard must know exactly who she is. For all you know the telephone girls may even listen in. It's against the rules, but I'm sure they do when they suspect something is going on, and they aren't always being supervised. How often does she ring you here? Every day?'

'No, she doesn't. So there must be something wrong. Why didn't you let me speak to her?'

'Because I don't approve of what you're doing and I don't want to have any part of it. Don't you understand how difficult this is for me, and how dangerous it is for your career? To say nothing of the damage a scandal involving Sara Armstrong and yourself could do to the Bank at this time? I know we've talked about it but I can't stand back and watch you throw everything away. And don't think it's because I'm either a prude or a dried-up old man who can't remember what it's all about. I'm not a prude and I'm not so old I can't remember. But Sara and you are being too open about the whole thing.'

'I'm sorry,' Bob interrupted, 'but I just can't give her up.'

'All right,' Tennent conceded, 'I admire you for that, but there are ways of doing things. And the way you're handling this is not right – not right for you, for Sara or for the Bank. Take the advice of an older man and try to calm down the whole affair, at least until we can get this Clan Oil business settled.'

Bob recognised the older man's genuine concern and saw too that he was embarrassed by his accidental use of the phrase 'whole affair,' from the way he tried to make amends for it by continuing, 'And there are a lot of people in this building who would be only too happy to use it against you – particularly just now.'

Bob knew that this was true. He knew that he should follow Tennent's advice, but he knew also that Sara was too important to him to be a mere factor in his business career. But he had been telling the truth when he had convinced Sara in the Bahamas that he would not tolerate criticism of their love from anyone and that included Tennent to whose patronage he knew he owed most of his success to date.

'James, I appreciate that what you say is the sensible thing to do.

But this just isn't a sensible situation—directors of banks aren't supposed to want to marry customers' wives—at least not while they're still married to the customers. I'll be careful if I can, but I make no promises. I don't want Sara to be hurt. As regards the job here, you know better than anyone how much I want it, and you also know that I would do it better than anyone else. So I'll let my record speak for itself.'

He knew that in the Bank, as in every large organisation, the top job was only available once to each succeeding generation of aspirants. If he missed this chance he would never get another. He saw too that Tennent was trying to protect him. In all their years of close contact Tennent had laid much store by the idea that in business great opportunities had to be grasped first time; that luck was important, but it had to be recognised and seized upon. He hoped that his mentor would see that he didn't mean to squander his only chance. But at the same time he wasn't prepared to give up Sara to ensure it.

Bob started gathering his papers and notes together and said, affection in his voice, 'You more than any man have helped me to become what I am. Help me now by believing in me. Now if you will excuse me I've got a lot of telephoning to do before lunch if I'm to set up all the things I want to do and the people I want to see this afternoon.'

Back in his own office, Bob used his private line to dial Sara.

'Hello. It's me. What's wrong?'

'Darling, I'm sorry. Please don't give your telephonist a row. She told me you were with James Tennent, and even so, I insisted she put me through. But I've decided I don't want to go on living separately from you—I want to come and live with you. Can I? Will you have me? Will it be all right?'

'What, today?'

'Yes, Right now if possible. It would be dishonest to stay apart any longer.'

Momentarily Bob felt trapped. Of course he wanted Sara to come and live with him. But her appeal was so sudden, so badly timed! And he knew, none better, just how small their world was in Edinburgh, where with luck they would live out their life together. He had always said that he wanted Sara and Mark to be completely finished before they moved in with each other. But with Mark not prepared to divorce Sara over their affair, Bob knew that the initiative would have to switch to Sara: she would have to take Mark to court on the grounds of the breakdown of their marriage, and she would be mentally better prepared for this if they were together. At the same time he was a realist and knew that the malicious gossipers of the small city and business community would have a field day if she and he shared a flat in Edinburgh before there had been any announcement whatsoever about a divorce.

'Darling, trust me. It would be wrong for you to come to my flat to begin with. Instead, go to Melrose and wait for me at Bankhead. Mrs Little and her husband will look after you until I get there this evening. Everything will be OK.'

Bankhead had been his parents' house. They were both dead and the house was looked after by his old nanny, Mary Little, and her husband. All his life Bob had turned to Mary in times of need and she had never let him down: from important things, like who broke the garage window when he was eight; to little things like hiding a fishing rod by the river for him when he was supposed to be studying for his university exams.

'Can't you come now? I need to have you with me now. Please.'

Bob could hear in Sara's voice the need for confirmation that she came first, but felt that it would be wrong to give in, that she would have to cope for the moment on her own. But he was gentle as he replied. 'No darling, I can't. There are things I've got to do today that might affect the whole of the rest of our lives. But I'll be down as soon as I can, it will only take me about fifty minutes as soon as I can get away. I'll talk to you then. Take care. I love you.'

'I love you too.'

He had caught the note of decision in her voice—perhaps it had been magnified by the telephone. It made him feel protective towards her. As he put the receiver down, he felt angry at the thought of her wasted years with Mark. Then his thoughts turned to what they had already had together, the things they had shared, the things to come.

He had had many women in his life. Some had meant a lot to him, but none enough for him to want to marry them. Always he had known that in the end one who meant everything to him and he to her would appear. He was not a demonstrative man but he had felt near to tears of pleasure after Sara and he had made love on the beach for the first time in the Bahamas—he could sense the way they were right for each other and how different it was for her. She would be safe at Melrose. It must have been difficult for her to decide to do what she had—particularly now, with Mark and he so heavily involved.

'I'll make it up to her,' he thought. 'I'll make up for the miserable years, make her forget them.'

Bob dialled a new number. The voice on the end of the line was a little wary, an elderly voice, mistrustful of telephones, feeling them to be harbingers of bad tidings.

'Melrose 7744, Mrs Little speaking,' it said.

'Mary, it's me. Sorry to be a nuisance, but can you get two bedrooms ready for this evening?'

There was evident pleasure in the elderly woman's voice. 'Oh, it's yourself. You've never been a nuisance and yes, I can. When will you be arriving? And will you be wanting dinner?'

'Mrs Armstrong will be down on her own in about an hour. Give her some lunch and we'll just have a light supper this evening – I'll be down later, about seven. And we'll just have it in the family room.'

'Are you sure?' Mary's voice was indignant almost to the point of taking offence. 'It would be no trouble to get the dining-room ready.' For Bob, nothing was too much trouble.

'No, I don't want any fuss. Just a quiet evening – with only two of us we'd be lost in the dining-room. And Mary, see if you can find things for Mrs Armstrong to do this afternoon. She's got a lot on her mind, and I don't want her sitting around all afternoon and evening until I get down, doing nothing. All right?'

Bob rang off, knowing that Mary would soon think of ways to keep Sara busy – she always kept the whole house ready for him, even though most of the time he lived in his flat in Edinburgh and in the last few years had only gone down for occasional weekends.

Hamish Blair was his next call. He was at a meeting. Bob had asked his secretary if he was free for lunch, but she had thought that he wasn't. Bob explained that it was urgent that they meet, and she promised to pass a message in to him during the meeting. She rang back a few minutes later to say that Mr Blair had cancelled his appointment and would meet him in the Oyster Bar of the Café Royal at one, if that was convenient.

Bob spent the next hour going over the entire Clan Oil operation as seen from the Bank's point of view. One after another his two assistants and several experts from different divisions of the Bank went through all the current ramifications. When he'd finished he sent the other executive directors a synopsis of what he was doing and planning. After that he rang four of the Bank's most senior governors and while he didn't discuss Clan Oil with them he did use the few minutes with each to impress them with his grasp of the business climate and their own sectors in particular. Then he set out to walk the length of George Street to the Café Royal, only a few hundred yards from the Scottish Office in New St Andrew's House. Just before he left the Bank, he was tackled in the foyer by Tom Morrison, the commissionaire.

'Mr Robertson,' said Morrison, taking his time about opening the main door. 'We seem to be giving Mr Armstrong a rough time. I hope we're going to be able to help him. He's a friend of mine. And he's relying on this Bank. I hope we won't let him down.'

'Tom,' Bob tried to look offended, 'you can't expect me to tell you things that are confidential.'

'No, no, Mr Robertson. Just give me a wee hint! That's all.'

Bob grinned and patted Morrison in an understanding way on the shoulder as he said, 'You'll get us both into trouble. But if it makes you feel any better, I'm doing the best I can.'

Morrison's relief was obvious. 'That's good enough for me. Your best is the best this Bank can do, Mr Robertson.' Drawing himself up, Morrison gave a salute that would have been smart enough for the Brigade of Guards, but was marred by a fleeting wink.

As he walked to the Café Royal Bob thought over the problems other than financial which would have to be faced in developing the Scotia Field. Only the day before he had been talking to one of the Bank's oil consultants about the difficulties of making production platforms for the North Sea. The man had been talking about some of the problems related to these giant structures that many people seem to have ignored and he finished off, 'Most of the platforms, both steel and concrete, that are in or being built for the North Sea have a life expectancy of forty years. Nobody, including government, seems to have given any serious thought so far to what they will do with these platforms when the oil, as expected, runs out early in the next century.' There was almost a note of despair or disbelief in the man's voice as he lectured Bob. 'Most people are just hoping that technical ability by then will provide an answer on how to float them off again. The theory is, although there is no practical data to back this up, that the steel ones can be cut at sea level, the legs sealed and the whole structure moved somewhere else—not to be used again, since the steelwork will all have perished. No-one seems to have any idea of how to float off the concrete monsters that weigh 600,000 tons when loaded with ballast. Since they are partially kept in position by the pressure of the sea there would seem to be no way of approaching that problem.'

Bob had asked a question about the working life of different types of platform.

'That's just the sort of thing I mean. Although all the platforms are supposed to have a life expectancy of forty years, there is already evidence to suggest this might not be the case. Like the tower blocks in London and other cities, they are supposed to be pliant enough to move plus or minus one foot over a height of four hundred feet from the sea-bed. Recently, one oil company carried out tests to placate workers who thought their platform was moving violently. Using equipment that can measure movement to one thousandth of an inch they showed that the movement was only two inches. This delighted the workers and the public relations people, who issued the story to the Press. But it horrified the design engineers. It showed the structure was too rigid, it was over-designed and the lack of movement could lead to metal fatigue and early failure. They predicted the life of the platform might be as short as two to three years. How are they going to solve all these problems?'

Before he had left for the Café Royal Bob had asked that same man to accelerate the negotiations he had been having with a particular company in London.

'I know we've had this on ice for a few weeks. But I now think it is essential for these people to get together with Clan Oil. I'll tell Mark Armstrong later today that we're setting up a meeting between them this evening if you can arrange it.'

Bob dwelt on his plan and speculated as he walked on how his Governors would react to the news that Clan Oil were going to have to raise a lot more money without having a penny of income to show to date. Mark had burned up the first loan at a rate of four million pounds a week—every week for two years. Even the Delta platform wouldn't begin to earn any revenue for a few months. Never in its entire history, going back to 1698, had the bank had a customer in this position—in absolute deficit to the tune of hundreds of millions of pounds. The Governors were going to need strong nerves—stronger than any of their predecessors, who had seen Scotland give away its nationhood, the monarchy at risk, Napoleon threaten Britain's dominance of the civilised world, the industrial revolution change the seat of power for ever, the loss of the American colonies, world war, and every other major upheaval over the last three hundred years. Would they have the commercial resolution to continue to pump funding into Clan Oil's seemingly bottomless hole in the North Sea? He grinned wryly to himself as he pictured his colleagues agonising over their decision—and I'll have to get Hamish Blair to co-operate in calling off the hounds from the Treasury.

MARK

MARK HAD DECIDED that the one person who could help him most with the proposed Press conference was Bill Gordon. He drove to the offices of Gordon Advertising in Heriot Row on the edge of the New Town—a curious name nowadays for a part of the city that is more than two hundred years old. The office was just a few doors away from where the author Robert Louis Stevenson once lived.

He always found the Agency an exciting and stimulating place—

full of extrovert and strong-minded people who were quite different from most of the other men he met in business, men who dealt with the harsh facts of oil production. Gordon's staff were men of decided opinions, never shy to give their view on anything and everything, sometimes wrong but more often right, using their intuition and the experience they had gained working for clients in many different businesses to give them a general understanding and appreciation of the overall business scene. He knew, of course, that it was easy for them to have strong views—they were a small tight team and didn't have a large labour force or trade unions to contend with. And, since they didn't have large assets and a lot of capital tied up in their company, it was simpler for them just to look at the narrow area of how they could communicate creatively with their clients' customers: the public.

The beautifully-proportioned Georgian offices had been fully restored, and there was the quiet constant hum of a busy professional office. Mark was shown straight in to Bill Gordon's own office, where Gordon as usual was working in his shirt-sleeves surrounded by layouts and ideas for a forthcoming campaign for one of his clients.

'Hi Mark, how are things with you? Just let me put these away and then I'll be with you.' Gordon put aside some full-colour proofs of a Christmas campaign for one of his whisky clients. 'By the way, time's getting on—can you join us for lunch?'

Mark hadn't thought about lunch, but accepted readily, knowing that the Agency's directors' dining-room had one of the best cooks in Edinburgh—a Cordon Bleu who was so good that most of the directors and regular guests had to go on to a strict diet every so often.

'The Caledonian Bank are making threatening noises,' said Mark. 'What's the matter, Bill, I thought you were doing so well?"

Gordon dismissed the suggestion. 'I suppose Bob Robertson told you that, but it's nothing serious. And I'm pretty confident that we can ride out the storm. We've got a couple of potential bad debts on our hands, and we've just lost a big knitwear account because they've been taken over by a group from the south.'

'But you must carry insurance against bad debts, don't you?'

'Yes. At least we do on one of the companies concerned. The other was a new direct mail company. We couldn't get insurance on them because they were so new—you know how insurance companies won't insure new people to begin with and they were right in this case! But I think we should recover some of our losses. It'll just take some time, that's all. We are going to be OK, the Caledonian Bank are over-reacting.' Gordon strode abruptly across the room and pulled open his door. From outside Mark could hear constantly ringing telephones, people coming and going in the main reception, a telex clattering somewhere above and a paging system asking two people to pick up the nearest outside telephone. 'Does that,' said Gordon closing the door, 'sound to you like an office that is having to look for business?'

'What are you doing about it?' asked Mark as Gordon sat down again. 'Can you retrieve the situation? How's business generally – not just for you but for everyone else?'

'Good,' said Gordon with a grin. 'But then when did you ever hear anyone who's a salesman as I am say anything else? The best cure for any doubts about an advertising agency is a couple of new accounts. And we are close to getting two – the Scottish National Bank and a new unit trust company that is being set up by one of the insurance companies. Sorry I can't tell you who it is yet – it's all very confidential stuff. If we get these two quickly, everything should be back to normal. Take my word for it. We won't need to call on your guarantee. On a day-to-day basis we are a healthy company and I'm sure in the end the Caledonian Bank will recognise that – they would be fools not to.'

'I can't do anything about the unit trust,' said Mark. 'But I might be able to help with the Scottish National Bank. Who are you dealing with there? They won't be very happy about any suggestion of your being rocky though – it would show a fault in their judgement if they appointed you and you then went bust. It would be a public mistake.'

'We're not rocky. And we won't go bust.' Gordon was snappy and assertive. 'In fact, you know I believe that the only policy that pays off in business is complete honesty – and I've let them see our books and explained the whole situation to them. They say it won't make any difference to them – they want the agency that can do the best job of promoting them to the public. I'm pretty confident that we will get that one – we're the obvious choice as the other two main agencies already handle the Royal Bank and the Bank of Scotland. Our contact there is Bob Robertson.'

Mark could see the logic of Gordon's comments. With Tennent leaving the Bank soon, the Executive Board would probably review all their advisors, and the appointment of a new advertising agency to promote a new stance might well be the logical outcome of such a review. He nodded to Gordon. 'OK. I haven't known you for all these years without being able to see you're going to get things together. I'll see if I can help by putting in a word to Bob Robertson. In spite of our personal difficulties I think he still respects my judgement. In fact, it's him and his Bank I really came to talk to you about.'

'I guessed as much,' said Gordon, 'although how you and Bob can still do business together after what is going on with Sara is beyond me.'

Mark brushed the remark aside. He wasn't prepared to discuss Sara even with an old friend like Gordon. For the moment he and Bob needed each other and there wasn't any point in attempting to justify their interdependence to other people.

Gordon could see from Mark's face that he had rubbed a raw nerve. He stood up. 'Shall I lead the way? As it happens, I've already arranged for the head of our public relations company, Iain Smith, whom I think you've met before, to be at lunch today. You're going to need a lot of help with this. It seems to me that Iain is exactly the right person. He's good. Very quick. And he won't try to flannel you – or the Press, or the public. Listen to what he and my other colleagues have to suggest.'

Gordon then showed why he had been so successful and how well he kept the pulse of Scottish business, giving an inspired outsider's version of what was being said about Clan Oil's problems – having first of all asked Iain Smith and the others to join them in the small ante-room that led onto the dining-room. Gordon gave a very thorough briefing to Smith. All Mark had to do was to nod, and from time to time correct some of the interpretations and assumptions Gordon made although they were all surprised when he told them, just before they went through for lunch, about the threatened nationalisation of Clan Oil.

Mark explained that he wanted to call a press conference for later that day, but said that he didn't have any idea of how to set it up, in spite of all the contact he had had with the press over the last few years.

'You see,' he said, looking round at Gordon and his fellow directors as they sat at a well-polished table that had been made when George III was on the throne, 'the press have always been chasing me. Stories about our first strike, the orders for our platforms – things like that. I've never approached them, it's always been the other way round, and that worries me. A friend of mine who is the European director of one of the big American oil giants said to me only a few weeks ago that the press always get everything wrong, that they slant their stories and are biased against big business. In fact, he suggested that the only way to get something right in print is to give the press wrong and inaccurate facts in the first place!'

'Rubbish!' said Smith. 'What they need to do is take the time to make sure the media – both press and television – understand all the ins and outs to begin with. No reporter wants to get a story wrong. They have their own credibility with their editors to think of.'

'Well, if you're right, how do I ensure that?' asked Mark.

Smith hesitated, and glanced at Bill Gordon who said, 'I think we can take it as read that as of now Mark and Clan Oil are a client – we can argue about the fee tomorrow. Let's get on with the job.'

'Fine,' agreed Iain Smith. 'Normally press conferences run for commercial companies are pretty dull affairs – a new product, annual results, a consumer competition – that sort of thing. Obviously they are valuable – but they are much more relevant to the company concerned than they are to the media. That's not the case with you. Here we've got a real hard news story. What we have to ensure is that our point of view is the one presented in tomorrow's papers and on tonight's television and radio programmes. I take it, Mark, that you would have no qualms about taking questions? You're sure of your case? Confident you can present it properly, willing to take questions on any aspect of it?'

'No and yes. But what will they ask?'

'We'll come to that. What you have to remember is that when these characters write up their story it's got to be good enough to get past their hard-nosed news editors. And it's also got to be short enough to stand some pretty hairy-arsed cutting by sub-editors who are always short of space. So don't flannel. Don't prevaricate. Keep it short if possible. Present your side of the story. And above all, tell the truth. If the story's worth running they'll research it. Right?'

'No flannel is our watchword at the moment,' interrupted Gordon.

'Right,' said Mark. 'But, how will you get anyone to turn up?'

Smith smiled confidently. 'That's my job. On what you've given me so far I can get enough people interested enough to come along – but you must remember I can't give any guarantees about how they'll handle the story. Every paper will treat it differently. The heavies – *The Times, Telegraph* and the quality Sundays – will assign informed industrial and financial writers and will probably handle the story in depth against the background of the complete North Sea development. The populars – the *Daily Mail, Express* and *Sun* and so on – will be frothy and may well play on you, the theoretical multi-millionaire in trouble. The Scottish papers will tend to be sympathetic. But if we prepare properly all of them will understand what you are saying and what you are trying to get across. Also, we can ensure that they have all the background information they need. How they interpret what we give them, all the same, is up to the individual reporter and their own organisation's editorial position. Understood?'

'Understood,' said Mark, smiling faintly at Smith's little lecture. 'Where do we have it and when? I thought our boardroom would be best. And what about booze and things to eat?'

'Forget the food. The press will come if the story merits it; and yours does. And yes, we'll have it in your boardroom at – five o'clock. That's a good time, gives them time to write their piece and allows their editors to make any checks or to seek the opposition's opinion before they put the paper to bed at about ten o'clock. That means they'll have the story ready to print for the first editions of the nationals – they are the ones that come up on the night trains to Scotland, so it's important that we make them as well as the Scottish papers. We'll give them a drink only because it's convention. With a story as good as this they don't need it, but they'll appreciate it.'

'How many should we allow for?' Mark wanted to know.

'About thirty-five, which will allow for all the main Scottish papers and the correspondents and stringers for the national papers. As you probably know, stringers are local reporters who freelance for some of the nationals who don't have their own people up here. And of course we'll have to allow for TV and radio as well. But remember, unless you've got something to hide, they'll be on your side: you'll be getting your story in first.' Smith looked around for agreement. 'The opposition will be caught because they will have to react to a story that will already be breaking and will have its own momentum and bias. That is much more difficult than just trying to put your own case.'

Smith pushed his almost untouched plate away from him and rose to his feet. 'Look, I'll have to leave you for a while just to get things under way. Give Mark a hard time on the sort of awkward questions he's likely to have to field. And when I get back we can run over the whole thing. OK?' he turned to their guest. 'Mark, up until now everything that's ever been written about you has been done by a feature writer who was looking for a success story to write about. This time you've got to sell yourself and your story, so make sure that when the fan starts turning, the shit is pointing in the right direction – away from us and towards the opposition!'

Smith left the room and all hell broke loose. Mark was bombarded with questions and advice from men whose job day by day was the use of words and images and the communication of ideas. It was exciting, as they showed him how to make a point, how to emphasise what he had to say; how to ignore one lead and follow another that would help him to put his case more clearly; how to play down one aspect and to highlight another; how to give an answer but at the same time ignore the question. But it was also upsetting, as they showed him just as readily how he had exposed a weakness in his argument and how it could be exploited.

When Iain Smith returned about an hour later, he seemed excited and optimistic. He obviously expected a good turnout from all the nationals and the Scottish papers, and the radio and TV stations had all promised to send people as well. He said that he had hinted at what was in the wind, what the conference was for. Everyone saw it was a good story and saw that it was in their interests to have their own representative there.

'Right, that's enough,' said Smith, calling a halt to the barrage of advice. 'Let's go over the whole thing again and make sure we agree the line we're going to take.'

He sketched out the problem and the answer as Mark and his company saw it, and suggested the guidelines and benchmarks for their approach.

'That wraps it up,' he said to Mark. 'We'll see you in your office at five.'

As Mark got up to leave Bill Gordon looked him straight in the eye and said, 'Don't oversell your ideas. Tell it as it is. If you're right, tomorrow you'll be a national hero. If you're wrong there won't be anywhere in Scotland for you to hide. Iain can only help you so far. Once the thing gets under way you'll have to handle all sorts of questions from the floor. Take your time if you have to. It'll be much better to wait a few seconds to get the right answer.'

Mark had been surprised at the close attention Iain Smith had given to all the arrangements for the press conference. As Smith had said, up until now all the editorials he had ever had had arisen from a press enquiry. He saw now how very different it was when you had a point of view to get across and wanted the media to write and talk about you in a particular way.

Although Smith seemed to be confident that lots of people were going to turn up, Mark could not help worrying that some of them might be coming in the hope of seeing him make a fool of himself. He decided to prepare properly, and on the way back to his office in the Ferrari with music playing softly on the radio, he went over the whole story bit by bit, trying to see it from all sides, debating with himself on how to produce his trump cards. He wondered if people would see things as he did. He knew enough about journalists to respect their brains and knew also that they often saw things very differently from the majority of people and made a habit of being able to see both sides of an argument. He wondered if he should have taken Gordon into his confidence about Sunray, but decided that Mackay would think the risk too great.

He tried to put himself in the position of both government and the Bank—tried arguing with himself and with Clan Oil's position. His preparation was the way he always got ready for any major business meeting which was why he was always so well briefed. At last he was satisfied, but just to be sure, he wrote a few single-line prompt notes for himself, which he could glance at during the conference if he needed them, which he didn't expect he would.

This just has to go well, he thought. A cock-up at this stage could be disastrous. I've just got to get them to see my side of things. I must get them to criticise both government and the Scottish Office. Stop them dead in their tracks. Stop them taking Clan Oil over, doing us harm. At the same time, I've got to embarrass the Bank into having to give me the rest of the money.

Hamish Blair was already seated at his favourite table in the Oyster Bar. The mahogany, brass and stained glass windows of the Café Royal gave it the atmosphere of an earlier age—one where there was more time to do everything. During the day it was popular with the senior civil service, banking and insurance people, whose offices were in and around St Andrew's Square. At night, the main room next door, with its huge circular bar, was filled to overflowing with students and working men.

'Hello, Bob,' said Blair, rising to his feet. 'I hope you'll forgive me sitting down already but I thought I'd start with a glass of wine and it seemed more sensible to have it sitting here rather than at the bar. Would you like something stronger?' Blair looked very much the senior civil servant in his obviously expensive double-breasted navy-blue suit and blue-and-white striped shirt, worn with a subdued dark-coloured tie set off by a loosely rumpled bright red pocket handkerchief, another handkerchief, white this time, poking out of his left sleeve. A small, slim, sinewy man with sandy-coloured hair speckled with grey, Blair looked elegant and well-groomed—newly scrubbed and polished.

'No, thanks,' said Bob as he sat down. 'I'll join you in the wine. It was good of you to rearrange your schedule to fit me in. Thank you.'

'My girl said it was urgent—and since I heard you don't exaggerate and since I also guessed what it might be, I was happy to cancel what would probably have been a very dull lunch with my lawyer.' With a sweep of his hand Blair took in the whole room. 'It's much nicer to be here. More interesting. And better company! Would I be right in thinking that we are going to discuss the affairs of a certain company engaged in the development of some of our country's natural resources and in which we both have a considerable interest, if perhaps for different reasons?'

Bob understood why his reference to Clan Oil was so determinedly oblique when he saw Blair smile hello to some fellow diners over his shoulder. He realised that Blair didn't want to use any names in public. Gratefully he followed his example.

'You're right. The situation is becoming somewhat complicated. We find ourselves in what looks remarkably like a pig-in-the-middle position. On the one hand we have a customer with what seems to be a promising future, and on the other a threat from your masters, who are showing what can only be described as intense interest with not the slightest intention of being honourable. We want to help if we can and we need help if we can get it. I thought you might be able to give some advice and direction and some of the help we need.'

Blair smiled, acknowledging the way that Bob had taken his lead. 'Well put. We don't exactly live in ivory towers in the Scottish Office, and disturbing news has been reaching us all morning. Still, I would have thought your customer would be in a good position to defend himself from attack, provided you're willing to help. Or is that the problem? Have you gone as far as you can go?' Blair was anxious to determine how much help the Bank was prepared to give.

Bob wondered where Blair had got his information but he didn't ask, knowing it was unlikely that Blair would be willing to reveal his source, and that he would be embarrassed by having to refuse. He knew that there are hundreds of visitors every day at New St Andrew's House – people attending meetings, conferences, committees, briefings – all connected with every aspect of life and living in Scotland.

The Scottish Office is the government in Scotland and New St Andrew's House the principal centre where the Secretary of State and four junior Ministers co-ordinate the roles of the great national departments of State in Whitehall, carrying out the functions of the Home Office, Department of Industry, the Education Department and many others. It controls the purse strings and directs policy in hundreds of different areas: the police, education, housing, transport, industry, the fire service, crime prevention, health, tourism and agriculture. With its block grant from the Treasury it also funds a number of quasi-independent organisations reporting to it.

Blair and his aides could have been told by any one of those visitors or, as was much more likely, simply put together a whole lot of apparently unrelated details from several people and come up with the right answer.

Bob explained. 'Yes and no. Yes, the general position is good. But our friend is now stretched to the limit. He owes literally hundreds of millions to his creditors. And in confidence, he's well over his personal limit with us which shouldn't colour our response. But bankers have been bankers for a long time and like everything to be neat and tidy. To help develop his considerable potential he is going to have to raise another thousand million pounds more than he thought originally – before there will be any significant income. Obviously he has to be in a strong position to do this, and there must be no doubts about his financial standing, credit and abilities.'

Blair spoke up. 'You are aware, of course, that I have also been talking to your headmaster, telling him of our own mercenary interest in your customer? Presumably that is why you are here. Right?'

'Yes,' Bob said, smiling in spite of himself at the thought of the sometimes schoolmasterly Tennent as his headmaster. 'We can't see why you should be so interested. After all, under British Government regulations covering the UK Offshore Oil and Gas Policy, the government could have a majority interest anyway. I know that policy is already extremely unpopular with the oil companies. They think it's bad enough giving fifty-one percent to the government. They are going to be very unhappy if you suddenly take all of the cake in relation to our customer. They may think it will be their turn next for a one-sided courtship.'

Blair had been studying the menu. Instead of answering Bob's queries, he said, 'Why don't we order now, enjoy our lunch and then go for a walk in Princes Street gardens afterwards? We can chat as we walk. We, or at least I, will feel much freer to talk under those circumstances.'

They ate well but quickly, and forty minutes later found themselves, looking a little out of place in their formal suits, amongst the casually dressed tourists of many different nationalities in the city's famous gardens. After the beautiful sunny start to the morning, the sky was now filling from the north with dark-grey clouds. But for the moment it was still warm and the Festival visitors who were adding to the city's normal bustle were for the most part in shirt sleeves and summer dresses although Bob suspected they would be scurrying for their raincoats before the afternoon was out. After chatting about nothing in particular over lunch and on the way down to the gardens, Blair seemed content to continue to gossip, as if he hadn't a care in the world.

'Your home is in Melrose, isn't it?' he said apparently casually.

'Yes.' Bob suddenly wondered if Blair could possibly know about Sara. Then he dismissed the thought and decided it had been one of those coincidences which occur, where there is no connection unless the person involved makes one.

At last Blair got down to the matter in hand. 'To return to your customer, Clan Oil. You were right, of course. Normally the government would be content just to participate in the development of the Scotia Field. But there are exceptional circumstances in this case. You more than anyone know how much pressure there is on the economy these days – it seems to me that there's always pressure on the economy. And with an election within the next couple of years, the Chancellor is looking around for some bold single stroke – something big enough to be significant to the voters, and also, and perhaps more important, something that will reassure the much quoted foreign bankers and investors.'

Blair dropped his voice. 'It would appear that in Clan Oil he has the perfect vehicle for such an action. The company is small, and with no large labour force there will be no union problem to deal with. There are virtually no shareholders, again good since the action could be swift and decisive, or could be seen to be. At this stage there is no huge cost involved, not at any rate for the government – just a few extra figures somewhere, in a budget which is largely out of control anyway. There will be the exploration and development costs to date, which, as you know, considering the potential are not great, plus presumably some compensation for Mark Armstrong and his fellow shareholders. Cromarty Promotions still have a stake, don't they? And of course by putting all the resources of the Treasury behind the development of the Scotia Field it could come on-stream much more quickly. The trouble is this lot promised a little too much in opposition. Now they're finding it almost impossible to put the policy they planned into practice. Each of them seems to make the same mistake each time. Now they're probably banking on, in fact my colleagues in London tell me they're positively praying for, the impact the Petroleum Revenue Tax will have on the entire economy in the mid-eighties. As you know, by then all the development allowances for the oil companies in the North Sea will be used up and they will all be fully operational. This is going to mean an extra £15 billion a year in taxes and other royalties to the ever capacious Treasury. The nationalisation of Clan Oil now would be a very welcome appetiser. In fact, the foreign bankers would not just be reassured; they would probably break into spontaneous applause.'

They were negotiating the traffic around the Royal Scottish Academy when Blair suddenly asked, 'Didn't I see you at the preview of the Summer Exhibition a couple of weeks ago?'

'Yes,' Bob agreed reluctantly, feeling that Blair might well have seen him arrive on his own but leave with Sara.

When they went down the steps, past the giant floral clock surrounded as always by visitors, Blair insisted on having a look at it.

'Always like to see if it's correct,' he said, checking his gold pocket watch. It was an infuriating gesture, in view of Bob's obvious impatience.

They set off down the path. Bob pressed on. 'But wouldn't it be unwise to nationalise Clan Oil? In fact, I'm surprised that the government would even consider it. There is no broadly-based acceptance for the concept of public ownership of industry in this country. Also, the oil industry in particular seems to need the vision and commercial flair of private enterprise. And that's not all. The public in Scotland will resent the idea of an arbitrary take-over from London – it's just the sort of thoughtless disregard for public opinion that fuelled the last great rise of nationalism here. All

Scots, no matter how they vote, are nationalists to some extent, proud of their heritage and suspicious of Whitehall. Surely your present masters don't want to risk another northern uprising?'

'Ah,' said Blair blandly, 'Now you have hit exactly on why the Scottish Office have been asked to look into the whole thing. How will the nationalists react, both those with a capital N and those with a small n? What about ordinary people throughout Scotland? Above all, what about the MPs in the House? Without at least their support and understanding the government's programme will be difficult to push through. It is really quite surprising how much delay and confusion even a few political guerrillas can achieve by constant sniping from the back benches. What do you think? We would value your opinion, not just as regards Clan Oil itself, but on how the rest of the business and commercial community in Scotland would feel. We would have to take that too into consideration when we decide to move, if, indeed, we move at all.'

Bob replied without hesitation, knowing that there was no room for ambiguity. 'My initial reaction is that all hell would break loose. You must be mad, even to think of such a thing at this time. I am not a Nationalist, as you know, but I sympathise with many of their aims, as do most Scottish businessmen.' He warmed to his theme. 'We're all sick to death of remote, ill-informed and uninvolved rule from Westminster. What you are suggesting will play into the hands of the people who say that London has lost the ability, if it ever had it, to feel the pulse of Scotland and the Scots. This criticism doesn't apply just to Scotland. I've heard the same thing from men from the North East, the North West, Wales—even the Midlands wonder if London knows they exist. You would be quite rightly accused of being totally out of touch with public thinking.'

Blair forestalled any further comment by suggesting that they listened to the band of one of the Scottish regiments in the pavilion they were passing. Bob instinctively felt that Blair knew 11 Downing Street were wrong. The references to Melrose, to the floral clock, the attention he paid to the band, were his means of taking some of the heat out of things, of giving him a chance to gather his thoughts and digest what they had been talking about.

Blair had no choice but to agree. 'That is the feeling of most of my colleagues and the few other people we have felt able to sound out so far. However, it would be imprudent to underestimate a Chancellor with his dander up and with the Treasury in full support, if not full pursuit. Once they get an idea into their heads it is very difficult to dissuade them. Believe me.'

That was, Bob could see, as much of a hint as he would get from Blair on where his personal preferences lay. Yet he realised that Blair wanted his help. 'Mark Armstrong is holding a press conference later today, and perhaps it would be a good thing if we were to flush the whole business out into the open. Do you agree? Would this help your situation? Would it achieve what I think we both have in mind?'

Blair couldn't resist the chance to score a point. 'We were wondering exactly what that press conference was about. Our constant companions, the lobby correspondents, were on to us within twenty minutes of its being announced, looking to see if our industry people could give them any background material. But the answer to your question is, I do, and I think it would. Armstrong will, I assume, be presenting himself as David beset by the Goliath of central government. I take it you have indicated our interest to him?' Blair paused and pursed his lips in a pretence of disapproval. 'In confidence of course. And of course he has no intention whatsoever of keeping that confidence, if he has any sense—and I presume he has a great deal of sense.'

'You're right,' said Bob, smiling wryly at his decription of the fight to come. They were now walking back towards the floral clock. Bob would have to leave Blair there in order to have time to get back to his office for his meeting with his oil division people. He had, however, one more thing to clear up. 'What about the Bank's position? I don't want us taking action that might cut across government policy.'

'I will trust to your judgement in that. Our discussion with your managing director earlier today was unofficial. We just wanted you to know of our possible interest: off the record. Our own little talk was the same. What you now do is up to you. I take it you have friends in the House of Commons?'

'Yes, we do.' Bob knew that Blair would be aware that like all the banks his own had a number of MPs from the two major parties on permanent retainer to look after its interests both in London, and, increasingly, in Brussels. 'However, I think I might be able to suggest an awkward question to a genuinely friendly Liberal—much better that it come from someone not too committed. And we'll see what we can do through our merchant banking subsidiary to help raise the next tranche of funding for Clan Oil and the Scotia Field.'

'Good. Your MP friend will probably put down a PQ. I think it would be as well if we kept in touch. Where will you be this evening in case I need to get hold of you?'

'At Melrose. The number is 7744: it's in the book.'

Blair glanced again at the floral clock as they went back up the steps leading past it, and said with a smile, 'This is exactly the same distance from our respective offices, so I think we can part here without having to worry about either of us losing face by having to accompany the other. By the way, I take it Armstrong has told you about his early morning telephone call?' Bob nodded. 'I see. Well it is too soon to judge how serious it is. The Chief Constable came to see my Minister and has assured him that the man in charge is the best he has, and that the police are hoping to contain the incident for as long as they can. But if they can't they have available all the resources they might need. Let's hope it doesn't come to that.' He turned to leave. 'Goodbye. I have enjoyed our talk. Most useful. And thank you for lunch, even if the choice of venue was mine.'

'Before you go, what exactly is a PQ? At least, I know what it is, but how do they work? Are they really effective?'

Blair was precise. He delighted as always in lifting the curtain from the machinery of government. 'A PQ is, as you probably know, short for a Parliamentary Question asked in the House of Commons and requiring an answer from the Minister whose responsibility is covered by the question. A PQ for the Scottish Office goes into a yellow file which is circulated in New St Andrew's House for immediate response by the senior civil servant responsible for the activities covered by the question. Within the Scottish Office they are known as "Yellow Folders" and one retired civil servant was once heard to remark that a Yellow Folder landing on a desk in the Scottish Office causes sweat to leak first from the bootlaces and then from under the door of the recipient's office. Usually the questions are awkward. Invariably they are the brainchild of an MP trying to ruffle the Minister concerned. And always they have to be answered at speed—no matter who is inconvenienced, or for how long. And of course because of the speed, some of the answers given are suspect from time to time. But they always cause a great deal of fuss, which is just what you and I want. We have an interest in raising a great deal of concern about what government is apparently considering doing. It might help us to get them to change their minds.'

Back in his office, Bob made a telephone call before meeting with his own staff. It was to a Liberal member for a Highland constituency. The man thanked him for the tip and promised fireworks in the House later that day. 'Just the sort of thing for a PQ that will rattle the front benches. If you have any more like that let me know.' The man's malicious anticipation was clear even over the telephone.

Bob hoped that the PQ was going to be as effective as Blair and the MP had suggested it would be. It's time some of this business started to go our way, he thought.

WHEN MARK GOT back to his own building he kept away from Mackay and his men. Once he'd established there was nothing they wanted him to do, he spent the next two hours working with his own executives. They used the time to bring him up to date with the normal strains and exigencies of their individual operations. One or two of the more perceptive ones probed him about what was going on on his floor and he fielded their questions carefully and gave nothing away. Privately he wondered how long it would be before the Sunray threat burst into the open.

At five to five he went up to the boardroom and watched Iain Smith making his final arrangements—checking everything, leaving nothing to chance. He made a last minute check with David Mackay to see if there was any news. But there was nothing. Mackay had begged him to be careful and not mention Sunray during the press conference. 'If by any remote chance it is raised, come down and get me. The press have an uncanny knack of uncovering this sort of thing—mainly by intuition—because we have to be much more circumspect with them than we normally are. However, I must say that they will keep the lid on a story if we ask them to and give them a good reason.'

Mark looked around the room. A catering firm, called in at short notice, had set up a mobile bar complete with a white-coated barman at one end of the room. At the other end was a long table, behind which were three chairs, and on which was a pitcher of iced water and three glasses. Facing the table were about thirty chairs in rows, with ashtrays dotted amongst them for the expected journalists.

When Bob Robertson arrived, he drew Mark aside to whisper to him. 'I've had a meeting with the Scottish Office. It may be that things are not as bad there as we had imagined. The government is serious, but I think we've got a friend and supporter in Hamish Blair. He'll help if he can—depending on how things develop. For the moment however we'll have to wait and see if he can dissuade his seniors at the Treasury. He can't promise anything but I get the impression he'll do his damnedest. His interpretation is that the Chancellor is looking for some flamboyant way of indicating that the government is prepared to take drastic action—even against its natural inclination—if such action will produce a swift and considerable benefit to the country. It's probably just bad luck that all the publicity about the extra funding drew his and his officials' attention to Clan Oil.'

Mark thanked him abruptly and went and sat down. With his head in his hands Mark stared out moodily at the rows of empty chairs, turning over his mixed emotions about Sara. He recognised that it was hurt pride at the public loss of his wife that was really what was nagging at him; not love for Sara but a wish to stop Bob Robertson taking her from him. He realised that as usual his preoccupation with Clan Oil and its problems were pushing Sara to the back of his mind – forcing him to admit to himself that Sara was only a minor problem at the moment, at least in comparison to his other problems. As if Sunray were not bad enough. Now the government itself was further complicating already complex negotiations with the Bank. The stars in their courses, he felt, were fighting Mark and Clan Oil.

Tension in the room built up. It was almost five o'clock and as yet no reporters had appeared. Everyone glanced nervously at everyone else. Iain Smith gave a sort of snort and said, 'Don't worry, it's always like this. You think no-one will turn up – but they will. During the last hour I've spoken on the phone to almost all of the people we expect. It's the only way – you have to have a last minute round-up. They'll come.'

He was right. Suddenly journalists of all shapes and sizes seemed to pour through the door. Smith's three assistants were going frantic trying to get them all a drink and a seat. Soon it was obvious that if anything they had underestimated the interest of the media. There were about forty men and women from the press already seated, some on extra chairs hastily arranged, when the television and radio people arrived and as usual started to quarrel with everyone in sight. They wanted the best seats; they wanted power points for their lights; they wanted a clear line for their cameras and directional microphones.

Smith dealt with them expertly and refused to bow to their unreasonable demands. With great aplomb he thrust himself into the argument, sweeping their complaints aside. 'Can't we make do with one set of lights in here, for both BBC and ITV? You can record the conference as it goes, if you like, and both Mr Armstrong and Mr Robertson will be available for TV and radio interviews as soon as they have dealt with questions from the floor. OK? That suit everybody?'

The warring TV men grinned amiably at each other, acknowledging that the conference was being run by someone who knew his business. Satisfied that their rivals weren't going to steal a march on them, they hurriedly got themselves drinks, and by the toss of a coin, ignoring union manning rules, agreed who would provide the lighting and who would do the first interview afterwards.

Smith sat down and tapped on the table for attention. Gradually the room quietened, and when he had everybody's attention, he began. 'First of all, thank you for coming. When we've finished, do, if you want, stay for a drink or, as I think most of you will prefer, use the telephones in all the offices on this floor to phone in your story. All the phones have an outside line, but the telephonists will still be on duty to help if needed.'

Several people nodded approval as he went on, 'Most of you will know the gentlemen sitting on either side of me: Mark Armstrong, who is chairman and managing director of Clan Oil, and Robert Robertson – Bob to most of us – the development director of the Scottish National Bank, who are bankers to Clan Oil. We have prepared a background brief covering most of the points these gentlemen will be making, which is being handed round now. And if you need any further information, no matter how late tonight, when you are re-writing your stories you'll find my home number on the brief. Their's are also there, but it will probably be easier to reach me.

'We'd like to start now with a statement from Mark Armstrong and Clan Oil.'

Mark looked around at the expectant faces – old, young, men, women, interested, or cynical, but all giving him their full attention, pens and pencils poised over all shapes of pads and papers. He was acutely conscious of the heat that was building up from the TV lights, and of the way the room was filling with smoke. He made a mental note to instal air-conditioning in case they ever had to do this again. He started to put his case.

'I too would like to thank you for coming here this evening, and I hope you will find it has been worthwhile. As you know, Clan Oil has in the Scotia Field potentially the richest oilfield in the whole of the North Sea. This is good news for us but it's also good news for the country as a whole – ensuring a better balance of payments situation and bringing a lot of new jobs to Scotland. But believe it or not, Clan Oil are now threatened on two sides.' Inwardly he thought briefly of the threat on the third side from Sunray and the effect the announcement of that would have on his audience. Instead he went on with his intended approach. 'As you know, we are under pressure to bring the Scotia Field on-stream as soon as possible. We're running behind schedule – we've explained in detail why, on the brief you've been given. And now we are having to go back to our Bank to raise extra money.'

'How much?' shouted a voice from the floor. Mark recognised the voice as belonging to a radio journalist who had done a hostile piece on the possibility of spillage from the Delta One platform and the harm that this might do to local lobster fishermen. He decided not to acknowledge him by name. 'A thousand million pounds.'

There was a gasp from the floor, and he went on quickly, 'I know it's a hell of a lot of money, especially as we haven't yet repaid a single penny of our original loans. We're asking people to trust us, to trust us again, to believe in us and in what lies out there under the North Sea.'

Now there could be no doubt that Mark had everyone's attention. He pressed on.

'And as though that wasn't enough . . .' He paused, deliberately allowing the tension to build, knowing that he had to get what followed absolutely right. 'There are rumours—and they are very strong rumours this afternoon—that central government is considering nationalising Clan Oil. In fact, at this very moment a high-powered team at the Scottish Office is completing a feasibility study on this for the Secretary of State and for Downing Street.'

Even his hard-bitten audience was taken aback and for a few moments people whispered to their neighbours. He could tell that not a single journalist had had even a suspicion of the second part of his statement. The Scottish Office had done well to keep such a big story under wraps. He presumed they must have limited the number of people who knew of it on a need-to-know basis to cut down the chances of a leak. Mark held up his hand for quiet. He could see from their faces that this was going to be the main news story of the day. He thought fleetingly of how Smith's colleagues at lunch had told him that the story was so important that most editors—or more accurately, deputy editors, who really run newspapers day-to-day—would want to make the story the main news splash of the day. There would probably be a complete two-page spread with a main report of the press conference and supporting articles by journalistic experts on oil and its financing, and possibly comment in the leader columns. He imagined the frantic search through extensive picture libraries for pictures of himself, Bob, the Delta One platform and anything else relating to the story, in spite of the fact that Smith had included photographs in the brief he had handed out. This, Smith had explained, would be because each paper would want to have different photographs from their competitors. When the excited buzz died down, he went on. 'I want to make it quite clear that we can raise all the money we need.' His confident voice became even firmer. 'We do not intend to stand by and watch government nationalise us. We hope that we can change their minds. What we do intend to do as quickly as possible is to float Clan Oil on the stock market, giving everyone who wants to and is able to, a chance to invest in this most exciting example of capitalism at work, with a guarantee of success as near cast-iron as dammit. Now there's a lot more detail in the brief, but if there are any questions we'll be happy to try to answer them.'

Mark sat down, and immediately more than half the journalists were on their feet with questions. Several drinks were sent flying and people bumped each other as they vied for attention. Flash-bulbs exploded again and again and there was the constant whirr and click of motor-driven cameras. One or two people went quickly out of the room without waiting for the question session, anxious to be the first to get their stories to their editors.

Mark remembered again his earlier conversation with Smith. 'Will the government try to suppress the story? Can they do that? What about a D notice?'

Smith had been adamant. 'No, they wouldn't dare. A D Notice is used only to protect the national interest or to avoid breaches of security. It is used nowadays almost solely for security matters. No government would ever risk issuing one on something which editors might ignore – such as this. If that ever happened the system would never work again.'

The chaos was getting out of hand and Iain Smith once again took control of things, gesturing impatiently for everyone to sit down.

Gradually order was restored, and he could make himself heard. 'Mark will take one question at a time. Somebody has to referee, so he'll take them from people whose names and affiliations I will indicate to him so he knows who he's talking to. OK. That suit everybody?'

The questions came one after another, with nobody showing any trace of bias in their voices. Most people stood up to help them make their points.

'How do we know what you say about the Scottish Office is true? How do you know exactly what they're doing?'

Mark told a careful lie to protect Blair as Bob had asked him to do. 'To mount the sort of action they are taking involves a lot of people. They've got to ask a lot of questions, talk to a lot of people. We've been getting calls about it all afternoon from all sorts of people. I'm surprised your editors haven't heard themselves.' It was a legitimate dig, and one or two media people, aware of their inclination to needle, had the grace to look abashed.

'Do you think you do have the ability to manage the development of the Scotia Field? Is it perhaps not a fair criticism to say you may have run out of goodwill, that you've failed to win your spurs?'

'Yes, I and my team have the management ability. No, I don't think we've run out of goodwill or of people who'll be willing to back us.'

Occasionally people would not let go of a point. 'Can I repeat, what is the source of your information about the government's plans to nationalise your company?'

'I don't want to be evasive, but I'm sorry I can't reveal that. It is what I believe is known as "an informed and normally reliable source."'

'How many jobs would be at risk if you can't raise the thousand million?'

'Well, we employ about two thousand people ourselves. But there are many more involved in supplying services to us. And of course we are about to give an order for four more production platforms—to yards in Scotland who have no other orders at the moment. Perhaps ten thousand jobs in all.'

'Do you really think you can raise enough money by going public, particularly now? Do people have money to invest on the scale necessary? Particularly at this time?'

'Yes, we do think that we can raise the money. The project is exciting simply because of the scale of its operation, but there is very little risk involved. We know the oil is there, we've proved that. All we have to do is get it out of the ground. On current predictions North Sea oil will produce to the operating companies a return of more than thirty percent after tax—that's a far higher return than is possible in almost any other industry nowadays.'

'Why don't you just get the money from the Scottish National Bank?'

Mark glanced at Bob, who accepted the invitation to field the question.

'Because no single Scottish bank could provide funding on this scale. By nature Scottish banks are conservative with a small c and we would never consider having so many of our eggs in the one basket, no matter how safe the investment. But I'm confident that our merchant banking facilities can themselves put up a significant part of the money needed, that the Bank can raise the rest of the money, partly by helping Clan Oil to go public and partly by persuading other major financial institutions to join us.'

'Mr Robertson. Would you consider it wise for the British Government to be considering nationalising Clan Oil? Can you argue it isn't prudent?'

'I can see the attractions: long-term benefits to our balance of payments situation; not too big a capital investment at this stage because so far all Clan Oil have done is to find the oil and make a start on the development. On the other hand, I would have thought that such an action in the current climate would cause grave concern to all the other companies operating in the North Sea. Our promises and contracts would begin to look no better than the ones which have been abandoned by less stable governments in the Middle East. And I would also have thought that politically such a decision would have devastating repercussions both here and internationally.'

Mark took up Bob's point. 'Apart from anything else, it's so damned unfair. We took the risks at the beginning. Why step in now? They didn't participate when there was no guarantee of success. That's no way to ensure co-operation between government and private enterprise. And why single out us?' Mark's anger showed. 'Either they take over every single exploration rig, production platform and field in the North Sea or they should be content with the staggering taxes they can take from us.'

For another ten minutes the questions came without a break. Mark and Bob coped between them, each taking the appropriate question. Then gradually the journalists started to drift away, some to phone the Scottish Office, most to phone their papers. Iain Smith brought the conference to a close and started to discuss with the TV and radio people how they wanted to do their interviews. Twenty minutes later, it was all over and the films and tapes were being rushed to the stations in time for the six o'clock news bulletins. Everyone still in the room drifted to the bar for a drink, and then sat around looking drained and tired, wondering if Mark and Bob had got their message across properly.

'How do you think it went?' asked Mark.

'OK,' said Smith. 'But we'll know for sure in a few minutes. One of my people is on his way with a portable TV set. We should just about make the main news programmes. I liked the way they asked their questions—I think we have most of them with us now.'

Both Mark and Bob congratulated Smith on the way he had organised the conference and said that if they hadn't got their position across they would have no-one but themselves to blame. In the strictest confidence Mark told him about the Sunray threat but said there was nothing he could do about that except refer any reporter who got onto it to Mackay.

*

At the Scottish Office, the Director of Information was inundated with calls. Most people rang Archie Donald's private number asking if Mark's allegations about the proposed nationalisation were true. Donald took the first couple of calls himself, gave a firm but friendly 'no comment for the moment' and promised to ring back inside the hour. He then didn't answer the phone when it rang, and the automatic hunter system re-channelled the calls after a few seconds to whichever of his staff was free, in order of seniority. Meanwhile he had contacted Hamish Blair, and the two of them had arranged to discuss the changing situation with the Minister, John Pallin, immediately.

Donald had said to Blair on the telephone, 'All hell is about to break loose. As we expected, the story about the possibility of nationalising Clan Oil is breaking. We're going to have to work like blazes to get across an acceptable version from our point of view. And I've said we'll have a statement ready as soon as we can.' As he rang off Donald groaned to himself at the prospect ahead. Most senior officials had probably just left to go home. How many were he and his staff going to have to contact and even bring back in? Pallin would be beside himself with excitement and fear, alarmed by his unusual situation of responsibility with power. He knew that every editor in the country would be planning to have this as his main splash tomorrow and God alone knew what would happen if Blair was right and the Sunray threat leaked out as well!

CLAN OIL

THE STORY OF the fight for control of Clan Oil was the first item in the early-evening news programmes on both channels. In both cases it was followed by informed comment from both industrial and political experts on the government's motives. The consensus seemed to be that Armstrong had played a shrewd card by bringing the whole thing out into the open. His side of the story was presented sympathetically whereas the government, in the shape of the Scottish Office, came in for a lot of criticism for being secretive, and in the opinion of the television experts at least, of being out of touch with public opinion in attempting to nationalise such an obviously Scottish asset. Many correspondents expressed misgivings about whether or not the Scottish National Bank would be able to help their customer even if they wanted to. How could they raise so much more financial backing for a venture that so far had failed to deliver any revenue and had also failed to meet every deadline in its development programme – no matter whose fault that was? The BBC economics editor sounded a chilling warning at the end of his review. 'It would be a mistake for Clan Oil to underestimate the steps the government could take in this battle. Through the Bank of England they could tighten the normally ignored banking corset on the Scottish National Bank and make it impossible for them to increase their level of lending to anyone until such time as it suited their book – and that would assuredly be too late for Mark Armstrong.'

After the first televised reports, when it was clear that the message had got across, Bob forgot about the TV and began to brief Mark on the people and performance of European Oil Developments Limited – a London-based company who operated, in spite of their name, in offshore developments around the world, including Venezuela and Nigeria. The Bank's own Oil Division had identified them as the ideal partner for Clan Oil and knew of them because they were customers at one of the Bank's big branches in the West End of London. Started ten years ago, EOD, as they were known, had pioneered new techniques and skills in offshore management.

Bob was most anxious to involve EOD in Clan Oil's future.

'They are still a small company and they have no oilfields of their own. Instead they make their money by offering a complete package of management and technicians. They employ only the best, irrespective of nationality. I think you should talk to them. They will beef up your technical skills, make you more acceptable to the money men. They would allay any misgivings about your ability to develop the Scotia Field. After all, you must admit that all your expertise has been grafted on bit by bit as circumstances dictated. Here is a chance to get all the benefits of real professionalism in exactly the area you need. For their part they are interested because they will no longer have to rely on contracts from companies and countries they can't wholly trust – that is the one weakness in their business.'

Mark could see the value of the suggestion but was suspicious and resentful that the Bank, through Bob, was bringing such pressure to bear on him to change his company.

'Why should they want to join up with us now?' he wanted to know. 'What's in it for them? Why them? Why not someone else? I've heard of them, but I've never met any of their people – perhaps we wouldn't get on.'

Bob was adamant. 'Because it is an ideal opportunity for you both. You both have a lot to offer each other. You'll get on because there'll be so much in the deal for both companies. To realise your full potentials you need each other. I expect there will be some pretty hard bargaining on both sides, but an agreement is there to be reached. Our Oil Division has been looking for some time for the ideal partner for both of you and there is no way the arrangement would be one-sided. They are much smaller, of course, so that will be reflected in the share of the equity they can negotiate with you in Clan Oil in exchange for their own shares, but they'll be able to demand very comprehensive salary, bonus and other benefit packages. I've arranged for you to meet them at eight this evening at the North British Hotel. All right? Can you make that? Perhaps have dinner with them?'

'Yes.' Mark recognised that he had nothing against EOD themselves. And Clan Oil's needs were paramount, as always. 'That'll leave me just enough time to go home first.'

They were joined by Iain Smith, looking very pleased with himself, who said, 'We were the main news item on both channels and in all the radio programmes as well. That's a pretty good start. And I've just had Collin Munro of BBC's Counterpoint programme on. You know, he does those big news programmes two or three nights a week. He likes to go where the news is – either using one of the new electronic news-gathering units or local facilities where they exist. He wants to do a special programme this evening with you, Mark, live from the BBC's studio here in Edinburgh and he wants to know if you'll agree to appear. Let's hope that he or his researchers don't uncover the Sunray story between now and then. You would have to be at the studio in Queen Street at ten fifteen. Can you manage that?'

'Yes. Or at least I think I can. Will I get any advance warning of what his questions will be?' Mark was worried. He had often seen Munro's abrasive style and questioning reduce hardened businessmen and senior politicians to stuttering impotent rage. He wondered how he would manage after only a couple of hours' advice from Smith and his colleagues. He once again regretted that he had never found time to instal a public relations function in Clan Oil with a professional manager who could have helped him at a time like this. It was just another pressure that they hadn't been able to cope with. 'Will he be sympathetic? Can we guarantee that? Will he be on our side?'

'No,' said Smith. 'But he'll do a rehearsal with you using similar questions. You'll have to keep your wits about you. I said at lunchtime that you should go on one of those training courses which prepare people for television interviews. Well, there's no time now. You're going in at the deep end. The best advice I can give you is to try and relax and have confidence in that he'll be working from notes and that you really know your subject backwards.'

Smith took out a pad and said that he ought to take a note of where they were both going to during the evening, in case he needed to get in touch with them. Mark said that he would be at home and then at the North British, and Bob that he was going to Melrose.

Out of the hearing of the few people left Mark told Bob that he was going down to his own office to see how the police were getting on and asked him if he wanted to come too. Away from the tension of the conference and the support of other people they were cold and distant to each other as they walked down the one flight of stairs.

*

At the Scottish Office John Pallin put down the telephone after a few uncomfortable minutes with the Chancellor. With an outsize silk handkerchief he mopped his brow, then turned to Hamish Blair and Archie Donald, sitting uneasily at the other side of his desk, and said, 'You probably gathered that we are to take a plane to London. We'll be met by a car and taken straight to a meeting with the Chancellor and the PM. It looks as though it's going to be a late night.'

Blair asked permission, then picked up the telephone and dialled his principal assistant.

'The Minister, Mr Donald and I are going to London immediately. The Prime Minister's office is arranging a flight through RAF Turnhouse. Let me have a complete minute on the present state of affairs regarding Clan Oil before we leave.'

Archie Donald said, 'I had better get my deputy to speak to all the people who rang. He can say that we can't have a firm statement ready until later tonight. Not that it will help much – he'll be badgered non-stop until we get something ready or until it's too late for tomorrow's papers, and if that happens the editors will go with whatever they have, trying to guess what our true position is and more importantly why we're avoiding them.'

*

In the House of Commons business was over for the moment, and MPs were leaving the chamber. Nigel Barron, the Scottish Nationalist member for Waverley, made his way purposefully towards the office of his opposite number, David Arthur, the government Chief Whip. He had to avoid several assistants and government back-benchers in the outer office as he swept past them, ignoring their questions and their half-hearted attempts to stop him. He thrust open the door and checked for a moment as the large and very untidy room seemed to be empty. A grunt from behind the over-flowing and much scarred desk reassured him. David Arthur was retrieving some papers which must have fallen from the desk and as he heaved himself upright his large fat face was suffused with exertion. He greeted Barron with an engaging although sheepish smile.

Barron had to remind himself, not for the first time, that this puffing fat man was in many people's opinion the most skilled member of the present government's team.

'Ah Nigel,' said Arthur, mopping his brow. He rose and dodged, with that lightness of foot that fat men often have, through and around several piles of books and documents strewn over the floor as he came forward to shake hands. 'I thought you'd be along. What kept you? The news has been out for at least ten minutes!'

'I wanted a quick word with several other members of my party and people in the other minority parties,' said Barron peevishly in his high-pitched Cockney accent. His parents had left Scotland when he was four and his strong Scottish feelings were somehow accentuated by his heavy London accent.

He was not mollified by the other man's friendliness. 'We are agreed. If the government pursues this idea of nationalising Clan Oil we will have to review whether or not we can continue to support certain other of your policies.'

'Very delicately put, Nigel. And just what I would have said myself in your place. Rest assured that this office knew nothing about this plan in advance. I'm sure it's a brainwave of the Chancellor's – aided and abetted by the Treasury. I shall do everything in my power to have it stopped. I've already spoken to the Prime Minister and we'll be having a meeting later this evening. As you know, we value and appreciate your support when you feel you can give it – we've got quite enough trouble as it is with the main opposition. I shall convey your doubts about the continuation of that support in the strongest possible way. Have no fear: in the strongest possible way.'

*

Mark had to knock to get himself and Bob admitted to his own office. Mackay apologised, but one glance was enough to show why the precaution was necessary. Mark's office and the others connecting were now crowded with shirt-sleeved policemen. The electronic recording gear that Mark had seen arriving earlier was now wired up to the flex of his telephone. In addition, there was a large radio console with three officers using headset microphones. They were producing a constant stream of reports which were being handed out to the twenty or so detectives who were manning large display boards giving visual indicators of all the forces now under Mackay's command. Mackay had answered Bob's query about keeping such an operation secret, particularly with the press conference just finished above, by saying, 'The lift no longer stops on this floor – my electrical genius has just fixed that. Also I've got, as you saw when you came down, two men posted on the stairs. In fact there is one poor reporter who innocently wandered down here just before the conference started and bluffed his way in. He's now in custody in our nice new police headquarters and will have a somewhat restricted view of Fettes College from there until this whole thing is over. I'll have trouble from his editor when he finds out what we did, but I'll just have to risk that. We got all our equipment up with the help of Mark's security people. We carried it up the stairs piecemeal.' As Mackay finished speaking, the telephone on Mark's desk rang.

Everybody froze. They knew that all normal calls were being

re-routed to Mark's secretary in a temporary office several floors below. Both Mark and Mackay rushed to the desk.

'It's for you, Mr Armstrong,' said the telephone supervisor. 'The caller refused to say who it was, but you said to put through anyone who asked for you personally.'

'Put it on,' Mark signalled to Mackay as he had been told to. In turn Mackay indicated to Jock Henderson that he should start up his equipment and then fitted earphones on himself.

It was the same calm flat voice as before. 'Armstrong? Sunray here.' Mark nodded to the others as he listened and saw the strain on their faces at being so near and yet so far from the source of the threat to Clan Oil. 'We've been watching the news with interest and hope you get the money you need.' Mark had no chance to reply before the voice continued. 'By the way, we presume you have contacted the police and that they are with you or are recording this call, hoping to trace it. It won't help—we'll break contact in thirty seconds. We're going to put on a little demonstration for you of how serious we are. If it doesn't convince you, it certainly will convince the police. The money will be paid in diamonds. No other form of payment will do. The police will understand. How you get them is your problem. We'll give delivery details later.'

The phone went dead before Mark could think of anything to say and he looked round helplessly at the others, the receiver still in his hand.

Henderson rewound the tape instantly, flicked a switch and everyone strained to hear every detail as the one-sided conversation filled the room. As it ended even Mackay's nerves seemed frayed. 'Again,' he snapped at Henderson as his junior started to rewind the tape back to replay it.

'Christ,' he said when it had finished. 'They are keeping one jump ahead of us.'

'Very professional,' agreed Henderson.

'Too professional.' Mackay was obviously concerned. 'If they keep up this standard of operation we won't get anywhere near them. I wonder what the hell they mean by a demonstration to impress us.'

A stocky man of about thirty, in military combat uniform with no insignia of rank, but referred to as 'major' by an identically dressed colleague, spoke up. The two had been arguing about something with Mackay when Mark and Bob had arrived and Mackay had not introduced them. 'They could strike anywhere,' he said, his voice harsh, with an edge of authority. 'Now you'll have to let me take over. We've been specially trained for this.'

John Graham whispered to Mark and Bob. 'This is some guy from the SAS. He and Mackay have not exactly hit it off together. He and his men flew into Edinburgh this afternoon.'

Mackay exploded with anger. He leapt to his feet and strode over to tower above the major who neither stood up, nor flinched as Mackay shouted at him, although his aide moved towards them crouching slightly, balancing on the balls of his feet. 'No. How many times do I have to tell you? No! I'm in charge of this operation and until such time as I think I've lost control of it, I'll use my own policemen. I don't want us to over-react. Your training is no help until we know what they're going to do. Then and only then, can we hope to plan any sensible counter-measures. You will hold yourself in reserve—and with luck we won't need you. Unless there are political implications—which doesn't seem to be the case yet—I probably won't use you at all. Maybe there's no political angle. Maybe they're not terrorists—just gunmen.'

The major obviously didn't agree. 'Why take chances? All your men are just ordinary bobbies who've been taught to shoot. My men have trained for years for just such a situation as this. Why not use them?'

'Because I don't want to. I want the police to be seen to be able to handle it,' Mackay insisted more calmly. 'One good thing, the weather has closed in even more in the North Sea. The fog is thicker and there's a very heavy sea running. Nothing can get at the platforms while it lasts, and the RAF tell us that it will be at least forty-eight hours. That leaves this office and the landfall complex—and I've got men at both.'

'I still think we should take charge,' said the major. 'It's getting out of hand. And we'll only have to clear up the mess in the end.'

Mackay's temper surged again. 'Look, soldier, if I think I need to use your Tactical Response Group I'll use you. This has nothing to do with rivalry or jealousy. I happen to think that in this country the public should be able to rely on the police resolving almost all breaches of law, not a bunch of death or glory boys whose only ability is to meet threat with threat, death with death.'

The major's face was like granite, his cold grey eyes staring at Mackay as he went on. 'Nor do I think you're infallible. I've seen the report on your colleagues in the SAS and their near disaster at the Iranian Embassy last year. You were lucky. The man at the back abseiling down with a frame charge to blow the window and almost hanging himself as his ropes snarled! The explosion from that dropped charge meant you had to go in. I'm not detracting from the bravery, just reminding you we're all human and that means we can make human errors. And for the moment Sunray have the edge—they are mobile and we don't know who or where they are. There is nothing for you to make a pre-emptive strike against. We just don't know who or what they'll mount their demonstration against although we know it won't be Mr Armstrong—he's their link.'

The major strode across to the telephone and gestured angrily at the recording equipment. 'Switch your stuff off. I want to make a call and I don't want anybody to hear who to.' When the telephonist answered he said curtly, 'A line,' then turned his back to shield the dialling from the others.

His call was answered immediately. 'Edinburgh.' It was obviously his identifying code and he had to wait a moment for the connection he was seeking. 'We've had another contact, sir. They were short and no leads. The money is to be paid in diamonds. But I'm speaking to you because I am meeting local resistance to our involvement. Can I have our position confirmed from a higher authority?' He paused for a question from the other end. 'I've got all my people at Redford Barracks less than five miles away. The officer in charge is a Chief Superintendent David Mackay.' He put the telephone down and turned to the others. 'I'm sorry, but we might as well get this out in the open now.'

Mark and Bob looked at Mackay and smiled their sympathy as he shrugged his shoulders in frustration and turned to Jock. 'Get me Commander Bell in London. We'll have to see what they can do about the diamonds.' He turned back to Mark. 'I don't think that you are in any personal danger – they need you as a link – but we just have to keep on waiting for them to make a move, hoping they'll make a mistake. It may seem to you that we are making no progress. It's a hell of a thing to admit but we've got to wait and see how they develop their moves before anything we do will make sense. Their insistence on diamonds is indicative – they know that they are virtually impossible to trace.' He pointed at Jock who was speaking to someone at New Scotland Yard. 'Am I right in presuming that in the end you would be willing to hand over the diamonds to the full amount if we can't terminate this before then?'

Mark looked at Bob and after only a moment's hesitation they both nodded agreement.

'Commander Bell,' said Jock, holding out the telephone for Mackay.

'Hello, Tom. David Mackay here. I need your help. We have a serious ransom demand situation here. Can you get us fifty million pounds' worth of diamonds in the next few hours? And get them up here to Edinburgh immediately? It's a commercial company and they will, if necessary in the end, pay the demand. We will telex you an authorisation reference, and the company's bank – the Scottish National Bank – will issue confirmation requisitions as usual from their main London office.' He looked at Bob who nodded agreement. Mackay then explained his dilemma to the other man, obviously an old friend. He finished off with a bitter, humourless laugh. 'Oh yes, we'll give you a receipt.'

Almost as soon as he put the phone down it rang again. Everyone tensed as he picked it up, expecting it to be Sunray again.

'It's my Chief Constable,' he explained, covering the mouthpiece hastily. 'Hello, sir. You what? You want the conference facility switched on?' Mackay's face showed his concern, but he told Jock to comply with the order.

'Is the major also there?'

'Yes sir, he is.'

'David, what is your view of the situation? I have just had a very angry Home Secretary on the line, saying that you are not co-operating with the TRG people. Is that right?'

'No, it's not. For the moment there is nothing to do. For us or them. We don't know much more than we did when I briefed you two hours ago.'

'The Home Secretary is concerned that we should not let inter-force rivalry get in the way of our objective. And as you know the TRG is one of his pet interests—you remember he was in the SAS himself during the war.'

'With respect, sir, I would not allow those sort of considerations to affect my assessment of the situation. As you know, I believe that units like the TRG should only be used in the last resort. The public expect us, the police, to protect them. The only exception is, as you know, anything political.'

'Surely that's only right, David, up to a certain point. Then we would be failing in our duty if we didn't harness all the resources available to us.'

'That is the essence of my position, sir. At the moment we have nothing to target against. We don't know the identity or affiliation, if any, of Sunray. There is nothing for the major and his TRG to retaliate against. Please believe me that the instant I feel that we should use him I will, although I do have one major misgiving.'

'What?'

'Sunray have been so well organised to date, so well planned and apparently so well disciplined that I am starting to think that they either have experience of our counter-terrorist measures or they have a very good mind in charge, someone who has carefully studied all other similar groups and where they have gone wrong. I think we are going to need a break of some kind to throw them out of kilter, to give us something to work on.'

'Perhaps you're right. Do you want me to come up and take charge personally?'

'No, sir, I don't. Thank you for the offer but I am confident I can handle this myself. Confident that on the evidence they are more likely to be gunmen than terrorists.'

'Very well, David, the choice is yours. Can I just say that the Home Secretary reminded me that the last two big jobs were filled by policemen from Scotland? The Metropolitan Commissioner in London and the recent head of the security services. He said that he was hoping that you might make it three in a row—you must have had some sort of interview even I didn't know about. So it looks as if there might be a lot riding on the outcome of this for you personally, although the old boy did say that having met you he would accept your recommendations without a qualm.'

'I'm sorry about the interview, sir. But I was told to take a week's leave and tell no one.'

'That's all right. Perhaps I'll have to use the "sir" if you get the job. Can I now speak to your major? What's his name? Put him on.'

'I don't know what his name is, sir. He didn't and doesn't seem to want to give it. He says that that is the way they prefer it nowadays,' said Mackay, as he handed the major the telephone.

'Chief Constable?'

'It wouldn't have cost you too much, young man, to have said sir. You heard everything?'

'Yes—sir.'

'The guidelines for this sort of co-ordinated exercise are clear. The senior policeman *in situ* is in charge. You will take your instructions from Chief Superintendent Mackay—without question or any attempt to circumvent or undermine his authority. Is that clear? Or do you want me to speak to your Director?'

'No, sir. It is perfectly clear.'

'Good. Then I wish you all luck.'

A second after the line went dead the major slammed the earpiece into the cradle and snarled, 'Well, Mackay, you'd better get it all right. You're in the centre of the stage now, and if you don't you'll be lucky to have control of the traffic wardens in Edinburgh in the future—instead of a new job!'

Mackay ignored the provocation and turned to Mark and Bob. 'Sorry about airing our dirty washing in public. Didn't you both say you were about to leave just before the first phone call?'

'Yes,' Mark nodded. 'I'm going home, then to the North British Hotel and afterwards the BBC. You can contact me at any of those. Or even in my car as you know.'

'What about you—er Bob?' Mackay hesitated before using Bob's first name. 'The Bank's not really involved in this, but perhaps I should know where you are too.'

Mark must have seen and interpreted the quick glance Bob shot at him. Before Bob could answer he snapped, 'He's probably off to see my wife.'

Everyone was disconcerted and busied themselves with trivia—Mackay checked his notes with unnecessary care, Jock fiddled with the switches and dials on his equipment, and the major adjusted and readjusted his uniform. Bob came straight back. 'For God's sake! Why now, in front of these people who're not involved? All you're doing is embarrassing them with our problem, which won't get any better with a public slanging match.'

Bob turned back to Mackay. 'I'm going to my home in Melrose. The number is in the book. Before I go I'll call in at the Bank and give the necessary authorisation for the fifty million pounds for the diamonds.'

*

In London's Hatton Garden a number of Britain's leading diamond dealers who were working late and quite a few of their colleagues who had gone home to comfortable villas in fashionable suburbs were being persuaded to unlock their safes and strong-rooms. None of them had ever had such a request before, and Commander Bell and his men had to use the full authority of the Commissioner of the Metropolitan Police and their own strength of character to get their diamonds—backed up by signed but blank purchase orders from the Scottish National Bank. Even so several particularly suspicious dealers insisted on telephoning the Metropolitan Commissioner personally. His well-known Glaswegian voice calmed their misgivings and he made a great play of thanking them in advance for the public-spirited help to his hard-pressed officers. In the end they were able to get the whole fifty million pounds' worth from only eleven leading merchants. An hour later a patrol car with three motorcycle escorts took an armed Chief Inspector and two Sergeants to Heathrow Airport and the last Shuttle to Edinburgh carried the most costly cargo in its history.

BOB AND SARA

Bob drove south through the softness of the rain-washed September evening towards Melrose in the powerful V12 Daimler supplied to him by the Bank—not his own choice of car, but one meant to reflect his position and status. Normally it was a journey he enjoyed—the long climb up Soutra Hill and afterwards the gentle rolling countryside of the Borders. When he was through the foothills the rain stopped and the whole countryside had a clean fresh look in the evening sun. But now he was in a hurry, and just forty minutes after leaving the offices of Clan Oil he was turning off the main road at Leaderfoot onto the narrow road to Melrose. A couple of hundred yards through the hamlet of Newstead he turned right through the gates of Bankhead. There was a well-kept, shrub-bordered drive of about three hundred yards ending in a circle of white gravel in front of the house which had been a typical large Scottish farmhouse until Bob's parents had bought and converted it. Painted white, with black woodwork and doors, the house had clean simple lines: two storeys in the centre with matching single-storey wings on either side. With its small-paned windows, red pantile slate roof and landscaped garden, the house looked welcoming and well cared-for.

Bob pulled up with a crunch on the gravel sweep. The front door, as always, was unlocked. His hand was still on the handle as he called Sara's name—to be greeted instead by Mary Little.

'Mrs Armstrong is in the garden. And she's crying her eyes out,' she said reproachfully.

He hurried through the house to where French windows led out from the sitting-room to the garden, which was Willie Little's greatest joy. For a hundred yards it sloped gently down to the river Tweed. Formal at first, it became progressively more natural until it ended at the river's edge as a rough lawn from which Bob often went to fish before breakfast. During the spring and summer Willie would sometimes work in the garden for sixteen hours a day—and it showed. Anything and everything that could be grown in the rich red soil did well. Bob sometimes tried to persuade Willie that he was too old to work so hard. The reply was always the same: 'If I didna like it, I wouldna do it.'

Bob could see Sara sitting in an old-fashioned but comfortable canvas chair, the sort that film directors always seem to use, on a south-facing lawn which had been cut out of a steep bank, the sides and the front faced in stones from the river. The evening sun glinted in her hair. She was watching a pair of swans gliding effortlessly on the river and didn't hear him coming until he was only a few feet away.

He could see that she had been crying. But she leapt up with a welcoming smile and ran to him. 'Darling, you're here at last. I thought you were never coming,' she said, her face buried in his chest. She hugged him for comfort. His arms tightened around her in return. After a moment, he smoothed her hair and smiled down at her.

'Why have you been crying?' he asked, leading her back to her chair and sitting down beside her in another, put there earlier no doubt by Willie. 'What's wrong?'

'Nothing. Nothing at all. I think it's just relief and reaction. But I was worried about whether I had forced myself on you this morning on the phone when you couldn't really refuse me. I didn't, did I?'

Smiling at her, Bob replied, 'Believe me, if I hadn't wanted you to move in with me I would have said so. I did. You just decided to do things a bit quicker than I had imagined they would happen. What about Mark? Did you talk to him?' He thought how pretty she looked in spite of her recent tears and saw no reason to upset her further by telling her that the relationship between him and Mark was deteriorating. He decided to play down what had happened during the day.

'No. I didn't want to talk to him about this or about anything else. We have nothing more to say to each other. Or at least there is nothing I have to say to him—we've already had a couple of silly verbal scuffles.'

'Perhaps I should call him? Let him know where you are? He might be worried if he tries to contact you.'

'It will probably be several days before he notices I've gone. We don't meet, and we talk only on the phone. Don't call him, please, I feel safe here. Don't let him know where I am. I'll tell him later—or he'll guess.'

Bob agreed not to call, and offered to bring her a drink. He went back into the house to get bottles, glasses and ice.

Mary Little was in the kitchen. She sniffed and said, almost accusingly, 'I think Willie and I will go and visit my sister at Jedburgh tonight. You'll want the house to yourselves. I can see you've got a lot to talk about. I've done the supper—cold lobster and salad, and cheese. It's in the fridge. Can you help yourselves? We'll be back in the morning. Will that be all right?'

Mary always gave him lobster if she thought there was something wrong. This was her way of showing she could see that Sara and he were upset; that she wanted to help, even to the extent of spending the night with her sister, who as far as Bob could remember she didn't like very much and saw very rarely.

'Yes, we'll manage fine. Thank you, Mary. We'll see you in the morning.'

Sara smiled at him when he arrived carrying the tray. He mixed a gin and tonic for her, a weak one as he knew she liked it, and a whisky, a strong one, for himself, because he thought he needed it.

He raised the glass in mock salute. 'Here's to us. A new start.'

'To us,' Sara agreed.

They both sipped their drinks, each lost for a moment in their own thoughts—Sara revelling in her relief at being with Bob, at having moved out of her own flat at last, and physically into Bob's life; Bob, sharing her excitement at their being together, was anticipating some of the difficulties that undoubtedly lay ahead.

Sara was wearing Levis, a checked shirt and flip-flop sandals. Bob glanced ruefully down at his own formal business suit.

'I think I'll go and change into something else. I look a little stuffy next to your jeans. Will you be OK for a few minutes?'

'Yes, of course. Off you go and change.'

In his bedroom Bob took off his clothes and put them all away carefully, a habit he had picked up at school and which he had never broken. He put on a pair of old jeans and pulled a V-necked cashmere sweater over his shirt and went back out to the garden. On the way he heard the Little's Mini set off down the drive.

'Let's go for a walk,' he said, taking Sara's hand in his.

They walked for over an hour. They started out along the river. The Tweed is wide and slow by the time it reaches Melrose except where it breaks over large rocks and the gentle rush and bubbling of the clear water was a soft background to their talking. Then they walked along the top of the wide wall which was supposed to have been built by the earliest monks from Melrose Abbey in the twelfth century, and Bob showed her the Devil's Hoofprint—a cloven hoofmark clearly imprinted on one of the top stones of the wall, a stone otherwise perfect; then past the iron bridge to Gattonside across the river; past the ruins of the Abbey where the heart of Robert the Bruce is supposed to be buried at the base of one of the broken pillars; round past the rugby ground, The Greenyards, where the game of rugby sevens was invented in 1883 by Ned Haig the local butcher. As they walked Bob gently told her about all the things they passed, about the people who lived in the town and about the surrounding area. His deliberately casual chatter was designed to relax her obvious tension, to overcome her desire to talk almost continuously—telling him how much she loved him, and why. He hadn't realised until then how very big a step she felt she'd taken. He was slightly shamed to realise that he'd believed that the problems were all his.

After a while the warmth went out of the air. Sara shivered slightly and Bob turned for home. Taking off his sweater he made her put it on.

Suddenly she was crying again. 'That's the sort of thing Mark would never do. He's so wrapped up in himself.' She shivered again and hugged the warmth of the cashmere to her. 'I don't hate him, I just feel sorry for him. He needs someone who will make him feel needed. Not me.'

Bob put his arm round her shoulder. 'There's no point in worrying about the past.'

'But I do worry. Mark doesn't like his possessions being taken from him. And he looks on me as one of his prize possessions.'

All the way back to Bankhead, Bob worked hard at reassuring her, telling her there was nothing Mark could do, that he, Bob, would look after her—not just in this crisis but for the rest of her life. And all the time, although he marvelled that this beautiful, independent, gifted woman could be so frightened by her own daring, he was glad that she had turned to him.

They walked back along the river, the setting sun turning it into a rippling blaze of copper. They stopped to watch a family of mallards, two parents and five ducklings. They were making for the river's edge at the end of the day, the dull browns of the duck set off by the brilliant colours of the drake. Both were watching their young, shepherding them to the security of the bank for the night.

As they watched they were both lost in thought. Sara compared Bob's gentle caring to Mark's indifference; marvelled again at how he seemed to want to share everything with her, to live everything with her, and yet to protect her. Bob found himself wondering if she had turned to him as a reflex, seeking security after her rejection by Mark. He glanced at her profile, beautiful against the blaze of colour from the river and knew that this was not the case. What they now shared had taken a long time to grow. It might never have come to anything if Mark had been a better husband. He wasn't an alternative to Mark. On the contrary, he was filling a position Mark had never managed to fill properly, had never even known existed.

When they got back to the house he lit the fire in the small sitting-room. The room was filled with old comfortable furniture and Bob's favourite pictures and treasured mementos of growing up. It was not a showpiece but a room for living in. Soon it was warm and cosy and cheery, and they ate their supper there, sitting on the floor in front of the fire with soft soothing music playing on the stereo.

Bob talked and talked, telling her of his plans for them. They laughed together when he spoke of children to come and what they would share with them. And he told her about his work, of how he expected soon to get confirmation of the top job at the Bank. He discussed what had happened that afternoon and how he saw the future for Clan Oil. He told her of the threat from Sunray and then glossed it over, saying it was a problem for Mark and the police. They watched Mark's interview on television and Bob told her the background to what he and Mark were trying to achieve.

'I still like Mark, as a businessman,' he finished. 'Which is just as well, since we're going to have to do a lot of business together. I think he'll be reasonable once he gets over his hurt pride.'

The fire died down. They made love in its warm glow, lying on the rug in front of it, slowly, gently and with concern for each other.

Sara was even more beautiful in the soft light, her hair spilled across the rug and her tanned healthy body languid and relaxed.

'Almost too beautiful to be true. It makes me feel humble,' he told her, as he ran his hands across her breasts and down across her stomach and thighs.

In turn she told him the light made him look bronzed and interesting. 'I'm glad you're not handsome in the conventional way—I like you just as you are. Compact and tough. Rugged.' For a moment she tried to look coy and innocent, and cocking her head on one side she smiled and asked, 'By the way, just for the look of things, do you think I should rumple the bed in the spare room? Just in case Mary notices.'

Laughing, he helped her to her feet and they went upstairs to his bedroom. Lying in the dark they talked on about their plans, repeating to each other, like children, the things that gave them pleasure. Sara drifted off to sleep after about an hour. But Bob found himself suddenly restless and he shuddered involuntarily as a vision of what Sunray might be flashed through his thoughts as a series of dark images.

BLAIR

PALLIN, BLAIR AND Donald were driven out to the airport from New St Andrew's House in the Minister's Rover. It was rush hour and the normally heavy traffic was swelled by the number of Festival visitors hurrying to the first of the evening's receptions, concerts, plays, previews, exhibitions and the dozens of other events that make up every night's entertainment during the three weeks of the Edinburgh International Festival. The seven mile journey took almost an hour and all three of them were fidgeting and bad-tempered by the time they reached the airport. However, their ruffled feathers were soothed to some extent since all the arrangements had been made in advance and their passage through the terminal was carried out with the minimum of fuss and bother: no checking in, no queues, no worrying if they might miss the plane, none of the agitation usually associated with trying to get an important flight. All three of them allowed themselves some justifiable pleasure in their temporary elevation above the hundreds of ordinary passengers milling around the airport, pushing and barging and struggling with luggage of all shapes and sizes. As well as the usual passengers and friends meeting or saying goodbye, there were musicians, actors, authors, singers, dancers and film-makers of every imaginable nationality—too many maestros and too many egos for any airport to deal with at once—so they appreciated the way they were shepherded past the turmoil.

They were accompanied to the steps of their aircraft by the airport manager, obviously impressed by the apparent importance of their journey, and there turned over to the Royal Air Force.

The Adjutant of RAF Turnhouse, a short bustling Squadron Leader, had everything under control. They didn't quite rank the purple alert which clears the airspace for a Royal flight, but the jet-engined HS125 of RAF Transport was ready and waiting for them. Their journey had been cleared with the Civil Aviation Authority and less than five minutes after arriving at the airport they were airborne. The flight was completely uneventful and fifty-five minutes later they were landing at Heathrow.

'Somebody is trying to tell us that this meeting is important,' Blair hissed to Archie Donald as they made their way down the steps of the plane.

A woman driver from Dover House, the Scottish Office's headquarters in London, was standing by another gleaming black Rover. The three climbed in—Pallin rather obviously choosing to sit in front with the driver as his little personal display of democracy—and they sped off towards London. The traffic was light at that time of evening and the journey to the city centre was swift and without hold-up. On the way the driver explained that she had been told to take them to the Prime Minister's own home. Like several of his recent predecessors, the country's chief executive had chosen to live in his own house rather than in Downing Street, preferring to keep Number 10 for the more formal business of government. On more than one occasion he had been heard to say, 'Downing Street is like living above the shop—you can never escape, even for a moment. For some reason people think twice before pestering a chap in his own house.' The remark was hardly original but it always raised a smile.

Within thirty minutes they were being saluted by the two policemen on duty at the front door. This was the only thing that made the house different from the others in the street—solid, comfortable, predictable and middle-class. No-one seemed to expect them, and feeling rather self-conscious after all the build-up, they stood awkwardly in the hall—chatting in a strained way with the detective who looked after the Premier's wife. 'I expect they forgot to warn us you were coming,' he suggested. 'It sometimes happens. Even the best systems break down from time to time.' He left them in no doubt that he felt himself to be part of the inner circle.

After a couple of minutes the Prime Minister's wife came hurrying out to greet them. A pretty woman in her late forties, she was much more attractive now than she had been when younger. She was breathless and blushing slightly in a way that made her seem all the more appealing and somehow girlish – one doesn't expect to see a Prime Minister's wife blushing, Blair thought.

'I'm so sorry you've been kept waiting. My husband's office has only just rung through to say you were coming. He'll be here shortly and has asked me to lay on some sandwiches and beer in the sitting-room.' She smiled at Pallin, whom she had known as her husband's friend over more than two decades, both in and out of office. 'John, you know where it is. Take the others in and I'll go and make you all something to eat. I expect you're hungry.'

Pallin led the way. The room was large and took up most of the ground floor. There were at least eight armchairs, but the room still had a comfortable, used-every-day feeling. Blair could see why the Prime Minister would prefer to have the familiar surroundings of such a room to relax in rather than the formal, under-the-microscope atmosphere of Downing Street. The furniture was of no particular period but the total effect was one of natural style. Around the walls were many photographs and mementos of more than twenty years in public life – the great man with other great men and women representing much of the political life of Britain and the world.

Whilst the other two looked around the walls, Pallin sat in one of the chairs with his eyes closed, occasionally asking questions to himself or making a point to the other two, clearly nervous as he was about to be confronted by his leader. The evening was warm and humid and the three of them were uncomfortably hot as they waited uneasily for the country's Premier. A blue-bottle which was trapped in the window irritated them with its constant buzzing until Blair picked a copy of Punch from the coffee table and swatted it, flicking the dead fly into the empty grate.

The sandwiches and beer and the Prime Minister arrived simultaneously, causing some confusion. With the PM were the Chancellor, David Arthur the Chief Whip, and the Premier's political and private secretaries. The Prime Minister was one of the few men Hamish Blair knew of who really did look in real life like his television image. Slim, five feet ten, dark features, he was a wise and cheerful man with an open honest face that most people felt they could trust.

'Ah darling,' he said. 'Sandwiches. Hope you made some of my favourites, with cheese and onion. Do try one,' he encouraged everyone as he helped himself.' And take off your jackets if it's too warm.' He himself didn't, so none of the others did.

'Thank you for coming down so quickly,' he went on. 'I take it you all know one another? Let's all take a plate of these—and there's beer or lager. Then we can settle down and look at this Clan Oil business. I had to keep you waiting because I was booked to go to a reception of local government big-wigs but got away after half an hour by pleading "affairs of state". The only speech I had to listen to was my own. Rank, it seems, really does occasionally have its privileges.'

As everyone settled down, the Prime Minister looked at Pallin over his bottle of beer—his wife having remembered the opener but forgotten to bring any glasses. His cheerful good humour had vanished as though it had never been.

'Well, John, we know the Chancellor's views on this—I've been listening to them all day. Perhaps you could bring us up-to-date with your side of things? We won't bother taking minutes just yet. In fact, I don't think we'll take any minutes at all. We'll all remember what is said. Won't we?'

The significance of this was lost on none of them. They all realised that it was a signal that the Prime Minister didn't want any official record of the meeting, that he wanted the freedom to manoeuvre in the future as he saw fit without the restraint of having to explain or justify his actions. Perhaps, thought Blair cynically, he wanted to deny his subordinates ammunition for the memoirs which they would undoubtedly one day be tempted to write.

Pallin coughed nervously, looked round at his Scottish Office colleagues for support, and began. 'Certainly, Prime Minister. As you know, the Secretary of State is ill and I was asked by the Chancellor to report as quickly as possible on whether or not it would be advisable for us to consider nationalising Clan Oil. Normally this would not be within the remit of the Scottish Office, but the Chancellor wanted a speedy and on-the-spot opinion. Our study was well under way when somehow news of it leaked out. Now all hell has broken loose, particularly after the press conference held by Clan Oil earlier this evening.'

David Arthur interrupted. 'What I want to know is who on earth authorised the study in the first place? What is being suggested would cut right across our stated policy on North Sea oil. And as you can imagine, it is antagonising the Nationalist MPs and other members as well. If we're not careful we can say goodbye to any co-operation from them and the other minority parties in the future. I repeat, whose authority was used? Who set this whole thing in motion?'

The Chancellor shifted his bulk in his chair and growled through the remains of a sandwich. 'I did. On my own authority.' He had, of course, had tacit agreement from the Prime Minister, but had agreed to deny this if, as was now obvious, complications and opposition should develop. 'But naturally I meant it to be completely confidential and wouldn't have taken any further action until we had had a chance to discuss it in Cabinet. But, and I'm serious about this, it could be a very important step for us to take at the moment. We could get Clan Oil on the cheap and it would go down very well with a lot of influential people abroad – people I have to deal with.'

'But it might, it seems, go down very badly with a lot more people here at home – people we all need, particularly at this point in our Parliamentary life and with our Parliamentary programme,' said the Prime Minister. Privately he was thankful that he had insisted that the Chancellor act on his own. He had been sure the plan couldn't be pushed through but it had been attractive enough to try, provided he could get the government to come out of the affair with its nose clean. He went on, 'What do you think, Blair?' Unable to get over a basic distrust of civil servants, he always used their surnames.

After two years in power he still resented how much real power in central government was vested in the hands of senior administrators like Blair – power which he knew they always disclaimed. Too often, however, he had seen his own and his senior ministers' best intentions thwarted by nothing more than the grindingly slow pace of civil service machinery. Somehow senior men seemed able to adjust that pace to their own ends – a negative approach which he, on the other hand, usually contrasted with their unwillingness to take any new initiative.

Blair was formal, his thirty-five years in the Civil Service showing in his reaction to the Prime Minister.

'First of all, sir, it would be misleading of me if I didn't admit that it may have been through some of my own inquiries that the story leaked. There were so many people to talk to in such a short time that this was perhaps inevitable,' he said, admitting that he was the source of the breach of security without actually admitting the form it took. 'My department has doubts about both the actual and psychological advantages that might be gained from nationalising Clan Oil. However, I have to be guided by the Treasury, and they appear to be adamant. As they always are, however little they are able to justify their strong opinions.'

This was too much for the Chancellor. 'That is pejorative, Blair. And quite unnecessary. I refute the suggestion that my officials would ever take such a high-handed attitude.'

Blair refused to be deflected. 'Most of my senior colleagues agree that the action the Chancellor and the Treasury are proposing would attract, and indeed generate, a great deal of hostile comment in the press. We also feel that it would antagonise most of the Scottish public, and that it would worry the business community.

And of course it would unsettle all the other companies operating or planning to operate in the North Sea—it could sour our, and by "our" I mean government, relations with them for a long time.'

He paused, sighed and then continued. 'However, having said that, there is no doubt that a swift and complete take-over could be made with almost negligible cost to the country at this stage, with very handsome returns coming within two years.' The Chancellor beamed smugly as Blair finished talking.

As he always did, Blair had stated fairly the pros and cons of the problem his political masters were wrestling with, although not at this stage attempting to lead them in their decision. This he would only do if he saw the actual decision going against what he felt was the correct course of action.

The Prime Minister, of course, saw through this but didn't press him for the moment. Instead he turned to the Director of Information whom he had known for many years since Archie Donald had been his own information chief when he was a junior Minister ten years before. He trusted Donald, appreciated his ability to judge the mood of the Scottish press and people, and didn't look on him as a real civil servant since he knew that originally Donald had been editor of a local newspaper. In fact, in a sea of constantly changing faces in his party, he looked on Donald as a friend, someone permanent, someone he could turn to for advice that he valued, someone removed from his party's internecine struggles but who at the same time would be concerned to see the Scottish Office presented in the best possible light.

'Archie, what do you feel? I have a lot of faith in how you see things up there. What do you think. Is it too hot to handle?'

Donald savoured his position in the limelight. Blair winced inwardly at the way Donald was speaking only to the Prime Minister—he recognised a man only a few years from retirement, with an eye carefully on his knighthood.

'I am convinced, Prime Minister, that there is no way that we could justify this action. At this moment every newspaper in Scotland will be preparing the Clan Oil story as their front page lead for tomorrow's papers. Incidentally, my people have been assuring them all that we will make a statement before eleven o'clock—I very much hope that that will be possible. As you know, the press trust me, and if possible, I must repay that trust by giving them a story when I say I will.' Blair wondered how often the press were disappointed by governments of both parties who promised clarification but then found it expedient to shelter behind the blander position of no comment.

'The main part of this story, as you know, was released by Armstrong, the head of Clan Oil, at a press conference this evening. He in turn was reacting to the story in yesterday's papers about his cash problems – he is presenting himself to the public as a man attacked on all sides. That is exactly the sort of story the press and the public like and with good advice he could keep this whole thing alive for quite a long time.'

The Prime Minister, who knew that Donald was stretching his brief, signalled his thanks by reaching across and patting Donald on the arm, nodding to him.

David Arthur burst in again. 'I don't think we can take this sort of risk. As you know, Prime Minister, we need every vote we can muster in the House over the coming weeks. My job as Chief Whip will be impossible if I can't rely on some support from the Nationalists, the Liberals and the other small parties, all of whose reaction will be the same. We simply don't have a big enough majority for that sort of old-fashioned cavalier attitude. They don't always support us, but there are a number of Bills where their help is going to be absolutely essential. I cannot emphasise this too much. I am going to need them over the next few months, not only in the House but in a number of key committees.'

The discussion went on for another half hour, the Chancellor presenting his case well, based on his brief from his Treasury officials. Blair saw, as he had so many times over the years, the classical battle lines: emotions and gut feelings ranged against a seemingly invincible battery of facts and figures. All of them, he realised, were resenting the pressure of the absent Treasury officials, and slowly but surely the misgivings of Donald and the Prime Minister, allied to that resentment, began to tip the scales in favour of his own advocacy.

Seeing how the argument was going the Chancellor eventually began to shift tack and to float the idea that he didn't want to see the government's plans set aside so easily. Everyone realised that what he really meant was that he didn't want his own prestige damaged and his Treasury officials exposed to sneers from the rest of Whitehall.

Finally the Prime Minister cut in. 'Right, I don't think we can pursue this further in this way. We could be held up to ridicule by the press, accused of being insensitive to public reaction in Scotland. But I agree, it mustn't look as though we've been pressurised so easily.' He demonstrated how fast on his feet he could be when the need arose. 'I suggest a statement tonight confirming that an inquiry is being conducted – not on the possibility of nationalising Clan Oil but to see how the Scottish Office might be able to help with the funds for developing that field, whatever it is, as quickly as possible. That would fit the facts too, wouldn't it?'

He turned from the Chancellor to whom he had been speaking directly, and was positive and full of the authority of his great office as he gave instructions to Blair. 'And you, Blair, had better set up a meeting of the relevant people tomorrow. Then with luck you should be able to present a much more favourable picture of the whole thing by tomorrow evening. Who knows? By close co-operation with the Treasury in speedily developing Clan Oil's potential you might be able to let the Chancellor have the best of both worlds, his cake without having to eat it, don't you think? Eh? And you have my full authority to do all that is necessary to clear up this mess. Use the weight of my office if you have to.'

For a few minutes they discussed the details of what the Prime Minister had in mind. Although he was looking at Pallin it was obvious to everyone that he was briefing Blair.

'Something else you had all better know—the people from Edinburgh know already—is that Clan Oil are under some sort of terrorist threat. The police have contained the situation to date—there has been no publicity. The Home Secretary got a message to me at my dinner about all this only an hour ago. He has a lot of faith in the way the local police will handle things. There is already a unit from the Tactical Response Group on hand, although the local Chief Constable doesn't want to use them unless he has to. And he's right, of course. There is no suggestion so far that this group—what's their name?' he turned to Blair, 'Yes, Sunray. No suggestion so far that Sunray has any political connection. And if that is so, then the local officer in charge will only call in the SAS Tactical Response Group if he feels his own men can't cope. The Home Secretary doesn't feel, at least not yet, the need to draw together the members of the Cabinet Office Briefing Room. As you all know we really only use COBRA when terrorists are trying to coerce government for political ends. The police are treating Sunray seriously but it in no way impinges on our area of responsibility. No matter what the outcome is, Sunray is a problem for today—we're looking at the whole future of Clan Oil.'

As the Prime Minister finished his instructions and outlined what their position should now be, Blair could see why he was the leader of his party. If Blair could get the sort of co-operation he was suggesting, the government would be able to turn a disaster into success and at the same time attract nothing but praise for their actions from the Scottish public and business community alike—just what he had privately been hoping to achieve.

Brisk farewells over, Pallin, Blair and Donald left in their Rover for Dover House to prepare their statement, leaving the other three still haggling—the Chief Whip cock-a-hoop and already on the phone trying to find Nigel Barron to give his opposite number the news and the inside story of how he put the case for him, knowing that he could count on a favour in the future; the Prime Minister fending off the Chancellor who had plenty of favours he wanted now in return for giving way.

At the mainly darkened and deserted Dover House there were almost thirty phone messages for either Pallin or Donald – all from the media. Donald's deputy director, who was based at Dover House, had his full team of press officers standing by, and the statement outlined by the Prime Minister was soon ready and being relayed by telex and telephone to the Scottish papers and by hand to the London-based national dailies and the television and radio network news services. Donald called all the journalists in Scotland who were waiting for him to call back.

Eventually the three of them climbed wearily into their first-class compartments on the one o'clock sleeper from Kings Cross to Edinburgh. After the hustle and bustle and importance of their meeting with the Prime Minister they had to settle for an ordinary taxi to get them to the station – all the car-pool drivers at Dover House had gone home hours before. They were disappointed to discover on the train that none of the early editions had used their release. All the London papers were carrying the story with the bias always towards Clan Oil's point of view and all of them were advising against the proposed nationalisation rumour. It was obvious that they had a long way to go before they could establish their new position.

MARK

SINCE CLAN OIL's headquarters and his home were both on the Western outskirts of the city Mark avoided the heavy traffic that bogged down Pallin, Blair and Donald as he drove home after the press conference. The weather which was thin and bleak with driving rain reflected his mood of growing depression as he drove down the drive to his home. The police had taken away the two burnt out wrecks but the dark scorch marks on the gravel were reminders enough for him of the now growing threat to his company. He wanted to speak to Sara and tried several times to phone her without success. He wanted to talk to her, to unload on her his resentment towards Bob.

He tried ringing several mutual friends to see if they knew where she was and eventually tried Jenny Scott. Talking to her he realised that Sara had made some sort of move that day. He knew how close they both were, and Jenny's careful lack of knowledge, although she didn't actually say anything, made him sure she knew that something was happening. He knew that Jenny liked him and her denials were all the stranger for that. He sat and tried to think about Sara, but his problems with Clan Oil kept intruding. He realised, none better, that losing control of his company would be more devastating for him than losing his wife, and that his thoughts about her were bound up with convention and loss of face. First of all I've got to get the company thing straight, he thought. Sara can come later.

After a quick bath and change, Mark drove back into town for his meeting with the directors of European Oil Developments. As he parked his car opposite the North British Hotel his eye took in the large green and white road sign beside him on the pavement. The A7; the old road to the Borders; Galashiels; Hawick, with a spur off to Melrose.

Melrose! Bob Robertson had said he was going to Melrose tonight. But Mark knew that he never went there during the week. Sara must be with him. She must. On impulse he turned to get back into the car and drive down there. Then he realised that his meeting would have to come first. It was too important. And he couldn't miss the television interview either; he needed public opinion on his side. Melrose could wait. Clan Oil could not.

Inside the hotel the head porter, who had known him for years, greeted him. 'Your friends are waiting for you in the American Bar, Mr Armstrong.'

The two EOD directors were young, bright, enthusiastic and as hard as nails. Mark liked them instantly and they liked him. The meeting went well: both sides knew how much was at stake and how important success was for them all. The Bank had obviously done the groundwork well: the concept of the take-over was right, the two companies were completely complementary. The board of EOD knew that they ran a good company but they had taken it as far as they could. To expand they would have to knit their expertise into a much bigger base. Otherwise they would still be doing the same thing and be the same size in ten years' time. After two hours and some pretty hard bargaining on both sides they were in complete agreement. EOD would merge with Clan Oil; the three of them would form the new Executive Board; and the new company would carry on the name Clan Oil, since it was the better name. The technical details of the merger they decided could be left to their respective lawyers, accountants and their common Bank to work out. But the deal was struck. There was so much in it for all of them it could not fail to be. EOD would disappear but their directors would give Clan Oil the management expertise it needed at the top.

Mark commented as they accompanied him back to the foyer, 'That must be a record of some kind, setting up a takeover so quickly. But it makes such obvious sense that I have no doubts about it at all. I hope you don't mind if I announce our agreement tonight? It's important that I do.' They agreed. The three of them shook hands on it before Mark left on his way down to the television studio.

In the foyer of the BBC's offices, Mark explained to the duty commissionaire, who at first hadn't noticed him as he sat watching the end of a film, that he had a meeting with Collin Munro. The commissionaire looked sheepish. He explained, 'You gave me quite a start there, sir. When we're sitting watching television here, we're supposed to watch the BBC. And if we do watch independent television, we're supposed to turn the set away from the front door.'

Mark laughed. His rapport with the commissionaire was genuine. He had always found that it helped him to see people who didn't want to see him, or who had other appointments, if he made a good impression on receptionists and secretaries.

Asked to wait, Mark sat down in one of the uncomfortable chairs in the dismal reception area. The whole place seemed to have about it an air of being run down – everywhere the paint was dull and chipped and scarred. The seats were worn and stained. It was nothing like he had imagined a television and radio station to be like. It wasn't glamorous; just another busy office and, like most offices, showing the wear and tear of every-day use. Mark was interested to see that there were still a lot of people around, including some well-known faces.

The commissionaire chatted to him as he waited. 'The whole place could do with a lick of paint. And a bit of spit and polish. Smarten it up a bit.'

'Yes. I must say it's not at all how I thought it would be. This is my first visit, and the first time I've had a big interview like this.'

'Oh you'll be all right, sir. The studios are fine. And Mr Munro'll look after you.'

At that moment Munro arrived and took Mark up to have his face made up. Munro was short and running to fat. His girth was emphasised by his thick tweed suit, complete with matching waistcoat and large flowery bow-tie. His hair was thick and frizzy, standing out like a grey halo. He had the mild appearance of an amiable professor rather than the look of a seasoned and feared interviewer. Mark noticed that he also had tanning make-up on his hands and asked him why.

'Because I can't cure myself of a habit of putting my hand up to my face as I talk. On the screen it looks terrible against my face, like a white slug, unless I have it made-up to match.'

After make-up they went through to the studio for a rehearsal. It was bright and bustling, as the commissionaire had promised. Everywhere there seemed to be young men and women giving and receiving instructions as though the fate of the world depended on them getting their programme right. Munro explained that at exactly eleven o'clock they would be linked up live to the anchor-man in the Counterpoint studio in London, for a twelve-minute interview. He also mentioned that Counterpoint was now the top rating current affairs programme—the most popular current affairs programme there had ever been in Britain—and the interview would be seen by more than fifteen million people.

'But what should be of particular interest to you,' Munro pointed out, 'is that it is a quality audience. It is now accepted that Counterpoint is the favourite television programme of the influential opinion leaders and management groups in the country, so everyone you want to reach with your story about Clan Oil will be watching. It is the perfect way for you to get your point of view across to the people who count.'

The rehearsal went well. Mark soon got used to the intense heat from the Klieg lights which was even worse than it had been at the press conference earlier. Munro was friendly and smiled a lot. Mark noticed that Munro's chair looked more comfortable than his own, which was fixed and didn't swivel. He saw too that the cameras seemed to take a fixed position on Munro but that for him they changed and were even sometimes aimed from almost floor level, which he rightly suspected would provide a most unflattering angle.

The questions were very general at first—was he married, where was he born, and so on, just to give him something to say and to familiarise him with the strange environment—but then came the questions about Clan Oil and its problems. Mark relaxed, although he still found it difficult to believe as he sat in the tiny studio in Edinburgh, the cameras only a few feet from Munro and himself in their chairs, that he was soon to be watched by millions of people throughout the length and breadth of Britain.

After about five or six minutes the director of the programme asked if the cameraman was happy with the lights, and if the sound technicians were satisfied with voice levels. Both said they were, and the rehearsal was stopped. Then he and Munro took Mark through the winding corridors—years before, the offices had been two separate town houses—to the spartan canteen for a cup of coffee. Again Mark was surprised by its shabbiness.

At ten to eleven they were back in the studio. There were lots of last-minute adjustments. Munro even changed his tie for another he had in his pocket. Mark was surprised to see that they were both made-up and were fixed by elastic. The floor manager prowled around giving and taking instructions and swore as he bumped into the low table at which they were sitting, knocking it off centre.

'Hell! Why wasn't that fixed down?' he said, blaming some unknown technician for his own shortcomings.

As the tension started to build up, Munro seemed to be trying to put Mark at ease, chatting to him as he took instructions from the director through his almost invisible headphone. Mark could feel his mouth drying, his hands growing clammy. He was suddenly terrified that he was going to freeze up, be unable to say anything at all, let alone anything sensible. He gripped the arms of his chair and forced his mind to go over the brief he had prepared for himself that afternoon for the press conference. He could feel sweat forming on his upper lip. He took out his handkerchief to remove it, remembering to dab and not to wipe since that might smear his make-up, so he had been told. The simple physical action helped him get control of himself. The tightening in his stomach and the pounding in his chest died away. He reached forward for a sip of water from the carafe on the table in front of him. He saw that Munro was doing the same, smiling at him. With a surge of fellow-feeling he saw that even this most seasoned of television current affairs men was also anxious, suffering from nerves as the hands on the studio clock came up to eleven. He felt reassured and could feel himself relaxing into his chair.

The monitor set sitting opposite flickered into life, with the well-known signature tune of the Counterpoint programme. Mark watched as first of all the presenter in London gave other news and then began to talk about the fight for control of Clan Oil. Then his own face appeared on the monitor, and he heard the announcer say, 'With Collin Munro in Edinburgh is Mr Mark Armstrong, chairman and managing director of Clan Oil.'

Munro began the interview with an excellent resumé of the current situation regarding Britain's oil. 'Out in the harsh and hostile environment of the North Sea, over ten thousand feet below the sea-bed, lies this country's greatest single asset for the next twenty years – North Sea oil. Billions and billions of barrels of it. Between the early seventies and this year more then £20 billion will have been invested by oil companies large and small in bringing all the present oil finds to full production in the British sector alone. This is probably the biggest commercial venture ever attempted anywhere in the world and it has all been taking place in the space of only a few years.' Mark could see on the monitor that the London station was now projecting behind Munro and himself a giant picture of a production platform being lashed by a gale. In the Edinburgh studio the wall was blank.

'Even allowing for this gigantic investment the oil companies are going to make a lot of money out of North Sea oil. It will be a bigger bonanza than the Californian Gold Rush in the eighteen fifties which, even though we've had constant inflation since then, produced only a total of $350 million worth of gold. Most people have been surprised at how long it has taken to bring the country up to a state of self-sufficiency in oil, at why the petrol in our tanks isn't cheaper and why our government ties the price of our oil to the price all the other producing countries charge. It now seems likely that more and more successful wells will be found in the British sector—even if they are further and further out in the North Sea and in the Atlantic to the west of Shetland—and cost more and more to develop. BP raised almost £400 million—at the time the biggest loan ever raised by a commercial company—to help fund the development of the Forties Field—and matched it with an even greater amount from their own resources.

'The prize is worth it. A guaranteed supply of oil is not the only benefit. Because we are a stable industrial democracy with our own energy resources we do and will continue to attract billions of pounds from around the world—the mobile money which looks for a temporary but safe home. That money too is buttressing and building up the underlying strength of Britain's economy. The people who invest that money would risk their lives before they would risk their money and their clients' money. For as long as they see us as having the unique combination of stability and an abundance of hydro-carbon fuels—oil and gas—they'll continue to pump money into the London money markets. And for the foreseeable future there doesn't look as though they will have a serious alternative. Others have the energy, some have the stability—but virtually nobody else has both.

'In this one single huge industry with all its faults, and its dangers, all its financial risks, Britain is pinning its hopes for the future. In some ways our political leaders are over-awed by the scale of what is happening out in the harsh primitive conditions of the North Sea. Almost it seems they are afraid to talk of how it will transform our economy as though they fear it is an illusion that will disappear. But it will not. The risks are great but the rewards are almost beyond belief— never before have we had such a natural resource as this. On its own it can make Britain great again.'

'But the prize is only available at a huge cost of entry. More than half of the money that will be needed for all this development will come from the capital money market. Some experts say, however, that to date the total investment in North Sea oil by all the British banks is tiny. The risks have been taken by other people—mainly foreign oil companies and foreign banks and syndicates. Against this background, Clan Oil is trying to get the Scottish National

Bank in Edinburgh to help it fight off possible takeover by the government and to persuade it to back its help with around a thousand million pounds which it needs now, or at least within the next two years.'

Mark had been nodding as Munro had been making some of his points. Then Munro turned to him, and before his eyes Munro seemed to become a totally different person. Mark could scarcely believe his ears as in a flat, unfriendly voice he described the fight for control of the wealth in the Scotia Field. The sympathetic questions of half an hour ago were gone. Instead Munro seemed almost to be trying to goad him. It was not just that he was indicating that the government had a reasonable claim to Clan Oil, but to Mark's over-sensitive ears he seemed to be criticising Clan Oil for wanting to hang on to control. At the same time he seemed to suggest that the actions of the Scottish Office were nothing more than some astute civil servants trying to obtain for the nation a share of the immense wealth represented by the Scotia Field. But Mark kept his head, and answered all the questions clearly and fairly while simultaneously his mind raced, trying to see how he might take the initiative. He could, of course, have walked out. He remembered seeing other people put on the rack of trial-by-television and wondering why they hadn't just got up and left. But now he could see that the pressure not to do this was enormous. He wanted to tell his story, to make a good impression. He felt hemmed in, trapped in the small room under the bright lights. Above all, he didn't want to make a fool of himself.

At last he got a chance, when Munro claimed that Clan Oil had no real development and production expertise and that this was why they had got into trouble and were running behind schedule. Patiently and thoroughly he explained the evening's deal with European Oil Developments and its significance for Clan Oil's future operations, how it would give them all the extra production expertise necessary.

After that, things went better. Munro seemed friendlier and his questions slightly more sympathetic to Mark's problems, more understanding. Mark got into top gear and made an excellent job of presenting his case, backing it up with an array of facts and figures, subtly playing the angle that he wanted both to keep control in Scotland and to keep the company in the private sector. Much sooner than he had expected, Munro was winding up and thanking him for taking part, returning the viewers to the Counterpoint studio in London.

The monitor died, the lights came on in the darkness around them as the camera lights dimmed and the technicians and studio hands started chatting together. The tension seemed to drain away and Munro smiled as he took his headphone off. 'That was good television, he said. 'Very good.'

Mark was blazing. 'What the hell were you trying to do to me? That was nothing like the rehearsal. It was nothing like any of the questions you asked me while we were waiting. What's going on? What were you trying to prove?'

'Relax,' said Munro. 'It was good. You were very good. Your story came across well. I couldn't just sit there and act as your public relations man. Our viewers deserve to hear both, or in this case all three, sides of the story: yours, the government's and all the people who have invested so much already in the Scotia Field. I happen to sympathise with you personally, but that doesn't count – my director sets the questions. And remember that most of the people watching weren't Scots – your story is national news.' He paused to nod acknowledgement and thanks to the congratulations of a passing cameraman. 'But you did well, as well as I've ever seen anyone do who's not used to this game. And if at the rehearsal I'd tipped the wink to you of what I was going to do it wouldn't have gone nearly as well. Once you reached the point of almost losing your temper you were so keyed up you were bound to do well. I was relying on you really knowing your subject and not drying up in a rage. Well done. It was great. There's no way any of the papers will be able to ignore that as a story – you'll see, tomorrow morning. Everyone will be talking about it.'

Mollified, Mark agreed that he had probably been expecting too easy a ride. He thanked Munro and left. Outside it was raining heavily. He made a dash for the Ferrari and sat there for a few minutes listening to the rain drumming on the roof of his car. He wondered if he should go home but decided not to. And as the engine fired he did a U-turn in Queen Street and set off for Melrose. After the excitement of the television interview he was elated, the adrenalin pumping round his system, making him feel he could conquer the world. He planned how he would confront Bob Robertson, how he would have it out with Bob and Sara once and for all.

It rained all the way to Melrose. Driving was difficult. The headlights of cars going in the other direction seemed to rear up threateningly before they rushed past in a splatter of extra spray. Mark had to concentrate on the road, which was awash with surface water. Slowly his elation wore off, leaving him instead morose and wondering whether to turn back. He couldn't pick a fight with Bob Robertson: apart from anything else he wasn't sure that Robertson wouldn't win. Also, he needed Bob's help, or at least the Bank's help, and that came to the same thing, to keep control of Clan Oil. For a moment he allowed himself to wallow in self-pity as he thought of the complications of his situation.

Parking the car on the road just beyond the entrance to the drive, he walked through the rain up to Bankhead. He had been there often in the early days of his friendship with Bob. Now, standing under the rain-sodden, wind-lashed trees in front of the darkened house he was soaked to the skin. Drearily he wondered what he was doing there.

After a few minutes, he walked across the gravel circle to the front door and knocked. There was no response, and as he stood there disconsolately he could feel the rain beating through his jacket and shirt into his back. He knocked again and looked up as a light came on upstairs, showing the rain driving almost horizontally against the window.

After a moment the door was unlocked and Bob, who had thrown on a sweater and trousers but no shoes, looked out.

'Mark! God, man, you're soaked. Where's your car?' Bob seemed both surprised and concerned. 'Come in,' he said, with genuine sympathy.

Mark's response was dispirited. 'I parked it at the bottom of the drive and walked up to give myself time to think. But it didn't work. Even after turning it over all the way down here in the car, I still don't know what to say.' He shivered, showing how cold he was. 'Where's Sara? Is she here? What are we going to do? You were my friend. Your help has made possible the growth of Clan Oil until now. We've got to sort this out.'

'Come into the sitting-room,' said Bob. 'The fire's still on. Sara's upstairs. You and I had better talk.'

GORMAN

JUST BEFORE ELEVEN-THIRTY Gorman led his group out of Glenn House, locking the doors behind them. They, in common with almost fifteen million other people around the country, had watched the interview between Mark and Collin Munro, winking to each other and grinning at Munro's summing up; Clan Oil would have to get their thousand million pounds from somewhere, either the government or the bank. Otherwise the potential in the Scotia Field would be wasted.

The men all formed into small groups by their Range Rovers hunching down in their cagouls against the rain. In their identical uniforms of semi-military fawn-coloured shirts, matching corduroy trousers and thick rubber-tread tan boots, they looked fit and confident, loaded down as they were with their weapons and other equipment.

'Right,' said Gorman, 'you all know what to do. The initial operations must all take place at exactly one o'clock. Just after one, the back-up group up here will phone Armstrong and then go to their waiting station to see whether or not they are needed later. The London group checked in just before we came out and said they're already in position if needed. All the rest of us will wait for the helicopter pick-up on Arthur's Seat. And we will arrange to pick up the group who have been out with Sara Armstrong all day.

'Off we go.' Gorman said, as he swung up into his Range Rover. He stopped as his head came up to the level of the roof and he called out to them, wanting them to share his excitement. 'We now have Sunray running.'

In the dim glow from the interior lights of the Range Rovers they all checked that their weapons, explosives and other equipment were in place. Then at five minute intervals each group set off in the order they had already agreed, depending on their target, towards the distinctive orange glow, created by the low pressure sodium bulbs of the Edinburgh street lamps lighting up the night sky in the distance. Leaving last, the back-up group turned west towards their holding position on the Langwhang moor at the foothills of the Pentland Hills.

An hour later the three attack groups were in position—each only a mile and a half from their targets, ready to move exactly on schedule. The months of training and rehearsal had paid off. Gorman had been able to inculcate in all of them his own striving for perfection, for precision, for order. They all knew exactly what the task of each group was and could all cover for each other if something went wrong or they had casualties. They were all on station at exactly the moment Gorman had said they should be—sticking to his instruction that they should be close to their targets with time in hand and not driving into the city from far out with the possibility of a mistake occurring in the synchronised timing of their attacks.

*

At twenty-five to one McQuillan moved off with his four men including the Irishman Paul, and Ishmail, who had chewed his fingernails down beyond the quick and was expelling all the air in his lungs with long slow breaths—to get in as much oxygen as possible which he knew would help contain his growing nervous anticipation. Even McQuillan was having to slow himself down, forcing himself to think only of the job in hand and stop his mind racing over all that they had to do in the next two days. He stopped his Range Rover outside the short drive of a large stone-built house on the western outskirts of the city, only a few minutes from the head office of Clan Oil. It was the home of Captain Iain Thomson, the senior pilot in the group of ten who worked for Clan Oil. In the house, McQuillan knew, were Thomson, his wife Jean and their three young children. For weeks he and his group had studied Thomson's work routine and personal life, spending hours shadowing his wife and family so that now they knew the family's habits and interests better even than did their relatives or close friends.

Silently McQuillan and his four men approached the back of the house. They broke in with ease, cutting a pane in the kitchen window with a glazier's ordinary tungsten glass cutter and removing it silently with a child's rubber suction arrow to stop the noise of falling glass alerting anyone inside. They sniggered quietly to themselves at the inadequate protection of the locked window.

As they moved up the stairs they could hear low voices and see a dim light from what they knew was the Thomson's own bedroom. They froze and listened. McQuillan grinned at the others as they recognised the soft personal noises of people making love. He motioned to two of the men to cover the landing to the children's bedrooms. Then he and the other two eased silently into the main bedroom, the door of which was open so that the Thomsons could hear any sounds from their children in the night.

For a few seconds they stood motionless watching Thomson and his wife. The only light came from a small bulb in a bedside lamp on the floor by the bed, put there either by Thomson or his wife to give a softer light for their intimacy. Thomson was sitting sideways on the bed, his back to the intruders, with his legs thrust out in front of him and his wife Jean was lying back on his thighs in front of him, her legs splayed out to either side and her arms thrown wide. Thomson fondled her breasts. She smiled and said softly, 'Lift me up. I like it when you lift me up.'

Thomson put both hands under her armpits and swept her up in a single movement. The excitement and wonder in her eyes as the action sent him deep inside her shattered in terror as her head came up beside his and she saw the three threatening shapes staring down at them.

Although he was facing away from the door, instinctively Thomson felt something was wrong and tried to turn round, startled disbelief fading from his face as McQuillan thrust the muzzle of the SMG against his bare neck. As always, McQuillan's cold measured voice gave even greater weight to what he was saying. 'No sound, Captain Thomson. There are five of us—two more on the landing. And we don't want to wake your children. But please take my word for it that we will do whatever is necessary to get you to do as we want for the next few hours.'

McQuillan whirled round in temper as Paul said suggestively, 'I'd rather spend a few hours with her,' nudging the man next to him as he spoke. 'Shut your mouth and keep your mind on the job,' he snapped. 'Do it right and you can buy all the women you'll ever need.' He turned back to Thomson. 'Now I suggest your wife gets back into bed and that you put your uniform on.'

Jean Thomson scrambled off her husband and under the covers—her thoughts a wild mixture of terror and of embarrassment at the way her and Iain's intimacy had been interrupted.

Thomson began to recover his composure as he confronted his attackers and reached for his clothes. His years of training and experience in a tough, difficult job helped to keep him calm, his voice steady. 'What do you want?'

'We want you to take us on a little helicopter trip, Captain Thomson. And don't bother protesting that you can't: we know that sudden unexpected trips are commonplace,' said McQuillan.

'But where to?' Thomson was surprised and concerned. 'What about my wife and family?'

McQuillan's order was flat and direct. 'Out to Delta One. Your family will be all right provided you do what we want. And I'm sure I don't have to enlarge on what might happen to them if you don't co-operate—some of us will be staying with them.'

'But the weather out there has closed in,' Thomson protested. 'The entire helicopter service has been stood down. No-one can get out to the platform at the moment.'

'Then no-one will be expecting us,' said McQuillan. 'We'll make it. It's only a few miles and your radar will pick up the platform easily enough. Once we're there, there will be no problem. During the war, before radar-controlled landings, in heavy fog they lined the runways with barrels of burning tar and the flames just burned off the fog—enough for them to land, anyway. The flare-stack will do the same around the platform. You'll be able to land all right. Take my word for it.'

Thomson agreed reluctantly that the theory might work as he started to get up from the bed on McQuillan's silent order, given by raising the muzzle of his gun twice. 'I've heard of that, too—but not from anyone who's ever seen it work.' He paused as he was pulling on his trousers. 'What guarantee do I have that my wife and children will not be harmed?'

McQuillan shrugged. 'None. But they're of no real interest to us. The men we're leaving behind will be picked up in less than an hour. It's you we need. If they do as they're told they'll have nothing to fear.' He paused to add emphasis to what he said. 'Neither of you has any option. So let's get on with it.'

As Thomson finished getting dressed, McQuillan told Jean to stay in the bedroom after they had left. 'Keep quiet, and as I said nothing will happen.'

Jean was starting to panic. 'But what about the children? They often wake. What if they do?' She looked beyond McQuillan at his men.

He could see and understand her fears—that her nakedness might have aroused them. 'My men will stay with you in here—you in bed and them by the door. Believe me, they will do as they are told because I told them—which means that they do it. Just act naturally with the children if they wake, and everything will be OK.'

McQuillan saw the Thomsons look quickly at each other and waved aside their unspoken protests as he threw Jean's nightgown to her from the floor.

'Believe me, you will be in no danger. My men have a lot more than rape on their minds at the moment. It's only for an hour, but if you want to see your husband again you will wait until he contacts you. You will not ring the police. It will be unpleasant, but not dangerous, if you do as I tell you.'

McQuillan gave last-minute whispered instructions to the men who were staying behind. Meanwhile Paul the ex-Fleet Air Arm pilot was putting on an identical uniform to Thomson's which he had been carrying in a rucksack on his back. Thomson squeezed his wife's arm just before he was pushed out of the room by McQuillan. Outside he hesitated before climbing into the Range Rover. Ishmail hit him a cruel crunching blow in the kidneys. McQuillan looked at him and said, 'Up here. Beside me. Don't argue, don't put up a fight. I can assure you Ishmail can do much worse than that.' Thomson grunted in pain and pulled himself up, wincing, and stretching to ease his back. Ishmail slammed the door and ran to the back to jump aboard as McQuillan gunned the engine and set off.

The action in the helicopter park went without a hitch. As they approached, McQuillan had said in a matter-of-fact voice to Thomson, 'You'd better convince the security people we're on the level. Because we won't shoot you, we'll shoot them. Dead!' The worsening weather was the perfect excuse for the protective clothing and plastic cagouls which McQuillan and his men, except Paul, were wearing and which covered their weapons from casual inspection. The windows of the Range Rover were steamed up and difficult to see out of, let alone to see in through.

The security guard recognised Thomson and waved him through, habit and the familiar face overcoming the extra warnings about being careful they had had when they came on duty. They didn't even call over to the police Granada parked only a few hundred yards away.

They had only one misgiving. 'But there's no ground staff here, Captain Thomson. They've all gone home.'

'That's all right. The six of us can manage. The choppers are ready to go, they always are. I checked with the chief engineer. He was upset that we needed to go.' The lie worked well, the guard sharing Thomson's strained laugh.

As they got to the helicopters McQuillan showed again the value of his and Gorman's meticulous preparation. 'I know it normally takes four or five minutes for a correct warm-up. But not tonight. Watch for the word from my pilot. On his signal, fire the engine and go.' He held up his hand to stop Thomson arguing. 'I know it's dangerous. But do it. And do it right. It'll work. Maximum power instantly and then go.' Thomson shook his head in doubt and McQuillan lifted the SMG towards his face as he repeated, 'It'll work—it has to.'

At exactly one o'clock they lifted off with a thunderous surge of power—McQuillan and Thomson to a holding position on the dark bulk of Arthur's Seat, the other helicopter turning south towards the Borders.

As they soared into the air McQuillan glanced at his watch and down through the now driving rain at the other helicopters parked below and wondered where Gorman was and why he was behind schedule, and if he would see the police car as he arrived. As he looked back watching for Gorman and his men, he saw the city unroll below them. The Castle was dramatic in its floodlighting. Off to one side, the Scottish National Bank's headquarters glowed in its own illumination. Dense traffic lit up Princes Street, in marked contrast to the darkness of the park. Thomson peered out anxiously as they approached the eight hundred foot high mass of Arthur's Seat brooding over the city. Thomson had followed McQuillan's instructions to the letter, and had kept their height down to two hundred and fifty feet above the ground to ensure that they wouldn't be picked up on the Turnhouse radar system. At that height, almost any change in contour was a potential hazard and Thomson strained to follow the shape of the hill as it loomed towards them.

*

The second group, led by the other Irishman, John, roared into the deserted car park in front of New St Andrew's House. Not even the bustling traffic of a busy Festival night had upset their timetable by a minute. They crashed straight through the black-and-white metal stanchions meant to block the road, snapping off their useless locks just as Gorman had said they would. The Range Rover didn't even slow as they powered through and skidded to a halt in the rain-drenched courtyard.

The three men dismounted, swinging their SMGs. John carried a loud-hailer which he switched on as his two men took up position on either side of him. In the dimly-lit hall they could see a few security guards chatting to some cleaning ladies. At the sound of their arrival, the group swung round to peer out at them.

'Stand away from the windows and doors. Stand away now. Stand away now!' boomed John through the loud-hailer, repeating the strident instructions as Gorman had told him to. Gorman's experience with the SAS had shown him that people in panic find it almost impossible to ignore a strong, repeated instruction. The voice sounded mechanical and inhuman in its magnification.

The three men fanned out. Each had a magazine in position, with another taped to it to ensure no waste of time in reloading and several more prepared in the same way in their waistbands.

It took only two minutes for them to shatter the two hundred and forty seven windows facing on to the car park, starting from the sixth floor and working down. The enclosed area with the height of the Scottish Office on one side and the older buildings opposite acted as a sounding board for the noise and confusion. As the smoke and smell of cordite from the SMGs drifted upwards the noise of the hammering guns, bullets spewing out at a rate of over five hundred and forty rounds a minute, and the crash and shattering of falling glass was deafening, terrifying. It merged into a single reverberation of sound that blotted out every other sense.

As they started on the giant sheets of glass on the ground floor one of the security men inside foolishly began to move towards the door, trying to overcome the numbing brought on by the terrible battering of the gunfire and the crashing and breaking glass. Just as he reached for the door, the twelve-foot high window beside it burst inwards, and a huge triangular shard of glass decapitated him, like an almost horizontal guillotine.

The cacophony stopped as abruptly as it had started—except for the panic-stricken shouts of the other security guards and the screaming of the cleaning ladies. The sudden hush was broken only by the crystal tinkle of the last few falling slivers of glass.

John and his two companions raced back to the Range Rover. The fat tyres squealed and hissed in the rain as they hurtled down the underpass into the traffic, heading towards the park and Arthur's Seat.

*

At two minutes to one the Range Rover with the two men who had been shadowing Sara all day turned slowly into the drive of

Bankhead. With no lights on it was almost invisible in the driving rain and darkness. They approached from the wrong direction to see the red Ferrari parked by the side of the road just beyond the end of the drive.

After trailing Sara to Melrose they had kept an eye on Bankhead with binoculars throughout the afternoon and evening and had even followed Bob and Sara at a distance during their walk around the town. Neither had noticed them as they posed as fishermen, tourists, walkers or just passers-by, according to the circumstances.

They stopped short of the circle outside the front door so as not to announce their arrival by the scrunching of tyres on the gravel. Climbing down from the vehicle they left their doors open and crept up to the front door, checking their guns on the way. It was not locked and opened easily and silently to their touch.

They paused in the hall, surprised by the sound of two male voices raised in argument coming from the sitting-room. They had expected only Bob and Sara. They had watched the Littles drive away earlier, and in the dark and the rain they had missed the arrival of Mark, fifteen minutes before.

They shrugged and with a nod to each other burst into the sitting-room – both firing half a dozen shots into the ceiling as they went through the door. Gorman's instructions had been that the shock of the sound of shots in a confined space, added to the disorientation of falling plaster, is the best way of throwing people in a confined space off balance.

*

Gorman and his team had parked in a quiet side street and were just about to move off when, a hundred yards down the road, a dozen youths came towards them singing and shouting obscenities, as they pushed and pulled at each other in rough horseplay, ignoring the rain and splashing in the puddles in the gutter. Between the youths and Gorman's group, four middle-aged people, two couples, hurried out of a house and got into a Triumph 2500 parked in the road. Even in the bad light Gorman could see the look of distaste on their faces as they looked towards the youths.

Gorman watched the two men locking the doors from the inside as the youths ran towards them. But the driver panicked as he tried to start the engine and move away quickly. The car stalled. In a moment it was surrounded, and the gang started to bang on the roof and to rock the car to and fro on its springs, shouting and whooping as they enjoyed the older people's panic. One of them began to urinate on one of the back windows, leering at the two women inside through the spread of yellow liquid. At last the engine caught and the car inched forward, but the driver could do no more than crawl, with three of the gang right in front of him. His nerve failed him, he stalled again rather than use the bumper to brush aside the louts who were threatening him.

Gorman seethed. Here was an example of all that was worst in society as he saw it – vandals attacking and terrorising innocent people. But there was nothing he could do about it. They had to move now to make the one o'clock deadline.

He started the Range Rover and began to move along the road, hoping that the sight of his side lights would scare off the vandals.

It didn't. Just before the Range Rover drew level with the youths, the good humour evaporated, leaving a hard core of violence behind. The vandals began to beat frenziedly on the car. Two of them had taken rocks from a garden wall and were pounding them on the roof. The driver blared his horn. The two wives screamed and wept. The windscreen shattered into thousands of milky pieces as one of the rocks was thrown at it. The engine stalled again.

As Gorman watched them, he saw the prayer for help on the faces of the men and could hear the women screaming. The jeering and obscene gestures were too much for him. His upbringing, his whole being was revolted by what was happening. He couldn't ignore the pleas for help. He glanced at his watch and saw his whole timetable was in jeopardy. McQuillan would have driven on, but Gorman knew that he would have to intervene, to strike back – not for himself but for his past, for his old values. He braked. As he leapt down, his five men followed his command of 'Come on'.

The vandals stopped and turned to face him. They showed no fear, their arrogance and numbers gave them confidence. 'What's it to you, grandpa?' sneered the pimply youth who appeared to be their leader. 'You and your other old men on an old folks' outing?'

As he had leapt from the car, Gorman had picked up the heavy lead he had used for his Labrador. To his abiding sorrow, and secret shame, he had had the dog put down a few days earlier since he knew he couldn't take him with him. The lead had been left in the car, two feet of thick leather attached to another two feet of heavy choker chain.

Without a word he lashed the chain across the leading vandal's face, splitting it from jaw to the ear, exposing white bone through the blood and flesh. The youth stumbled off, screaming and holding his face. Gorman crouched to face another of the gang. As he did so, his men launched themselves on the rest. The whole scene was lit up by a street lamp beside the car – the older men crouching in a defensive position in a circle facing outwards, the rain driving down and highlighted by the car's headlamps. No command was issued by Gorman. The only sounds were the grunts, groans and curses of the gang as they were battered senseless. Three of them ran away – the others were badly beaten up by Gorman and his men. They meted out punishment they knew the louts would understand. Ribs were kicked in. Fingers were stamped to pulp. Faces were laid open. Then the vandals began slowly to drag themselves away, all dripping blood and limping. Two lay where they had fallen. Their comrades did not stay around to come to their aid.

The lethal scuffle over, Gorman moved back towards the Range Rover, calling to his men, 'We're late, it's almost one o'clock now.'

'OK, Colonel. We're coming.'

He brushed aside the thanks of the two men who, to their credit, had got out of their car and joined in the rout. Frantic with haste, he smashed through his gears and raced off, his engine revving wildly.

His time-table was a shambles. Gorman had to throw caution and his carefully prepared plans aside. He rebriefed his men as they hurtled towards Clan Oil's headquarters. 'Just get the job done. Everything must dovetail—everything must come together as a whole. With luck we'll still have the element of surprise.'

As they roared round the last corner on the approach to the entrance to the helicopter park Gorman saw a black Granada parked by the perimeter wall a short distance from the gate. In his headlights the four armed policemen inside were clearly visible as they swung their weapons up and started to open the car doors, alerted by the speed of Gorman's arrival. Watching the police, Gorman saw out of the corner of his eye two helicopters soar from nowhere into the night sky. He reacted almost without thinking, his scruples about not harming the innocent abandoned at the first threat to his plan. Instinctively he changed direction and rammed the police car from the side, shouting a warning to his men to brace themselves, just before the impact. The policemen didn't stand a chance—their car collapsed under the impact as though it was made of cardboard. The driver and passenger compartment was crushed between the wall and the Range Rover, and the roof buckled upwards like an obscene metal blister. The wreck looked like an enormous battered biscuit tin, less than three feet wide. Almost before the sound of collision had faded, blood began to seep under the shattered doors.

Gorman reversed harshly, slammed into first, and crashed straight through the high wire gates as the security guards came running out. Two of his men dropped out and took up defensive positions facing the now wide-open gate. The security guards knew better than to move against the guns of the rearguard. Not so their two Alsatian dogs—and both dogs died, killed by single shots in the head, fully twenty-five feet short of the intruders. Gorman and the remaining men used grenades with shortened fuses and raced the Range Rover down the line of parked helicopters. The first were exploding before they had reached the end of the line. The whole night was lit up as balls of fire and smoke belched upwards.

When he reached the last helicopter Gorman spun the wheel and the Range Rover lurched as he turned at speed and went back for his two men. He barely slowed, and the two were lifted on board without stopping, thrusting their arms through loops of thick rope held out for them on each side. 'Now comes the risky bit,' said Gorman, more to himself than the others. 'I'll have to slow down in a minute. Take the side roads and just trust to luck that we don't meet a patrol car. That was one risk we couldn't eliminate. But the police are going to be so stretched over the whole city, the odds should be with us.'

He swung the Range Rover into the car park, and at a signal his men raked the vehicles, which he guessed were police cars, with bullets. At least there was no chance of pursuit from that quarter.

'Right,' Gorman said calmly, heading for the main road. 'First we pick up the men at Thomson's house. Then up to Arthur's Seat.'

*

High in Clan Oil's main building Chief Superintendent Mackay had heard the unexpected sound of the two helicopters lifting off. As he turned to run from the room the telephone rang. He couldn't ignore it: only one source was able to get calls through to Mark's phone.

'Sunray here.' The voice was not the one Mackay had heard dozens of times as he had played and replayed the recordings of the earlier calls. 'We have just taken Sara Armstrong; shot up the Scottish Office; blown up your helicopters. All simultaneously. All at one o'clock exactly. All to impress you that we mean business. We will contact you again.'

Mackay slammed the receiver down as the connection was broken. 'Christ! They've got us on the run.' He shouted at some of his men in the next room. 'Go and see what's happening out there.' He turned back. 'Did you all hear?'

Jock and the major nodded.

Mackay pinched the bridge of his nose between thumb and forefinger as he concentrated. He looked up suddenly and with hope. 'Simultaneously? Bloody hell, they're behind schedule. They said they'd blown up the helicopters—they can't have, we'd have heard.'

'Come on.'

They all rushed to the lift. As they got there the night was split by a series of explosions. They turned to the windows and saw below them the shapes of the individual helicopters momentarily visible as their fuel tanks blew up. Then a single huge explosion, and flames roared, reaching a hundred feet high. The heat had ruptured a fuel tanker nearby.

Silhouetted against the flames they could see a speeding Range Rover. They saw two men swing themselves aboard the vehicle as it slowed down but didn't stop. They saw it turn into the car park below and heard the distant crack of automatic fire as the half-dozen unmarked police cars in the otherwise deserted area were raked with bullets. Impotently, they watched the big vehicle drive off into the darkness, leaving roaring mayhem in its wake.

Mackay forced himself to go back to Mark's office, realising he could do nothing to help outside. He told Jock to mobilise all police cars in the city, although he suspected the terrorists would be well away before he could organise any sensible search or set up a pursuit amongst the tens of thousands of Festival-goers who would be swelling the normal traffic to almost rush-hour proportions as the audiences from dozens of concerts, plays, reviews, poetry readings, recitals and the late session of the military tattoo would all still be milling around the centre of the city. Reluctantly he had to admire Sunray's timing.

'I blame myself, Jock,' he said a few minutes later. 'We should have had armed men all over the place, and with the helicopters, as well as at this office. What happened to the men with weapons we did have down there?'

'I don't know, sir. They must have been immobilised somehow. We're waiting for a report now. I don't think we can blame ourselves. They seem very well organised to me. They would probably just have picked off more men before they started. Then you'd feel even worse.' Jock tried to reassure him. 'One thing, though, they're human: something went wrong with their co-ordination – even if it was only by a couple of minutes.'

'Yes. Get on to the incident room at Headquarters and tell them I want hourly reports on anything unusual that is reported tonight. And ask for details about the Scottish Office – what did they mean shot up? And Mrs Armstrong: ask if there's any news about her. Where did they take her from? I thought she and her husband were completely separated. Try to raise Mark Armstrong on his mobile phone: we'll have to tell him about his wife. Sunray obviously doesn't know they are no longer together. And see if the navy or the RAF can track those two helicopters that took off. I'll have the major pestering me again saying this is proof that we need to use his group. But I'm damned if I will – this is still a job for the police. We could never have anticipated this. Three attacks at once. There is no way that the TRG could have helped to deal with that. Their strength is a single fast reaction in force against a static position. What we need is some information to work on – something to give us an edge over Sunray.'

He stopped as a uniformed inspector burst into the room. 'Four of our men dead, sir. Crushed like beetles in a matchbox.'

Mackay said nothing and turned to look out the window, not seeing the fire and the arriving fire engines below but lost in his own thoughts as he cursed Sunray and the savagery of the attack. He could imagine the confusion in the control room at police headquarters as hundreds of calls poured in about the shootings and the fires. He knew how easy it would be for the Sunray people to melt into the background of a busy Festival Friday night, and policemen all over the city caught up in trivial misdemeanours and traffic snarl-ups.

SARA

SARA HAD BEEN drowsy with sleep and pleasure when Bob had got up to answer the knock on the door but sat up in alarm when a few minutes later she heard shouting from below. She put on Bob's dressing-gown and went downstairs. She was frightened when she went into the sitting-room and saw Mark. He and Bob were standing at opposite sides of the fireplace. Bob had thrown some logs and coal onto the fire which had almost died out. Both men were tense and hardly noticed her coming into the room. Mark looked soaked through and Bob was wearing no socks or shoes. She went straight to Bob's side. The sight of her with Bob and wearing his dressing-gown started Mark shouting again.

'She can't live here with you, she's still my wife. What would people think? How will the bank react?'

'They can think what they like.' Bob could see that his and Mark's business interdependence was temporarily forgotten. Now the whole issue was stripped down to basic emotions. He tried to help the other man see things in perspective. 'Good God, man, is what people think all you care about? We're talking about flesh and blood, not possessions, not business.'

'It just doesn't seem right. You and I have got so much to do together. The whole situation is going to seem so bloody peculiar.'

'Well, I can live with that,' Bob snapped. 'What is happening between Sara and me won't affect any of the decisions I have to make at the Bank. I believe in Clan Oil just as much as you do, and I'll do my damnedest to make sure you get the funds you need.'

It was precisely at that moment that the door burst open and two identically dressed men crashed into the room. Both crouched and fired a number of shots into the ceiling from the machine-guns they were carrying. The noise and dust were appalling. Sara screamed. Bob and Mark stood dazed and staring as table lamps and ornaments were toppled to the floor by chunks of falling plaster.

'Stay still. Stay still. Stay very still,' said one of the men, emulating exactly the style of orders his colleague was giving at that very moment outside the Scottish Office.

Mark and Bob looked at each other. Neither moved. Each of them could sense the tension and they were being covered by the muzzles of the SMGs which didn't move from their midriffs as the two men watched their eyes, knowing that any signal of resistance would show there first.

'Just keep it like that,' said one of the men, 'and nothing will happen to you.' He grabbed Sara's arm. 'We're going to take Mrs Armstrong with us.'

Bob took an involuntary step forward. As he did so, the man pulled Sara closer to him and said, 'Don't be silly. If we had wanted to kill you we would have done so already. But you will give us no choice if you don't do as I say.'

'What do you want with Mrs Armstrong?' shouted Bob. 'Why her?'

'Her husband will tell you,' the man said coldly. 'Now we are going to leave. If either of you come out of the house before we reach our vehicle we'll shoot you—and we'll shoot to kill. Also, if you value Mrs Armstrong's life you won't try to follow us.'

The three of them backed out of the room, and the lock on the sitting-room door clicked behind them. Outside the house, as they passed Bob's Daimler, the one who wasn't holding Sara sent a burst of fire into the bonnet. The heavy calibre nine millimetre bullets punched gaping one-inch holes through the bodywork and crunched through the carburettor, distributor and radiator beneath. One single round ricocheted off into the dark with a curious musical whine. They ran to the Range Rover, dragging Sara with them, leapt in, and drove off. Sara was pushed into the front beside the drive. The other man sat behind, pressing the muzzle of his gun against the back of her neck.

At the sound of gunfire Mark and Bob came to life and threw themselves against the locked door. It wouldn't give, and they turned to the window to get out. They lost precious seconds opening it, and by the time they were outside the Range Rover had reached the end of the drive and was turning left. They also saw what the gunfire had done to Bob's Daimler.

'My car's outside on the road, just beyond the end of the drive,' shouted Mark. 'I think they might miss it. Come on!' With their heads down to protect themselves they ran through the pouring rain, Bob not even noticing the pain of the white gravel chips biting into his bare feet.

Mark was right. Two minutes later they were roaring after the kidnappers.

Sara slumped back in her seat as the Range Rover hurtled through the night. The rain was still lashing down but the driver took no notice. Even the narrow twisting road didn't slow him and trees and walls flashed past, sometimes only inches away.

Sara turned to the driver. 'Where are you taking me? What do you want?'

'You'll see in good time. Just shut up!'

She glanced nervously at the speedometer which was creeping up and up as they careered on to the A68 and turned towards Edinburgh at the new bridge at Leaderfoot. Far below, the swollen metallic ribbon of the river Tweed glinted in the darkness.

'But why me? What can you want with me?' Sara pleaded.

'Shut up,' snarled the man, 'and let me concentrate on driving.'

The rain was now heavier than before and torrents were running along the side of the road, sometimes meeting in the middle. The windscreen wipers could barely cope with the rain and spray as they drove through deep pools of rain-lashed water. 'The rendezvous is only a couple of miles on,' said the driver, without taking his eyes off the road. The lights of the village of Earlston were receding behind them when he did turn to say something to the man behind Sara. Just as he turned, the front wheels lost their grip, and the vehicle began aquaplaning.

The driver lost control. He braked violently. The Range Rover slewed one way, then the other, veered to the right, hit the bank, teetered for a moment on two wheels, then crashed onto its side, ploughing back across the road at right angles, straight through the inadequate crash barrier, built to take glancing impact but not full power head on, and over the edge where there was an almost sheer fall of three hundred feet to the river below.

To Sara it all seemed to happen in slow motion. As the car turned on its side she could see through the window a shower of steely blue sparks only inches from her face. She felt no sudden movement but was aware of pain in her left shoulder. For a moment the corrugated barrier filled her vision and faded slowly away on either side. And all the time there was a terrible screeching and grinding of metal ripping on tarmac and a high-powered screaming as the wheels, no longer in contact with the road, continued to turn under full power from the engine, the panic-stricken driver's foot jammed hard on the accelerator having slipped off the brake.

It was quiet as they went over the edge. With a part of her awareness Sara was conscious of the two men being thrown about like rag dolls.

The Range Rover stopped with a sickening crunch. Sara's eyes seemed backlit with flashing images—the tree they struck, the bonnet folding slowly back towards her as her face smashed into and through the windscreen, and the driver's single high-pitched scream of agony as the steering wheel crushed his chest like an egg-shell. Her last conscious sight was of his hands frozen like talons as they reached towards his chest for a fraction of a second before death came to relieve the terrible pain.

The headlights went out. It was dark—darkness that almost had a feel to it.

*

It was quiet. Deathly quiet. Sara stirred, could hear only the drumming of the rain. But she could smell something. What? Petrol. And then above the rain she could hear the growing crackle of flames. The car was on fire. She couldn't see! She couldn't move! The two men weren't moving or making any sound.

Please God, she thought, as she lost consciousness again, can't somebody help me?

*

As they drove Mark and Bob agreed that the kidnapping must be tied in with the threats to Clan Oil and that this must be part of the demonstration Sunray had said would come. 'This must be what they meant. But the police didn't think there was any risk to Sara.' He pointed to the dashboard in front of Bob. 'Use the phone. There. Just pick it up and the office will answer. Ask for David Mackay. Surely he'll still be in my office.'

In fact it took several minutes for Bob to get any response, although the instrument was activated immediately Bob released it from its cradle. The glowing indicators showed it was automatically searching for a free channel with a burr, burr—just like an ordinary telephone—coming from the loudspeaker, to show that one had been located. Eventually a girl came on and said, 'Mr Armstrong! Where are you? We've been trying to get hold of you. We've got a terrible situation here—bombs and shooting.'

'It's not Mr Armstrong. It's Mr Robertson from the Bank. Let me speak to Chief Superintendent Mackay immediately.'

As they waited Mark threw the car at each new bend with more and more disregard for safety, stretching it and himself to the limit of ability. He made mistakes in the unfamiliar car and often they powered out of rainfilled bends in a four-wheel drift—fighting to steer against losing control completely. On one long badly cambered corner he overconnected and only the steep grassy bank threw them back onto the road.

'Yes, Mr Robertson. What can I do for you?' It was Mackay's voice. Steady. Reassuring.

'I'm with Mark Armstrong,' Bob explained. 'We're chasing a Range Rover heading north on the A68. In it are two men who have kidnapped Mrs Armstrong at gunpoint.'

Mackay sounded strained as he asked, 'Where exactly are you? Can you see the Range Rover?'

'We're about two miles south of Earlston. And no, we can't see them—they're about two or three minutes ahead of us.' He glanced at the needle of the speedometer which was now touching 120 as Mark accelerated even more on a rare straight. 'At this speed, we must be catching them up.'

'Keep this line open,' Mackay insisted. 'I'll put my assistant on at this end. Meanwhile we'll alert all patrol cars in the area and let you know how soon they can be with you. If you do spot the Range Rover, do not try to stop it. Just keep it in sight but stay back. These are not the sort of people to try any heroics with. We've just had four men killed here, two helicopters stolen and all the others blown up. Don't take chances.'

A few minutes later just after they had passed through Earlston Bob's heart thundered in his chest as he saw the signs of the crash and the flickering of flames from below the level of the road, casting great shadows from the dripping trees. He wondered if almost at the moment of totally winning Sara he was going to lose her, killed in an accident with two nameless maniacs. The sense of impending loss and dread appalled him. He reached for the phone again. The car screeched to a stop. Mark leapt out and looked over the edge. He called back, 'It is them.'

Bob shouted into the phone. 'They've crashed. A mile north of Earlston. We're going to help.'

'Right, Mr Robertson,' came the reply. 'We've contacted a patrol car only a few miles north of you, just off the main road. They'll be with you in a few minutes. And take care: these men are dangerous.' Bob didn't hear the instructions as he threw himself from the warmth of the car into the rain and wind after Mark.

They plunged down the steep bank to where the Range Rover had stopped fifty feet below the road. It was difficult to stay upright—layers of wet slippery leaves gave way beneath them and the dripping bracken they snatched at broke off with their weight. Bob found it easier to get a grip with his bare feet and beat Mark to the wreck. A sawn-off tree stump had ripped the petrol tank from its mountings. Flames flickered around it. For the moment the blaze seemed confined to the spilled fuel all around but had not reached the vehicle itself, which was back on four wheels, but was swaying slightly in the wind, balanced unevenly on an outcrop of rock with a vertical drop immediately below it.

Mark seemed to hang back. 'Come on, Mark! Help me,' said Bob, reaching out for the buckled and torn passenger door. As he pulled on it, the car rocked violently and he watched in horror as it toppled sickenly on its side—turning away from him. He tested to see how firm it was, then climbed up on to it ignoring the further slip that the extra pressure brought.

'Come on!' he shouted to Mark.

'I can't. I can't. It's the fire!'

'For Christ's sake, man. We've probably only got a few minutes to get Sara out of here. Come on up. Take my hand.'

All his life Mark had had a fear of fire which Bob had noticed years ago on the visit to the production platform. No-one could explain the reason for his deep-rooted fear but it had been with him all his life. He saw Bob stretching out his hand—not the hand of friendship, but a symbol of his willingness to risk his life to save Sara. And he knew that Bob would do just as much in a different way to save Clan Oil for him. For the first time he appreciated a simple gut reaction—he deserved to lose Sara. He had put his own fear above her danger as he had always put his own preoccupations above her needs.

Bob was straining with the buckled door. 'Mark. Get up here. I can't shift this on my own. I need your help.'

Mark was jolted out of his agony of indecision by the force of Bob's plea. Ignoring his panic and racing heart, fighting down his instinct to turn and run he pulled himself up beside Bob. Together they got a grip on the twisted door and started to pull. On the third heave it came away suddenly in their hands and they almost fell off as the car swayed again. They threw the door into the darkness.

The fresh air from the open door fanned the fire and the back of the Range Rover burst into flames. By the extra light they could see inside. Sara was slumped over—from the angle in which it was lying, her left arm was obviously broken; her face was covered in blood, and lacerated with dozens of splinters of glass. Bob's white dressing gown had fallen open. Beyond her was the driver, his face a terrifying mask of death above the steering wheel embedded in his chest. The other terrorist lay limp across the back seat.

Reaching for Sara, Bob shouted, 'Darling, can you hear me? Are you all right?' But there was no response.

'I'll have to go in,' said Bob, after they had tried to pull her out but had failed to get any purchase because of the awkward angle.

Mark had to force himself to stay and help. The scene inside the car was almost more than he could bear—Sara unconscious and hurt, her tanned body exposed indecently by the gaping dressing gown, its thick creamy white towelling now soaked in blood; the dead driver; the second terrorist out cold; Bob sweating and grunting and the fire growing, casting ever-longer, ever-brighter red flickering shadows. It was his worst nightmare come true, and with the added danger that at any moment the petrol tank might blow up. Desperately he concentrated and sucked in great lungfuls of air to calm himself. Then he saw what was needed and shouted to Bob. 'Try to force her seat up. Her foot is caught.'

Bob nodded, groaning with the effort of trying to prise the seat up. It wouldn't give. As he struggled, the heat from the fire grew and grew and the smoke was beginning to make it difficult to see. At last the seat gave a little and Sara's foot came free. He pushed her up towards the open door and Mark lifted her out.

'All right, sir. Pass her down to us,' said a voice firm and steady beyond its years. Mark turned in amazement and saw two young policemen. He passed Sara down.

'What about the other two?' he shouted to Bob, resisting the impulse to jump down and away from the heat of the growing fire and flames.

'The driver's dead. The other one doesn't seem to have a mark on him but he's unconscious. I'll see if I can move him.'

Somehow Bob lifted the man towards the door and Mark and one of the policemen hauled him out. Bob's hands were badly burned, the flesh raw and angry as he scrambled out himself. The others were on the ground, and as he jumped down with relief the sudden movement as he pushed off set the Range Rover moving again, slowly at first, but then with gathering speed, crashing and banging from tree to tree.

'In a film it would have exploded,' said one of the policemen.

As they turned back to Sara and the still unconscious terrorist, the car erupted with a great whoosh in a huge single ball of flame far below them beside the river. For a brief moment the whole countryside was lit up: the trees, the twisting river, fields beyond, the grimace of the policeman who had spoken.

Mark and Bob carried Sara back up the slope while the two policemen brought the terrorist. Going up was even more difficult than their sliding progress down, and all the time they were trying to avoid dropping or jolting Sara, trying not to hurt her more.

As they reached the top another police car and an ambulance were pulling up, blue lights flashing. Bob could have wept with relief at the sight of the ambulance.

'We sent for the ambulance,' said the younger of the two policemen. 'We're only a few miles from the hospital and luckily it was on its way back there from a false alarm.'

As the ambulance men examined Sara and the terrorist, Bob and

Mark told the police what had happened. Then the police contacted their headquarters for advice. The ambulance men carefully and gently eased Sara's arm down by her side. She cried out in pain without recovering consciousness. They peered closely at her face and one said to the other, 'Lucky. It all missed her eyes. Think what it would have been like if it hadn't.'

Bob felt sick. He rested his head against the coolness and wetness of the roof of one of the police cars. He felt drained. His hands throbbed with pain. But he didn't notice them as he thought how near he had come to losing Sara.

Mark spoke to him. 'Thanks. And sorry. You deserve her. I couldn't do anything because of the fire. Thank God you were here.'

Bob realised for the first time why people don't attack each other after road accidents – the relief at being alive swallows up all inclination for action. He was so relieved that Sara was still alive he had to choke back tears.

'Forget it,' he said. 'But keep away from her from now on. She's not an issue for you any more.' As he spoke Bob saw that he had won; that Mark accepted that Sara and he were finished.

The ambulance men had completed their initial examinations. Bob was impressed by their quiet efficiency.

'The lady's arm is broken,' one of the men said. 'We don't want to touch her face – think a doctor had better do that first. The man seems only to be concussed – he's still pretty groggy though. We'd better get both of them to the cottage hospital in Galashiels as quickly as possible before the lady comes round – she's going to need some help to cope with the pain. You too, sir,' he said, turning to Bob. 'These burns are going to need some attention.'

The police sergeant who had been in the second car took over. 'Right. We've had instructions from Edinburgh. The two injured will travel in the ambulance with one officer and me and we'll handcuff the man just in case. The other two gentlemen will follow in one of the patrol cars. The other car can wait here until we get back. I've sent for reinforcements to get down to the wreck. I want to get these guns you said you saw in it,' he finished, looking at Bob.

Just as they were about to set off they all heard the distinctive clatter of an approaching helicopter. It hovered for a few moments above them – the revolving blue lights on the police cars and the ambulance showing up the whole scene clearly – then headed north. 'Is that yours too?' asked Bob. The sergeant shook his head. 'Not as far as I know, sir. Odd, don't you think?' He nodded at the terrorist. 'Something to do with our friend here perhaps?'

*

Back at Clan Oil Mackay put the phone down. He turned to Jock, unable to hide his excitement. 'We've got one of them. Now perhaps we'll see if we can't start to take the initiative.'

DELTA ONE

THE RAIN LASHED across the windscreen as Gorman turned his Range Rover off the road through Queen's Park and onto the lower slopes of Arthur's Seat, the high hill that thrusts straight up from the centre of Edinburgh. After a few hundred yards, even the Range Rover's four-wheel drive couldn't cope with the wet slippery slope so Gorman and his men abandoned it and climbed the last few hundred feet to the helicopter waiting on the flat ground just below the peak. He wondered if this part of his planning would work. He had explained to McQuillan and the others that if the helicopters kept their flying height down beneath five hundred feet they would not be picked up on radar control, either by the civilian authorities at Turnhouse Airport or by the RAF system based in Fife. But he knew he might not be up to date with the latest advances in radar technology.

The whole city was spread out below them like a huge illuminated map as all the men reported to Gorman their successes and what had gone wrong. Captain Thomson was shaken as he heard the unemotional reports of the deaths of so many people. He protested to Gorman, 'I was told my wife and family would be in no danger if I co-operated with you. But how can I believe that now, hearing what you've done to other people?'

Gorman cut him short. 'Because you have to. We need you, and we need your co-operation. Nothing will happen to your family: they are already free. In any case, you have no option but to fly for us now if you want to live.' He signalled to one of his men to take Thomson aside as he turned to McQuillan. 'It could have been worse, Douglas. I was banking on the police wanting to tackle this sort of thing on their own. Which they did. We might have run into an ambush at the offices of Clan Oil, but fortunately they had no idea of our strength or of where or what we might hit. However, they'll be a lot sharper now, and unless I'm mistaken our erstwhile colleagues will be brought in too.' He glanced at his watch, squinting at the luminous figures in the darkness. 'One twenty-five. The other chopper should be back in ten minutes. All we can do is wait for them. Set a guard just in case any idiot decides to come wandering up here on a night like this.'

After the burst of intense activity, the waiting seemed endless by contrast. Each man was alone in the dark with his doubts and misgivings. Each looked at his watch time and time again, willing the minutes to pass more quickly. All of them were nervous and keyed-up and they over-reacted to the sounds caused by colleagues shifting position or bumping against the bare rock. At last, from the south, they heard the throbbing clatter of the helicopter. It was showing no lights but they were able to pick it out as a shadow against the glow from the city's suburbs. They heard it rear up as it reached the dark mass of the park and then seconds later the enormous bulk – large enough to carry forty men – was hovering down beside them. On instruction from McQuillan, Thomson switched on the lights of his identical craft for ten seconds as a last-minute guide.

Even before the rotor blades had started to slow down, Paul leapt out of the pilot's door and shouted, as he ran towards Gorman and McQuillan, 'We didn't get her. The others crashed. The police were there as we arrived overhead. We decided it was best to abort.'

Gorman didn't waste time on a pointless post-mortem. 'Right, let's get out to the platform. Paul, you follow one minute behind us. You'll see us on your radar. But, as you know, we'll be so low over the sea that the altimeters are bound to be inaccurate, so for God's sake be careful.'

The flight to Delta One was a nightmare. As soon as they flew over the coastline the rain stopped and the fog closed in. Several times Thomson insisted that all their navigation aids, however sophisticated, were suspect and they should turn back. Each time Gorman ignored him. They flew through absolute darkness, seemingly cut off from the rest of the world. The only light, the dim glow from the instruments panel, revealed the strain on Thomson's face. His jawline was rigid as he clenched his teeth, his arms stiff almost to shaking point as he gripped the controls. He nodded as Gorman gave him last minute instructions for his touchdown. 'I'll do it if I can,' he said bitterly, 'but this is madness.'

Gorman's gamble paid off. After quarter of an hour they picked up the blip of Delta One on their radar. When they were exactly over it they switched on their landing lights and started to descend slowly, inching their way down. They could see nothing, nothing but the solid bank of fog reflecting back the beams from their lights. The tension was almost unbearable as the altimeter showed their height as zero and yet there was still nothing to see, nothing but the all-enveloping fog, dense and impenetrable. Thomson looked at Gorman and shook his head in despair. Gorman only grunted and continued to stare out. Thomson was flying as he had never had to fly before, coaxing his helicopter forward at less than walking pace, delicately controlling his massive charge.

'Christ!' Gorman's oath was involuntary. With no warning the platform legs had loomed up, filling the windows, only feet in front of them. Their theory had been right. The heat from the flare stack was burning off the fog and they had inched in under the huge overhang of the platform which towered above and below them like a ten storey building with lights blazing everywhere.

Pale with effort, sweat shining on his upper lip and running down his forehead, Thomson eased his way back from the soaring bulk of the platform, out and up over the overhang. He hovered six feet above the landing deck as Gorman and all his men, except the one left to guard Thomson, jumped down and fanned out over to their individually rehearsed targets. Behind them the second helicopter clattered to a safe landing. Since they knew the platform radar system wouldn't have picked them up, they didn't anticipate any warning of their approach.

Bruce Barr and Peter Klein were with the duty operator, Sparkie Brown, in the radio-room as Gorman and two of his men burst in. 'Don't move,' Gorman shouted. 'Don't move. And nobody will get hurt.'

Bruce Barr stepped forward to protest and Sparkie Brown reached forward impulsively to his console. Without any communication Gorman and his two men reacted simultaneously. One slammed Bruce Barr back against the wall, the other reached Peter Klein as he started to rise out of his chair and smashed him back down into it with the steel butt of his SMG. Gorman reached Brown, the radio operator, in two strides, pulling a dagger from his belt as he moved. The dagger flashed in the bright fluorescent lighting as he drove it downwards, pinning the radioman's hand to the table. Brown screamed and fainted.

'Perhaps from now on you'll believe me when I say something,' Gorman snarled as he turned to face the other two.

In the dining-room almost twenty men stared in disbelief as McQuillan and three men fired long bursts into the ceiling. 'Stay where you are! Stay where you are! Don't move until we tell you to,' shouted McQuillan, as the firing stopped and the echoing noise died down. Nobody moved.

In the small cinema the same technique worked with the other men who were enjoying a few hours off duty. The sudden lights, the firing and noise, again reduced any idea of resistance. Only one big red-headed roustabout moved, lunging towards Ishmail. When he was still two feet away, Ishmail lifted his SMG and slashed the muzzle across the man's face, smashing his nose and all his front teeth. The man collapsed on the floor holding his face.

All over the platform it was the same. The surprise and viciousness of the attack crushed any thought of challenge. Deck by deck Gorman's men did what they had trained for months to do: they took complete control of Delta One within three minutes of landing on it.

In the radio-room Gorman was telling Bruce Barr what to do next as Barr tried to comfort Brown who had regained consciousness as Gorman was pulling the dagger from his hand. 'Just do as I tell you without arguing,' said Gorman, handing Barr the microphone of the public address system and turning the volume to maximum.

Barr took the instrument, exchanging doubtful glances with his toolpusher as he switched it on. 'Hear this. Hear this. This is Bruce Barr. Close down all operations immediately and assemble in the dining-room now. The platform is in control of a number of armed men. Do as they tell you without question. We don't want any accidents. Don't provoke them.'

Barr's voice boomed at full volume throughout the platform, interrupting everything and everyone on the entire structure. Even men sunk in deep sleep after twelve hours of exhausting duty were wakened by it with a start.

Gorman took the microphone from Barr. His hard voice was emphasised by the harshness of the magnification. 'Let me repeat: do as you are told. Heroics won't help anyone. They'll simply mean you'll be shot. Assemble by the lift on each deck and my men will allow you to come up to the dining-room. Don't underestimate our strength. Each of my men is being covered by a colleague. Move only as they tell you.'

Ten minutes later they had a hundred men jammed into the dining-room under constant guard from watchful suspicious eyes. All over the platform explosives were being placed in high risk areas—on the blow-out preventor, on the fuel tanks, and on the bottom of the flare stack. Within a matter of minutes, Delta One had become a time-bomb—with a hundred prisoners on board.

Back in the radio-room Gorman and McQuillan grinned at each other as they watched Bruce Barr start to raise his headquarters.

*

At Peel Hospital Bob had insisted on being allowed in to see Sara as soon as his own hands had been cleaned and bandaged. A kindly porter had lent him a pair of slippers.

Sara was conscious. A young doctor had already picked out all the bits of glass from her face and she smiled ruefully at Bob as he came into the room, pointing with her free hand to the stitches and bruises that were showing through the bright yellow ointment that had been applied. The doctor let the nurse carry on finishing the plaster they were fitting to Sara's broken arm and turned to Bob. 'I believe you want to take Mrs Armstrong home when we're finished?' He looked a bit dubious as Bob nodded and smiled at Sara. 'At first I was worried that she might suffer some delayed shock. But I now think that won't happen. She was very clear when she was giving her statement to the police. If you promise to make sure she takes things easy, then she can go.'

'That's a promise,' agreed Bob. 'I've already given my story to the constable so we can leave just as soon as you say we can go.

'We'll be a few more minutes,' said the doctor. 'You can wait outside now while we finish off.'

In the foyer Bob and Mark were alone for the first time since the accident.

'How is she?' Mark's voice was dull and his face drawn.

'She's all right now. The doctor's just finishing off a plaster on her arm – it's broken just below the shoulder. Her face looks a mess but he assures me it looks a lot worse than it really is. The cuts are all superficial and there will be no scarring.' He reached out and put his hand on Mark's shoulder. 'She's coming home with me for good.'

Mark just nodded and turned away. 'I'm sorry,' said Bob, 'but, scandal or no scandal, that's the way it is.'

The awkward silence was broken by one of the policemen coming in from outside. 'We're ready to leave now, Mr Armstrong.'

Mark turned to Bob. 'I've been speaking to David Mackay on the telephone. I'm going back up to the office. There's been some sort of attack on them there as you know and Mackay thinks I should return right away. The police are going to take me and bring my car up later.' He paused and as he turned to leave he added, 'He thinks Sara should have a permanent guard until all this is over. I told him that she would be with you.'

'I know. The sergeant just told me too,' said Bob. 'And I'll get in touch with you later today when James Tennent and I have anything to tell you on the loan. Will you be in your office?' Mark said yes. 'Then I'll ring you there.'

The policeman wanted to say goodbye. 'I haven't said this to many men, sir, but it's been an honour to meet you. It took a lot of guts to go into that car.'

Bob shrugged off the compliment. 'I didn't stop to think – I just had to get them out. And I couldn't have done it without Mr Armstrong. By the way, where's the man who survived?'

'He's gone up to Edinburgh already. They wanted him as soon as possible when they heard he was OK. But I don't think they'll get much out of him. He wouldn't even give us his name, told us to sod off. Which is what I'd better do. All the best, sir. Hope the lady's OK.'

In the back of the police car on the way to Bankhead Sara was drowsy with reaction and from the effects of the painkillers the doctor had given her just before they left. Bob held her good hand and squeezed it occasionally when she looked at him..

It was almost light when they got back to Melrose. The front door of the house was still open and the lights were still blazing through the shattered sitting-room window just as he and Mark had left them, what seemed like a lifetime ago. Bob carried Sara up to the bed they had left only a few hours before.

As he settled her into bed he said, 'I'm just going downstairs to say goodnight and thank you to the police.' He could see that Sara was already drifting towards sleep as the doctor had said she would when the powerful painkillers took effect and she relaxed. 'Also, I've got to leave a message for Mary to contact the local doctor as soon as she gets back and arrange for him to come in tomorrow morning—I mean this morning.' Sara managed a half smile. 'She'll have to ring my secretary,' he went on, 'and tell her I won't be in until lunchtime at the earliest.'

Bob locked up the house and left his note for Mary. When he got back to the bedroom Sara was already fast asleep. Ignoring the pain in his hands he set up a make-shift bed beside her on the floor. Just before he got into it he glanced out of the window and saw the two armed policemen meet on their patrol of the house. He'd asked them to explain things to Mary when she arrived and to tell her to let Sara and him sleep in. As he drifted off to sleep he was aware of a warm glow. Beside him was Sara and he had a satisfactory feeling that he'd earned her.

*

Mackay was almost beside himself with rage, but his icy control made his temper even more forbidding. 'For Christ's sake, Inspector,' he hissed at Jock. 'I know we've had all hell here for the last hour but two bloody great helicopters can't just have disappeared into thin air. The air traffic control people must have picked them up.'

Jock who had just seen Mackay climb down and admit to the major that he had perhaps misjudged the situation, made allowances for the strain his boss was obviously suffering. 'They say that no helicopters have been operative in the Edinburgh airspace during the last hour. Or if they have, they are operating under their radar umbrella and that means less than five hundred feet above the ground they're flying over. That's probably the answer.' Jock broke off as he saw Mackay and the major nod to each other. 'It's not for me to say, sir,' he went on, 'but I think we were right to try and contain our response to our own people and not bring in the major and his push right at the beginning. We never could have anticipated such a massive action by Sunray—there was nothing to suggest they had anything like the resources they have.'

Mackay grimaced his thanks and said, 'Thanks, Jock. It's good of you to support me, but I was wrong. I don't know exactly what we could have done but the major's right. I underestimated and misjudged what our response should be and that was what I was supposed to get right. That's what I'm paid for.'

The major was about to say something but he stopped as the telephone on Mark's desk began to ring. Mackay picked it up and they all heard the operator say, 'I'm patching this call in from Delta One through our radio control.'

The voice on the end of the line was strained and obviously the speaker was under pressure. 'Mark. This is Bruce Barr. The platform has been taken over by an armed group. We had no chance. We weren't expecting any flights because of the fog and with the constant noise on the platform we didn't hear two choppers coming in.'

The voice stopped. There was nothing but background hiss for several seconds. Then a different but familiar voice: 'This is Sunray. Do you hear me, Mr Armstrong? This is Sunray.'

'Mr Armstrong is not here. This is Chief Superintendent Mackay. I know the whole picture; you can talk to me.'

The voice took on a slightly supercilious edge. 'I was wondering when the police would make contact. Well, Chief Superintendent, we have a hundred hostages here and the platform is wired to blow up at a moment's notice. Do not attempt to storm it.'

'We can't,' said Mackay. 'The weather's too bad.'

'Don't interrupt. We managed it. So could you. I presume that you have your recording equipment there so I will not repeat my instructions.

'We will pick up the diamonds at twenty-one hundred hours tomorrow evening. They are to be in one hundred separate pouches each containing half a million pounds' worth of stones, but gathered in one bundle and placed exactly in the centre of Murrayfield rugby ground. We will make the pick-up by helicopter and will be able to see the entire area of Murrayfield, the pitches and car parks around it. We will have twenty hostages with us and unless we are convinced the area is clear we will drop hostages from the helicopter at the rate of one every five minutes from a height of a thousand feet. These hostages, and the remainder left on the platform with the other half of our group, will be released when we have checked the diamonds and are sure that we ourselves are in no danger.

'Is that all clear, Chief Superintendent? Did you get it all?'

'Yes.' Mackay's confirmation was steady. 'We got it all.'

'Good. We will have final instructions for you at twenty hundred hours. That is all.'

Mackay wanted to keep the contact and try to rattle his opponent. He knew from his training and the experience of other police forces that by keeping Sunray talking he would have a better chance of understanding him and of getting to know him, and that if he got him to talk for long enough he would start to make mistakes and perhaps give away gaps in his preparation. 'Your plan to kidnap Mrs Armstrong failed,' he said.

The voice altered not at all. 'We know. Our second helicopter reported the crash.' Then even Gorman's training cracked for a moment as he was drawn momentarily into communicating with Mackay. 'What happened to our two men?'

'They're both dead,' lied Mackay, knowing the advantage of having a captive source of information that Sunray believed was dead.

'Perhaps, Chief Superintendent.' Gorman was confident his men would never talk even if they had been taken alive. 'But perhaps not. I made the mistake there of asking you a question. I won't do that again. We will contact you tomorrow.'

For ten minutes Mackay tried without success to raise Sunray again on Delta One. Then he gave up, and with the major went back to join Jock and his men sifting through all the police reports that were pouring in, covering every reported incident in the city during the last few hours.

Just after three o'clock Mackay got a message from the policeman who was now on duty at the front door of the building that the prisoner was being brought up.

When the man was brought in Mackay and the major stared at him in silence for several minutes trying to unnerve him. The man was obviously tough and had completely recovered from his temporary concussion. He stood erect and alert. He was fit and looked like a soldier in his matching shirt, trousers and boots, the dried blood from Sara and his colleague adding to the impression. They'd had a radio message earlier that he was refusing to talk and so far they didn't even know his name.

For an hour Mackay and Jock harangued and harried him, keeping him standing as they circled and prowled round him. But they couldn't break his resolve—he simply refused to reveal anything, not even his name.

Finally, Mackay gave up. 'Take him next door, Jock. Put some of the others to work on him. Keep him up all night if necessary. Nothing to eat. Nothing to drink. No visiting the loo. Just keep at him. And keep him standing up.'

The major wanted to be tougher. 'Let me have him for ten minutes. He'll be glad to talk then. I'll take the responsibility.'

Mackay looked at him for several seconds. 'I can't sanction that. You're suggesting that we go down to their level – an eye for an eye. I can't agree to that. Several hours of pressure will make him break.'

'But we need every bit of information we can get now,' the major insisted. 'This is no time to be soft. There's only one thing a man like that will bow to, and that's someone who's tougher than he is. That's the only thing he respects.'

Mackay was equally adamant. 'No. We do it my way. Maybe you can try yours if I make no progress with mine.'

An hour later they got the break they were looking for. The two elderly couples in the Triumph car had reported the attack on themselves and the routing of the vandals by the identically dressed men in the Range Rover. As soon as he saw the report, Mackay sent patrol cars to bring the two couples in to see him. He started by apologising when they arrived, for inconveniencing them when they were obviously tired and upset and had already given a full report of what had happened. Then he took them over what had happened again and again, trying to get something to work on. He was patient and considerate, each time drawing out a little more detail of the incident and of the men who had taken part in it. The driver of the attacked car gave him what he was looking for, as he told his story for the fourth time, and a fragment of detail surfaced in his memory.

'Oh, and somebody called the one in charge with the old-school tie, "Colonel". He had a pistol in a shoulder holster – I'm sure I saw it when his anorak swung open.'

Mackay held his breath as he asked without emphasis. 'What school was it?'

'Eton!' said the man, surprised at himself. 'I'd forgotten until now. But I've always liked it as a tie, the dark background with the pale blue stripes. Silly of me. I recognised it at the time even under the artificial lights and it just slipped my mind until now. Didn't seem important.'

As the man finished giving his description of Gorman, Mackay turned to Jock and the major, unable to conceal his excitement. 'Colonel! Sunray! One is usually the other in the army. Now Eton! Put all three together . . . we'll find him now, find out who the bastard is.'

*

Just about the time Mackay and Jock and the major were congratulating themselves on their breakthrough, relief cancelling out their fatigue as they started to put their new knowledge to work, one of Sunray's back-up teams was driving into Edinburgh. The Range Rover was inconspicuous in the heavy traffic of the morning rush-hour. Ahmed, who was driving, went straight to the West End, to the first objective in his deadly mission to protect Sunray from counter-attack.

BLAIR

THOUGH THE HEAVY rain of the night before had stopped, Edinburgh was damp and waterlogged under a weak sun as Pallin, Blair and Donald got off the sleeper together at Waverley Station, all of them tired after having been woken several times in the night. They were irritable and felt dirty since they had had no overnight things with them.

'Why don't we have a decent breakfast in the North British?' suggested Pallin.

The others agreed and they took the lift which goes direct from the station up to the hotel. Unfortunately, whoever thought of this excellent idea fell down on detail and, like almost everyone else who uses that lift, they got lost in the rabbit warren of corridors below the hotel's main reception area until they were rescued by a member of the staff. They had an excellent breakfast in the dining-room sitting at a window table with a diagonal view down Princes Street, the Scott Monument in the foreground and the Castle dominating the skyline. At any other time it was a view to be enjoyed; this morning it was merely a backdrop in the clearing weather.

As they ate they studied the Scottish morning papers. The Clan Oil story was covered by them all—in every case on the front page—but none had details of the terrorists' attacks on the Scottish Office and Clan Oil because they had taken place too late to be included. Almost all the stories had included photographs of Mark Armstrong and they all had a decided bias towards his version of events. The government came in for a lot of stick for being so insensitive as to consider such action at this time.

'My God,' said Pallin, patting the pile of discarded papers beside him. 'We're coming out of this even worse than I expected. This is very serious. A lot of the blame is going to be directed at me personally. What can we do?' He looked almost accusingly at Blair. 'It's up to you two to think of something. I need to be advised.'

Blair carefully folded the papers he had been reading. 'The best thing will be to attack with our new instructions from the Prime Minister. It's obvious that the press release we put out last night came too late. I also think, Minister, that you should leave today's meetings and actions to me. You keep back from the firing-line for the moment. Carry out the programme that you had already planned and announced for the day. Archie Donald should perhaps spend the day briefing the editors and senior correspondents and if all goes well we'll be in a better position by five o'clock, and able to put out a stronger line this evening. Nothing can be done until then in any case; all the evening papers will already have their stories written and the television and radio programmes will carry the present line on their news broadcasts until such time as we change our stance.'

The others agreed. But Pallin was still nervous. He could see in his mind's eye another scathing attack in the popular papers. 'Are you sure you are absolutely clear on the action we should take? The PM wasn't very precise about that last night. He seemed to be leaving a lot to us. Are you sure you'll get it right?'

'I think that he was being deliberately vague, leaving his options open so that he won't be too closely linked with what we're doing until we get it right.' Blair was firm. He wanted to do what he had to on his own and didn't want anyone else interfering. 'I'm sure in my own mind what we have to do. If you'll trust me, I'll report back to you during the day. Archie Donald will do the same as regards the media. Between us we'll get it right.'

As they were leaving the hotel Blair said, 'I think a shave and face massage would make me feel a lot better, freshen me up for the rest of the day. I fear it's going to be a long one again. I'll leave you here if you don't mind.'

It took Blair only a few minutes to walk from his hairdressers to New St Andrew's House, the main centre of the Scottish Office which has many other offices throughout Scotland. He walked with renewed vigour and a spring in his step, a shave followed by ten minutes of alternately hot and cold towels having refreshed him for the action ahead. He felt a hundred percent better and ready to take on anything the day threw at him.

He was appalled and concerned when he saw what had been done to the front of New St Andrew's House. Every window on every floor was a gaping sore. A gang of workmen was clearing up the broken glass and dozens of civil servants of all ranks were frantically gathering up thousands of bits of paper and files that had blown out of the empty windows during the night and were scattered, soaked and forlorn, all over the car park. Blair bent down and picked up some stapled sheets that were headed "Strictly Secret. Minister's Eyes Only". The papers were snatched from his hand by a uniformed security man who recognised him too late. The man hastily transferred the papers to his left hand as he saluted. 'Sorry, sir,' he said. 'Didn't recognise you. We've had a terrible night.' As he regained his composure he went on, 'I'm surprised you got in, sir. We told the police that no-one was to get in.'

Blair smiled weakly. 'They seemed to be busy with all the other people gathered round but ignored me as I walked past.' He indicated his suit, and his briefcase with its official crest in gold. 'Perhaps I look official and like a public servant.' He pointed to the building. 'Tell me. What on earth has been happening here?'

In his own office which fortunately was sited at the back of the building it only took Blair about a quarter of an hour to line up a whole series of people he would want to see during the coming day. The one person he couldn't reach was Bob Robertson who wasn't at the Bank. His secretary had been discreet, but, pressed, she admitted that Mr Robertson had been delayed in the Borders and didn't know when he would get back to Edinburgh. Blair made her promise to ensure that he rang as soon as he arrived back at the Bank's headquarters.

'It is vital that I speak to him as soon as possible – a great deal may depend on it.'

His first meeting was with as many of his fellow Secretaries at the Scottish Office as could come to his promised briefing. In spite of the chaos most managed to turn up. They could sense a major development.

As they crowded into his office there was a good deal of in-joke ribbing for Blair and the predicament he and his Minister found themselves in – given and taken in the best humour.

'Someone seems to have a spite against you and your target Hamish!' said one with whom he had a friendly rivalry. 'Or at least it seems like that on the front side of the office.'

'I see, Hamish, that you are reported this morning as being the senior man at the Scottish Office. Congratulations on your promotion.'

'I was not aware, Hamish, that your remit covers the taking-over of private commercial concerns.'

'Hamish, it is good of you to spare us all a few minutes of your valuable time away from the affairs of state.'

'Is it true, Hamish, that you are steam-rolling plans through in spite of massive opposition from all of us?'

'Hamish, your cat appears to be well and truly out of the bag and with several lives to go!'

'I didn't know, Hamish, that yours was the hand behind so many of this office's successful operations in the last few years.'

Blair grinned around at these men he trusted and admired. Although he didn't necessarily like all of them, he knew that they put service to Scotland above all else.

'All right, all right. You've had your fun. We all know that no matter how carefully we brief the press they seem to get the facts wrong.' He smiled round the room. 'Although in this case I must admit they are a little too close to the truth for comfort.'

'Hamish, your Minister looks a little exposed and without friends this morning. Have you been looking after him properly?' asked an up-and-coming young assistant who had just completed a two-year assignment in the Cabinet Office.

'Your concern is touching.' Blair's sarcasm was not entirely feigned. 'Presumably it is tinged with relief that it was my department, and not your own, that has been looking after this! However, to be serious, I wonder if I might now bring you all up to date.

'As you have seen from this morning's papers the proposed nationalisation of Clan Oil, against which my department spoke out from the beginning, has produced the most unfortunate reaction, as we all forecast. The entire role of the Scottish Office has been called into doubt. My Minister and I were instructed late last night by the Prime Minister and the Chancellor to take all sensible steps to retrieve the situation.'

Blair looked around him. He could see everyone was turning over the many alternatives as they waited for him to continue.

'Our main concern is to dismiss from everyone's thoughts as soon as possible the idea that the nationalisation of Clan Oil has ever been a serious proposition, without suggesting that our masters have been turned from their plan by the weight of opposition and opinion in Scotland. I should say in passing that the Chancellor and the Treasury were acting to a large extent on their own initiative.' He felt no regret at this mild deception, knowing that it was likely that a leak indicating the Prime Minister's prior approval would reach the media. His colleagues would undoubtedly gossip and one of them might even deliberately release the story to a reporter friend or contact. 'At least we have the pleasure of knowing they were wrong yet again, although of course we'll never get them to admit that.

'I am proposing the following action. I will inform the Scottish National Bank who are bankers to Clan Oil, in confidence, that there is no possibility of our pursuing the idea of the take-over. Incidentally, for the moment I am unable to meet with Mr

Robertson of the Bank because of some personal problem of his which is delaying him out of town. Simultaneously, I hope to persuade the Scottish Development Agency to invest in a minority stake in the development of the Scotia Field. As you know, this should perhaps be done more properly by the British National Oil Corporation but I feel very strongly that any government action at this stage should have a strong Scottish base—for the look of things. And the Prime Minister agreed that this would be right at this time. However, this situation is subject to change in due course.

'If, or rather when, I have done this, I hope the SDA commitment will help to persuade the Scottish National Bank to back the raising of the rest of the finance for the Scotia Field. You will have seen that they have already indicated some willingness to try to do this although so much money is required that they will need all the help they can get. Then, and only then, will I call a press conference, and on behalf of my Minister, will explain how the true nature of our interest in Clan Oil was to put together a powerful financial package to ensure the speedy development of the Scotia Field. Press speculation regarding my department over the last few days has been wholly unjustified.'

Blair leant back in his chair.

'Well, do you approve? Can you suggest any other course?'

'Is anyone going to believe this?' The recent Cabinet Office experience showed in the assistant's question.

'Will you get away with it? Best of luck to you anyway,' said a man who was usually more of a rival.

'Will the SDA co-operate? After all, they cherish their independence. What's in it for them? Why should they help us?' The Permanent Under Secretary of State had joined them.

'What about these terrorist attacks?' asked Blair's own assistant.

'I think they are something separate,' replied Blair. 'Presumably the police will sort it all out in time. It's a short-term problem and it shouldn't affect the overall picture once it is contained.'

There were lots of questions and details to be covered, but Blair was finally able to convince his colleagues that he had the authority to do what he was planning. 'I have the full authority of the Prime Minister's office. For once in my life I can take any action I believe will help in what I'm trying to achieve.' His satisfaction was patent, and there wasn't a man in the room who didn't envy him.

The meeting broke up on his promise to keep them informed during the day as the situation developed. Blair rubbed his hands. Things were going well. He asked his secretary to place a telephone call to the SDA.

Twenty minutes later Blair was on his way to Glasgow by train to the meeting he had set up with the commercial director of the

Scottish Development Agency. In view of his mission he had felt it better that he went to him rather than the other way round, knowing this would give the other man a psychological advantage —he would feel safer on his home ground.

Forty five minutes later he was instructing a Glasgow taxi driver at Queen Street station. 'The Scottish Development Agency, Bothwell Street.'

The SDA had been set up by a previous government as a vehicle for the regeneration of the Scottish economy. Blair was hoping that his scheme would be attractive to the Agency since it would certainly generate jobs and get a lot of publicity.

But the meeting started badly. The commercial director quickly worked out the true state of things and was disinclined to help, and said so. 'You are asking too much, Blair. why should we pull your chestnuts for you? We've got plenty of problems of our own at the moment. Plenty of projects with more justifiable priority than what you're asking.'

They argued back and forth. Blair could see his adversary's objection wearing thin—but not his resolve. Finally, his defence was money. And he fell back on this.

'We are too far into this year's programme. And as you know our budgetary restraints don't allow us to overspend. We just simply can't afford to help at this time in spite of the revenue that might be generated in the future. We don't have available funds on the scale you are looking for.'

Blair relaxed, certain he could now carry the argument. 'Ah, well, perhaps we can help there. I am confident that a request for supplementary funding would get a sympathetic hearing for this particular project, even although at the moment we can't say exactly how much would be involved. I feel sure that we will be able to vote you the money—if only you will take on publicly the responsibility for what we are suggesting.'

Eventually agreement was reached. The commercial director could see that the arrangement would be a good one from the Agency's point of view. He confessed that his opposition was not real, but just a reaction to interference from outside, and a lack of money.

'We are anxious to preserve our autonomy. And it is galling to find that you can vote us such large extra funds part-way through the year when it happens to suit your and your masters' own ends.' Blair apologised for the inconsistency and pleaded direction from the highest level.

The commercial director suggested an immediate meeting with the Agency's chief executive and the rest of the directors and Blair was able to start back towards Queen Street station an hour later with agreement in principle to his plan.

He decided to walk to the station. He was in no hurry now and would be back in Edinburgh in time for a late lunch. As he strolled along he pondered to himself. Well, that's one part done. Now for Bob Robertson, wherever he is. I hope he can pull off the next part with his Bank. That it won't be too much for them.

BOB

As Hamish Blair's meeting broke up in Edinburgh, in Melrose Mary Little was knocking on the door. At Bob's reply, she came bustling into the bedroom. Drawing back the curtains, she said, 'It's eleven o'clock. Here's breakfast for you both. How are you feeling, Mrs Armstrong? Better, I hope. The two policemen on duty downstairs were asking after you as well.' As she turned and saw Sara's face she said accusingly to Bob. 'I got your note, but didn't think it would be anything like as bad as this.' She busied herself around them for a few minutes then left, leaving behind a tray heaped with orange juice, bacon and egg, toast, butter, marmalade and coffee for two.

The sun streamed through the open curtains. The contrast from the appalling conditions of the night before was startling, as good weather from the south pushed north and they could feel the warmth of the sun even through the glass of the window.

'Well, well,' said Bob, getting up from his bed on the floor and smiling at Sara. 'She never brought me breakfast in bed in my life. It's you she's spoiling.' He reached over and touched her face gently, turning her head to the light. 'How are you feeling? Did you sleep? Is your arm sore? You've got the two blackest black eyes I've ever seen, all purple and yellow. Very becoming, I must say.' Sara winced as she sat up. He helped her sort her pillows, thinking to himself that she looked a lot better than he had expected she would. Her face was swollen but the angry red colour of the cuts had died down during her sleep.

Sara stretched up her good arm towards him, and he leant down and hugged and kissed her gently. 'I'm fine,' she said. 'I woke up once or twice, but there's no pain – just a numbness. How are you?' She looked concerned. 'Shouldn't you be at work? I know how important today is going to be for you with Mark and Clan Oil.'

'I'm OK,' Bob insisted. 'Work can wait for the moment. I'm a little tired but otherwise fine. Let's eat. I hope you're hungry, otherwise Mary's going to be offended. She will never forgive us if we leave a scrap: she's old-fashioned about food and doesn't like to see any wasted.'

'I could eat a horse. But you're going to have to help me. I won't be able to use a knife with this,' she said, indicating her broken arm.

'And these will make it difficult for me,' replied Bob, holding up his two bandaged hands. Laughing together at Bob's difficulty with the knives and forks, they ate and talked, Bob preparing things for her like a child.

Afterwards he rang the local doctor and told him what had happened. The doctor said he would finish his surgery shortly and come and see Sara in about thirty minutes.

When he arrived, Bob started fussing, agitatedly giving advice, telling him what had happened and what to do.

'Look, Bob, I've already rung the hospital and got a report on Mrs Armstrong's accident and the X-rays. Why don't you get dressed and leave us alone for a while? We'll get on a lot better without you.'

Feeling like a schoolboy who has been put in his place, Bob did just that. He walked up to the newsagents in the Square to get all the morning papers and a packet of cigarettes for one of the policemen who had run out of his own. Clan Oil's financial situation was covered in depth by all the papers. On the way back to Bankhead he met the doctor, who stopped his car to have words with him.

'She's fine. Some pain, mainly numbness but that's only to be expected. No after-effects of shock.' He got out of the car. 'What she needs most is rest. I've given her something to make her sleep and told Mary exactly what to do when she wakes up. Let her sleep – she'll probably drift in and out of sleep for most of the day.' He patted Bob reassuringly on the shoulder. 'I'll look in again after evening surgery, just after seven. The main thing is that she is to rest and lie quiet. You go off to work. But first of all let me have a look at your hands.' Sitting comfortably in the warm sunshine on the bank of the river, he changed the dressings on Bob's burns and replaced them with smaller more manageable ones, but warned him that he shouldn't drive his car.

Bob thanked him, and realising that there was nothing more he could do for Sara for the time being, decided he would go up to Edinburgh. He rang his secretary to arrange for a car. Before he left he had a last word with Mary Little, telling her to ring him if he was needed, saying that his secretary would know where he was throughout the day.

*

Hamish Blair was obviously relieved to see Bob and greeted him warmly as he was shown into his office just after lunch. 'Hello, Bob. Take a seat. What's happened to your hands? You'll have heard the news about the attack here and have seen the damage on the way in. My assistant has been trying to set up a meeting with you since this morning. Things have ben moving along.'

Bob told him briefly what had happened during the night. Blair was concerned and insisted on knowing if Sara was truly all right.

'Yes, she is. Or at least she will be. All she needs now is rest. Incidentally, did you know about us? I mean, had you heard anything?'

'Yes, I did. But since it is none of my business, I was waiting for you to mention it. You didn't. So I didn't.'

'Thanks.' Bob nodded. 'The police are keeping a constant guard on her now—there are two armed policemen on duty at Bankhead and they'll be there until this whole terrorist business is cleared up.'

In turn Blair gave a resumé of his actions including his success with the SDA, and finished off by asking, 'Well, what do you think? How are we shaping up? Can we pull it off?' His enthusiasm and concern showed us as he dropped his normally courteous manner. 'Will it all work?'

'Well, it's better than it was yesterday,' said Bob, 'a lot better. None of us except Mark Armstrong is getting a very good press although I get the feeling that all the papers now expect the Bank to help.'

Blair nodded. 'I agree. But your letting the cat out of the bag regarding the plans for nationalising Clan Oil worked. All our energies are now directed to helping Armstrong. Can I assume that this is also the Bank's intention?' He leant forward to give emphasis to his question. 'You will be able to provide all the money they are going to need?'

'Yes and no. That has always been my aim. But there are limits to the help we can give. As you know, financing on the scale now needed by Clan Oil is beyond our own resources. And even if it wasn't, it is the policy of all Scottish banks to be sparing with their venture capital.' Bob paused and sounded apologetic. 'Now before you protest, I know that Clan Oil is a special case, but I still have to convince my Board of this.' As he spoke, Bob wondered if he could rely on his directors' backing for such an enormous commitment. 'I'm hopeful that I can, but it's by no means certain, and even so, we would still have to go to the market for the rest of the money needed—even with the help you hope to arrange from the SDA, although I must admit that that will be an important psychological boost. Just at the right time. Can you announce it today?' Blair nodded.

'By the way,' Bob changed the subject, 'haven't you over-stepped your normal brief with what you've been doing this morning?'

'Yes, but for a long time I've felt that we senior civil servants should actually exercise the immense power everybody says we have. Normally, of course, we avoid the issue by hiding behind our Ministers – I'm glad to say this was neither practicable nor possible in this case. I have had to act on my own initiative.' Blair sounded pleased. 'And I've enjoyed the freedom the Prime Minister gave me.'

Bob was about to speak when there was a knock on the door. Blair's assistant came in and handed him a note without comment and left.

'Ah, action!' said Blair, feigning surprise. 'There are no fewer than three questions down for answer by the Prime Minister today on the subject of nationalising Clan Oil. I think we can take it he will emphatically declare that this was never his government's intention. Looks like Clan Oil have got quite a few allies. Your friendly Liberal seems to be earning his keep.'

'Good,' said Bob, reading the note when Blair passed it to him. 'I knew he would.'

They rounded off their meeting by briefing each other on their next moves. Bob was driven the short distance to his office and when he got there found that James Tennent had arranged a meeting with Mark Armstrong for four o'clock, and that there was to be a specifically called meeting of the Bank's Board of Governors at five. There were only three items on the agenda –

1 Minutes of previous meeting
2 Future funding for Clan Oil
3 Mr James Tennent's successor

A note on the agenda said that executive directors would withdraw after item two.

GORMAN

ALL DAY LONG Mackay's men in Mark's office made slow painstaking progress, while down below two dozen uniformed officers kept refusing to allow into the building any reporters who were following up the attack of the night before.

Jock, who was a fastidious man and a non-smoker, moved from

room to room wrinkling his nose in disgust at the overflowing ashtrays, empty coffee cups, partly eaten sandwiches. At first he said nothing – neither about the mess nor the rumpled sweat-stained shirts his men, who had had no time to change, were wearing. He did, however, ring his wife to ask her to bring in his electric razor and some clean shirts. From mid-morning he couldn't stand the mess and guddle any more and insisted that everyone break for ten minutes every two hours to clear up, sort the growing piles of paper and reports, and to freshen up by washing and by taking a couple of minutes of fresh air outside, on the roof of the building.

Mackay called in the help of the Army Records Office. Detectives were sent to interview the existing headmaster of Eton in his Cornish holiday cottage, and to contact four surviving predecessors throughout Britain. A whole team of detectives examined the only six copies of the Old Etonian Association List that could be found in Edinburgh (and these were broken up so that more people could work with them) after the major had said quietly, 'If my memory serves me right, we have an officer in the Regiment who was at Eton and he once told me that only Old Etonians who join the Association are allowed to wear the tie.' He had telephoned the SAS headquarters at Hereford and checked with the officer, who had told him he was right but that virtually everybody joined the Association when they left the school.

Unfortunately the list was alphabetical and not chronological, so the detectives started from different points in the book – front, back, middle – looking for men with military careers and high rank who had left the school between the years 1938 and 1953, their ages now between forty-five and sixty. Before each name was the year the man left Eton and then came his present address. In some cases the search was made easy because the rank was shown. But sometimes the only clue they got was a military address. They had to allow also for people who had left the army and were no longer using their rank. This was their prime target group and a lot of them showed no military connection in their listing – for example, people who had inherited titles and land and now used their title rather than rank. There were 11,150 names in the list, six generations of men who had attended the famous school, and the dates they were interested in threw up almost 2500 men who fitted their target.

The Army Records Office helped as much as they could. All the information on past and present officers was of course carried on their central computer. But it was malfunctioning and they could not feed in a new programme to identify Old Etonian officers. What they could do, they said, was provide a report within ten seconds on any name the police themselves traced.

Mackay had to call in the help of every police force in Britain as bit by bit and hour by hour they singled out men whose activities over the last forty-eight hours they wanted to check out physically. They had one or two interesting cameos as a result – a distinguished Scottish laird was astonished to have his Highland castle surrounded by armed policemen who stormed in and caught him and a dozen local dignitaries relaxing in the castle's great hall with hard-core blue films, some excellent marijuana and two dozen very young ladies who had been flown up from London specially for a long weekend, all of them with nothing to cover their initial embarrassment; in the gazebo of a beautiful park in Oxfordshire, an ex-Guards half colonel was found giving a poetry reading to two fourteen year old boys who, along with the ex-soldier, had left their clothes outside so that nothing would interfere with their appreciation of the verse!

But mostly it was just a slow, grinding slog – the sort of examination which, Mackay said in an aside, was in the end the only way the police could ever make progress in this sort of case. 'No matter how good our electronic aids get, Jock, we are always going to have to revert occasionally to this kind of human effort. We were unlucky about the Army's computer – but even with it we would only have gained an initial advantage. All the prospects have to be followed up by bobbies the length and breadth of the country. I reckon we must have about two thousand policemen from other forces working for us now. Our Chief Constable is going to owe most of his peers a favour by the time we finish this.'

Throughout most of the day Mark stayed in his office watching the policemen and helping when he could, from time to time assisting Mackay in some point of information about Clan Oil and the background to the money he was trying to raise. At four he explained that he had at last had a summons to the Bank. All day he had had to wait for Bob to contact him about the progress on the thousand million pounds.

*

In Melrose Sara spent the day in bed, with Mary Little buzzing around her attentively, bringing her food and drink and asking if there was anything she particularly liked or wanted. Several times she tidied the room which didn't need it and straightened the bed, which did. She offered to get her newspapers or magazines, or anything else she might like. But Sara didn't feel like reading. She was very tired and stiff, but not sleepy in spite of the drugs. She kept asking Mary questions about Bob when he was a young man, and about Melrose and the other people who lived there. At first Mary was reserved, but after a while Sara's free and easy American way broke down her resistance and she drew up a chair to the side of the bed and, with much of her affection showing through, told Sara her version of Bob's life to date, and about the small friendly society of Melrose where everyone knows everyone else and what they're doing.

That day Sara learned much about Bob that she had never known, but had guessed—his strength of character; how he never ducked an awkward issue; the way he was unaffected by his wealth, always ready to pass the time with someone who interested him whether the person was a farm worker or a landowner; how he had helped many people over the years, sometimes Mary suspected with money, but more often by taking an interest in them and helping them to help themselves. She learned of the mistakes he'd made. 'But nobody's perfect,' Mary had said, excusing him all of them.

Sara asked about his parents, who had owned the house before him; who were his friends in Melrose; and much more. All of it Mary told her, more like a doting aunt than an employee, and through it all shone her affection for Bob.

When she got up, saying it was time to make tea, she blushed and said, 'I've never told anyone about lots of these things. But I've enjoyed telling you, Mrs Armstrong. You see, I've never seen Mr Bob as happy as he is, in spite of your accident. I hope what I think is happening between you two is happening. It'll be the best thing to happen in this house for a long time.'

Sara was touched by the older woman's affection and honesty. 'I hope so too, Mary. And thank you for telling me all these things. It will be our secret. Without you I wouldn't ever have known most of them.'

As Mary left to make tea, Sara sank back hugging to herself all that she had just learned about Bob, turning over in her mind the things about him she loved—the rather conservative way he dressed; his strong voice; the way he always said what he was thinking; the way his love for her showed in almost every little thing they did together. And as she drifted off to sleep, she thought how lucky she was to have found a man like him who loved her the way he did. 'I wonder how it's all going to work out,' she mused. 'Will it affect his career? What a beautiful house this will be to live in, but will he want to travel to Edinburgh and back every day? Will Mark leave us in peace?'

When Mary came back with the tray Sara was asleep. Closing the door as quietly as she could Mary went back to the kitchen where her husband Willie was tucking into a huge mug of tea and some doorstep-size sandwiches.

'She's asleep,' said Mary, as she sat down. 'And I for one hope that she's going to sleep in that bed for ever more.'

*

Most of the people in New St Andrew's House were going home as Archie Donald walked in to Hamish Blair's office. Blair explained to him that he had called him because he had finished his task and now wanted to present the new position to the press and public.

After Blair's morning briefing he had been anticipating this and Donald had alerted a number of senior journalists during the day to expect a press conference at short notice—people he felt he could rely on to present their new version of the story. Within half an hour he had called twenty-five of them to Conference Room Number One on the first floor of the building. As they settled back in the comfortable and expensive tan-coloured leather and steel chairs, he delivered a forceful and complete picture of the arrangements Hamish Blair had negotiated with the Scottish Development Agency.

Blair was also there, and he and Donald fielded the inevitable questions easily and confidently, giving the impression that the government's interest all along had been nothing more than a feasibility study to see how best the Scottish Office could help in the development of the Scotia Field—as quickly as possible in view of its vast potential, implying that the nationalisation rumours had been nothing more than a distortion of their honourable interest.

'Throughout we had envisaged the development being carried out by Clan Oil under its own management and we hope that the participation of the SDA will speed up that development.'

Jim Todd, an old and experienced reporter from Glasgow, caught Archie Donald's eye. 'Forgive an old man his cynicism. But I have just been whispering to my young colleague here that this is a lot of balls.' He grinned round at his fellow reporters. 'Is it not the case that the Scottish Office has been caught out? Caught with your hand in the till so to speak, and that this new involvement of the SDA is a cover up?'

Without a moment's hesitation Hamish Blair replied, 'Even if that were the case, surely you wouldn't expect us to admit it? I repeat: speculation on the role of my department yesterday was premature. We have gone to great lengths today to ensure that you appreciate exactly what our interest now is.'

Todd grinned again. 'Thank you, Mr Blair. That was delightfully evasive. But I take your point. No matter what we may suspect, you will be sticking to your story.'

There were one or two questions on Sunray's attack on the Scottish Office but Blair turned these aside, saying that that was outside his area of responsibility and that he understood the police were making no comment at all for the moment.

Just before half past five the meeting broke up, and the newspaper men and women made full use of the telephone facilities offered to them. Within minutes, the major news agencies were flashing the story the length and breadth of the country – 'Scottish Office deny take-over bid for Clan Oil stop announce firm intention of SDA to invest one hundred million pounds in development of Scotia Field immediately in return for a minority stake.'

*

As they waited for Mark to join them, Bob brought Tennent up to date on all that had been happening: the attempted kidnapping of Sara; and the attacks on Clan Oil. In the cool hushed calm of the Bank's head office on a sunny afternoon Bob played down the drama of the previous night and indeed found it difficult to recall the terror and the lashing rain. Tennent was concerned, not about the terrorists which he immediately assumed the police would deal with, but about Bob and Sara. Even at such a late date it raised a doubt in his mind. 'How are you going to be able to deal with Armstrong if his wife is living with you? Surely this is going to make for a very awkward situation? Should you perhaps withdraw and let someone else work with Armstrong? Even if it does damage your chances of taking over from me.' The phone rang, and Tennent paused to answer it. 'He's here,' he said, replacing the receiver. 'He's coming up now. Are you sure you can still work with him?'

'I've thought about that a lot. But I think we can handle it – Mark and I, I mean. You see, I am convinced that Clan Oil is much more important to him than Sara is.'

This was beyond Tennent's personal experience and his view of an ordered world. 'You can't be serious. No man would think like that.'

'I am, and I know I'm right.' Bob was emphatic. 'You'll see.'

Mark was shown in by Tennent's secretary. 'James.' He turned to Bob as well. 'Bob. Well, where do we start?' Bob gave a fleeting wink to Tennent as Mark turned to sit down. The older man nodded slightly to acknowledge the accuracy of Bob's prediction. Mark had shaken hands with him and patted Bob's shoulder in a friendly way as he greeted him.

They all sat down and Bob began. 'I'm glad to see you're looking all right. No after-effects from last night? Good. Then straight to business. The tactic of calling the press conference seems to have worked in our favour – your Mr Gordon seems to have more than earned his fee. The press reports couldn't be more in your favour if you'd written them yourself. The whole business is right out in the open.'

Again Mark surprised Tennent by using Bob's first name –

obviously friendly, obviously without malice. 'What now, Bob? Are you going to help? We've still got the government to deal with. What has been happening with them today? They've been very quiet.'

Tennent cut in, relieved that Bob was right about the two men working together but careful to make no sign. 'We've been working pretty hard on your behalf, Mark. Bob has been in very close touch with the Scottish Office, and has a lot of news, haven't you, Bob?'

'Yes, although we must be careful how we handle what I'm about to tell you. The idea of nationalising Clan Oil had no firm foundation of support within the government, or at least that is the position which they have now taken up. It's a complete reversal of what was actually the case yesterday. However, the government and the Scottish Office have been placed in a potentially embarrassing situation. After a meeting in London last night with the Prime Minister, Hamish Blair has been charged with the job of extracting the Scottish Office and the government without loss of face.'

Bob leant back and made a steeple with his bandaged hands as he went on. 'To my mind, he has been extremely bold and imaginative in the way he proposes to do this. He has found a means of coming out of the whole affair with glory – and at the same time explaining the government's initial interest in your company.'

'Has he?' said Mark. 'Well, I'd like to know what he's planning.'

Bob continued. 'He has persuaded the Scottish Development Agency that they should put up some of the financing necessary for the next stage of the development of the Scotia Field . . .'

'But that's just the same as the government getting control,' Mark interrupted irritably. 'I'm not standing for that.'

'No, it isn't,' Bob said firmly 'It is not at all the same thing. The SDA would have only a minority interest. And in fact Blair is having to find the actual money from elsewhere since the SDA has already committed most of its budget. But the injection of funds by the Agency just now will be a tremendous boost to us as we try to raise the rest of the financing needed. The plan is that they will sell off their ten percent stake to the public in five years' time.'

'I still don't like it.' Mark was truculent. 'It seems like a different version of the same thing.'

Tennent joined in. 'Mark, have faith in us, we have nothing but your, and,' he added honestly, 'our, best interests at heart. The amount of money we are going to have to raise is frightening. We need all the help we can get. But I'll let Bob explain the rest of it. He has been working out all the details.'

'Provided James and I can get approval at a Board meeting at five o'clock, the Bank will provide facilities to raise the thousand million pounds. There will be conditions, of course – a share in the equity of Clan Oil, and our own representative on your Board.

'The bulk of the money we will raise by forming a syndicate as we've discussed before, using non-recourse financing – in other words, the guaranteed profitability of the Scotia Field as security, which as you know is fairly standard in the oil industry. Our merchant banking division is convinced that the combination of involvement by the SDA and ourselves, allied to the known reserves, will prove irresistible to the investing public who haven't had a share like this to play with since Poseidon in 1970. We will, of course have to underwrite the complete loan so our own exposure will be enormous.'

Mark still wasn't happy, and showed it. 'But bit by bit you're giving away my company. I'm losing control of it – perhaps not immediately but in the long run. Why the hell should I let other people in? It won't be mine any more.'

Tennent's tone was placatory as he expanded on what Bob had said. 'In a way that is true. But what Bob is trying to do is to put together a package which will allow you to keep a major stake in the company, and enable you to continue as managing director. You see, there is no way that you can continue to develop the Scotia Field as a private company. We've gone over this with you for months. Our feeling is that this is feasible only for a strong well-balanced public company, which will mean changes. The arrangements you have completed with European Oil Developments are an important ingredient in these changes. The way you have presented yourself and Clan Oil to the public and press over the last couple of days has helped as well – I've already had some very favourable comment on that today, from people in London as well as here in Edinburgh. What we will finish up with is Clan Oil floated as a public company, responsible to thousands of shareholders.'

'But almost ninety percent belongs to me at the moment,' Mark protested. 'Why should I let it go? How much of a holding would I have at the end? How much of it is still going to be mine? Cromarty Promotions and EOD are already in.'

Bob took it up. 'A lot will depend on what sort of proposal our merchant banking people think will be acceptable, to the public and particularly to the Stock Exchange and the major institutions, who will also have to find the offer attractive. If you ask me to hazard a guess right now, I would expect you to retain about fifteen percent of the equity.' He turned to Tennent for agreement. He nodded. Bob went on, 'It doesn't sound a lot, I know, considering that you own almost the whole thing just now. But it will make you one of the richest men in the whole country. You will give up a big slice of the equity but the fifteen percent you will have left will be worth many times the value of what you're giving up in the company as it stands. And you'll still have a very important job to do as well. And let me emphasise this is the only course of action open to you. The

Scotia Field must be developed as quickly as possible; everyone can see that. If you don't agree to what we are suggesting I would not be surprised to see the government change their tack again and press their case for a compulsory take-over.'

Mark considered Bob's argument in silence, and the other two didn't interrupt him, realising that he was facing the need for far greater concessions than he had probably bargained for. As always he faced the big decisions in business easily and after a few moments he said, 'Oh well, if that's what's got to be done, we'd better do it. Quite honestly, you have been able to do much more than at one time I ever thought possible. By the way, James, you said there would be other changes needed. What else do you have in mind?—as though what you've mentioned isn't change enough!'

Tennent looked embarrassed and cleared his throat before he spoke. 'Well, Mark, as you know it is very important for a large public company to have a chairman who is well-known and respected—a figurehead who will lend weight and authority to the company, someone removed from the day-to-day executive control. We feel it will be essential to attract such a person to Clan Oil. This doesn't in any way reflect on yourself, it's just that we believe this would ensure . . .'

Mark surprised them. 'Of course, it reflects on me. But luckily I'm not worried about hanging on to the job of chairman. In fact, I don't like it. I would far rather devote all my energies to running the company. I don't care about chairing board meetings and being the head of the company.'

'Well, there will be more to it than that, because of the scope of your operations in the future. There will be a lot of delicate negotiations with many people. But I'm glad you feel like that. At the moment we don't have anyone in mind, but we'll take some soundings and discuss the matter again. Perhaps Bob might also consult his friends at the Scottish Office to see if they have any suggestions. Whoever it is, is going to have a lot to do with them in the next few years.'

'I take it,' said Mark as he got ready to leave, 'that the terrorist business and their blackmail doesn't affect what we've been discussing, since you haven't mentioned it?'

'That's right,' replied Tennent. 'For years we've known that sooner or later a customer, or even ourselves, would be in such a position. We don't think it is something we ought to be involved in. We hope the police can solve it. If not, we would hope that the demands can be contained,' he finished primly.

Mark smiled wryly. 'I hope so too. Meanwhile I'm going back to see if the police have made any progress. You can reach me at the office when you have some news.' He paused. 'Which I hope will be that your Board agrees with you.'

He turned to Bob and said deliberately, aiming at Tennent, 'I don't suppose you and I will ever be on the same footing again. But thank you for your help. And take care of Sara – she deserves more than I've given her.'

*

In Mark's office the tension was building up as information was fed in from all the police sources working on the problem of Sunray's identity.

At last Jock gave a bellow as he came off the telephone. 'Got him! Got him, David,' forgetting himself in his excitement and using Mackay's first name in front of junior officers. 'It's Lieutenant Colonel William Gorman, Glenn House, Kirkhill, Midlothian – fifteen miles out from Edinburgh on the Langwhang Road.'

'Are you sure?' Mackay couldn't believe it. 'Right on our doorstep?'

'Yes. One hundred percent. We can account for everyone else. And everything about him fits: the local station even confirmed that he's gone a bit odd in the last year.'

'Right,' Mackay gave instructions to another of his senior officers. 'Get our anti-terrorist group out to keep the house under surveillance – but out of sight, well back. I'll join them as soon as I can. Set up radio contact with headquarters back here. I'll telephone the Chief Constable myself. And bring the prisoner in. Let's see if we can shake something out of him now.'

Throughout the day the captured terrorist had been questioned constantly, given water but no food. He was exhausted and showing signs of fear but had still refused to say anything. He had been forced to stand from the time he'd been brought in by the policemen from the Borders.

Mackay was speaking to his Chief Constable as the terrorist was brought in. 'Yes, sir. Glenn House, Kirkhill. One of my groups will be out there in twenty-five minutes. I'm staying here because Sunray is due to contact us again in two minutes, at eight o'clock.'

'I think it would be unwise of us to underestimate him. Can you sanction a full alert throughout the whole force?'

'Yes, sir. I will keep you informed.'

Mackay turned from the telephone to see the prisoner gazing at the clock on the wall with the second-hand creeping round to eight, a look of anticipation cutting through the man's exhaustion.

'I see you know the plan in detail. Well, we now know who your leader is and where you've been operating from: Gorman and Glenn House. I think you had better tell us what his next moves are going to be.'

Before the man could reply, the connection that had been linked up to the radio room crackled into life. 'Hello, Clan Oil. Delta One. Delta One here. This is Sunray.'

THE BANK

THE BOARDROOM OF the Scottish National Bank exuded a sense of established power even when it was empty. The solid, expensive furniture was set off by the astregalled windows which looked out from the first floor over Charlotte Square—to many the seat of influence not only in Edinburgh but throughout Scotland. On the walls were a dozen fine portraits of the Bank's famous directors and officials through the last two hundred and eighty years, impressive-looking men who frowned down on the actions of their present day successors. Each director had his own chair, solidly built in mahogany, finished in rich dark red leather with on the back the Bank's crest picked out in gold leaf. The full Board of Governors numbered thirty in all and an earlier chairman had discovered that having a Board table with sides which sloped inwards on both sides from his end was the only way he could actually see everyone at the same time down the length of the polished mahogany surface. Each chair faced a microphone which the Governors used, indicating that they wanted to speak by pressing a button which activated a small red light to attract the chairman's attention. The secretariat who recorded the meetings and the decisions sat along the narrow base of the table, opposite the chairman.

As Tennent and Robertson entered the room a few minutes before the meeting was due to start, Bob saw at a glance that it didn't look as though there were going to be any absentees. The two main items on the agenda were so important that all of the Governors would want to play a part in such major decisions.

Tennent went immediately to where his chairman, Lord Drumsheugh, was holding court by the fireplace. Bob wandered around nodding to everyone and greeting the few people he didn't meet regularly. He noticed that the other four executive directors who were his only serious rivals were doing the same. He wondered momentarily if his bandaged hands—it was clear the story of his night's adventures had got around—would give him an edge, and smiled wryly to himself at his vanity. Perhaps the indiscretions would outweigh the bravery—who could tell?

Lord Drumsheugh cleared his throat noisily instead of using the ornate ivory and brass gavel before him, and sat down. 'Gentlemen. If you're ready, please.'

Tennent sat on Lord Drumsheugh's immediate right. Bob took his place much further down the table with the other executive directors. As he sat down he looked at the men whose decisions in the next hour would affect his life so much. All of them were successful in their own fields and many of them chairmen of their own companies. All of business life in Scotland was represented—insurance, shipbuilding, investment and unit-trust management, distilling and brewing, engineering and electronics—together, of course, with a number of senior partners from the country's leading law and accountancy firms, and a world-renowned surgeon. They were all shapes and sizes. Most were near the end rather than the beginning of their careers, but there were half a dozen in their late thirties or early forties from whom Bob expected the backbone of his support to come—men he would be working with for the next twenty years. Some had inherited their wealth but most of them had made their own, and even the ones who had been born rich had greatly added to it by their own efforts. A duke and two earls represented old wealth based on land.

The formalities at the beginning of the meeting were soon over. The minutes of the previous meeting had been circulated and were quickly agreed. Several major decisions that normally would have generated a great deal of discussion and argument were nodded through, so to speak. Everyone was eager to get on. But first Drumsheugh told them the bare facts about the ransom demand. 'This is, of course, gentlemen, in the strictest confidence. The police have no wish for the demands to become public. However, James Tennent felt that since all our business together is completely confidential you should know of the threat.'

Drumsheugh looked around for complete attention and introduced the subject of the loan for Clan Oil. 'Now, as you know, normally the lending policy of the Bank towards any one borrower is agreed by the Executive. We are only called upon to ratify the executive decision. However, the case of Clan Oil is unique in the size of the funding sought and the decision has quite properly been left to us. Can I say in passing that the terrorism and the ransom demands that Clan Oil has been subjected to in the last two days are no concern of ours. Our business is to look only at the financial side of the company. The police will deal with the rest, no matter how long it takes.

'I would like James Tennent to outline the situation and alternatives to us. James?'

As Drumsheugh was speaking, Bob was conscious of two things. He had already promised both Hamish Blair and Mark Armstrong that the Bank would help, while the chairman's remarks implied doubt. He could only hope James Tennent would carry the day. And he saw that the other executive directors were looking resentful. He realised, as they did, that if the decisions to fund Clan Oil went through, his challenge for the top job would be that much stronger. If it failed, his career would fail with it.

He was still considering the implications when he was conscious that Tennent was speaking. 'Most of you will have seen the recent coverage on Clan Oil. I will return to that later. The situation in a nutshell is that Clan Oil by luck and application has the potential to become the largest and most successful organisation Scotland has ever seen. But it does not have the access to the funds at the moment needed to realise its potential since it has used up the original facilities we helped to arrange.

'However, the management is sound, and because of steps it has taken recently my executives and I are confident that it can successfully develop the Scotia Field—provided this Bank helps them to raise the necessary finance. If we don't Clan Oil will undoubtedly approach one of our rivals. Alternatively control will pass elsewhere, perhaps even abroad.

'Now I would like Bob Robertson to give you a detailed breakdown of how he sees the situation.'

There were a couple of loud interruptions. Drumsheugh was ignoring the lights on their microphones, and it was strength of voice and personality that carried the day.

'How much money are we talking about?' asked a large bustling brewer, smoothing the lapels of his pin-striped suit.

'What's the point if the government is going to nationalise the whole thing?' said the duke who always tended to side with the Establishment, a sensible attitude for the ninth of his family to hold the title.

With a surge of gratitude Bob saw that Tennent was letting him put the Clan Oil case personally as a means of furthering his own. He didn't let him down. Carefully he explained the scale of operations involved; how European Oil Developments had been brought in; how the proven potential of the Scotia Field would be used as security; that the Bank's investment would be safe and that they would have a significant shareholding and a seat on the Board. He circulated a single-page paper giving all the salient figures. He couldn't give details of the SDA funds since that was still confidential, but he did hint at a favourable attitude from central government. He finished by saying, 'Therefore, Mr Chairman, I am recommending that we raise a syndicated loan, by sharing the risk with all other Scottish financial institutions interested.

Through our merchant bank division I propose that we raise the rest of the money needed by seeking a public quotation on the Stock Exchange and by underwriting it for them. The total sum involved is one thousand million pounds—that is how much we would have to underwrite, to guarantee.'

The meeting erupted. Even Drumsheugh with his years of experience wasn't able to restore order although he pounded on the block with his gavel. Eventually he resigned himself to this and announced, 'There will be a ten minute break for personal consultations.'

Drumsheugh, Tennent and Bob sat where they were, but most of the other members of the Board milled about the room taking soundings. Bob could see that a number of people were literally staggered by the scale of the funding needed, together with the guarantees the Bank would have to give, and he hoped that they wouldn't be frightened into playing safe and voting against it, preferring, as banks tend to all over the world, to do nothing rather than risk doing something that could go wrong. Several had obviously thought the press reports were exaggerating the amount needed.

When things had quietened down again Drumsheugh brought them back to order and asked for questions, which he let Tennent or Bob answer. They took the questions well, both confident that what they were recommending was right. Gradually people started to come round but there were still some doubters.

'You still haven't convinced me that the government don't intend to nationalise the company in the country's interest. It said so on the news last night,' persisted the duke, looking petulantly at his neighbours.

'We've never been involved in a single financing deal of this size. We aren't geared for something on this scale,' said the senior accountant from Glasgow.

'Isn't there still the point that Armstrong's personal finances are not as they should be? He owes us a lot of money, as I understand it. And I also know he has a guarantee out to the Caledonian Bank that may be called in.' The brewer was smug in his assumption of inside information.

Bob was about to answer them when there was a knock on the Boardroom door. Everyone looked at each other in amazement. There was an unbreakable rule that Board meetings were never interrupted. No-one had ever heard of it happening.

Bob spoke up. 'Mr Chairman. Forgive me, but I think that may be a message that is vital to our discussions.'

There were grumblings. 'Bloody irregular.' 'Can't we have any peace?' But Drumsheugh called out, 'Come in.'

In came Bob's secretary. She flushed, and searched desperately around the faces at the table for him but at first couldn't find him. He stood up to let her see where he was and walked towards her holding out his hand for the tearsheet from the ticker tape machine she was holding.

'Thank you, Betty.' She nodded and almost ran out.

Bob glanced at the tearsheet and nodded to Tennent.

Drumsheugh waved his right hand towards the rest of the Board asking, 'What is so important, Bob, that it justifies an intrusion into our meeting?' There was a trace of sarcasm in his crisp voice.

'Sir, I'm sorry about the interruption but this is a newsflash which has only been released. James Tennent and I had hoped this would happen. It has just been announced from the Scottish Office that the government has no plans to nationalise Clan Oil but instead is intending to invest a hundred million pounds in the development of the Scotia Field by Clan Oil as an investment from the Scottish Development Agency, provided the rest of the money can be raised from the private sector.'

Drumsheugh turned helplessly to Tennent as once again the meeting collapsed. He let the discussion go for a few minutes, then rapped on the table with his pen for attention, frowning peevishly when he saw that he had marked the surface.

'Gentlemen, please. Bob. Continue.'

'Well, sir, I think that's that. Let me deal with the last three points in turn.

'First, a possible government take-over. That has been emphatically denied.

'Second, Mr Armstrong's personal finances. These do not cause any concern to the Executive. He seems to be fairly typical of the successful businessman who doesn't pay enough attention to his own affairs. I am sure we can get them straightened out to everyone's satisfaction.

'Third, the sheer size of this deal. I agree that one thousand million is a far bigger accommodation than we have ever contemplated before. But I submit that the circumstances are also exceptional. To some extent I feel that all Scotland is watching to see how we react on this one. We are expected to give a lead. I hope we won't be found wanting.'

The arguments raged, for and against. The conservatives were against such a major single commitment by the Bank. The progressives were anxious to prove their progressiveness. But in the end no-one could argue that the investment didn't seem to be sound, was in the country's interest, would make money and would reflect creditably on the Bank. One point was lost on no-one – they were so far in already that the only hope they really had of getting their initial investment back was to continue to support Armstrong.

The senior partner from Scotland's largest law firm tried a last argument. 'We can't dismiss the terrorists. What they are doing just emphasises how vulnerable our investment would be.'

Bob disagreed with him. 'This is an isolated incident. Every major customer we have could be open to such an attack at any time. It shouldn't in any way affect our decision: it's a threat which any business may have to cope with in the future.'

Drumsheugh decided to allow no more discussion and put the proposal to a vote, making it obvious that it was something he thought the Bank should do. His summing up showed that he too had done his homework.

'In many ways it is fitting that this Bank has the chance to play such an important role in the development of North Sea oil. The modern oil industry was started by a Scot – Dr James Paraffin Young who patented the extraction of oil from coal and shale in the 1840s. It is in his footsteps that we now have a chance to follow, leading this country towards a new era of prosperity and ending forever these dreadful cycles of stop and go in our economy. How can we refuse to take up the challenge of the Scotia Field? How would we face our fellow Scots in the future?'

'All those in favour of our raising facilities for Clan Oil Limited by another one thousand million pounds for the express purpose of developing the Scotia Field?'

The vote was unanimous, even those with reservations being caught up in the end by the prevailing excitement.

'Thank you, gentlemen.' Drumsheugh beamed round at them all, congratulating them on their collective wisdom in agreeing with him. 'Now perhaps the executive directors and the secretariat will retire whilst we discuss item three on the agenda.'

Bob joined his fellow aspirants in the anteroom. The finance director, a kindly man in his late fifties who could only really hope at best for a caretaker appointment, smiled at him. 'You didn't do yourself any harm there. And you have obviously got a friend at court in the chairman. I think we should all go back to our own offices. I'll ask Tom Morrison to wait in here and notify us when they want us back in. Agreed?'

No-one disagreed. From his own office Bob rang Mark who was waiting for the call. 'It's OK. We've agreed to do it. The whole thousand million. We'll handle the launching of the quotation for the Stock Market. And I hope to be able to clear up the Gordon Advertising thing tomorrow.'

Mark said nothing.

Did you hear?'

'Yes. Thank you. I know it isn't enough, but in the circumstances all I can say is thank you. Perhaps later. I've still got a lot on my mind – this terrorist thing is coming to a head.'

'Thank you is quite enough. Don't forget we expect to make

money out of this as well. I hope the police have got the Sunray business under control. Let me know what happens.'

Bob telephoned the Bank's director of external relations and its public relations officer and asked them to join him. He had warned them to wait behind. He briefed them on the financing that had been arranged for Clan Oil and asked them to get a press release out immediately outlining the Bank's intentions. As a courtesy he suggested they clear the draft with Mark Armstrong and make sure he had no objections to what was said.

Tom Morrison came to call Bob back to the Board meeting. As they walked he put his head cheekily on one side and asked, 'Will Mr Armstrong be getting his money, then?'

'How do you know we were discussing that?' Bob pretended surprise at the man's knowledge of what was going on in the Bank.

'Och, I know everything that goes on in this Bank, Mr Robertson, everything.'

'Well, there's no harm in telling you, since the news is going out right now. Yes, he will.'

'Great, Mr Robertson, great. I knew we wouldn't let him down.'

As he moved ahead to open the door, Morrison showed he really did have his finger on all that happened in the head office.

'I hope it's you that's got the job, Mr Robertson.'

Bob laughed. 'Well, if it is, Tom, I think I'll keep in with you in the future.'

*

Board meetings are like all other big meetings—when there has been a real fight on one subject people have a tendency to close ranks for the rest of the agenda.

Tennent had proposed Bob as his successor. Two of the other executive directors were proposed but they were quickly discounted because of lack of support. A complete outsider was advocated but dismissed immediately because he could have no understanding of the complexities of the Bank's organisation and business. There was brief support for an idea that was floated to ask James Tennent to carry on for a couple of years. Tennent scorned the suggestion and claimed they were only putting off a decision that had to be made and he even threatened to resign to ensure that they had to take a decision. He did, however, agree to accept a directorship for five years, a compromise that he felt would help his protégé although normally the outgoing managing director severed all contact with the Bank.

The only real criticism of Bob was his relationship with Sara. All of them were worried about a scandal.

'Particularly,' as the duke put it with Calvinistic disapproval, 'since it is a customer's wife that is concerned. It's bad enough with anyone, but a customer's wife! What will the papers say? What will people say around town?'

Tennent answered him. 'I've developed a lot of faith in the papers in the last couple of days. We've got a lot of friends there.'

Lord Drumsheugh showed his hand at last, his colleagues' discussion having strengthened his growing resolve. 'This is the last quarter of the twentieth century. This sort of thing happens all the time. It is unfortunate that Armstrong's wife is the lady concerned, but we'll all get used to it. I think you'll find that we will worry about it a lot more than people outside will. Customers can come and go – but the managing director of this Bank should be the best man for the job. If this is the only objection to Robertson then I suggest we can learn to live with it. Does anyone have any other points to make? No? Right, then, can I have your votes on the appointment of Bob Robertson as managing director designate of this Bank? First of all, a proposer and then a seconder.'

Once more there was not a vote against. The executive directors were invited back in. Bob was congratulated by everyone – including the losers, who were too senior and too skilled to show any resentment to the man who would shortly be their boss.

Forgetfully, Drumsheugh rapped the table again with his pen and looked forlornly at the new marks.

'Dammit, I must remember to use that bloody hammer properly. Thank you, gentlemen. I don't want any other business. I suggest we now have a drink. Perhaps with his new-found authority Mr Robertson will ring for the steward, since he is nearest the bell.'

BOB AND SARA

Bob got back to Melrose about seven thirty. He drove fast – excited by both his news and the thought that Sara was at his house waiting for him to come home. Sara was awake and sitting up in bed.

'Darling.' He sat on the edge of the bed and hugged her gently. 'How are you feeling? Mary told me as I came in that you've been asleep most of the day.' He looked at her tenderly, not seeing the swollen and discoloured face or the plaster cast, but just the Sara he knew normally.

'I'm fine. Almost no pain now. Just numb. And the doctor's just left. He said I could get up when you came back so long as I take things easy. So don't worry.' She took his hand carefully, and asked, 'How did things go at the Bank? How's Mark? What about the terrorists?'

Bob leapt up, wanting her to share his excitement in his success. Ignoring his bandages, he smashed his right fist into the palm of his left hand as he said, 'We won. I got the job, Clan Oil will get the money, and the police are keeping a lid on the terrorist story as far as they can.'

Bob was like a boy on his birthday. He prowled around the bedroom giving her the details of the Board meeting, telling her what everyone had said, repeating the good moments and savouring them again himself.

'James Tennent was tremendous. He stood back and let me take all the credit. As for Mark, he seems fine. He's got what he wants: he'll keep control of Clan Oil, although in a different way from how he imagined. There was something different about him, though. It's as though he has come to terms with himself. I can't explain it. Our dealings are still strained, but he needs me, and seems to accept it.'

They talked on. Sara was pleased that as he told her of the day's events Bob gave credit to other people—not, as she knew many men did, giving only his own side of the story and taking all of the glory to himself. She was reassured when he said that the police would be leaving the armed policemen with her until the whole terrorist business was finished and delighted that he seemed to want her to share every little detail of the day with him. She mentioned that she had just been speaking to Jenny Scott on the telephone and that Jenny was going to come down the next day and stay for a few days until she felt better.

Bob helped her get up and dress. They had supper in the drawingroom. Mary had lit the fire there and made it cosier for them by drawing the three sofas in closer to the fireplace, serving supper on the big coffee table.

'One of the first things you must do when you feel up to it,' said Bob, 'is to plan how we're going to redecorate the small room next door after what happened last night. Then it will be truly our room.'

They watched the nine o'clock news on BBC. The main item was Clan Oil and the thousand million pounds the Bank and the SDA were making available to it. There was a brief mention of the attack on New St Andrew's House and the shooting and explosions at Scotia House the night before. There was a short film, taken weeks ago, of Mark looking out over the sea from Delta One. Just at the end of the item a black-and-white still photograph of Bob flashed up on the screen and the presenter said, 'The Scottish National Bank also announced tonight that Bob Robertson, who masterminded the Clan Oil deal, will be their new managing director.

Talking over the rest of the news Sara said, 'Darling, how famous you are. And how odd to see you both on television. But why was the picture of you in black-and-white? And how did they get it on the news so quickly? They only decided this evening.'

Bob laughed. 'It's amazing that they had a photograph of me at all. My public relations people must have had a terrible evening getting it to them after the story was released. I think I'll give them a ring and say thank you.'

As he looked up the number in his pocket book and dialled, Sara thought that this simple little action was typical of what made him special to her and to other people.

'Hello, Mrs Cunningham, it's Bob Robertson from the Bank. Sorry to disturb you but can I have a word with your husband . . . Hello, Jim. I just rang to say thank you. Your people did a great job getting the story out tonight. No, we only saw BBC. Was it? Well, we spend enough money advertising on ITV—it's time they did us a favour.

'Tomorrow? A new photograph in colour? OK, will you fix it with my secretary? Thank you again, and goodnight.'

The news coverage added to their celebration of the day's great events. Sara had been forbidden to drink by the doctor, but Bob poured himself a brandy and leant back on the sofa at her side.

'When I've finished this I think we should go to bed,' he suggested.

In the hall they saw Mary in her dressing gown, also on her way to bed.

'I just came down to do a hot water bottle for Mrs Armstrong,' she said, looking slightly flustered and pulling her dressing-gown tighter.

'Mary, I'd like you to know that once we've sorted out a few little problems Mrs Armstrong and I are going to be married.'

'Oh Bob, how wonderful. How marvellous. That's the best news I've had for a very long time.'

Bob hugged her. 'I agree. And I'm going to rely on you to look after her. OK?'

In the dark of the bedroom they lay holding each other and planning their life together, the things they would do and share. Just before they fell asleep Sara asked if they would live in Bankhead.

Bob saw that the house had a symbolic significance representing both change and security to her.

'Yes and no. It would be too far for me to travel every day in the winter. I think we should also have a new flat in the city, don't you? We would stay in it during the week when the weather's bad and come down here at weekends, but be here all the time during the rest of the year.'

'Oh yes. I think that would be almost perfect, the best of both worlds.'

MACKAY

MACKAY AND THE major listened in disbelief to Sunray's instructions. Mark stared back at them stonily as the familiar icy voice boomed out. Everyone else stopped what they were doing and listened too. The call had come at the end of one of Jock's enforced ten-minute breaks and all the policemen had been just about to start again on their task of sifting every scrap of information built up during the night and day of their colleagues' efforts.

'It is twenty hundred hours. One hour till our pick-up of the diamonds. We will make the pick-up at Murrayfield rugby ground as we have already indicated, at the exact centre of the pitch.'

'You and the police will be elsewhere, looking for bombs placed today by our back-up groups to go off at twenty-one hundred hours—looking in the airport, in the Usher Hall, at Waverley Station, on the Forth Road Bridge, at the cinema centre, and on this platform, which we will vacate in forty minutes and which you are not to approach until we are off.

'Take my word for it—there really are bombs in two of the places I have named. And you will have only twenty minutes to get everyone off this platform once we leave.'

The radio went dead and once more Sunray would not respond to calls from Mackay. For the first time he showed the strain he was under as he desperately tried to get Gorman to answer. After several minutes of trying he turned to the others as he regained his composure. 'He has thought out, or they have, every move. He is always one step ahead of us, out-thinking us. This possible bomb threat is to absorb all our energies while they get the diamonds and then escape. I'll have to do just what they expect. We'll have to find these bombs. With tens of thousands of people here in Edinburgh for the Festival the repercussions could be world-wide if one went off.'

Mackay briefed his Chief Constable and alerted thousands of police and other services he had been holding in reserve for the last few hours all over the city and surrounding area. He contacted his group out at Glenn House and told them to stand by. 'It looks to me as though they will get to you at about nine-fifteen if I'm reading everything correctly. I'm assuming – which I have to – that they are going back there.' He asked the major to contact the Army's bomb disposal unit and to warm up his helicopters parked below the office with his men waiting around them.

'Why don't you call in the TRG?' Mark asked.

'I'm going to now. The major here can get out to Glenn House and take charge there.'

Mackay was stretched to the limit as the police operation got under way throughout the city. Out at Delta One the shepherd boat moved in as close as possible to the platform in readiness to take off the crew. He spoke briefly to the superintendent sitting in a car just inside the Murrayfield perimeter. The officer had reported an hour earlier that he and his escort had arrived in position after taking delivery of their diamonds at Turnhouse airport. 'Take the pouches to the centre of the ground now. Go on your own and as soon as they are in position, clear everyone out of the entire area. No-one in. If necessary, arrest anyone who might argue.'

Mackay's first priority was the Usher Hall where a packed audience of 2570 people was listening to Beethoven's Sixth Symphony – the Pastoral – played by the Israel National Orchestra; the cinema centre where all three cinemas were playing to full houses was also a problem, but his experience told him that just by stopping the films it would be easier to get everyone out of the modern building with its many fire doors.

The Usher Hall, antiquated and over-crowded, was going to be a completely different matter. A Chief Inspector called him a few minutes later from outside the concert hall.

'Sir, there is no way I can evacuate these people with safety. The building is old, the stairs and corridors narrow and winding. Panic would probably do more harm than a bomb – if there's one here.'

'Hold your position and do nothing,' said Mackay. 'I will contact you again as soon as I can. A bomb disposal expert should be with you and at all the other possible targets in a few minutes.'

Mackay turned as he heard a scream from the room next door. 'What's that?'

Mark answered. 'The major took the captured terrorist in there when you were on the telephone. He said this was no time for fighting fair and for stiff upper lips.'

Almost on cue the major reappeared in Mark's office holding a long thin blood-stained knife in his hand. He snarled with satisfaction. 'It's the platform and the Usher Hall. All over the platform and under the stage at the Usher Hall. The bastard knew everything—it just took a little bit of effort to get him to remember.'

Mark and Mackay were appalled as the terrorist was brought back in by the major's aide and a constable. His face was a swollen and bloody mass. His hands ran red from where the long thin blade had been thrust up under his fingernails and he held them stiffly in front of him. He could barely see through his swollen eyes.

Mackay let out a cry of anger and lunged at the major as Mark looked with horrid fascination at what had been done.

'You're as bad as they are,' shouted Mackay. 'There is no way we can justify what you've done.'

The major brushed Mackay's protests aside. 'Forget it. Report me later if you like, but mine was the only way in the time available. There was no time for finesse and playing by the book.' The major knew that Mackay resented the freedom of action he had and his anonymity within the bland identity of the SAS.

Exhausted and in pain as he was, the terrorist tried to make a break. Gorman had insisted that they should never give up and that he would ensure that, until a man was known to be dead or captured, his share of the ransom would be kept for him. But it wouldn't be kept for men who betrayed them. The prisoner knew that now Sunray would want him killed—vengeance for putting everyone else at risk.

Momentarily the row between Mackay and the major had given him a chance as everyone else in the room was watching them. The man started for the door but he was weak and stumbling. The major's reactions were instantaneous. He overtook the man in the doorway and grabbed his shirt with his left hand and his neck with the right. The man turned to struggle as the major hissed at him, 'No way, friend. No way you're going to get out of this.' He tightened his iron grip on the man's throat and released the shirt, reaching with his left hand for his knife. Before the knife cleared its sheath the man died. He just buckled at the knees and fell against the major. A post-mortem later showed that the major's fingers were pressing into the vagus nerve and the man died of vagal inhibition—literally fear of dying. The major stared down at him in some surprise. 'He just died,' he said, an almost plaintive note in his voice.

'Get out to Glenn House now,' Mackay said, ignoring the dead body. 'That is where this will all finish up just before nine thirty. Stay at least a mile back from the house, under cover. Remember, they might be able to see everything as they fly in—if that's where they plan to go—although they'll be keeping low as usual. I'll join you when we've dealt with the Usher Hall. But first of all get half of your men out by helicopter to a hold position by Delta One. Tell them not to make any move at all until they see the Sunray helicopters lift off from there. And tell them to take some bomb-disposal people with them.'

Mackay left the office almost at a run, spraying orders broadside as he went. He transferred his command post to a Jaguar police car with an amazing array of radio equipment that his Chief Constable had made available earlier in the day. Mark went with him since Mackay now felt that he might be a late target for Sunray—a last-minute hostage.

They raced to the Usher Hall and with the bomb-disposal lieutenant who had arrived separately Mackay went straight into the concert hall from the back and down under the stage to where the bomb had been discovered minutes before. Awkwardly, they carried the lieutenant's bulky bag of equipment between them.

In the cramped space, no more than four feet high, they saw the bomb—a crude device with a dozen sticks of dynamite joined to an everyday alarm clock and a plastic drum of two gallons of petrol, with a six-volt battery to supply the moment of power. From above came the haunting melodies of Beethoven—a strange counterpoint to the danger and sweat of what they were doing. The heat was intolerable, the end of a very warm late summer's day, the tension unbearable.

Gorman trusted his men but that trust had been misplaced in one of the back-up group—Ahmed, the Arab. When he had seen that morning who was to perform in the evening—the Israelis, his sworn enemies—he had set the clock ten minutes early. The primer for the dynamite was attached by wire to the alarm hand of the clock which had had its glass removed. Wires almost as thin as human hair stretched from a blob of solder on the alarm hand and another blob on the face of the clock at exactly eight fifty. There were dozens of other wires and dozens of blobs on the main clock face making it look like an insanely constructed spider's web. Even Mackay, who knew nothing about bombs, could see that, with the two main blobs less than half an inch away from each other, all the rest of the tense wires were an amazingly effective protection for the mechanism. Any cut wire which sprung up on being cut would make the fatal connection. And he could imagine the devastation that the combination of the explosives and the petrol would make.

'Jesus,' whispered Mackay, pointing to his watch with his torch. 'We've only got three minutes.'

'I see,' said the soldier. 'No time now to get everyone out. I'll just have to stop it. You get out.'

Mackay said nothing, but waited, giving companionship but no practical help to the young soldier as he worked. Ahmed had taken the final precaution of protecting his obscenity by pouring some of the petrol all round the dynamite and the timber joist on which it was lying. The fumes from the petrol added to their discomfort as Mackay and the soldier crouched above it. After two minutes of careful probing, the soldier said, 'We'll have to take a terrible risk. There is no time to dismantle either the wires or the clock's own mechanism. I'll have to lift it up and get the primer from under the clock out of the dynamite.' He paused to wipe away the sweat from his eyes and nose. He reached into his bag. 'Can you insert this sheet of mica between the blob on the end of the alarm hand and the one on the alarm face to insulate them? It's the only chance we have. And we have to pray as I pick it up that there is no back-up system and that none of the other wires connect to the alarm hand.'

Mackay nodded and took the thin sheet of mica. He held his breath to steady his hand and with infinite care placed it between the blobs which were now no more than a sixteenth of an inch apart. He could feel his stomach turning over and his heart racing as the mica touched the blobs of solder on each side.

The lieutenant leant against him as he slowly lifted the bomb up a few inches and tilted it away from them. Holding it with one hand as Mackay strained to keep the mica in position, he grasped the thin black primer and pulled it out. With the cutters he had attached round his neck he cut the wires running into it. Then he sighed with relief and said to Mackay, 'That's it.'

Both of them almost had a heart attack as Mackay took out his mica strip and leant back – the alarm went off. Simultaneously they grabbed for the stop button. In the moment of relief the music from above came through for the first time and the lieutenant said, 'Beautiful, isn't it? I couldn't have done that without your help. Thank God you didn't panic. I couldn't have lifted it and held the mica in place at the same time.' He picked up the bomb and threw it into his canvas bag. 'It's no more dangerous than a stick of rock now. The man who made it must have been told originally to do it in such a way that we could disarm it in time. Pity whoever was in charge didn't have a way of ensuring the whole clock wasn't set ahead of time. Or perhaps it was intentional?'

Mackay clapped him on the back in congratulation and scrambled out from beneath the stage. As he rushed along the empty corridors, the music just audible in the background, he briefed the chief inspector in charge. 'No fuss. No excitement. Get that soldier's opinions about the style of the bomb and get the forensic and fingerprint people in to examine it. But keep everybody out of sight from the audience during the interval.' Back at the police car outside, he once more gave instructions by radio. Then with Mark still in the back of the car, he set off down the

Western Approach Road, passing on their right the empty splendour of Murrayfield with its huge stand and terraces capable of holding more than eighty thousand delirious or despondent Scots rugby supporters. As they passed, Mark said to Mackay, 'It seems almost unbelievable that fifty million pounds in diamonds are lying in the centre of that ground with no-one on guard.'

Mackay only grunted and went back to his radio telephone. As they turned off the Approach Road, a helicopter came swooping in low from the west. It rose steeply over the back of the stand and then hovered almost stationary in the evening sky over the centre of the ground.

'Right, no horns, no lights, until we're on the open road. Just get us to Glenn House. And no lights or horns for the last two miles,' said Mackay to his driver as the car picked up speed and was joined by others behind.

*

'So far so good,' said Gorman to McQuillan as he signalled to Captain Thomson to land now that they were satisfied that there were no police anywhere in or around the huge stadium.

The big Sikorsky settled down like an ungainly dragon-fly beside the bundle of chamois leather pouches. McQuillan took less than thirty seconds to leap out and scoop them up and then vault back through the chopper's open door. Even before he sat down they were lurching upwards. 'Doesn't look like fifty million pounds' worth to me,' he said suspiciously.

Gorman slapped him on the back and laughed as he said, 'That's exactly why I wanted them.' He slit open one of the pouches and let a stream of glittering stones run into his hand. 'This is the truly international currency. Virtually impossible to trace and acceptable anywhere. Some poor bloody policeman must have been working hard to get them all collected for us in time.' The others laughed as he picked one of the larger stones and wrote with it on the glass of the helicopter's window: SUNRAY. 'Just checking,' he laughed, 'that they are the real thing. Not that they could run the risk of trying to fool us when we have so many hostages.'

Gorman became serious. 'We'll divide them up when we get back to the house.' He went back up to the flight deck, relieved the guard watching Thomson and gave instructions for Thomson to land on the edge of the Langwhang Moor.

*

The second Sunray helicopter lifted off from Delta One and in the now clear evening sunlight headed towards Edinburgh. The army helicopter which had been hanging invisible a mile off with the setting sun behind it immediately headed for the platform's landing deck and below, the two Royal Navy frigates started closing in. The SAS soldiers of the Tactical Response Group and the bomb disposal men with them swarmed out as they landed.

The captain in charge shouted at Bruce Barr as he ran towards them having broken open the locked diningroom door. 'Who's in charge here?'

'I am,' shouted Barr. 'There are bombs all over this platform set to go off in twenty minutes.'

'I know,' said the captain. 'Evacuate all your people now. We'll take care of them.'

'Like hell,' Barr turned as he spoke. 'We'll find them a damn sight quicker than you will.'

The captain grabbed his arm. 'Do as you're told. Get everyone off this platform now. You'll just get in our way.'

Barr lost his temper. 'Look, sonny. I've given two years of my life to bringing this bitch on-stream. Nobody's going to blow it up now. It's mine – I'm in charge here. We're just wasting time arguing. I know the few places where a bomb could do real damage. I'll find them. You deal with them.'

He was right. Or at least almost right. Within five minutes five of the bombs had been located. The fifteen minutes left were more than enough time for the bomb disposal experts to neutralise them. But the sixth – on the blow-out preventor – was awkward to get at. He and a bomb disposal captain tried to disarm it in time. But it went off. Barr and the captain just disappeared as the explosion ignited the oil and a white hot jet of flame only two feet wide leapt three hundred feet into the clear evening sky.

In the radio-room Sparkie Brown sent out his message with his left hand as the SAS paramedic checked his stab wound. 'Mayday! Mayday! Delta One! Delta One! We are on fire! Request all possible assistance!' The SAS supervised the abandoning of Delta One on instructions from one of the frigates which also said that the emergency services were on their way.

*

Gorman watched Paul land the helicopter beside them on the edge of the reservoir. The Sunray group transferred to the second chopper as Paul ordered his hostages to join their colleagues in Thomson's Sikorsky. Gorman waved his last two men away and turned to Captain Thomson and the hostages watching from the open door. 'You're free now. You can go. We've taken one or two bits of your radio so you can't use it.' He spoke directly to Thomson. 'Your wife and family are unharmed. I'm sorry if they were frightened.'

Thomson said nothing and as Gorman looked into the other man's eyes he could see both hatred and disgust. He shrugged and ran forward to the helicopter, shouting as he scrambled in to Paul to take off.

*

Thomson watched Gorman's helicopter fly off hugging the contours of the moor, then got everyone into his chopper, insisting, 'Let's get back to Edinburgh. We can't do anything out here or contact anybody.' He took off and turned back towards the city. Almost as soon as he gained height, he saw what looked like a convoy of police cars racing towards the Langwhang on the lonely road, their blue lights flashing. He brought the Sikorsky down onto the road about a mile ahead of them with all his lights on and stood in front to greet the policemen, the other hostages behind him.

Mackay's car snaked as it skidded to a stop and Mackay was the first to reach Thomson. 'What the hell are you doing?' Then he saw the Clan Oil livery on the fuselage and realised who he was talking to. 'Are you Captain Thomson?'

It only took a few minutes for Thomson to fill him in on all that had happened to him. Mackay asked him to fly directly to police headquarters in Edinburgh, saying that he would radio ahead to warn them he was coming in for debriefing.

Back in the car Mackay raised the major on the radio. 'We've got them now.' He couldn't contain his excitement. 'They should be with you any minute now and they've no longer got any hostages. At last the bastard's made a mistake. He's so sure of his security that he's going back to Glenn House. He thinks we haven't had the time or any means of working out who he is, or where he's been operating from.'

The major cut in. 'There's a chopper coming in now.'

Mackay didn't want any mistakes at this late stage. 'Major, make no move until I arrive. I know that the situation is now exactly the kind that your group exists for. But I want to make a personal assessment before you move in. Do you hear what I'm saying? I have witnesses with me.'

'I hear you,' replied the major. 'How long before you reach us? How long before we can move?'

Mackay looked to his driver who, in spite of their terrifying speed, took his hand off the steering wheel and held up three fingers. 'Three minutes,' said Mackay. 'Three minutes.' He turned to Mark and told him to stay in the car when they arrived. 'You shouldn't really be with us.'

GLENN HOUSE

MACKAY SLID IN beside the major who was lying on the ground at the edge of a small wood. In the fast fading light of a clear summer's evening, Glenn House looked welcoming: all its lights were blazing and the sounds of laughter and shouting drifted across to them.

'I've set up road blocks all around the whole area,' said Mackay. 'How many of them are there? Captain Thomson thought about twenty—perhaps more.'

The major passed him a pair of light-gathering binoculars. 'Take a look yourself. We don't really know. The chopper landed in a yard behind the house where there's a hollow square formed by outbuildings, stables and so on. We couldn't count them as they disembarked since we couldn't see them—even though we've got men surrounding the place.'

Through the glasses Mackay could see happy men congratulating each other in most rooms in the house. He focussed on the drawing-room and was certain that he was looking at Gorman as he saw a tall distinguished-looking man holding forth by an ornate marble fireplace. He spoke to the major as he watched. 'We'll have to immobilise that helicopter. We can't chance them getting out in it.'

The major touched his arm and pointed to their far left. 'I've got four men there with grenades. There are no windows on that gable end of the house. They can get in, lob their grenades—two each—on slightly shortened fuses—which they're setting now—and be back under cover before they go off.' He paused. 'Except it might be better to leave them in there against the wall.' He spoke quickly into his radio, changing his instructions to the four commandos.

Mackay hesitated, wondering if he should start the operation without giving Gorman and his men a chance to surrender. But he felt immediately that they wouldn't. Already he had seen signs of heavy suitcases being carried down the main stairs, presumably preparations for a general departure. He nodded to the major and asked, 'What is your plan after that?'

The major made a grabbing action with his right hand. 'We attack on all sides simultaneously. They'll fight, but we have the advantage of mobility. We'll get them.'

'But at what cost?' asked Mackay. 'How many men are we going to lose in a frontal attack? Too many,' he answered himself. 'After the grenades I'll give them a minute to come out. I've got a loudhailer here. Any longer than that will just give them time to organise themselves. We've got to try and keep the initiative, use the element of surprise to ensure that for a change they are kept off balance.'

The major gave a dismissive shrug. 'You can try, if you like. But they're not going to surrender. They're trapped like rats in a sewer. The safe house they planned has become their downfall. These people always make a fatal mistake in the end. They won't accept that to begin with: their instinctive reaction, based on what we've seen of them so far, will be to fight their way out. But you're in charge as you keep telling me. So you decide. If it was up to me I'd shoot the bastards without any warning whatsoever.'

*

Gorman and McQuillan were handing out false passports and travelling money to all of their men. They were laughing and joking together, using the new names for the first time, all of them caught up in the party atmosphere of a difficult job well finished. The passports had been arranged weeks earlier by the simple method used for decades by criminals of assuming the identity of children who had died and were buried in local churchyards some thirty years earlier. Duplicate birth certificates cost only two pounds and Gorman had faked the signature of the local doctor on the application forms. Spaced out over several months, not one of the applications had been queried. Each man had a thousand pounds' travelling money—the residue from Gorman's sale of land six months earlier—and a complete set of new clothes. Each man also had his own pouch with a million and a half pounds' worth of diamonds. All of them were heading on one-way journeys to countries where not too many questions are asked about a man's possessions, such as Brazil, Liberia, Colombia, Panama and Switzerland. All of them had matching suitcases, into which the ex-armoury staff sergeant had fitted a half inch cavity along the whole base. Lined with soft rubber, the cavity was big enough to take the contents of a pouch without being noticeable except in the most vigorous search. Each man had the name of a diamond merchant in his final destination city—names sought out by McQuillan when pretending to be a freelance reporter months earlier in the main diamond markets of London and Antwerp. McQuillan had also met a shady Dutch financier with access to a diamond fence in Amsterdam. He had pumped the two Dutchmen dry of information on diamonds, moving money and possible contacts in the countries he was interested in. Then he had killed them both, making their deaths seem like gangland killings. There had been no publicity. Gorman had given them all the same advice. 'Travel slowly. Don't use planes where your luggage might be put through a scanner. Use cars, railways and ships. Travel as a visitor and always have one or two small items to declare at any customs post you go through. Have something you're not sure about, something you have to consult customs men about. They will be so anxious to exert their superiority they'll wave you through. Only with exceptional bad luck will your case ever be searched. Even then, don't panic. Try a quick bribe. If that doesn't work, pick up the suitcase and run. If you time your arrivals for during the day and always into major centres, you'll very likely never get caught. Think of Terminal One at London airport. There's a bunch of sleepy couldn't-care-less customs people there—anyone could get a suitcase back, sprint the last twenty yards and get out amongst the thousands of people, all carrying suitcases, on the main concourse. It would be easy to get lost just by slowing down.

'Not that I think that will be necessary. Your cases will probably never be opened. There will be an alert for a few days after today but in a week the vigilance will drop off, particularly if you join on to package tours, coaches or cross on one of the big ferries. Within Europe I don't ever remember having a suitcase checked in more than thirty years of travelling. You know how to behave under strain—keep cool, stay in the crowd.'

He had a last instruction for everyone as they collected their diamonds and money. 'Make contact with your dealer as soon as possible after you arrive. Change only some of your diamonds into cash and deposit it with a large bank. Wait a few weeks and then change some more which you should deposit with another bank. And so on. Then use your money—buy and sell high-value items, buildings, houses, antiques, anything. Even buy and sell a few small businesses. It doesn't matter if you make a loss here and there. Inside less than six months you will have laundered the whole lot. You'll be able to come and go as you please. If you get caught we'll read about it in the papers. We've got three million spare from the men the police told us were killed in the car crash. We'll find some way of looking after you when you get out.'

McQuillan handed Gorman a large brandy and said, 'Drink up, Bill. We should be going soon.'

Gorman looked at his watch and nodded. Nine thirty-five. 'The London back-up team will ring in five minutes for confirmation of standing down. You speak to them, Douglas, and remind them to make contact if you miss each other or if anything goes wrong. What was it you arranged—a job advertisement for a gamekeeper in the Daily Telegraph under a box number?'

'Yes,' said McQuillan, 'it's virtually foolproof. We only reply to them and arrange to meet in Switzerland. Not that we'll need it. Nothing can go wrong now.'

'Right.' Gorman finished his drink and put it down. 'I'm just going to say goodbye to everyone.'

At that moment they both heard a shout from the courtyard: 'Christ! Grenades.'

Two of their men dived through the back door into the hall. Everyone who heard was also on the floor and crawling towards abandoned weapons as the blasts from eight separate grenades hit the house, blowing out every single window.

*

At the police headquarters in Edinburgh the Chief Constable and his senior officers were doing their best to stop the media from following up the attacks on the Scottish Office and Scotia House. He had personally rung the editors of all the major newspapers and the radio and television news services, insisting that they should only give the barest details of the previous night's attacks and seeking their co-operation to help him bring the matter to a successful conclusion – promising full details then. But individual press, radio and television reporters had been working on the story since the middle of the night. Straws in the wind. Their own experience and leads from dozens of curious members of the public alerted them to the fact that somewhere in or near the city a major story was breaking. The number of police moving in a generally westward direction at last gave them an indication of where. The arrival of the Clan Oil helicopter with the released hostages who couldn't be kept quiet then told them more. And eventually an understandable slip by a young constable gave some persistent men the name of Glenn House. Nearly all of the reporters were stopped by the ring of roadblocks the police had set up on all roads leading near to Glenn House but a couple who had been roving far out got through after an early tip-off on their car radio.

*

The four Tactical Reponse Group commandos had pressed against the gable end of the house as they waited the four seconds for their grenades to go off. Under cover of the noise of the explosions and the much bigger one that followed a few seconds later as the helicopter's fuel tanks erupted, they launched their grappling irons and trailing ropes towards the roof of the house. Three of them caught and one fell back. They waited, taking the strain on the ropes, as Mackay's voice boomed out on a loudhailer.

'This is the police – Chief Superintendent Mackay. You are completely surrounded. Come out now.' As Mackay spoke every light in the house went out – someone had thrown the main fuse.

But the fire in the courtyard was now blazing brighter and brighter as it spread to one of the outbuildings, throwing the whole house into a flickering, changing silhouette. 'You have one minute to come out. One minute,' repeated Mackay.

Nothing happened. No-one moved or responded in the house. The major touched Mackay's arm as the minute was up.

'Wait,' Mackay snarled. 'Wait and see what they do.'

Another minute passed and then another, without action. And then Mackay and the major heard the ring of a telephone from the house. It rang twice. Then silence. Then from every window came the flash and the harsh barking of sub-machine guns firing on automatic.

Mackay cowered behind a larch tree as bullets thudded into the trees around him and whined off the ground in front. He could see the major and his men doing the same – some hugging the ground within small depressions, some, like himself, taking whatever cover the trees could give, and a few lucky ones keeping their heads down in an overgrown ditch. Mackay wondered how his own men were getting on further back in the trees.

'What now?' he shouted to the major who had crawled up directly behind him.

'I told you so!' The major also had to shout above the noise of two of his men aiming at each side of a window from which the SMGs were firing without a break. Suddenly the shooting from the house stopped, except for occasional bursts from a couple of guns. The rate of fire from the soldiers slowed down but continued regularly along the entire circle of their front.

The major spoke into his radio and then said to Mackay, 'My four men at the side of the house are going up onto the roof now. We're giving them covering fire until they get there. Sunray's trapped in there. So much for his planning now.'

As he spoke, half a dozen men started firing from the roof towards them. He cursed and spoke quickly into his radio again. He indicated with his arm to one of his sergeants to close in on him. 'Our men are isolated from the terrorists on the roof by a continuous bank of chimneys with a glass sunlight running the full length of it on their side. They can only get to the chimneys along the top of the front and back walls, where they'll be in full view of the enemy. See if we can pin the opposition down with sniper fire.' Before the sergeant could move, two Range Rovers came charging round from the courtyard behind the house with six guns in each pouring a non-stop hail of heavy calibre bullets into the scant cover the trees provided. They drove straight at the trees as the soldiers pounded them with automatic fire.

Mackay heard a soldier cry out, and turned to see him holding a smashed elbow as he stared in horror at his corporal whose face was now just a pulp of blood and two staring eyes. The terrorists crashed the two Range Rovers into the smaller trees at the front of the wood and forced their way further in. Mackay was appalled as he realised that in the dark wood the major's force was cut in two and the terrorists could now take them on from behind and at close quarters. The level of fire from the house had also greatly increased again.

*

On the roof McQuillan winced as he was struck in the face by fragments of sandstone blasted from the low parapet in front of him by a bullet from one of the sniper's rifles. He spoke urgently into his radio. 'Sunray, Sunray. We're pinned down by fire from all sides. And I'm certain there are soldiers on the part of the roof we can't reach. We're under sniper fire from the back but not from the front or the left flank. I'm going to try and get round the chimneys at the front. Do you hear me? Can you try and give me protection?'

In the wood Gorman stood absolutely still as he listened to McQuillan's voice in an earpiece in his right ear. The volume was turned completely down, which he was glad about since a sniper was lying prone on the ground only eight feet away from him. The soldier was lining up a light-intensifying night sight on an old Lee Enfield ·303 rifle—still regarded by most soldiers as the most accurate rifle ever made—as he picked his target carefully.

Gorman, who had a loudhailer on a strap on his back like a hunting horn, had taken several minutes to creep up on the soldier lying with his back to him, easing forward a step at a time, testing his weight with each foot before he moved. The soldier fired and quickly worked the bolt to push a new round into his breech. As he took aim, all his concentration on a figure more than three hundred yards away, Gorman leapt onto him from a mere four feet, driving his right knee into the small of his back. With all his weight bearing down on the soldier, he threw a garroting wire over his head and throttled him.

Still kneeling on the dead soldier, Gorman looked all round him carefully before he answered McQuillan softly. 'Sunray here. Go now! We have to keep them at bay for a few minutes more. We'll try to draw their fire. But stay in contact.' He turned to signal to his men to lay down heavy fire, sure in his own mind that they would be back to back and in no danger of shooting each other. Even before his hand was down to the bottom of his signal, the SMGs were spraying a deadly stream into the trees—firing blind but relying on the weight of their fire power, drawing the soldiers' attention away from the house.

Gorman himself picked up the sniper's rifle and set out to ensure that the soldiers on the roof had to stay down as McQuillan tried to get through to them. Through the night sight he could see McQuillan and other men reaching up to the gap between the tall chimney pots.

'Follow me as I go through,' whispered McQuillan to his men. 'But watch your step—there's a bloody great sunlight just on the other side.' Henri nodded and tried to ease up into the small space between the ornate pots.

The major hissed at his sergeant. 'It worked. Now!' The sergeant tapped the two snipers lying one on each side of him as he knelt facing the house. The major said to Mackay, 'We have not had any sniper fire from the front since we started. So they're trying to secure the roof, thinking we can't reach them accurately across the killing ground they've cleared.'

The Frenchman didn't even make a sound as the bullet tore through his neck. For a moment he turned to look directly at McQuillan, blood spurting from his jugular vein. Then he fell slowly forward. The glass in the sunlight seemed to bend for a second, then gave way as his body fell into the main hallway below.

The bullet which shattered McQuillan's left leg just below the knee was only a second behind the one that killed Henri. He felt the massive impact, then nothing, and lost his balance as more bullets crashed into the chimney-pots. He fell over the low parapet. As he fell he dropped his SMG and grabbed at the guttering. For a moment the cast iron held, but years of neglect had weakened it and it gave way under the dead weight of his twelve stone. All his instincts to survive and his training told him to turn over to try to break his fall. But there wasn't enough height. For a second he saw the wrought iron railings just before he was impaled on them. One spike drove through his chest, the other into the thigh of his already injured leg. His whole body writhed with pain as he shuddered in a nerve spasm. He screamed in agony.

Gorman swore as he raged at his loss. 'You fucking bastards. You'll pay for him,' he cried, hurling grenades into the trees to either side of him. In his earpiece he could hear the whimpering and moaning of McQuillan whose radio was still live. He could see the man he owed his life to arching his body in agony, trying to push himself off the railing spikes.

'Help me, Bill. Don't leave me like this. Please, Bill, it hurts so much. Bill. Please, Bill.'

He burst the strap of his loudhailer as he pulled it from his back. His voice boomed out. 'This is Sunray. This is Sunray. Do you hear me?' The shooting stopped, and men crying out in pain stopped too to listen. 'This is Sunray. Acknowledge.'

The major watched as Mackay switched on his loudhailer and turned round to face the direction the Sunray voice had come from.

Mackay's skin crawled with apprehension as he realised the voice had come directly from behind them, several hundred feet from the crashed Range Rovers.

'We hear you. Are you surrendering?'

Even through the booming volume Gorman's anger was naked. 'Like fuck. It is only a few minutes to ten o'clock. Go to the cottage on the main road and watch the news programme. You will see our fall-back protection, why you will have to withdraw. We have always recognised we might need to ensure our way out. Go and watch the news!'

'What the hell is he trying to pull?' asked the major softly. 'He can't expect us to fall for something like this.'

Mackay ignored him and brought his loudhailer up again. 'You can't be serious. We have you completely pinned down here. There is nothing you can do now to escape. Nothing.'

Gorman boomed out again almost before he had finished. 'Chief Superintendent, I'm deadly serious. Within minutes one of our back-up teams will strike. I'm not asking you to call off the army. Go on your own and see the news. Then come back and talk to me. But go now.'

Something in the man's voice told Mackay he had to go. 'All right, we'll go. What do you do in the meantime?'

'Nothing till you come back. We'll all stay as we are.' Gorman paused. 'Except that I want to go and get that man off the railings at the front door. OK? I'll come back here after I've got him off, if you want.'

Mackay moved out from the protection of the trees as he replied. 'Get him and stay by the door. We're going to the cottage as you suggest.'

He started running back to where his car was parked, shouting to the major to come with him. After telling his men to hold their positions, the major followed.

Gorman ran across the killing ground towards McQuillan, all the time hearing in his earpiece McQuillan's moans. The scene was grotesque. Parts of the house itself were now on fire; there were dead and wounded men everywhere; the air was rent by the whimpering of the injured; and his friend was skewered on the wrought-iron spears.

Just before he reached McQuillan, shouting broke out from the trees and a civilian ran out, just evading two soldiers who were trying to stop him. He carried a case in one hand and a microphone in the other. He made no attempt to protect himself and ran forward shouting, 'Television News, Television News,' as though the words were some sort of talisman.

When he was about twenty yards short of the house, Mac rushed out of the front door carrying one of Gorman's shotguns. 'Bugger off,' he shouted. 'Bugger off, you stupid little shit.' The man thrust the microphone towards him and said, 'Can I ask you what you hope to achieve here?' Mac fired both barrels at once. The man's microphone and hand literally vanished and he stared down in revulsion at the white stump of bone at the end of his arm. He began to cry and ran back towards the soldiers he had ignored, still carrying his case with a now useless wire trailing from it.

*

Gorman's foot slipped in a pool of blood as he reached the bottom step. He hesitated before he touched McQuillan's shoulder. 'Douglas. Can you hear what I'm saying?'

McQuillan's face was grey and twisted in pain. He said, 'Of course I can, Bill. Just need a little bit of help. Can't seem to move.' As he spoke his words were interrupted by his moans of agony. 'Can you get me down?'

Mac shook his head in despair at Gorman as he indicated to him to help lift McQuillan off the spikes. They tried to do it gently, but every time they applied any pressure McQuillan screamed and coughed bubbles of frothy blood. Gorman found himself screaming with him and then as he got himself under control whispered to Mac, 'We'll have to do it with one big lift. Now!'

McQuillan passed out as they lifted his body and wrenched it off the spikes. They laid him on the steps. Gorman held his hand as he regained consciousness and muttered through the ever-growing bubbles of blood. 'Will the back-up work, Bill?' He shuddered again and cried out.

Gorman smiled and nodded. 'Yes, it will. They've gone to the cottage now.'

McQuillan screamed again, a long agonising animal sound that died in a gurgle in his chest. For a minute he was quiet except for his involuntary whimpering. He reached for Gorman's arm, his eyes momentarily clear. 'I won't make it, Bill, will I?' Gorman squeezed his hand reassuringly but McQuillan insisted. 'I won't, Bill. Not like this. Wouldn't want to.' He pleaded. 'Can you do it for me? Don't want to do it myself. I'd do it for you.'

Ever since he had reached him Gorman had known what he was going to have to do. He drew his Smith and Wesson and placed the wide muzzle at McQuillan's temple, holding his neck with his free hand. 'Goodbye, friend,' he whispered as he pulled the trigger. Most of the top of McQuillan's head came off in one piece and slammed against the front door. Gorman turned and threw up for the first time since he was a child.

THE BACK-UP

As the major drove the police car back towards the main road across the moors, Mackay got through by radio to his headquarters and passed a message to his Chief Constable to watch the news programme. It was less than one minute to ten o'clock as the major braked to a stop outside the lonely single-storey cottage set back from the road.

Mackay and the major barged through the unlocked front door straight into the living-room where a couple, both in their sixties, were watching a play on a large colour television beside their fireplace. The couple climbed to their feet protesting. As Mackay produced his identity card, the major changed channels and the room was filled with the dramatic signature music of News at Ten. The elderly shepherd put his arm protectively round his wife's shoulders as Mackay quickly explained his sudden intrusion. They continued to stand as Mackay turned to the major and the music faded away.

'Why can they want us to watch this?' asked Mackay. The major replied that they could only wait and see.

*

The Range Rover had drawn up just beyond the Independent Television News studios' entrance in Wells Street. For the last hour the men in it had waited in a quiet side street, ignoring the hustle and bustle of central London on the first night of the weekend. The brief telephone instruction had set their back-up operation running. The four men moved slowly, not wishing to attract any attention to themselves. They were dressed like workmen and carried canvas bags with rope straps. They turned into the studios' main door.

At first the commissionaires were quite happy to let them into the building on the strength of their story of a serious water leak. Then one of them became suspicious. 'Ow come it tikes four of you, then?' he asked, reaching for his telephone to seek reassurance and authority from the duty manager. He and his mate died two seconds later, each stabbed through the heart.

While three of the terrorists raced to the lift and up to the news studio floor, one remained on guard in the entrance hall. As it turned out, no-one else appeared in the two and a half minutes it took to complete the operation.

Surprise, and the length of time it takes people to react to a completely unexpected attack, was the key to their success. As they burst into the studio they could hear the well-known voice of a famous newscaster presenting the world's latest news. He sat at the usual curved desk with his opposite number of the evening. They were stark and clear in the bright lights – a contrast to the cameras, electricians, assistants, and technicians clustered in front of them in a semi-circle.

The grenade was lobbed straight into the lap of the speaking newscaster, bouncing down off his chest. He stared at it in horror for a second before the short fuse went off. Where there had been a man there was nothing, nothing except blood. A growing spray of blood was hitting the plain wall behind his chair, an artery from his truncated body was pumping it in a steady stream from where his left thigh had been. Most of the curved desk had been destroyed but fortunately enough of it remained to hide the obscenity behind it from the cameras. The cameras had carried the whole thing – except for a slight wavering with the initial blast – to the watching nation.

The three terrorists had thrown themselves to the floor facing away from the explosion, knowing that everyone else in the room would be disorientated and in shock for the first few moments after it. Now one of them strode to the surviving newscaster who was bleeding from a shrapnel wound in his shoulder and thrust a paper at him. He snarled, 'Read it.' Then he turned and ran as the two other terrorists covered him. People were now screaming, some crying, but all of them too dazed to offer any resistance.

In the control room the programme's director faded the frightening picture from the screen. Isolated though he was from the terror of what had taken place even he had been slow to hit the panic button but now he brought up a still colourband card and background music.

The three terrorists raced down the stairs, not willing to risk being trapped in the lift. They and the man in the entrance hall abandoned their weapons inside the front door and with tremendous self-control walked to their Range Rover. They had driven off and turned out of Wells Street before anyone at ITN had even started to dial 999. In a few days they would travel north to where they knew their share of the diamonds would be hidden. They were confident that if they weren't there, Gorman's fall-back procedure would ensure that they would get their one and a half million pounds each later.

*

Mackay couldn't drag his eyes from the blank screen. 'Jesus Christ. Live coverage of their atrocities.' He stopped as a shaken voice came from the television set which still had only bands of colour showing on it.

'We have been told to read out this statement. The bomb you have just seen was the work of Sunray. Unless the main part of the Sunray group, who are surrounded by police near Edinburgh, are allowed to go free in the next fifteen minutes, attacks of this kind will be repeated.' The voice faded and music replaced it, together with a sign saying that normal service would be resumed as soon as possible.

'Oh no!' cried Mackay. 'We're being blackmailed in front of almost twenty million people.' He held his head in despair and spoke more to himself than to the others in the room. 'I'll have to let them go. They've beaten us. I can't risk anything else like that. The threat is too great. It's imprecise but at the same time too real after this for us to ignore.'

The major thrust his face close to him and shouted. 'No! We can't give in to them. You said yourself that the public expect us to win. If we let them go they could strike again: anywhere, at anytime. We must wipe them out while we've got them surrounded.' Mackay rested his head on his hands as he tried to think. The major shook him in frustration. 'We can't let them go,' he insisted.

Mackay stood up. 'You're wrong. I can't take the risk of another attack like that.' He pointed resignedly to the television set. 'These men are no ordinary terrorists. They are led by a man used to planning, a leader who has been able to out-think and outwit us ever since they first made contact with Mark Armstrong. They have beaten us by planning and organisation. How many back-up teams have they got? Perhaps only the one. But I can't take that risk. You've seen the speed with which they can react to a threat to themselves.' He tried to reassure the other man. 'There is nothing we can do – nothing we could do. Gorman has used the methods of modern terrorism, not for spurious publicity or political advantage, but for personal gain. His men are trained and disciplined, probably all ex-soldiers. They won't stop now. I've no choice, no choice at all. We must let them go.' He went on more to himself than to the soldier. 'Perhaps I was wrong even to use your group at all. This is nothing more than robbery. It has nothing to do with politics; there's no risk to national security. It's a job for the police, but beyond us, beyond anyone, to cope with.'

The major wouldn't give in. 'But I think they've shot their bolt. There has to be a limit to how many of them there are. I don't think there are any more back-up teams. I think we can take them all out now.'

Mackay shook his head. 'I've told you – I can't risk that. If the one we captured hadn't been killed we might know for sure.' He paused, then went on. 'They could strike anywhere—London Airport, a packed cinema in Manchester, a crowded bus station in Bristol. Anywhere!' He paused again. 'I over-ruled you before. Perhaps I was wrong then, although I still don't see how we could have prevented all that's happened. We couldn't know where they would attack. The initiative has always been with Sunray. At first there was nothing real to counter-attack. Now we can't strike back at them because of the danger to innocent people. He's always known that surprise, mobility and protection from what he called his back-up teams—more than one—in an action that has lasted less than three days would ensure he succeeded. We can't compete. We never could. We probably helped train him in the beginning. He was prepared to kill for what he wanted. Even with your help I could do nothing against him—his preparation was too good. By the time we even worked out who he was, his planning protected him.' He paused and his voice was firm as he finished. 'My command. My responsibility. My failure. I have to over-rule you again. You will tell your men to stand down, major. Now.'

On the short journey back in the car Mackay contacted his Chief Constable who had seen the television attack. He gave his confirmation that Gorman and his men should be allowed to leave and said he was ringing the Home Secretary to tell him.

Right up to the last minute the major kept arguing with Mackay, trying to persuade him to change his mind. 'Can't you see, man? If we give in once we'll be expected to give in always. We'll spawn a shoal of imitators who will think they can hold the whole country to ransom.'

Mackay was stung into replying. 'That's a risk we have to take. But these men are exceptional. Only with another Sunray—a Gorman—could the planning and initiative beat us. I have to think of the public's safety. The terrorists now have nothing to gain by surrendering. Obviously you could kill them all, or at least all the ones who're here at Glenn House. But so long as there is a possibility, no matter how slender, that they have others to strike against the public, we have no alternative but to let them go.'

The major had to fight to control his temper. In his heart he knew Mackay was right; but his training had not prepared him for failure and he could not admit absolute defeat. 'I'll find him. Gorman. Wherever that bastard goes, I'll find him,' he said as Mackay used the loudhailer to tell Gorman that he and his men could go.

After a moment Gorman's voice answered from the front steps of the house. 'My back-up teams will stay active for a week. Only I can stop their operation. Only my code-word. Realise that and don't make any attempt to intercept our escape. Only when I have heard that all my men are safely out of the country will I have them stand down. Only then will I stop Sunray.'

Mackay acknowledged that he understood and Gorman went on. 'Bury my dead, Chief Superintendent. I'll leave a note pinned to each of them giving their names – it doesn't matter now.'

Mackay watched them leave in Range Rovers and other cars which had been in the stables and had not been touched by the fire which was now raging through the entire house. Just before they left, eight bodies were brought out and laid on the clear ground a hundred yards in front of the house. Even in his defeat Mackay had to admire Gorman's planning, meticulous to the end. His seven-day deadline probably meant that the whole group would be able to leave the country. He walked back to his car where Mark and his other men were waiting to drive to Edinburgh to face the inquiry that would be held immediately to examine where the police response had failed and what could be learned from it. The major and his men had already left.

*

Gorman was on his own as he drove away from the burning shell that had been his home. Neither the thirty-three and a half million pounds' worth of diamonds – his own, McQuillan's and the other seven dead men's, plus the three million pounds for the two men waiting for him – nor the success of his final bluff about extra back-up teams gave him any pleasure. He had banked on the enormity of the television bombing to persuade the police to withdraw if he was trapped or in danger and that they wouldn't dare risk any retaliatory response inside his seven-day embargo but its use gave him no satisfaction.

He drove towards Galloway. Two hours later he was driving down the bumpy track to Ardwell Bay on the Irish Sea. In the clear night sky he could see the glow of Belfast, twenty miles off. Away to the left, out of sight, was the bulk of the Isle of Man and the open sea leading to the south.

Lying at anchor in the bay was an ocean-going yacht, *Le Bon Vent*, which the two men on board had hired in Cassis near Marseilles and sailed up to Stranraer during the last two weeks. All its lights were shining in the darkness of the bay. Gorman flashed his headlights three times. The lights on the yacht flashed twice in response.

Gorman turned his Range Rover and drove back up the track as he saw the yacht get under way. He then drove to Gallie Craig near the end of the peninsula. He drove the last few miles carefully and without lights. He turned off the narrow road a mile before the lighthouse. He parked the Range Rover fifty yards from the edge of the soaring cliff, got out with his backpack with its sixty seven pouches, leant in and let off the handbrake. The slope was not enough to set the Range Rover moving and he had to give it a push. At last it moved, slowly at first, then picking up speed as the slope increased. The cliff fell almost sheer for five hundred feet to the sea below—one of the most dangerous areas of Britain's entire coastline, where two tides converge and where a boat can't progress round the headland unless it can do more than seven knots. Gorman didn't even bother to look over—he knew that the deep water and the fast tides would hide the Range Rover for ever. He walked a mile back along the road and turned off down into West Tarbet Bay as the yacht came gliding round the rocks on the northern side of the bay. A rubber power-boat came in to collect him.

*

For three weeks they drifted gradually southwards towards the Mediterranean, behaving like three friends on a leisurely holiday, the diamonds carefully hidden from possible search in a double thickness of table-top and other surfaces in the galley. But they needn't have bothered with the precautions, for during the whole three weeks they weren't even hailed by another boat. After a couple of days Gorman threw off his despondency about the death of McQuillan, arguing to himself. 'We did everything we could. Douglas knew the risks and we agreed that we would take each other's share if anything went wrong.'

They parted company at Cassis. Gorman went ashore with all the diamonds and waited whilst the other two returned the yacht to its owner. They shook hands and Gorman set off to walk to Switzerland. During the three weeks he had grown a beard and had sun-bathed naked on the boat. Now dressed in shorts, faded shirt, thick socks and rubber-soled boots, he looked fit and handsome as he hiked towards Switzerland with all his belongings in a large pack. He took a long detour away from all roads as he approached the border. He lit no fires and saw no-one as he waited for three days in the thick forest. At last, satisfied that there was no chance of detection, he crossed over at four o'clock in the morning of the fourth day and by noon was just another hiker enjoying the splendours of the Swiss mountains in summer.

He gradually made his way towards Zurich, the main Swiss financial centre. He made contact by telephone with the diamond dealer McQuillan had identified for him. They met at the bear pit. There were no bears and no crowds as they sat on the wall of the pit and Gorman explained that he had more than thirty million pounds' worth of diamonds to dispose of. The dealer sucked in his breath as Gorman told him that he wanted him to act with him on the whole transaction. For several minutes he was silent. Then he said, 'First I will change only £50,000 worth. And that money I will bank on your behalf. You will take a villa near to Zurich. There we will plan the rest together. Do you agree?'

Gorman hated the villa, he hated Zurich and the people of Zurich whom he found smug and complacent. But he did as his new colleague instructed. He established himself as a conspicuous figure in the life of the city—eating in the best restaurants, going to concerts and other public entertainment. The dealer found a teacher to improve his rudimentary German. Over the months Gorman released the diamonds at a million pounds' worth a time to the dealer, who never even asked where he had them hidden. He would probably have been appalled to hear Gorman kept them in the self-service left luggage units at the main railway station—as safe a place as any, he had decided. He and the dealer had worked out their relationship right at the beginning. 'No bargaining,' Gorman had said, as he sipped coffee in an open-air cafe. 'No discounting the value. You get thirty percent of everything I get. Not more. Not less.' The dealer had agreed even before Gorman finished. 'And remember I won't tolerate anything less than a fair price. And I'll kill you if you even think of double-crossing me.' The dealer had known he meant it.

In eight weeks the dealer had completed his transactions. He introduced Gorman to a banker who ran a small family bank in Geneva with overseas branches in Lichtenstein and Panama, explaining, 'He owes me a favour. A big favour. Now he can repay it in one go. And you, my friend, can launder your funds through his bank into one of the big banks in return for his fee.'

Gorman had agreed, and with letters of introduction from his new bankers, had set about investing his fortune in the antiseptic world of Swiss finance. He decided finally that he would buy himself a substantial chalet in the village of Klosters beneath the vast skiing field of the Parsenn which Klosters shares with the more famous Davos.

*

At about exactly the moment Gorman was clambering aboard *Le Bon·Vent* the major was in London finishing his report to the Brigadier who directs the SAS Regiments. The Brigadier was abrupt and to the point as he always was. 'Find him. Find the others, too, if you can. But find Gorman.' He permitted himself a rare show of humour. 'Find him for the sake of the Regiment!'

The next day the Brigadier met the Home Secretary in the Carlton Club for lunch. The Brigadier explained over a glass of dry sherry what instructions he had given. On the way up to lunch he paused on the landing below the portrait of Spencer Perceval, the only British Prime Minister ever to be assassinated, and said to his superior, 'Not for the honour of the Regiment we both served in but because he shouldn't get away with it. We taught him. We have to catch him.'

BOB AND SARA

THEY WERE SITTING in the warm sun by the side of the house.

'It makes a change to read a newspaper without seeing something about you or Clan Oil,' said Sara, looking up. 'Not even in the Business News today.'

Bob put down his colour supplement and smiled at her. 'Oh, we're old news now. Ten days is a long time to the media. There are lots of new disasters for them to get on to. They much prefer bad news to good news. They seem to think it's more interesting and perhaps it is. Who wants to read about something that's going well.'

Bob got up and held out his hand to her. 'Let's go down to the river before the others come.'

Walking by the wide sweep of the Tweed they held hands. Sara was her old self. Ten days of sun-bathing in the unexpected Indian summer had returned her tan. She looked healthy and fit and even the arm-sling looked dashing, in bright colours. Her black eyes had almost disappeared and the scars on her face were healing. She had recovered her self-confidence and no longer kept touching her face and looking in the mirror.

They turned back towards the house, now no longer patrolled by armed policemen.

'You know, I walk here every day when you're at work,' she said, pointing up and down the river bank. 'I can't quite take in what has happened—it's all been so quick. And now it's so perfect: this house, your new job and us. Sometimes I cry because I think someone will take it away from us. That we are too happy. They won't, will they, Bob?'

Bob stopped and took both her hands in his. 'No. What we have now we have forever. No-one can take it away from us. No-one.'

He pulled her to him and nestled her head on his chest as he kissed her forehead. He looked up as he heard a car engine. 'But we're going to have to share it. Here comes Hamish Blair and his wife, from the sound of things. I haven't met his wife. But I hope you're going to like them both.'

'I will.' She laughed and skipped away from him. 'I like everybody at the moment.'

The Blairs were getting out of their car in front of the house as they arrived back in the garden.

'Bob, this is my wife, Susan.' Blair smiled as he made the introductions. 'Bob, and this must be Sara. I've been looking forward to meeting you.'

Mary had been given the day off, and while the two women were getting lunch – Susan insisting on helping in view of Sara's arm – Blair became mock serious for a moment. 'I thought you would like to know that my Minister is taking credit the length and breadth of Scotland for having solved the Clan Oil crisis himself, single-handed!'

They talked over the events of the fight for control of Clan Oil, telling each other the details of how they had persuaded and cajoled their respective colleagues into helping.

'I hope that people won't feel that I overplayed the Scottish Office's role in the whole thing. But there was so little time to consult people I just had to get on. I hope the business community will realise that.'

'I'm sure they will. We at the Bank certainly do. And I don't see how anyone else could have helped in any way. Only you and I acting together as we did kept the control of Clan Oil and the Scotia Field in Scotland. But I don't expect we'll get many thanks for it from anyone.'

'Oh, I don't know. Already I hear a great deal of talk about how the other major financial institutions are vying to get some of the action in Clan Oil. All the credit for that must be yours. And that is going to make it all so much easier to raise the rest of the money on the Stock Exchange.'

*

As soon as he reached his office the following Monday, Bob rang Bill Gordon and asked him to come and see him as soon as it was convenient.

When he was shown in Bob had his director of external affairs, Jim Cunningham, with him.

'Mr Gordon, we would like your agency to handle our advertising and public relations from next month. Is that possible?'

'Yes, indeed it is. This must be our lucky day. I got a letter this morning from a new unit trust company also appointing us.'

Bob smiled. 'It is. If you will move your business to our Branch in this building you can also use our facilities—and release Mark Armstrong from his guarantee to the Caledonian Bank.'

*

James Tennent's secretary was used to taking calls from important men but even she was impressed as she announced, 'It's Downing Street on the line, sir.'

'Tennent here.'

'Ah James,' said the Prime Minister, presuming on one or two meetings with Tennent over the years. 'We are concerned that Britain should provide a stable and calming presence in the councils of the oil-producing countries during the next few years, a stand I am sure you agree with.'

'Indeed I do, Prime Minister. We saw in the seventies how much damage the escalation of oil prices can do to the industrialised world.'

'Quite. Which leads me to the purpose of my call. It is being suggested to me by those people who are supposed to know about these things that Britain must exert more pressure now that we are self-sufficient in energy, and that the companies that provide that self-sufficiency must be able to represent our interests in the best way possible. They must be led by men of stature. Men such as yourself.' The Prime Minister ignored Tennent's protestations as he went on. 'Clan Oil will in a short time be one of the most influential oil companies in the world—certainly the most influential one in Europe. My Ministers and officials feel strongly that whoever leads Clan Oil must be a man of substance—a man of considerable experience. And they believe that man is you, James. They further believe that in their negotiations with Mark Armstrong in other areas where he is seeking governmental help they will be able to suggest that idea to him. In such a way, of course, that he will be unable to do other than agree. I hope that you too will agree.' He paused for Tennent's expected protest that such a position had never been in his mind, but that he would be delighted to accept. 'Good. Good. I understand that it will also go down well with the people who matter in the City—not an unimportant consideration when Clan Oil are launching their company onto the Stock Market.' He paused again and threw in, with the pretence of an afterthought, 'And of course some elevation in rank would be called for as well. Perhaps you can think of a suitable title?'

*

Mark Armstrong finished his call to New York. As he replaced the receiver he leant back and looked around his office. All evidence of the occupation by the police had been removed. He flipped through his diary—London, Hamburg, Washington, Singapore; meetings every day for weeks ahead with contractors, government officials, planners, engineers, computer experts, sales and marketing people, merchant bankers, stockbrokers, reporters, designers, lawyers and accountants. His company had come back to life. He had nothing else to worry about, nothing else to take up his time. Momentarily he thought of Sara and then dismissed her with the consolation, 'What the hell, there are plenty of fish in the sea. Nothing is more important now than getting Clan Oil going—making it one of the world's great oil companies.'

He picked up the telephone and asked for Jenny Scott. When she came on the line he said, 'Jenny, I was wondering if you would like to have lunch. Yes, today—now. Good.'

EPILOGUE

THE MAJOR WAS taken out of active duty and had only one job to do—find Gorman. He changed his combat uniform to blue and sometimes grey double-breasted pinstripe suits as his battleground became assorted government offices. He didn't resent the change. While his brother officers in the SAS continued their careful counter measures to terrorism in a dozen different countries, he tried to track down Gorman whom he saw as the ultimate gamekeeper turned poacher. To him, Gorman, who shared his own origins in Britain's Establishment had committed the unforgiveable—he had turned against the very system that had given him rank, position and authority. The major gloried in his pursuit—kept buoyant by his resolution to avenge the disgrace Gorman had generated with Sunray. Weeks stretched out into months as he travelled back and forth across the world following up every scrap of information that came to him. He had no support team as such, but he did have the authority to call on the services of every government department or agency that could help him in any way to close in on his quarry. He used their facilities to the full, to the point of being resented as his search extended beyond a year.

Since the major was divorced – his wife had been unable to cope with his aggression and the pressures of the security of his job – he had no-one else to consider. He couldn't even find time to see his two daughters. Occasionally he reported to the Brigadier, but never asked to be taken off the assignment. His obsession worried his chief who knew that the thin line between duty and personal vengeance had been breached. He stilled his own conscience, however, with the thought that someone had to get to Gorman and the major was good – dangerously good.

He had occasional successes which helped keep his hunting instincts going and suggested that in the end his perseverence would win through. After small mistakes which were usually financial indiscretions or overt profligacy, six of the Sunray group fell into his ever-widening net. But none of them could help him trace Gorman. He left the lengthy extradition process of the six to the police and turned his effort elsewhere.

He called in old favours from all around the world, using the accepted philosophy that a favour given is a favour owed. He got introductions from fellow officers and reminded foreign counterparts of past involvement and leadership by the SAS during the last twenty years in their problems: how when they needed it they called on the acknowledged supremacy of the SAS in the Western world's defence against subversion, terrorism, insurgency and guerrillas, whether the threat was from outside or within their own societies. SAS participation at Entebbe and Mogadishu, against the OAS in France, helping restrain both the extreme right and the extreme left in Germany and covert attacks against the rising militarism of the right wing in Japan and similar involvement in more then twenty other countries now had to be paid for. Always the pressure was the same – 'On ne peut pas se permettre d'avoir des gens qui changent de camps comme celà, pas vrai?' 'Wir können die Leute doch nicht zur anderen Seite überlaufen lassen, oder?' こうみごとに変身されるのはやりきれませんな。 לא נוכל להרשות לאנשים להחליף את עורם, לא כן?
'We can't have people changing sides, can we?'

Slowly but surely he mobilised the resources of the security and intelligence services of every major country in the free world, and a few behind the Iron Curtain. They were all motivated by the common spur of self-interest. To all of them the most appalling prospect of all were turncoats from within their own services – trained experts who knew not only their strengths but more importantly their weaknesses and who would be able to turn these weaknesses to their own personal, sectional or political advantage, wreaking havoc against the societies that had spawned and nurtured them in the first place.

The massive weight of both governmental treasuries and banking communities was directed against the secrecy of banks and other financial institutions in countries like Lichtenstein, Brazil, Switzerland, Lebanon and anywhere else that at one time was a safe haven or bolthole for wealth, the origins of which were difficult to trace or substantiate.

Bit by bit the effort and the pressure brought indicators that sent the major to Switzerland. It was December, and he was soon finished in the cities and heading up into the mountains. He had known that in the end the slow sifting of scraps of information and innuendo would lead him to Gorman; knew that the vast wealth of more than thirty million pounds' worth of diamonds would leave some ripples. It was too great a fortune to off-load without some risk. And sure enough, a second-rate diamond fence in Zurich had broken under pressure.

*

The Home Secretary was at least man enough to send for Mackay. He didn't, as others might have done, write to or telephone him. But he spoiled it by making a point of his directness. 'I always give a man bad news myself—face to face. Don't like to be thought too weak to do it any other way,' he said as Mackay was shown into his gloomy office in Whitehall. He didn't get up or offer to shake hands, but did indicate that Mackay should sit down on one of the two chairs on the opposite side of his heavy, leather-topped desk.

Mackay said nothing and the Minister swung his swivel chair round so that he was looking out of the tall windows and not at the policeman as he spoke. 'You're the right man for the job. No doubt about it. I've seen all the other candidates myself. We've taken almost a year to decide. And it would have been nice for Scotland to have provided the men for the three top jobs in a row—Commissioner of the Metropolitan Police, Head of the Intelligence Services, and then this one. Pleasing, too, that the first two came from Glasgow and you would have come from Edinburgh.' He turned back to face Mackay. 'But your failure with the Sunray business was much too public. Even Robert Peel himself would be unacceptable to my colleagues in Parliament after such censure in the press.' He paused. 'So, I'm afraid the job will go to another: in the great British way, a compromise candidate who has so far done nothing that has antagonised or upset anyone. But that was the risk you took. Success against Sunray would, on the other hand, have guaranteed the position as yours.'

He pressed a button on the underside of the desk which brought in an assistant immediately. He indicated the door with a wave of his hand to show that the interview was over and that further discussion would be pointless.

Mackay stood up. Since he wasn't in uniform he didn't salute but he hesitated before leaving and said, 'I'm sorry I haven't got the appointment. I have been expecting that, and I understand your position. However, I was right in what I did. There was no action we could have taken, short of mobilising the entire armed forces, that would have defeated Sunray. And even then we might have got it wrong. They could have struck anywhere, and we couldn't guard everything. We never can. If we, or rather I, had over-reacted after their first thrust, we would have been criticised for that too. Sunray's system was fail-safe. The initiative was always his. He or anyone like him would always be too well prepared for any defence we could ever arrange. We ourselves trained him, after all.' The Home Secretary ignored what he had said and picked up a file from his desk and opened it. Mackay left.

*

It was Christmas Eve, and a beautiful crisp clear day, a perfect Swiss day, as Gorman walked through the village of Klosters towards the cable car lift up to the Gotchnagrat. He was early, hoping to beat the queues that would build up later in the morning. As he walked along, tall and erect, carrying his skis easily on his shoulder, he looked fit and well, his face burned brown by the sun and wind after weeks of skiing. The locals he passed greeted him warmly as a now familiar face. Morgen, Herr Oberst, said twenty times in the ten minute walk, confirmed his acceptance as a South African diamond-mine owner who had decided to settle in Klosters after a successful career. His large but not ostentatious chalet beyond the ice-rink was open to all, his friendship freely given, his largesse restrained. He was exactly the sort of in-comer that the people of Klosters took to themselves; comfortable but not wasteful. And after two winters of personal tuition he was now a first-class skier.

In the cable car he got into conversation with a stocky young Englishman who was obviously fit and tough but who had a pale white face that contrasted with the tans of the locals and the regular skiers. The Englishman explained that he had only just arrived and sought Gorman's advice and instruction on the huge ski field they were approaching. Good humouredly, Gorman told him what he wanted to know and then, since the man had been planning to ski alone, agreed to the suggestion that he show him around to begin with. Gorman suggested he wax his skis to counteract the night's fresh snow and held his ski sticks as he applied the wax. As he handed back the ski sticks he commented that they were rather heavier than most these days and didn't seem to be well balanced. The Englishman thanked him for the use of the wax and took back the sticks, saying, 'They're not mine. I borrowed them when I lost my own from a friend who had them made for him.'

At the top station they chatted, exchanging information about each other as they fitted their skis on. Just before they set off the Englishman asked if they might start with the small run off to the left. 'It doesn't look very long and would give me a chance to get my ski-legs back before we go up to the main runs on the Parsenn. We can come back up on the chair lift.'

The run wasn't a favourite of Gorman's—normally he liked to get straight up to the open pistes of the Parsenn—but he agreed. At the bottom of the short run the Englishman, who had obviously had a lot of trouble getting back into his skiing technique—understandable since he explained he hadn't skied since the previous winter—took an age fiddling with his boot bindings and adjusting his skis. They missed several chairs on the lift that would take them back up but there weren't many people about and they were in no rush.

Finally they got on and sat side by side, a dozen empty chairs in front of them and no-one in sight behind. They chatted, holding their ski sticks, their skis dangling below them or resting on the bar. It was still only eight forty-five and the sun was creeping up over the mass of the moutains behind them, touching just the summits with gold and pink, a soft contrast to the continuous white of the snow.

'Beautiful, isn't it?' said the Englishman. 'It's worth coming all this way just to catch the sunrise.' He paused and seemed to be adjusting the ski sticks in his hand, then continued, 'Or to give it its much older name—to catch the sunray.'

The warning was almost enough for Gorman—but not quite. More than a year of good living had dulled his reactions. At the top of the lift the Englishman got off and skied away with one short and one normal-sized ski stick. He skied like an expert, safe and secure in his own ability, straight down the terrifying face of the Wang, the almost perpendicular and certainly the most difficult run in the whole Klosters area leading directly down to the village.

Gorman stayed in his chair as it went round the top of the lift, with much shouting from the operator who was still a bit sleepy. He stayed where he was as the chair went back down. Now other skiers and the operator at the bottom started shouting and pointing at him. Advice and abuse came in half a dozen languages at the strange sight of a man going down on a chairlift. The bottom operator stopped the whole system as Gorman reached him and came storming out of his hut to give him a piece of his mind.

He didn't. The man was dead. A long thin knife, its handle

fashioned like the top of a ski stick, had been plunged to the hilt into his heart.

*

Jock laid the telex on David Mackay's desk without saying a word. The city of origin was Zurich. The message was direct, with no signature. SUNRAY IS OVER AND OUT. As he re-read it Mackay wondered for the hundredth time what the major's name was.